ANNE ZOELLE

The Protection of REN CROWN

EXCELSINE PRESS

Other Books by Anne Zoelle:

The Awakening of Ren Crown

The Protection of Ren Crown

The Rise of Ren Crown

The Unleashing of Ren Crown

The Destiny of Ren Crown

House of Scepters

Cage of Shadows

Crown of Starlight

Tender of the Garden

Contents

Chapter One

WELCOME TO THE NEW WORLD

A FLYING CARPET whizzed down the hallway of the Second Layer Depot and two mages followed slowly in its path, engaged in a magical duel with fencing swords in one hand and tasers in the other. They danced past us, alternating between lunges and electrocuted spasms. Bubbles emerged with each clash of steel, then popped boldly in the air, producing an offbeat chorus of a battle hymn.

This was my world now. My insane, exhilarating, dangerously upended world.

"Olivia Price, requesting a refill," my roommate said crisply into a wall speaker as she pressed her palm to the wall along with an empty glass container shaped like a genie's bottle.

I leaned against the wall next to her and withdrew a pencil from my back pocket. In the air I drew a depiction of the taser-fencing fight. I hadn't quite gotten my air sketches to animate yet, but electrocuted hair was still pretty amusing in its stagnant state.

I forced my hand not to redraw one of the combatants as Alexander Dare, combat-mage-extraordinaire. I would have to add far more blood, destruction, and dying screams to the scene, if I did. Along with more intense, earth-shaking hotness.

"Identity confirmed," the wall responded to Olivia in a soothing feminine voice. "Olivia Helena Price. Sanctioned for defensive magic use in the First Layer. Refill activating."

The magic of the device enveloped both Olivia and the container, pulling out a small portion of Olivia's magic and directing it into the container in her hand. A navy blue ribbon stamped with a gold dragon wrapped around the container, sealing itself and the magic within. The unbroken seal would allow Olivia to pass into the non-magic world with active magic in hand.

It hadn't escaped my notice that out of the thousands of mages currently traversing the corridors of the largest transport hub in the world's Second Layer, that we had been the sole occupants in this alcove each of the three times we had come here for Olivia to refill her container. I had neither a container nor a permit, and despite there being a station for filling containers, I had seen no evidence of anyone else possessing one either.

"Refill complete," the wall-voice said.

Olivia tucked the container securely in a sling that crossed her torso, then tucked a single wayward brown hair back into her tight ponytail. "Finished."

I twirled my pencil into my back pocket, and threw the air drawing toward Olivia's bag. A stream of magic directed it to the first empty page of my sketchbook, where it should spread out and sink into the fibers. The possibility that, instead, the drawing would end up as pencil dust strewn inside Olivia's designer bag was too humorous and terrifying to contemplate.

"All magicked back up and ready to scare the daylights out of people in the non-magic world again, Liv?"

"That is not amusing, Ren," Olivia responded stiffly.

We were staying with my non-magical parents in the non-magical First Layer of the world over winter break, and last night Olivia had reacted a little explosively to someone bumping their cart into ours at the grocery store. The ice cream aisle there would never be the same.

"I should have been cited for that," she said. "My permit doesn't allow me to just randomly blow things up. That I wasn't cited is a problem that you have yet to grasp. Especially with everything else we've been doing."

"That the magical cops haven't come for us is a terrible, terrible thing."

She gave me the look that meant my wit was not appreciated and that I was three seconds away from a magical zap. "It means that either the reporting process isn't working as it should in the First Layer, or...or that they saw the magic and didn't cite me. I should have been dealt with brutally and immediately."

"And yet, with a nice monetary donation to the store and a judicious use of the daydream enchantment that affects people without magic, you are free as a bird, and falling in line with my diabolical desire to corrupt you."

She sighed. It ran through her entire body. "Ren..."

I smiled and hooked our arms together. "Library? Then home? It's my birthday. I am exempt from recrimination during daylight hours."

"Fine." The word was heavy, but there was a smile tugging Olivia's lips.

It was my new mission in life to make those smiles appear more often.

My old mission... Well, such shadowy thoughts were for the darkness of night. Daytime was for causing mischief. Exactly what my twin brother Christian and I would be doing on our birthday today, if he were still here.

I hip-bumped Olivia, which resulted in a haphazard series of snapped body crashes since our arms were still hooked. Olivia would have crushed me like a bug had I tried to shake her hand when we'd first met. But she had become increasingly tolerant of my physical contact and I was determined to desensitize her completely.

She hip-bumped me awkwardly back, restarting the drunken jostle.

I laughed, and my lingering melancholic thoughts departed, tucked away for later. I maneuvered us into a crowded hall leading to the northeast spoke of the Depot. Ducking flying objects—identified or unidentified—and skirting all manner of weird creatures and mechanical constructs, I made another appeal.

"If the magical law enforcement system isn't correctly registering magic use in the non-magical world, then we are seriously squandering—"

"No."

"But Will said that after my Awakening, if he hadn't called Marsgrove, we could have gone on a serious magical bender."

"William Tasky, while brilliant, is not who I would follow on a 'bender.'"

"Hey, Will's awesome."

And Phillip Marsgrove, Dean of Special Projects at our school, was not awesome, despite being Olivia's powerful, older cousin. Marsgrove's hatred of me was a sentiment I returned wholeheartedly. Speaking of which...

"We could use my new lockpicks." I pointed at her bag, where I'd stashed them. "See what hilarious things magical picks will do to ordinary doors." I had ordered a set of magical picks last week in case Marsgrove found a way to get around Olivia's contract magic in order to imprison me again. "Will would totally be in for helping."

She gave me a deadpan stare, unamused, as always, by lockpicks and delinquency. Last term, after being illegally enrolled, I had broken into her room each day for weeks pretending to be her newly assigned roommate. All term, I had convinced myself that I was getting away with it too, until the day Olivia had given me an actual room key and a scathing lecture about breaking and entering.

We were forced to separate as we turned into the corridor that led to the Library of Alexandria's port. Mages were entering and exiting the Depot in multitudes of fantastic ways from across the Second Layer, but the most intense magical domains were still travel-restricted to specific ports within the main transportation hub.

"You have skill in picking useful friends, Ren. But a moral compass, or perhaps more accurately, a legal compass, William is not."

"We have Neph for that," I said.

"As a moral compass?" Olivia scoffed. "Nephthys would follow you to Hell and say that it was lovely," she said as we entered the gilded Hall of Knowledge. The soaring, domed hall contained two-dozen ports and smelled of parchment and magic.

I pointed at Olivia. "And we would probably have a good adventure there. I'm just saying, we should—"

"No."

I threw my hands forward. "You don't even know what I was going to suggest."

"That we engage in some wild and 'awesome' magical treasure hunt across the non-magical tri-state area using my container magic."

I paused. "Okay, you knew exactly what I was going to suggest."

We stepped through the thin, but elaborate port into the largest library in the Second Layer and the strange whirring noise of the magical sensors buzzed in my ear like a swarm of mosquitoes.

"Think about it, though," I said as we grabbed the slips that spit out from a box on the side of the portal. "It could be fantastic."

I grinned at her, but then immediately grimaced as I read my visitation slip. The magical scan had allocated me with a one hour and five minute period in the library today. Five minutes less than yesterday, and ten minutes less than the day before.

If the sequence continued, I wasn't going to be able to enter at all. Or maybe I'd just be digested while stepping through the port one day.

Because, while the library was awesomely magical and contained a bit of everything from the magic world, the Library of Alexandria was sentient.

And carnivorous.

Thus, the real-time scanner that examined each mage and issued a slip, precisely allocating the time that the mage had before the library started chewing. While Olivia's one hour and forty minute allocation had stayed steady, the library was looking to chomp me sooner with every visit.

There was nothing I could do about that, at present, so I shoved the paper into my back pocket and continued needling my roommate.

"Besides, Olivia," I said, multitasking as I set a timer in my head, grabbed a cloak from a peg, and plotted the fastest way to the warding books and materials I needed. "You are the one who wants to take over the world. I imagine that includes all five layers of the Earth—the four magical ones and the non-magical one too."

Olivia glanced sharply at the guards stationed at the entrance to the library's soaring, sharply-curved, golden atrium. They were standing smartly at attention as if guarding Buckingham Palace, but their gazes looked even more vacant than usual.

"A 'magical bender' is not a path to dictatorial splendor," Olivia hissed.

I cheekily waved at the guards and, as expected, received no response. Olivia grabbed my hand from the air and pushed me into the atrium.

"Not a proven path," I said, letting her manhandle me. "But on our journey, we could come across some magical trinket that will ensure you a long and terrifying rule—like a ring, or a medallion, or a fiercely magical toenail. Think about it, Liv."

Her shoulders relaxed at the nickname. She would have shot me for assigning one to her weeks ago. "Wards first, splendor and terror second," Olivia said, dryly.

I grinned.

My grin slipped, though, as we walked through the portrait gallery just past the library's breathtaking entrance. Paintings covered every bit of wall space and were secured with thick spells. Deep alcoves contained individual observation benches and particularly special pieces. My gaze shifted to one alcove and one painting in particular, as it did every time I passed. The lovely woman draped in beautifully mixed oils was watching me. Again.

The hair on my neck stood on end.

Olivia deliberately picked up our pace, hurrying me past. We hadn't spoken of the portrait, but there was no doubt in my mind that the artist who had created the extraordinary piece in Ganymede Circus had created this one as well—Sergei Kinsky, the last mage capable of wielding Origin Magic, both a god and bogeyman.

Olivia didn't have to tell me that I didn't have the time to study the magnificent work of art. She also didn't have to explicitly state that I couldn't afford to be seen doing so.

As it had for the last three days, my heart only stopped racing when we broke from the main corridor and entered the gallery tunnel webbed by thousands of complex and interconnected wards. My fingers brushed the access panel and quickly pulled up visuals of the wards that were on my day's to-do list. Colored lines and shapes zipped and zoomed across the indexed screen and I pressed the button for "educational activation," which pulled my twelve selected wards from the web and into the area where I could study and internalize them individually.

I took a deep breath, centering my magic. Replicating each magic and setting it to paper would require the entirety of my allotted library time.

My parents had "acquired" twenty-seven new pieces of frameless art in the past two days. After today, a dozen more would be attached to their walls.

Using one of the library spells, Olivia conjured a table and two chairs next to the staging area. We dropped our bags on the tabletop.

"How much time do you have today?" she asked.

"Fifty-five minutes after the cloak." The cloak protected me from the library's 'taste sampling' inclinations so that I didn't have to expend the energy to protect myself. I had seen more than one screaming person run down the halls after being sampled. But everything had a cost, and time was one of the most precious bargaining chips here. By increasing the magic around me like it did, the cloak cost ten minutes of my allocated time.

I touched the first ward I was interested in replicating and wrapped it around me, absorbing it into my senses—taste, sight, sound, texture, purpose. The sensations coalesced into a dimensional picture in the eye of my mind and I stamped the image into memory, then sealed the associated sensations into the skin and bone of my fingers.

I released the ward and stepped back, shuddering at the discharge of the sensory overload. The real world snapped back around me. Not for the first time, I ached to discover what the other sections of the library could offer. Someday I would.

"I could live here and not be bored for a thousand years, Liv."

Unsurprisingly, Olivia rolled her eyes. She hated coming here and never left the table once she placed all the appropriate protections. There were too many elements outside of her control in the library, and she hated things out of her control.

"The library would suck you dry in the one minute succeeding your fifty-five allotted ones, then feast on your bones for that thousand years," she said.

"Might be worth it." I flipped open my folio and extracted the specially designed sheets of paper I had created during the last week of fall term. I had created them just for this purpose—to put wards to paper. To protect my family.

The sensation of the ward swirled beneath the skin of my fingers, ready to push through my pencil and come alive on the page.

"You ready?" Olivia asked. She was researching the protections that had been previously placed on my parents' house. We needed to make sure that what I was installing wouldn't conflict and destroy the house while the new wards were seeking to replace the old ones.

"Yes. Yesterday's batch settled in well. I'm feeling positive," I said.

"Using paper was smart, and you have a talent for this."

"The first time I died I was attached to a billion wards. That helps, I think." It also helped that the defensive wards were responding to my overwhelming need to protect.

"Having a photographic memory for images and the ability to put an exact likeness to paper likely helps just as much," Olivia remarked dryly.

"That too," I said, twirling my pencil. Using magic was exhilarating and art made my magic sing. If only I could use it everywhere.

If only I could draw directly on the walls of my parents' house... But using magic in the non-magical First Layer was impossible for normal mages without a container like Olivia's, and would, without a doubt, bring the magical spooks of the Department right to my door—the opposite of what I was trying to do.

So for the past three days while my parents had been under the assumption that I was showing Olivia around our town, we had been returning to the Second Layer, and bit by bit I was constructing new protection wards and embedding them in the fibers of the paper. Olivia was transporting the papers containing the wards through the checkpoint to the First Layer with the crazy all-access pass that similarly allowed her to take a container full of magic into the non-magic world.

I gave Olivia's foot a bump under the table and started drawing, making the ward become a physical representation on the page through color, design, dimension, and imbued purpose.

With Christian gone, my life's focus had been...redirected. My vital need to protect and attend him had transferred wholly to a small group of people, of which Olivia had moved dangerously close to center.

We were taking care of my parents' safety right now, so that when I left for school again after the holidays, I could leave without worrying that the repercussions from my actions last term would negatively affect them.

And so that I would not worry about the wards that were already in place on the house—the ones set by Raphael Verisetti, a notorious terrorist who killed without remorse. He had placed enchantments on my parents' house before my magical Awakening in order to hide my presence from the magical world. In order to hide me until he could use me, betray me, and collect my magic—along with the magic that had transferred to me when Christian had been murdered during his Awakening.

Despite the absolute beauty and intricacy of Raphael's wards, I could not let them remain in place without designing my own checkmate. I swallowed down my anger and got to work.

Thirty minutes in, the library desk ate my folio. Wooden jaws then reached up and grabbed my pencil. I released the vine charcoal just before the jaws clamped my uncovered fingers too. The library swallowed my magical pencil with a gulp.

Olivia sighed and gave me an irritated wave. "Go." This wasn't the first time the library had eaten my things, even with all the protections Olivia implemented each visit.

I rose and sprinted to the materials section, my cloak's hem flying wildly over marble floors. Hungry magical objects trailed behind me and swooped at my sides, trying to nip any part of me that the cloak revealed as I moved.

Each section in the library was delineated by its time period or subject matter. The materials section was constructed completely of magical materials. Every chair, table, lamp, and rug was an exquisite piece to study. There were books, tomes, scrolls, constructs, and screens, of course. But there were also objects that were far more unusual. Cutting edge magical technology. Every few minutes something new would appear when someone, somewhere, added a new piece of technology or magic to the collection.

However, sometimes the library bypassed the system and independently acquired pieces it thought ought to be included.

I located my folio and papers quickly in an "inbound" stack and grabbed them. An outraged roar from the southern wall didn't faze me this time, and I sprinted back to the warding gallery—passing a group of mages dragging long, purple boxes—while marble nipped at my heels.

The library ate knowledge and magic, incorporating everything into its catalogs and limitless memory. Even with the cloak, books flew out to brush along the bared skin of my fingers, chairs wrapped around me, and magic swirled through my hair, despite the enchantments in place. It tried this with me more than with Olivia, possibly because I was always doing stupid things unconsciously, like connecting to every little piece of the library that took my interest. I loved it here.

But Olivia had forced me to watch a traumatizing instructional video before we'd entered the halls the first time. The library would consume anyone who stayed past their time limit.

Excelsine's libraries, unlike Alexandria's, had special properties and wards that allowed enrolled students unlimited access within its walls—a priceless bonus. But because of the restrictions implicit in the allowance, Excelsine's libraries couldn't contain truly intense magics like those in the warding hall. Which was devastating, as the piddly little hour I was allowed here didn't include time for adventure.

Not like those lucky mages with four or five hours printed on their slips. So unfair.

I repeated the sentiment to Olivia as I collapsed back into my seat and took the ward stone she handed to me. I placed the stone on top of the folio and papers. Using the ward stone would shave three minutes off my allowance tally, but running again would expend five.

"Lucky?" She gave me an unimpressed look. "Normal magic users, the kind who get four hours here because the library can't be bothered to eat them sooner, can't do that." She pointed at the creations on my pages.

"I'm normal!" I argued. "People do crazy things at school all the time."

"Excelsine educates some of the most powerful young magic users anywhere." It sounded like she was reading from a brochure, her voice haughty and disdainful. "You aren't used to normal, Ren. Or average. Most mages would be jealous of your one-hour limit here and what it means."

"Eh," I said, equally dismissive, as I stood and approached the web of wards. "Bursts of madness are great, definitely, but if a mage is diligent, she can build magic into a device or ward over time and make powerful things no matter her power level."

And then spend as much time as she wanted here, enveloped by magic.

I wrapped myself in another ward and breathed it in before letting it go. I drew it with fast and sure fingers, then chewed the cap at the end of my pencil, examining the complicated image to make sure everything was correct.

"I think people underestimate the importance of diligence and working at something for years, Sistine Chapel style," I mused.

"Nothing you say will convince me that you would rather spend three months doing something that takes you twenty minutes now."

"Time itself? I could use a vacation."

Something akin to a growl came from Olivia.

"Being an idiot means I'm normal," I said cheerfully, tickled. The Olivia Price of two months ago wouldn't growl.

Ten minutes later, I had completed three more papers. Olivia poked a finger toward the clock in the corner. When I looked up, a single digit appeared on the face, indicating my remaining library time.

"Almost done. Do you think—?"

My query was lost in a massive boom that shook the entire building.

Olivia immediately swept everything into her bag and thrust her chair back.

I followed suit, fumbling with the strap of my bag as I shook off the arms of the chair that tried to pin me in place. "I have seven more minutes."

"No. This is an attack." She was already at the end of the gallery and peering around the corner before the sentence had fully left her lips. She frantically dug two small devices out of her bag and activated a small silver bracelet. A tangerine shield sprung around her.

"On the library?" I said incredulously.

"Artifacts, Ren." The devices she had grabbed from her bag whirled in her palms lighting her hazel eyes with the emerald halo of one device and the topaz of the other. "The library is full of priceless pieces that people want. But also full of magical protection—active, inactive, and sentient. Stupid thieves."

The marble beneath our feet started swirling, as if responding to her words about its sentience. Olivia looked at the marble with distaste and a little fear. "Ugh, I hate it here," she hissed.

Another boom shook the space around us. I waited for Olivia to take off running, but she kept her position.

"Does this happen often?" I whispered, watching the active marble swirl closer. But Olivia didn't move, even as other mages sprinted past us, down the main corridor, running toward the atrium and the single exit at the far end.

"No." Olivia gripped the emerald device. "The library exterminates all threats."

And just like that, the swirls in the marble gathered into a solid fist and shot out into the main corridor, like a predator chasing fleeing prey, and rammed one of the fleeing mages down into the stone floor.

My heart stopped beating, and sound grew confusing.

"...is very bad," I heard Olivia say, once my panic sharpened to tight focus.

Running the main corridor had just, very plainly, entered my "don't do it!" category. There were shortcuts throughout the library—hidden doors and windows and quicksand floors, books that sucked you in and spit you out of other books, hanging lights that switched you out of existence then switched you back on in a faraway wing, doors that folded and unfolded you from space.

The building was full of small portals that transported people from one spot in the library to another, but the paths were dangerous, unpredictable, and unknown to me. Olivia was always reminding me not to touch anything other than the parts of the warding gallery we'd painstakingly vetted. I didn't know any shortcuts.

But I did know there was only one exit to the building. And we were tantalizingly close to it, while being horribly far away as I watched mage after mage go down.

Guards were fighting mages cloaked from head to toe in black, while others were being swallowed by doorways and floors, and crushed by ceiling beams left and right. Rock, clay, marble, and wood exploded from each crash. Wall trim bent down to crush and rend, and picture frames snapped their jaws. The library had clearly switched to offense and it was winning.

Olivia and I, standing stock still and peering around the corner, had just enough defensive protection with her bracelet and my cloak, to remain out of the library's immediate notice.

We had seven minutes to figure this out—probably six, now. And maybe the library wouldn't remember me when my time ticked out. We could try to wait out the attack...spend my remaining six minutes devising a plan. Between us, Olivia and I would think of something in six minutes.

A cloaked mage threw something small and silver at a statue in the middle of the large atrium. Even a hundred yards from the atrium, the explosion knocked us off our feet.

And the library...screamed.

"Holy— Run!" Olivia shrieked, scrambling up.

Marbled hands thrust out from every wall, one punching straight for Olivia. I launched myself at her. Stone fingers tore my cloak straight off my frame as Olivia and I fell hard to the floor. We grappled with each other, elbows flailing everywhere, as we stumbled to our feet and lurched forward.

My last look at the atrium was of everyone—guards, terrorists, patrons—being swallowed by toothed arches and marble tiles.

We skidded down the main hall—away from the atrium, away from the exit—surfing the rumbling floors and dodging falling objects. Olivia slammed me into a wall, saving me from a chandelier hammering into the floor. I wiped the blood from my mouth, then tackled her just as draperies snapped out to behead her.

We scrambled to our feet again, sliding sideways as the marble buckled. A mage in black, racing toward us, shattered into a thousand clay-like pieces as he was violently crushed by hammering ceiling tiles.

We had to get out of here.

"We have to hide!" Olivia yelled amid the nightmare as we avoided the next crushing blow aimed our way. As if we could hide from something that we were already within.

Another tile crushed downward in a hammered fist and we threw ourselves against the wall, narrowly missing death. But the walls were no safer than anyplace else in the locked belly of the beast.

Locked? Wild thoughts bloomed. I grabbed the pencil in my back pocket.

"Shield!" I screeched as the library attacked. "Last stand! Last stand!"

Olivia threw a shield over us with everything she had left. The reverberation from the library's strike was deafening. We'd withstand two, maybe three more strikes, and that would be it.

"Door," I said, already drawing on the wall with one hand as I frantically reached over to fish my lock picks out of Olivia's bag with the other.

If only I had paint. But I didn't and I had zero time to cry about it. I had only the time to enact my burst of a plan.

I got the picks free and ducked instinctively as rocks burst against the shield Olivia was clutching around the two of us. Two more strikes.

My pencil tip flew over the corridor wall as I visualized and created what I wanted in a multi-dimensional landscape, schematics flipping through my mind too fast for conscious thought. I didn't even try to make it conscious, as I thrust the expanding mental balloon into the creation.

Magical travel was Will's passion, and port technology was one of his favorite discussion topics. Spending fifty-plus hours last term helping him on projects, and doing whatever he needed, had to have left a mark. That, and sheer insanity. I had no other option but to believe that this would work. Somewhere, my subconscious had to remember how to recreate the portal pad Raphael had ripped from my magic when I had Awakened.

There was, however, a chance this would kill us. Or suck us into some dimensional void.

"Faster," Olivia gritted out, holding the shield against the marble floor to also protect us from being swallowed from underneath. Another column of stone exploded.

I drew the last line while letting conversations with Will, equations, and internal images of magical locks focus the magic sliding along the rays of the mental pyramid construct I used to correctly bring together and balance the cornerstones of magic. I pressed the torque wrench and pick against the newly sketched door, pictured the rotating tumblers of a triple-grade magic lock, thought the word exit, and pushed.

The door swung inward, shocking me, just as the opposite side of the corridor erupted into a swirling magical vortex.

My fingers wrapped around the edge of the new doorframe reflexively as the vortex on the opposite wall spun faster and the suction increased. I reached out my hand for Olivia.

A black clad mage appeared and grasped Olivia before I could. Using the leverage of her body, he flung her backward—toward the vortex—and plunged himself through my door. I released the frame and dove toward Olivia, frantically grabbing her outstretched hand in both of mine.

Her torso jerked and her legs flew out behind her. Magic erupted from her toes—defensive spells cast at the vortex, and offensive ones flashing in every other direction. The vortex reacted, swirling faster and swallowing everything into its cyclonic throat. Olivia's magically thrown ropes, hooks, and fastenings snapped before they could attach—sweeping stone jaws eating all magic before it could connect.

The eyes of the library were directly upon us. My feet dragged along the floor toward the swirling hole of doom that was sucking us in, inch by inch. I tried to supplement Olivia's defensive magic with my own. My pencil and picks dug into our clasped palms.

Jagged teeth rent the mangled shield around us, chipping and gouging more holes in the magic with each chomp.

I pulled Olivia for all I was worth, digging my heels into the slippery marble, and arching back.

Olivia's legs swayed hypnotically behind her, like a snake in a death trance—the sucking vortex pulling us in while the library's corridor dove toward us for an early kill. No!

"Let go," Olivia said, her voice and gaze far too cynical and resigned.

"No way." My feet lost six more inches. Gaping jaws tore through the remaining pieces of the shield's top in one giant rip.

"We will both die," she said in a voice far too calm and cold. "I would let go of you."

Another inch of ground slipped beneath my feet. I looked back to see my door shutting—the library pushing it closed around my magic. Five more seconds and it would be gone.

Tick...

Six sets of jaws swept up the walls, converging on the ceiling, then together, dove toward us. There would be nothing to hamper their descent.

There was just one last thing to do. One action that I wouldn't survive, but Olivia might.

Tick, tick.

I thought of the Kinsky painting, of my Awakening paint. A drop of ultramarine dripped in my mind and magic exploded against the door behind me. The momentum flung me forward and I used the initial jerk of propulsion along with a burst of magic to fling Olivia over my head and through the closing door.

I flew toward the vortex instead.

"Ren!" The door shut on Olivia's scream.

Motion slowed, and the feel of the drop of paint in my mind lit the magic around me. I could see the magic, layering one thread, one line, one sheet, one slab...one upon another in an infinite sequence. I could see the possibilities of the world. And in that last moment...a possibility for myself. I flung my right hand around a glittering turquoise ward striping the air and pulled it to my chest, tangling it together with the pencil and picks in my left hand. Thrusting them in front of me, I hit the vortex as hard as if it was a brick wall and told it to let me through.

The library screamed as I was sucked harshly inside.

Stygian blackness, then a flash of light illuminated the gloriously mechanical and magical Hall of Locks—which I had desperately, and absurdly, wanted to visit—then darkness and another flash.

I was painfully spit onto a textured, multi-colored floor.

Olivia was crouched behind a padded bench on the floor—a floor that was strangely far below me. She was holding her midsection. Art glittered everywhere. We were in what appeared to be one of the deep alcoves near the atrium.

"Liv, up here," I wheezed.

Her head whipped up and she stared at me in horror. The skin around her eyes bunched, her lips painfully compressed. "You idiot."

"I know." I pushed roughly to my feet, coughing and spraying a mist of crimson toward the floor.

Instead of splatting on the floor, though, the blood swirled around my ankles like real mist. Unease gripped me. But Olivia was alive. That was such the important part of this equation. And, hey, me too, bonus! "Where—?"

Detonations echoed weirdly in the distance. The alcove was strangely inactive, but clay and rock littered the floor in front of Olivia's bench. Whatever the library was doing to people—turning them to stone before crushing them?—there was no blood to be seen other than that upon our skin. Unless the library was drinking down whatever fluids it spilled. And...it was better to think about other things.

"Don't touch her!" Olivia's voice was harsh as she reached toward me, then snatched her hand back. "Stop!"

I whipped around to see a woman walking toward me—a woman draped in beautifully mixed oils, with excitement vibrating her painted features. Ripples of her excitement flowed around us.

Flowed around us...on canvas.

Absolute terror crawled up my throat. I was inside the Kinsky painting. I had thought of it. I had thought of the painting before I'd thrown Olivia through the door. I'd been awash in thoughts of paint when I'd hit the vortex.

The woman's painted hand dipped inside the folds of her dress and she pulled out a piece of paper, similar to the paper that had been held by the painted woman in Ganymede Circus. She motioned me closer, her movements elegant, but edged by anticipation. The paper pushed against the texture of the air, riffling out the colors of the piece.

I stepped toward the woman without conscious thought, enthrallment swallowing my terror.

"Ren, don't!"

I turned as an explosion rocked the hall behind Olivia, cutting off any further words. Stone teeth descended from the alcove's arch. Olivia's yells had alerted the library to her presence. My heart leaped to my throat. I was not doing this again. No.

The paint turned liquid beneath my touch and rolled up my fingers, as I grabbed for my roommate. Library air pulsed around my freed fingers in waves echoing the beat of my heart. The cuff around my wrist—the one meant to keep my magic from acting on uncontrollable urges—sizzled as the surface coating of the paint touched the edge of the flexible metal. The paint streamed upward, like rivulets of lava slicing through the final pieces of something supposed to be unbreakable. My magic burst completely free.

I grabbed Olivia's wrist and before she could say anything, before the terror could completely form on her face, I pulled her inside, wrapping thoughts of safety around her as I did. The noises from the library turned distant.

I could feel Olivia's terror... I could feel...everything around me. I tucked her against my back, holding onto her wrist, as I turned to the painted woman.

The woman said nothing—she just smiled and extended her hand—but I could hear the echo of speech and nonverbal communication in the painted textures flowing and swirling around us. I carefully accepted the paper from her fingers.

Words drew upon the page as I pulled it toward my chest.

Over my shoulder, Olivia read the words aloud in a rasping voice. "What do you seek?"

The woman looked at me expectantly, then motioned to the note in my hand. "Answer, magic, direction," her paint whispered.

"A path home," I answered her, light-headed but certain.

"No." Olivia's voice held the strangest tone. "The Second Layer Depot."

Oils swirled around us and I struggled with the split-second decision, while uncontrolled magic surged everywhere. Trapping the magic in my mind, everything slowed, and loose drips of paint suspended in the air as others whirled around us.

"The Second Layer Depot," I said, concentrating on Olivia's directive instead of where my magic wanted to take us. The four words spread on the page.

I held the paper out to the woman. She covered my hand with hers and smiled. Kinship, need, aid, her paint said. Brilliant, swirling color replaced shadowed light and her features changed, the lines of her body swirling outward into the world around her, and pulling us inside.

Simply looking at Kinsky's paintings—both in the hall and in Ganymede—had moved me. His use of color and texture and emotion was extraordinary. But being inside that art was like nothing I had previously experienced. In the battle rooms at school, where simulations became real in the mage's mind, the experience was still the mage's own. Here...it was as if I was in another artist's mind, blending memories and echoes of feelings together and producing new reflections with every movement.

I kept a tight hold on Olivia's wrist even as I was overwhelmed with the world around us.

Colors mixed with snippets of sound. I could taste our desperation to escape from the library. No, I could taste Kinsky's desperation to escape from...shadows...darkness, a collar?

"Find it."

"Escape."

"Destroy."

The words were not mine, and they were not the vanished woman's, but they echoed in my head, trying to find purchase.

Turquoise mixed with fuchsia, sea salt, and rhubarb. Tastes, sounds, and textures mixed in patterns that made sudden, ringing sense for a split second—the secrets of the universe, unraveling in a single moment, only to be lost in the next.

Doorways formed in Munch-like whorls—brushstrokes that beckoned and repelled. No, not those. Not yet, a voice whispered in my head. The Second Layer Depot. I held the thought in the front of my mind and tightened my fingers on the paper still gripped in my left hand, and on Olivia who I gripped in my right. I didn't look back at her, in case this was a place of myth where she would be released should I turn. I moved through the paint, pulling oil along the interior path of the canvassed world. Half-expressed memories and emotions bombarded me with every movement.

It was overwhelming. I looked at the paper in my hand, trying to concentrate on the words written there in turquoise ink.

Whorls of a turquoise path curled in front of me. I followed it, feeling the paper tug me along.

What if I had asked for...something else? Possibilities stirred and doorways formed and swirled apart on my sides, underneath me, overhead.

What if I had asked for knowledge? The path in front of me abruptly changed to silver and Olivia's hand began to slip.

No. Protection. I crushed her slipping fingers in mine and screamed The Second Layer Depot in my head.

The turquoise path jerked back to center and a door at the end shot toward us, opening wide and swallowing us in kaleidoscopic paint.

We flew through endless space, then were spit out, face down on a mirrored floor.

Magic washed over me in a wave.

My mirrored image in the floor morphed—teal eyes turned brown, medium reddish-brown hair shortened to buzzed black. And––

"I'm a guy," I said, a little panicked. My magic overloaded and sent streams bouncing around the mirrors that composed every surface of the room, and the color streams reflected a thousand times in the infinitely-mirrored reflections.

"Shut up."

My magic stopped panicking at the familiar voice, and I looked over only to immediately panic anew when I saw a green-eyed, brunette male.

"Oh my God, I sucked us into an opposite dimension."

"No you didn't. Shut up."

Olivia grabbed my arm and her magic blunted the sudden, uncontrollable surge of mine. Overwhelmed by the trek through the painting, my thoughts were completely overloaded.

I snapped my panic-stricken lips closed. The active magic she was channeling grounded me and clued me in to other things as I touched the magic that had washed over me a moment before. I took a few deep breaths. Olivia's magic. Olivia had cast an enchantment, changing our features and rendering us males. That meant she knew where we were and thought we were still in danger.

"Later," she said forcefully. Even as a boy, she was the master of a tight-lipped "I will crush you, if you don't listen" expression. "I am furious with you. You are an idiot," she said, her voice shaking a bit.

From her bag, she tugged the control cuff that Marsgrove had given her days ago when we'd been in line to leave campus.

God, I didn't want that on my wrist. Especially after the temporary high of complete freedom in a world of paint. But reality was quickly returning. I had to wear a cuff. I had nearly destroyed my parents' house—and everyone in it—the last time I was without one. That I might lose control and act on fleeting desires unchecked by conscious thought was more terrifying than wearing something that stifled me.

I nodded stiffly and closed my eyes.

When I didn't feel it clamping onto my arm, I looked to see what the holdup was. She was staring at my wrist. More importantly, at the figures drawn there.

Two new butterflies drew forth from their cocoons, their wings touching.

A mage's shifting tattoos showed a direct insight into her current thoughts or an important event, and were thus, highly personal. There were fringe groups on campus who preached to the freedom of showing the tattoos at all times, but the vast majority of mages kept them covered, usually by the control cuffs which were legally required to be worn in the Second Layer.

Olivia snapped the cuff into place, her fingers shaking.

I felt a pang as my magic abruptly settled underneath, caging the beautiful feel of unrestrained glory.

Glory that would obliterate everything around me the moment I forgot to consciously regulate my magic. I didn't want to blow up my parents. Nor could I go bare-wristed to the government inquiry on campus that was scheduled after winter break. Heck, I'd probably be arrested the moment we stepped out of this room if I didn't have the cuff clamping my wrist.

Olivia checked her bag twice—unzipping, then zipping it again—before nodding, satisfied. She rose, all shakiness clamped by tight control. "Okay, Reno, let's go."

A hysterical laugh bubbled up as I looked at our reflections in the thousands of mirrors, large and small, distorted and clear, surrounding us on the walls, ceiling, and floor. It made me deeply hungry to know how the painting worked. It had tapped into a port system somehow. "Lead on, Oliver."

She grimaced, then limped toward a distorted mirror made of hundreds of bottle-glass bottoms, and swiftly turned one of the circles. The door opened and we stepped into a hallway in the Second Layer Depot.

A hundred different types of mages and strange creatures streamed by. My eyelids slid shut in relief. "Oh, thank God."

"Don't get giddy."

Alarms sounded and people cleared to the side with us as a group of mages with buckled collars shot past on a flying skiff. Heading toward the Hall of Knowledge, I'd bet.

"Take care with your words." Olivia's finger twitched and I looked in the indicated direction. There was nothing there for a moment, then suddenly there was—as if Olivia pointing it out had made it real. A disc on the wall blinked, a thousand eyes shifting in a thousand directions. There was something very sinister and menacing about it. "Physical spells are easily seen through if one is looking for them."

We turned a corner and the disc disappeared from view, but the tubes and tunnels and all of the mages and animals surrounding us were suddenly a lot less whimsical and fascinating.

Olivia's controlled and precise magic rippled over me as we walked through the halls that ran in twisting spokes from the central area of the Depot. I felt bits of the enchantment loosening, felt my hair grow longer the farther we walked. Surreptitiously glancing at her, I noticed her eyes were almost hazel once more, and her hair was one shade off from her natural color.

Mages in battle cloaks strode past, and chaos burst around us as people opened feeds and holograms, trying to see what was happening. My gaze fixed upon one group of soldiers in particular, and one mage in particular. Ultramarine eyes narrowed on me and I couldn't breathe until we turned the corner and I lost sight of Alexander Dare.

Two hall turns and three large crowds later—all filled with melees of magic, chaos, flying vehicles and creatures—Olivia and I were female again.

As we moved closer to the main room in the Depot, where the First Layer Checkpoint was, I found it harder to breathe. There was no way Dare had recognized me. And with Olivia's magic, no way was anyone tracking us. No way.

"Hurry and keep up." Olivia smoothed her hair. "We need to check most of our magical equipment in a locker and I will not be late returning to your house."

I wanted to talk about the mages in black cloaks. About us nearly getting eaten. About the vortex and door. About being engulfed in the painting.

She shot me a hard look and I nodded sharply to indicate that we would wait until we were home. Safer.

Everything would be fine.

My new metallic cuff glinted under the magical lights of the Depot.

Control had been washed away by paint, like everything else in my world. But apart from my previous control cuff, everything else had survived—Olivia, her bag, my bag, the ward papers.

We were fine.

I looked at the walls with their hidden discs and at the occasional person dressed completely in black with a gaze far too keen. I pushed against the pit in my stomach that said we were anything but fine.

Chapter Two
TWO WORLDS INTO ONE

"TEN MINUTES TO DINNER, Ren, Olivia, dear!" Mom's voice came from downstairs.

Olivia's expression turned unreadable at the "dear" on the end of Mom's statement, but she merely said, "Thank you, Mrs. Crown," in her coolly polite voice, raised just enough to reach downstairs at the perfect volume.

Three days in the non-magical world at my parents' house had showcased Olivia as the perfect guest. However, my parents, who were used to Christian's rowdy friends, weren't quite sure what to do with my utterly poised and coldly polite roommate who acted far more like a thirty-year-old than one only a few months past eighteen.

I drew my fingers along Christian's burial sketch that Olivia had slipped through the checkpoint for me our first day here, and took strength and solace from the flowers within the sketch that swayed with vitality on top of the burial mound, waving along with the gentle, interior breeze.

The winter sun had set in the aftermath of the afternoon's life-and-death situation, and evening, family time, and sorrow were now upon me.

I had never experienced a birthday the way most children did—where one special day was mine alone. And I wished with everything in me that I wasn't experiencing it now. That I didn't see my parents' smiles stretched and overly happy every time our gazes met—as if trying to remind themselves to be joyful of the fact that at least one of their children had lived to be eighteen.

I carefully put the sketch on my pillow and sat on the edge of the bed. I repeated the phrase from Dealing with Death for the hundredth time—grief took time, not magic—and focused on Olivia while itching the skin around my new cuff.

"Stop touching your cuff," Olivia said, without looking. "You don't need magic here. Concentrate on that. It is required practice for Second Layer magic users to spend extended periods of time in the non-magic world. Anyone too reliant on magic never has the sense to use their brain first."

Having said that, the container of magic Olivia refilled each day was only an inch away from her hand. But I understood. Magic had become so much a part of my life in the last few months that having it repressed completely was a strange and unwanted feeling, and one I didn't want her to have. Knowing that she could get out of trouble, if needed, made me feel better.

We had attached the hard-won new wards to the walls as soon as we had returned, then escaped from my parents to discuss our disastrous afternoon.

Olivia had never directly addressed my magic's proclivities...and even now she didn't directly say why I had been able to access Sergei Kinsky's painting. As if saying Origin Mage aloud would make it real.

We had found out after we had arrived back home that a dozen public libraries and museums across the Second Layer had been simultaneously attacked. The news feeds hadn't disclosed what was missing, if anything, but it was noted that all of the affected institutions contained Origin Magic collections.

Perched rigidly on my desk chair, Olivia observed the muddy paint, ink, and chalk that my magic had hideously mixed in the destruction of my room's artwork when my magic had awakened nearly ten weeks ago. The mediums had pooled and dried into a barfy brown at the base of my walls. Years of artwork destroyed in a ten-minute blitz of painted bloodletting.

"We should do some wall and ceiling art in our room at school," I said lightly, trying to think of regular art magic and not the kind of magic that made artistic creations actually pop out and come to life—or that allowed you to travel through them. "Fun stuff. The night sky? Real celestial events?"

She gave my walls another pointed look but made a note on her pad.

Warmth gripped me that she was considering it even with a lot of bad evidence surrounding my artistic tendencies.

She activated the internal magic of the pad so that the words rearranged themselves on the list, prioritizing each sentence, then she checked the little black gauge at her right that resembled a compass.

She had been eyeballing the gauge every time she used a bit of the magic stored in her container or in one of her checkpoint-approved magical devices. Like all mages, Olivia couldn't pull and use magic in the First Layer unless she had a bundled container of it that had been disconnected from the earth and atmosphere.

"What does the gauge do?"

"If you hadn't been staring at Alexander Dare when we were in line to leave campus three days ago, you would have heard William explain. It monitors the grid. I am allowed to use a specified amount of container magic in the First Layer, and each use shows up on the Department grid—or should. It is beneficial to know each impact."

"I...I was not staring at Dare," I said lamely. My cheeks heated, though, because I had been so distracted I couldn't remember seeing Will give Olivia anything. I hadn't even registered said conversation. And I hadn't said anything about seeing him in the Depot.

One of Olivia's perfect brows rose and she made a note, then flipped a switch on the gauge. The little meter lurched. "Event recorded," a voice announced in a perfect imitation of Olivia's.

She nodded, satisfied. "Excellent workmanship on William's part."

I watched the magic on her pad work again and the grid gauge bob. "How do you get everything through the checkpoint?" My brother's burial picture, though it had been neutralized of most of its active magic, had to be at least somewhat concerning at a checkpoint where people were arrested regularly for trying to sneak things into the non-magical world.

"Helen Price's daughter would never misuse magic," she said calmly, her gaze focused on the pad as words and sentences continued to follow her fingers. Her tone never wavered, but the natural magic I felt in connection to her, did.

At the checkpoint between the magical and non-magical world, Olivia cleared more magical items than anyone else in line simply by raising a brow and pointing at her last name––a gesture that never escaped me.

"Besides which, one or two extra items are easy to slip by since, as the child of a high-ranking government official, I require additional magical defense devices and stabilizers, and am cleared for their use."

I imagined some sort of allergy to the non-magical world and stabilizing pills that would help one acclimate. I scratched the skin around my cuff again. I could certainly use a pill like that. My magic had been urging me to return to the magical world since I had stepped out of it with my new and improved cuff.

"How did you get permission to come here?" My parents would lock me in the attic if they knew it would keep me out of danger.

"I didn't ask," she said coolly, looking up at me, her eyes just as chilly as her voice. "Besides, it would make Helen Price's week to sadly sacrifice the life of her abducted child in order to confirm that she will never compromise her agenda."

My uneasy feelings turned darker. "What? Olivia--"

"We need to get down to dinner. We have a timetable to keep." She brushed her fingers down her skirt, but didn't stand.

I looked through my window into the dark December night. "Maybe...we should stay in tonight."

"William, Nephthys, Mike, and Delia are meeting us in the city to celebrate your birthday." Her voice brooked no argument. "We are in the First Layer, and you promised that birthdays were fun. We are going to have fun." Her tone held a distinct "or else" vibe.

I smoothed a section of loose hair behind my right ear, and focused my gaze on the floor. "Yeah, about that guest list..."

She quickly interpreted my guilty expression. "If you tell me that you invited Constantine Leandred, I will be most put out."

I cringed as she crossed her ankles in the other direction. "He said he was mostly busy with something." My words got faster as I tried to get it over with. "He might drop in for a few minutes, after dinner, just to drop something off."

"Ren—"

"I know, I know," I said quickly. "But he might not come."

The savage delight that had been in his eyes when I had mentioned visiting the First Layer made me think otherwise, but saying so wouldn't help my argument.

"You told him where you live?"

I forced a bright smile. "Just a quick stop, then he'll be on his way."

"You told him where you live," she stated flatly. She made another note on her pad that I was sure was not in my favor. "We will discuss this later, after we celebrate," she said grimly. "With or without Leandred."

People either pined after or loathed Constantine. Very few people had feelings to the middle. "He's rather brilliant. Truly."

"I've never second-guessed the intellectual capabilities of the Leandred scion. Basil serpents are viciously clever too, even as they poison and consume you."

"He's..." Nice. Helpful. Loyal. None of those traits were descriptors that anyone else would use for Constantine. "He's a savvy businessman," I finished, lamely.

"He's a serpent. Without a single minion, because he devours the mice around him." Her mouth twisted.

I didn't dare to point out that Olivia didn't have minions either, regardless of her notes detailing plans to collect some. Minions required some trust be instilled, which neither Olivia nor Constantine possessed in any abundance.

Her gaze narrowed on me. "Do you realize—?"

"Ren, Olivia, dear, dinner!"

Saved. Olivia stood promptly, her words cut off and her expression strange once again at my mom's use of an endearment for her. I thought of Olivia's words about her mother sacrificing her.

I stuck my arm through hers and squeezed. "Mom made meatloaf. Horribly normal and

First Layerish. The first thing you should know about us is that comfort food is the key to our enslavement."

Olivia jotted a note instead of laughing—but she made the note without releasing my arm.

I rolled my eyes at the squiggling letters. "Come on, Genghis. Let's go."

Our reflection in the windowpane at the bend of the stairs made me tighten my arm with hers. Her hair was austerely styled while mine was wild, and her eyes were hazel to my mixed teal, but we looked right together with our arms hooked. Friends. I wished Christian were here to rib me about it. Or to flirt with my roommate. That would be something to witness.

Movement in the backyard caught my eye as shadows shifted along the fence. The wards on the house spiked, then echoed their pulse within me. I couldn't use magic in the First Layer, but I could still feel it. And I was intimately attuned to warding magic due to my first death in the art vault, when I had died attached to hundreds of powerful wards.

My second death, due to being crushed by the bone monster, had been far different.

"What?" Olivia's eyes narrowed and followed the path of mine to the window.

But there was nothing in the yard to see that might have caused such a spike. No man with a gold earring, a sly, twisted grin, and a swirling box in his hand. And no boy with ultramarine eyes.

"Nothing," I said too quickly. My imagination was running wild again.

~*~

For a meatloaf night and birthday celebration, dinner was painfully formal. Olivia's presence played a part in the formality, but celebrating Christian's birthday without Christian was far worse.

An aching sensation settled in my gut as I watched my parents with their over-bright smiles. We were still tiptoeing around each other. Two months spent living apart had healed some wounds and widened the chasm between us in other ways.

That I would do anything to protect them, though, would never be in question.

"Earthquakes and tornadoes, blizzards, ice storms, and droughts. This last month was particularly disturbing." Dad shook his head. "I'm relieved that both of you will be safe at school in the new year."

The skin under my new control cuff itched. The same chaotic magic that had produced the weather and geophysical problems my dad was speaking of—earthquakes and tornadoes, ice storms and droughts—could be traced to that which resided beneath the flexible metal on my wrist. Magic channeled by my repeated attempts to raise my brother from death.

Using power without respect for limits. Giving into desire without regard for consequences.

Responsibility nagged at me. Like too many comic book morals read in too short a span of time. And the idea that I might be...the villain of the series, held no comfort.

Olivia eyed me, glanced down at the repetitive, jerky bounces of my leg, then looked back at my dad. "The Layers bleed into each other sometimes, but Excelsine is one of the safest places to be in any Layer."

That prompted my parents to launch into a question session on the Layer system and the security at school. Olivia answered every question precisely, and if she glowed a bit at the attention, it could be explained away by the brightness of the chandelier's light on her skin.

But when my parents went to the kitchen to light the birthday cake, Olivia crossed her hands in her lap—a sure sign that I was going to get the third degree—and visually dissected me.

"You keep touching your cuff. And your leg won't stay still."

I forced the anxious bouncing to cease and looked down at the flexible metal band. "It's tight. Tighter around my wrist than my last, even when that one was first placed."

She seemed unsurprised. "Your body is readjusting to the full restriction of the new cuff."

"Marsgrove probably put some horrible spell in it." As a dean at Excelsine, he had a lot of control over my fate while I was a student.

"If he figured out a way around our agreement, then it is likely. You frighten him," she said.

The metal was cool against my skin, impersonal. I stared at it instead of looking at her. "Do I frighten you?"

"Don't be stupid," she said without inflection.

I wasn't sure what that meant. That I did frighten her? That I didn't? That our magical sympathy was so great that it overrode all else?

"Happy Birthday, to you!"

My parents came out singing, Dad, out of tune, and Mom's voice a little high. But I could see the love in their eyes, on top of the wistfulness and pain. My heart clenched in response.

"Happy Birthday, to you!"

I thought of the first ward I had erected for their protection—a complicated design full of spiked vengeance born from my fear and motivated by love. It would incapacitate anyone containing a magical spark and ill intention who tried to enter the house. If some enraged, ignorant, slightly magical door-to-door salesman got a foot in the door, it would be the last thing he would do for a long time.

"Happy Birthday, dear...Ren!"

The pause. The pause. For seventeen years it had been Christian and Ren.

"Happy Birthday—"

I would never allow another such pause to develop. No one under my watch would be vulnerable.

"—to you!"

I pasted on my brightest smile and made a big deal out of blowing out the candles—the first time I had ever done such a thing alone—then divvied up the best parts of the cake.

An hour later, with birthday cake consumed and wearing a new top and jeans, I stepped into the kitchen with Olivia.

"Going to meet some friends, Mom. We'll be back sometime tonight."

Mom's smile was superficial and strained as she finished wiping a platter with a soapy sponge. "Okay. Have a great time. We'll see you at 1:00."

I frowned. "What?"

I could count the number of times on one hand that I had been in my dorm room by 1:00 a.m. The main library, Battle Building, and Midlands were open twenty-four hours a day and I'd had quite the schedule to keep.

"Your curfew is 1:00 a.m., Ren." She smiled and continued soaping the pots and pans that were too large for the dishwasher, as if we were done with the conversation.

I hadn't argued about the restrictions they had imposed following Christian's death; I'd been too depressed at the time to care. But now...the issue of trust was coming to roost. "No way. I'm eighteen. And I'm in college." Or the magical equivalent of college. "I'm not coming home at 1:00," I said, throwing all of the debating tactics I had learned from Olivia right out the window.

Mom's lips pursed and she gripped a pan with tight, soapy fingers. "Ren—"

"We will be back in plenty of time tonight, Mrs. Crown," Olivia said, voice smooth. "Then tomorrow you and Ren can discuss a curfew and terms that please both of you."

Mom blinked, and not realizing the danger of ever agreeing with anything Olivia said, replied, "Very well."

Olivia gave me a pointed glance and walked from the kitchen, leaving me alone with my mom. Mom looked at me and despite the stubborn cast to her expression, I could see the love, and I could see the keening hurt that was still there, especially on this day, of all days.

I could tell her about Christian. About trying to raise him from the dead. About my failure. About his now-peaceful rest. I could reach for the solace I so desperately wanted, and the chance to share the burden with those I loved.

This was my chance.

I don't know who moved first, but her arms were firm around me. I held on tightly.

This was my chance.

"Thanks for dinner, Mom. It was great."

"Happy Birthday, Ren," she said softly into my hair.

"Thanks." Say it, say it. "Yeah." I cleared my throat. "See you later tonight."

I tore away, guilty words frozen, a stone heavy in my gut. Blindly making my way down the hall, I deliberately didn't look at the family photos adorning both walls.

Guilt twisted and increased my emotions into a mild panic.

I repeated the words from the stack of grief books everyone had given me. Christian was no longer here, but I had friends and family. There were many lights in my life.

Lights I could nurture.

Olivia was waiting for me in the foyer and a little of the tightness in my chest eased upon seeing her. The wards shivered as we exited the house. I stepped in front of her, but I couldn't sense anything dangerous in the shadows.

Olivia checked her little magical-detection device. "Nothing is out of place."

I nodded and we headed to my car, parked in the street. Olivia had flat out refused to take the train.

"Even if I come home before 1:00, Liv, that's not the point, you know," I said, as we got in. I ran my hands along the steering wheel where my brother's hands had rested just four months before. I had been happy as the eternal passenger. But that was no longer my life.

Olivia shrugged as I turned the key. "It's simple. Put together a presentation of why you should have no curfew. Tell her you will text her at midnight when you are out to let her know everything is okay. That will reassure her that you know she is worried about you. And is it any big deal to give in and let her have her comfort by going with the curfew? You can stay out until whenever you want at school. We'll be back there in a week." Olivia's points were all delivered smoothly, but her eyes were unreadable.

I pulled away from the curb. "Your points are well taken, but it's the principle of the thing. I'm eighteen. I'm an adult now. It's like magic. The clock ticked past twelve and poof––adult!"

"You are in the rocky period of a secure, parent-child relationship when the child is becoming an adult," she said, her calm delivery making my words seem more juvenile.

"Ha. I knew it." I pointed a finger at her. "Don't think I haven't seen those self-help books you have been trying to hide."

"I see the use in personal relationships now and am filling my knowledge gap," she said, primly.

I grinned. It was easy to shed dark thoughts when I focused on a friend—on Olivia, just as I had once done with Christian. The desire to tease her wiped away my lingering obstinacy and I nudged her after shifting into third. "You are filling the gap rather well. You will take over the world more easily with friends."

She nodded. "Of course I am, and, of course I will." It was said matter-of-factly, but I could hear the pleased tone, both at the compliment and the physical affection. Eight weeks ago, she would have blasted me for both.

She was right, of course. I just needed to figure out how to handle my mom. To balance the need to do my own thing with the part of me that still wanted to curl up on her lap and have her tell me that everything was going to be all right. I might have made peace with my inability to resurrect Christian, but the hole of his absence remained.

~*~

It was an hour's drive into the city and Olivia was in rare philosophical form the whole way—clarifying points from the books she had been reading, with their message of choices and alternatives, and arguing the authors' merits of how to determine what to do when presented with forks in the road. Listening to her made me smile.

Parking sucked in the city, as it always did, but when Olivia had refused to ride the train—saying there was no way she was getting in something non-magical that she had no way to exit—I had scoped online and found a neighborhood near the club that was known for 'sometimes' having available curb spots. It took four patient circuits around the neighborhood, but we finally got lucky. We locked the doors and started walking briskly in the cool December air.

An itchy feeling registered under my cuff almost immediately as we turned the corner out of the residential area. The street shadows jumped and a four-headed creature—with tusks and horns and talons—blinked into being ten feet away. It winked out of existence a half-second later, so quickly that my heart didn't get a chance to fully stutter to a stop.

"That was a flicker." Olivia's voice was calm, but her arms no longer swung casually at her sides. "The layers thinned in that spot for a moment. It happens sometimes. There are a thousand things that cause flickers. Ordinary people think they are merely daydreams or tricks of the imagination. Keep walking."

The itchy feeling wouldn't diminish. It was growing stronger. The industrial street around us was packed with parked cars and empty of life.

But we were being watched. I could feel the gaze, and I had neither a weapon nor magic.

"Olivia—"

"We need to join a large group of people immediately. The car's too far to turn back."

I could hear people laughing, maybe a block away. We picked up speed.

A tall figure stepped out of the shadows between two parked vans. My hand touched Olivia's arm automatically.

The figure sauntered into the light. Dark hair lazily fell around perfectly debauched features. Constantine headed toward us in all of his sexed-up, privileged glory.

"Hey," I said, sagging in relief. I ran to meet him halfway, giving him a hug. He wrapped long arms around me.

"I didn't think you were going to make it," I said. "You said you were coming to the house."

"I was unavoidably detained," he answered smoothly.

"You missed cake." I stepped back, beyond relieved that the danger I sensed in the shadows had been Constantine. The irony of that wasn't lost on me.

At Excelsine, his magic was never without a treacherous edge, and I could see that translated to his aura in the non-magic world as well. Fathers here probably made their daughters cross the street when they saw him.

"But the others should be here any minute if you want to come to the club with us?" I said.

I could feel Olivia's eyes boring holes in my back and imagined her mentally penciling down "Talk to roommate" on her pad.

Constantine's lazy eyes took in Olivia, then dismissed her. "Quaint, but I have to pass. I have little time."

A butter-soft, dark leather strap vertically hugged his torso, the messenger bag settled against his well-formed backside.

"You didn't need to travel all the way here," I pointed out. "I'd have seen you in a week or two."

"And miss the ten minutes I could claim of your birthday, even if you choose to celebrate it in this godforsaken place? Never." He avoided my friendly pinch. "I was held at the checkpoint. Amusing, but amusements consume time."

Olivia looked at him sharply, but said nothing.

"Really? What did you bring that caused the hold up?" I eyed his bag, curiosity pulling.

"Eying my assets, Crown?" His expression was lazy and amused. Upon first meeting him I had thought he might be some sort of sex demon. He was completely human, in actuality, but the reality of him wasn't far from my first impression.

"You know me, always ogling fine leather." It was easy to share in his amusement. "What did you bring?"

The establishment of a firm, friends-only relationship when we'd first started working together had been beyond the right move, and such a relationship made it very easy to get along with Constantine. He was not, and would never be, a nice boy, but he was darkly entertaining and brilliant, and a great business partner.

I tried to peek into his bag. He was tall enough that I had the perfect view. When he didn't object, I stuck a finger under the flap, lifted it, and peered inside.

"Something obviously brilliant," he said, posture slouched and casual, expression lazily expectant as I searched. "A present to equal yours necessitated a challenge." Our birthdays were six days apart, with his occurring while we'd still been on campus. The gift I had given him had greatly amused him.

He wasn't avoiding my poking. Which meant that anything good was well hidden. I paused for a moment, examining the interior details. There were a dozen interesting pockets lining the sides and an expensive-looking thin sweater puddled in the middle—possibly hiding a dozen more objects beneath.

I focused my gaze on the exterior hardware of the bag and ran my fingers along the large metal button that secured the front. Magic sparked inside of me, battering against my cuff and seeking an outlet it wasn't able to find.

Constantine twisted the bag away. Bingo! "Patience, Crown."

"Coming from the master of patience himself," I retorted, trying to get a better visual on the button.

"You acknowledge my supremacy. Finally."

"Ha. As if you—"

"We should get moving, Ren," Olivia said tightly. She was standing to the side, observing us with the unreadable expression she undertook right before she ripped into the prosecution's argument at school.

Constantine didn't look away from me. "What's the matter, Price? You think you'll find yourself under attack?" His voice was honey smooth.

Unease enveloped the atmosphere around us again.

"Idiocy and reckless disregard aren't traits I desire to possess." She started walking again, obviously expecting me to follow—which I did. "Your little toys won't work here, Leandred, if we are tagged."

"How could you know what I have up my sleeves, Price?" Constantine sauntered alongside me until we individually squeezed through a turnstile and into the industrial lot, a shortcut that would take us to the club. He cocked a brow in my direction. "I don't remember sleeping with her. Did I, Crown? I must have been drunk."

Without thinking, I put my hand on his arm and started to send a zap of magic as punishment. Olivia turned immediately and her hand clamped on my wrist, startling me enough that I stopped channeling the energy.

The three of us stood half-interlocked and unmoving in the empty, concrete space.

Laughter from the club's entrance around the corner rang out over our silence.

The reverberation of the magic I had to force back down echoed through my arm. I looked at my new control cuff, which had just tightened even more unpleasantly around my wrist.

Constantine brimmed with intensity and anticipation. His expression was definitely one of encouragement. He wanted me to try and zap him.

Olivia's lips pursed. "Ren…" The single word was a warning. "Magic use in the First Layer is continually monitored and since you don't have a container, you would both fail and be fined."

But Olivia wasn't positive I would fail or she wouldn't be holding on to my arm so tightly.

"Unless you have a device to hinder such things," Constantine said lazily, though his gaze was the furthest thing from idle. "Or are a mage who can tap into the magic of the Layer system. A very rare type of mage. There was strange talk concerning something that happened specifically during the attack on the Library of Alexandria today."

My heartbeat spiked.

Olivia kept her gaze focused on me as we maintained our motionless, broken triangle. "Such a mage would not want to be registered by the Department, which is exactly what would happen should said mage be caught on the grid," she said.

They would analyze my magic and my background. I'd be caged or exterminated. To be caught doing magic without the aid of a container in the First Layer would be devastating.

I nodded to her, releasing all intention to channel magic.

Thunder cracked and a green line zipped past my peripheral vision.

The three of us whirled to see a thirty-foot chartreuse dome suddenly encase us. Five men, armed to the teeth, stood just inside the perimeter.

"Hands where we can see them," one ordered.

Olivia's hand flew to her pocket, only to be ripped away and unnaturally extended a moment later. From the grimace on her face, she was fighting to lower her arm.

"Hands where we can see them, or we start removing limbs. And if you try to escape, the Containment Magic will kill you instantly." The man's expression indicated that this would please him immensely.

The Department had finally caught me.

Chapter Three
DANGER RE-ENGAGED

THE CHARTREUSE containment field leeched swirls of lime into the concrete and back up into the dome above us. There was a poisonous feel to the curves, as if they were streaked with venom.

And yet there was something—familiar, yet alien, comforting, yet enticing—about the magic. Like a beloved childhood stuffed animal that had resided in another person's house for a few years. The dome's magic looked familiar, but didn't smell right.

I stepped in front of my friends, hands outstretched. This was my fault. And I would take the full blame.

The man who had spoken moved forward as well. He was of average height, with short brown hair and deep-set brown eyes. His left ear was slightly larger than his right. In fact, all of the features on his left side were just slightly larger than the ones on the right, as if he had been created by an uneven hand.

I had seen this man. Earlier today, I had seen him in the library amidst the group lugging the purple boxes. On my way back from grabbing my papers, I had passed them in the hall. Right before the attack.

His unevenly set eyes flashed and focused on the top of my head. His expression faltered, and his gaze dropped to my face. His eyes narrowed as if he were memorizing my features like I had his.

"And who might you be with such an interesting set of shields? Step back with the Leandred and Price spawns. I'll deal with you later."

His words registered slowly and strangely. They weren't here for me.

Adrenaline surged and I positioned myself fully in front of Olivia and Constantine. Threat to friends was in an infinitely worse category than a threat to me. My brother had died the last time a strange magic user in the First Layer had asked me to step away.

And if this man had been at the library before the attack, he was likely not from the Department at all.

Magic leaped from my core and blasted upward. I had to get Olivia and Constantine out of the dome, or somehow call magical law enforcement to us. I'd be arrested for using magic, interrogated by the Department, and likely imprisoned in magical Siberia. I accepted those consequences.

I thrust my hands toward the men. Expecting a successful outward blast despite the new cuff, I was unprepared for the violent ricochet of failure. Magic exploded inside of me. I stumbled, vision blurring, my organs battered, bruised, and on fire.

In a blink of the eye, bolts of blue flew forward over my shoulder as Olivia attacked in the wake of my failure.

The blasts hit two of the men, sending them sprawling across the lot, but as the leader dove to the side, he spiraled an arm toward his injured comrades. The downed men sprang back to their feet, revitalized and battling once more. The five men separated in a move that bespoke long hours of practice drills—like Christian's football plays of coordinated attack and defense—and bolts of magic flew everywhere.

I pulled myself upright and tried to regain my equilibrium. My new cuff issued a threatening shock to my wrist against using magic again. But Olivia and Constantine were outnumbered five to two.

I'd done magic in the First Layer before, and there had been the unspoken communication a few moments prior between Olivia and Constantine that implied I was capable of doing it again. Something had to get through the cuff if I just tried hard enough.

What was the point of being the monster under the bed, if I couldn't use the monster's power?

Pulling my trusty mental pyramid into rotation, I separated the tip into five points, and let the spiked lines dance wildly around each of the five assailants, trying to lock into position like a fighter jet locking onto its target. Slippery and hard to control, two spikes nonetheless locked on and another one pulled tighter circles—nearly there.

Before I could fire, I was roughly pushed to the ground and my targeting mechanism broke.

Olivia and Constantine each dove to opposite sides of view. On my knees, I tried to shoot magic in the general vicinity of the outspread enemies, regardless of aim.

Nothing. I reflexively gripped my cuff, which was now strangling my wrist and cutting off circulation, and tried to rip it free. I gathered magic and targeted my cuff instead of targeting outward.

My body slammed flat into the ground, shattering my concentration. Silken threads snaked over me, binding me to the pavement, as firmly as any spider wrapping a fly. The parking lot lit with magic—electrified jolts illuminating the industrial buildings around the lot like the set of a horror movie.

A horrific nightmare trapping me.

The leader crouched next to me—the battle raging around us in a rippled, bolting chaos. His asymmetrical eyes were narrowed. He looked at the top of my head again, and his expression lost the last edge of confusion and turned straight to fury as his eyes flashed again.

"Verisetti." Anger and disgust didn't completely hide the fear in his voice as he said the name. "Playing his own game? I'll dissect you myself for the answers."

Two blasts thrust him backward. Constantine was suddenly at my side, launching into battle with the man. Any panic-stricken thoughts of the man mentioning Raphael Verisetti were firmly pushed aside by terror for my friends as full on warfare ensued. Olivia crouched, holding the edges of a shield to deflect their attacks, then raising the shield at intervals to send out beams of her own. One of her beams connected and thrust a man twenty feet through the air. His body bounced off the dome and joined another downed enemy at the edge.

Olivia was a powerful mage, but the kind of reflexes and quick lateral strategy that combat mages needed in battle weren't Olivia's strengths. She was a precise, exacting mage who deliberated extensively before she cast.

Her magic was always perfect, but her methods took time. If her shield went down, she was toast.

And the men were expending huge amounts of magic without any sign of lessening their siege. With their coordinated movements, they easily revived their downed companions. Like Alexander Dare and his team of combat mages, this group moved together cohesively—almost as if they were synced.

Why wasn't anyone running in to arrest us? Members of the Department, Marsgrove, anyone?

Painstakingly, I tried to peel the edge of the net from the ground, but it held firm. Any magic I tried to channel sparked fruitlessly, like a gas stove unable to light.

Constantine, like Olivia, was also under attack, but he casually deflected anything aimed his way without bothering to return fire. His smirk was lazy, but his gaze was sharp and kept track of me, his defensive movements never taking him far.

Neither Constantine nor Olivia attempted to fight together or pool resources. Both would run out of container magic soon.

I watched, helpless against the ground.

Olivia's shield flickered suddenly and a penetrating wave of buttercup yellow hit her, making her lurch to the right. Her shield pulsed.

Help her, not me! I tried to yell at Constantine, but no sound emerged.

I pushed and pushed at the net strands, anxiety making my caged magic frenzied, but impotent. Nausea rose within me at my complete inability to move or act.

Then Olivia fell. A scream rose within me. The sound and feeling of it choked my silent throat. A net engulfed her and she too was forced motionless beneath it, her face turned away.

Concentration turned en masse to Constantine, who stood in front of me but slightly to the side.

A device in the leader's hand was aimed at Olivia's head. "If you move," the leader said to Constantine as the others prowled closer. "The Price girl dies."

"Kill her then." Constantine's voice, usually dripping with false charm, was ice cold.

My throat constricted with the sounds I tried to make.

One of the men holding a net device edged close enough to grab Constantine's arm. As soon as his fingers touched Constantine's skin, the assailant shrieked—a high-pitched animal noise—and fell to his knees, screaming in absolute agony. He clutched his hand, wildly shaking it as if attempting to dislodge acid.

A compatriot grabbed his collar and scrambled backward with him— away from Constantine—while he rapidly cast healing spells on the man's hand, a hand that looked like it was crumbling.

Constantine smirked.

Sitting in his room making diabolical mixtures and practicing sex spells probably didn't engender a lot of tactical fighting savvy. Other than his blasts at the leader when he had knelt next to me, Constantine had been solely diverting magic aimed his way in the perennially bored manner he exuded outside of his workshop. But Constantine was Professor Stevens' protégé and a genius with materials. Whatever personal shields he wore obviously worked in the First Layer and had vicious defensive properties.

With his perpetual arrogance, though, Constantine was watching the pain he'd caused and missed the leader's asymmetrical features morphing in fury.

A huge wave of blackened purple flew from the man's hands and exploded against Constantine's face. Constantine stumbled, and magic peeled away like destroyed skin, eating away his shield set and exposing what lay beneath. A horrifying set of crisscrossing patterns twisted across Constantine's face.

His head bent toward me and I could see every disfiguring violet bloom. His expression twisted into something violent and lethal and his fingers gripped a jagged metallic star on his belt then threw it. As it coursed through the air, the metal changed properties, becoming silver mist. It attached like a web to the asymmetrical man, who fell to his knees, holding his throat, gasping the last breaths of a gutted fish.

Active magic and sound ceased completely and the parking lot lights eerily illuminated the deadened space.

Constantine's fingers slipped under his own shirt to grip his stomach. The disfiguring violet marks turned nearly black then receded, leaving clear, unmarked skin behind. His expression promised death, but whatever he had done to heal himself had taken its toll. The hand lifting from his shirt shook.

The other was gripping a second metallic star.

Above his mocking smile, Constantine's deadly gaze pinned the remaining two men—promising to give one last death before he was put down. "Who will it be?"

The men looked at their leader and edged closer together—away from Constantine.

The leader's eyes didn't stray from the star in Constantine's hand as the man painfully pressed a button on the device at his waist. The metallic mist burst away from the leader's skin and fell to the concrete in droplets. Then the droplets gathered together and reconfigured to form a silver star once more.

Rasping, wet breaths became measured pants, and the leader rose with great difficulty. His finger maintained contact with the device at his waist. He still had magic, but I concluded, from the wary way everyone was reacting, that unrecoverable death was a possibility with another hit like that.

"Take the Price girl only," the leader rasped at the man near Olivia, without turning his head. "Leave Leandred...and the other one."

It was an order to his men and a deal for Constantine.

No. No! I sent a mental plea to Constantine. I knew he didn't care about Olivia. When he had said to kill her, he had meant it. He had never given me the impression that he cared about anything other than what directly interested him at any given moment, but please, please!

The leader began to back away from us, satisfied with whatever he read in Constantine's expression.

Constantine knelt next to me, his gaze finally meeting mine.

Help her! Anything, I'll do anything!

The light in his caramel eyes spiked and a smile grew, the whole effect making him look somewhat feverish.

"Easy enough, Ren, love." His gaze switched back to the men, watching them for movement.

He carefully worked the metal button from the outside of his leather bag with one hand while in the other he continued to hold the silver star in a position where he could throw it, if threatened.

He avoided touching the net covering me as he slipped the button between the strands and against the inside of my elbow. I felt the magic in the net reaching for him—spreading and stretching silken fingers.

"Give permission to the magic of this device." Darkness and excitement permeated his barely audible voice. "And we will stop them from taking your friend."

The man next to Olivia put a gloved hand on her netted back and her frozen body turned, her face and empty expression rotating toward us.

I thrust permission to the button pressed against my skin. Magic flew into the device at my elbow and zipped past the cuff on my wrist, as if no restriction existed.

One thread of the net around me snapped, then a second, and a third. The crackling sound continued down the silken veins, then burst free.

Something else, a second coating of something I couldn't instantly identify and that I hadn't known had been there, broke free as well.

Magic jumped to my will, and I could feel Constantine's exhilaration and fervency so clearly that it felt like my own. My constantly rotating pyramid was ripped from me, abruptly and shockingly. The sky groaned and magic shot through my body, out of my control, down into the ground, erupting and shooting outward in a torrent of rage.

The blast sent everyone except the two of us sprawling. I frantically tried to regain control of my magic, but it ran free and unchecked...to Constantine. Everything in me, including my will to move, flowed into him in a pattern of choices and options that he controlled. His magic told me to stay still at his side, and I did.

Horrified, all I could do was watch as he crouched next to me, fingers touching the metal against my skin, and eyes fiendishly watched the flashes of magic flying from me—my magic completely under his control.

The green dome thickened to a few shades lighter than black and patterns formed and started to swirl in smoked circles of greenish black.

Olivia rolled with the blast that freed her.

The man near her stumbled upright, fury in his eyes as he glared at me. His intent was clearly malevolent as his arms rose.

A violent pull of my magic lit the interior of the dome and sent the man hurtling to the ground, his head cracking hard on the pavement. An echo of the earlier unearthly groan sounded—eerily similar to the sound of the magic from Raphael's box. And the circles... I knew those circles.

Another pull of magic stripped a nearby tree, entwining the branches over the man, pressing him against the ground, and securing him in a vicious parody of the magic net that had encompassed me.

I frantically tried to gather back my magic. Dear God.

Constantine's expression was one of perfect, deadly satisfaction as his eyes narrowed on the places where each new blast hit.

Grabbing, breathing, holding... I visualized pyramids, squares, diamonds... Nothing was working. I was locked in a mental box while my magic spilled free and unchecked.

The leader of the men grabbed a device at his waist and thrust it outward as he lunged toward the curved wall of the dome.

Constantine ripped magic from me so hard that I lost consciousness for a moment as he threw it toward the device. When the smoke cleared from my vision, five unmoving bodies were splayed on the concrete. The dome still pulsed overhead, but now it was swirling with hunger.

I felt another pull of magic. There was black death in the taste of it as it slithered over my tongue and through my pores. My magic was about to be used to kill someone.

Olivia lunged toward us, her arm moving as she sent a spell that ripped Constantine's hand and the metal button away from me. The button clattered to the ground and Constantine was pushed a few feet backward—leaving a furrow in the concrete, as if a bulldozer had forced the movement.

My magic abruptly went dormant and my cheek hit the ground as I tried to catch my breath. As I lay there panting, white stars drifted everywhere around me.

"Now, Price. That wasn't very nice." At Constantine's tone, a rush of adrenaline pumped through me, clearing my vision completely. Constantine's hands started to glow with power, and his expression was the same as when he'd thrown the silver star—he was about to do something especially cruel. I could feel it, as if we were still connected. He raised a hand toward Olivia.

I scrambled to my knees and threw myself at him, grasping his arm instinctively. "No."

I could feel the raging power beneath his skin.

"Please," I begged.

The currents beneath my hand slowed and the glow slowly faded from his fingers. Olivia's chest heaved, her bun was mussed, and locks of hair fell around her face.

I had never seen her so visibly affected and angry.

"As you wish," Constantine finally said. His cheeks were flushed and his caramel eyes nearly glowed gold.

Hate and antipathy passed between Constantine and Olivia in a festering stare.

Olivia quickly and viciously rifled through the five assailants' pockets, pulling out containers of different sizes. Her furious gaze continuously darted back to Constantine, checking his movement and the button's distance to me.

I sagged. The two of them were safe. I'd think about Constantine's actions later.

Olivia ripped the remaining magic from the assailants' containers and performed a long series of motions over the men. Her gaze was piercing as she worked. Precise, deliberate magic was her forte.

She finished her movements with a dark frown on her face, then she tore the remnants of the black box from the leader's belt. She stepped away, her face nearly as flushed with the use of illegal magic as Constantine's.

"A containment dome?" The muscles in Olivia's arms flexed as she gripped the shell of the broken device harder. "In the First Layer? And, there are enough regular usage containers here to give Axer Dare trouble," she spat. Her eyes moved to the silver star and metal button Constantine had picked up from the ground. "And you? Are the checkpoints even checking anything anymore?"

Constantine sniped back a response, but I'd stopped listening. My hands were clenching my thighs, and I had to force my muscles to relax, and my horribly obstructed anxiety, to work its way free. Thoughts of domes and containment and Origin Magic whirled through my mind.

The dome felt familiar, but odd. Reasons for why made me clench the denim beneath my fingers even tighter.

I had researched Origin Magic domes in my search for a good containment field last term. Ganymede Circus' dome had been one such example—a marvelous creation that Raphael Verisetti had destroyed in one blow using my stolen magic.

My stolen magic wielded by someone capable of horrible things.

I focused on the men splayed on the ground, and on the leader, specifically. 'Verisetti,' he had said while looking at the top of my head.

Marked. I had known conceptually that Raphael had done something to me, marked me somehow—as both he and Marsgrove had separately remarked upon it. I still didn't understand what that meant, but where that mark obviously resided was very unsettling.

Because like this man, and Marsgrove months ago, Professor Stevens had stared at the top of my head when I had first arrived at Excelsine. She had darkly examined me, then engineered a meeting in order to ask very specific questions about my loyalties.

Professor Stevens knew Raphael. The knowledge curled bitterly in my stomach. She had become a mentor. Another mentor, perhaps using me for her own ends. Magic roiled around inside me, poking at my cuff and vainly trying to connect to the blackened tendrils of the dome.

"Touch this again, darling," Constantine said at my side, holding the button in the palm of his hand once more.

"No. How dare you." Olivia grabbed my arm, pulling me up and away. Her gaze never left Constantine. "How did you get that through the checkpoint, Leandred? How do you have one?"

Olivia—calm, poised Olivia—was more flustered than I had ever seen her as she tried to file information that didn't fit into her perfectly constructed database. Olivia was used to verbally shredding people—holding a debate hall or courtroom in the palm of her hand. Today had severely put her off her normal game.

Constantine smiled. "Come now, Price. You act as if you didn't sneak prohibited items through the checkpoint as well. I consider the privilege to do so a 'get out of jail free card' courtesy of the ones who love us the most."

"You aren't using that on her ever again," she hissed.

"You have five more minutes to change your mind, Price. You hold the remnants of the device that created the dome—a device which is useless to us now." He reached out a hand, almost touching the dome's magic that was swirling madly in poisonous shades of green and black. He smiled strangely, curling his fingers back into his palm. "Five minutes—maybe six—before it explodes with us inside. Before the entire Department task force descends upon us. If we survive at all, what do you think will happen during questioning? What do you think will happen to your delectable roommate?"

A cracking sound in the dome underscored his words.

"What can you do?" I asked without emotion. I felt...removed, as if their argument was at a distance from me. I could hear the words, but the connection to any emotional response wasn't there. Delayed shock, the disconnected portion of my mind said.

He smiled slowly, a devastating thing for most females at Excelsine. It merely registered to me in an analytical way, though. I was lifeless. Wooden. Like a tree. Like Christian in my sketch.

A small bit of emotion broke through.

"I can permanently set the memories that your roommate just modified," he said. "A delicate operation that involves breaking into the Layer system and using the erasure spell that works on ordinary people, but instead directing it to mages. Delicate work, but I've been...doing a lot of research on the magic involved in the Layers lately."

"No," Olivia said harshly. "I won't allow it. The enchantment will stick on its own."

Constantine didn't even glance her way, his gaze never leaving mine. "More importantly, the dome must be collapsed correctly, unless you want a ten-block radius destroyed along with all the people inside of that radius."

Memories of Ganymede Circus rent my thoughts, letting more emotion through. My head shook as I wobbled it sideways in the negative. No good options.

Constantine's fingers touched my chin. "The Department will not be kind to any of us. Or to your ordinary family. I know what I'm doing. Trust me."

I stared at him. We had worked together frequently last term and I could read him pretty well most of the time. I knew exactly why he had been doing Layer research lately.

"You need me—my magic—in order to affect the Layer system."

It wasn't a question. I had spent my time last term researching necromancy, not Origin Magic, since Origin Magic couldn't bring my real brother back—it could only produce a pale approximation that echoed my thoughts and wishes. But I had absorbed a few uncomfortable and familiar facts about Origin Magic and how my own magic displayed.

And it had been obvious that Constantine had suspected things about my magic right from our first meeting.

I didn't want to think about being the monster everyone in the magic world feared. But Kinsky's paintings had reached out to me twice now, and one had transported me through it earlier today. A pretty big red flag of doom.

"No." Olivia's tone was dark and final. "You aren't doing it, Ren."

Constantine's fingers slipped from my chin and he extended to his full height, tapping his lower lip as he finally looked at her. "That little bit of stripping magic you just performed on their minds was quite dark, Price. Cause for immediate arrest. Does Mommy Dearest know what you do when you are angry?"

If we survived the collapse, the Department would come. They would arrest Olivia and find my house. And all of the faceless people celebrating in the ten-block radius around us would die. To join the Ganymede ghosts who already haunted my dreams. "Olivia—"

Olivia held out her hand, her fingers shaking with anger. "Not him. I'll do it."

"Not a chance," he said lazily, hand closing over the button. "You might damage Crown. I will do it or no one will."

I extended my hand to him, but Olivia grabbed it before Constantine could. Her face was blank and she didn't answer for a long moment as her gaze clashed with his. "You will only use it for this one task. And you will swear it."

His expression was one of dark satisfaction. "There's the selfish daughter of Helen Price who always looks out for number one. I will use this device today for the discussed purposes, by my magic I so do vow."

I could feel the thin threads of magic from one of the containers latch onto him, sealing the vow.

Olivia had to have felt it as well, but she lifted a device she had ripped from the leader's belt and held it in a position that people in action movies used with a knife.

"Now, now, Price. You might hurt yourself." Constantine's voice was lazy, but his eyes were narrowly focused.

Since vows worked on future magic, by including the word "today" in his declaration, Constantine was restricted from further use only for the next two hours before midnight. This obviously was not what Olivia had intended.

She was nearly spitting with rage as she faced Constantine. "Do you know how long it will take someone to drag your body back to a port after they get here to investigate, and after they see ranked terrorists on the ground? Do you think you will be revived in ten minutes, should you misstep with me?"

Exhaustion made my shoulders slump. I longed to go somewhere safe and draw and sleep and forget the craziness my world had become.

"I'm not going to hurt her." Constantine's words were clipped, as if he didn't want to admit them.

"You want something from her. Everyone does."

He sneered. "Including you."

"Of course I do. That doesn't mean I'm going to let anyone else do it."

"Great, wonderful," I said, just wanting to go home and not think about who wanted to use me and for what purpose. I flexed my magic, but it rebounded against my cuff again, useless.

"You really know how to do this?" I asked Constantine.

Constantine smoothly held out his hand. There was something fierce in his eyes as his gaze met mine. He gave a swift nod.

There were all sorts of things that people didn't agree with or like about Constantine Leandred. His brilliance and competence, though, had never been in question for me. And neither was my ability to take risks regardless of personal damage.

"No killing anyone even accidentally," I added.

He gave another swift nod, all business now. I removed my hand from Olivia's still resistant grip and put it in his, letting the cold metal of the button rest between our palms. Upon permission, my magic immediately pulled into the metal, into Constantine, then out, spreading to the five figures in front of us. A whisper of sound blew on the breeze, and crackling resonated through the air. The dome drew slowly downward, draping each of us and changing from a deathly greenish black to a clear, colorless barrier, like Saran wrap pulled tightly over each nook and cranny of our being.

I could see ribbon after ribbon of magic layering and adhering. The original strand slowly shifted color over the first body.

I frowned. The engineering, design, and magic of the procedure pushed my curiosity ahead of my still horrified emotions for a moment. That didn't...seem ideal. If I were doing the repair, I would ripple the change across the section there on the right—

A thread of magic sifted back into my control and the view zoomed closer.

Yes, there. If the ribbons were shifted, then I would—

The thread of magic was once more taken from me, though this time with a far gentler hand, and my thought process also suddenly sucked down the magic stream, through the button and into Constantine. The magic over the bodies moved into the thought pattern I had designated, except once again, the actuation was outside my control.

My very thoughts were being stolen.

Panic struck me, overriding everything else. Constantine shifted, his fingertips stroking mine, unnaturally soothing my tension, forcing a layer of reassuring calm over the panicked feelings swirling beneath.

Everything knit together in less than a minute and the magic sunk into the men. It sunk in quickly, as if their bodies, brains, and magic were perfectly awaiting change. The magic dissipated outward a few short seconds later. The dome followed, but in a less natural way, thundering and creaking as it went.

A slight breeze blew over us, then everything was still.

Laughter—incongruous and wrong—from the club around the corner registered once more.

An echo of the disfiguring purple markings stood out on Constantine's skin for a moment, as if they hadn't fully healed, then gold seeped into each divot and scar, filling them and strengthening his skin back to normal.

Strengthened all of his magical reserves, as well...because he wasn't using container magic. He was using live magic, just like he would in the magical world. Numb thoughts slogged through my brain.

Using live magic in the non-magical First Layer was an impossible feat for a normal mage because the connection to the magical veins of the Earth that was available in the other Layers was not present in the First Layer. The First Layer had been deliberately freed of magic, designed to protect the non-magical people of the world by giving them a magic-free safe haven. The only way to access magic here was by bringing it in via a container or device, or by breaking through the Layer system and making a connection to the Earth's magic by bypassing the system.

Bypassing the system compromised everyone's safety. Everyone's. There was a reason mages who could do such things were feared.

Even if the most upstanding member of society possessed such powers, if used as a conduit for someone else, world-ending disaster could result.

Constantine drew in a deep breath, then let out a sated smile. "Done."

His fingers slid from mine, leaving the button in my palm. My fingers closed over it in a tight fist. My eyes were unable to focus properly and my breath returned harshly, as if it too had been stolen, then suddenly returned.

"Look at you glow." I heard him say. "Exactly as you should."

I forced myself to look up, but it was hard to think beyond numb, looping thoughts.

Olivia stood rigid, her gaze focused entirely on Constantine. In contrast to the searing hate in her eyes, her words were calm and precise. "Leandred, I will report you for immediate termination if you ever use that—or one like it—again."

His face and body held a compelling sort of tension, as if he were intoxicated, with too much power rolling through him. He was brimming with it, like some sort of dark god. He flexed his fingers to show her his empty palms and my eyes watched the gilded lines of his hands. He waved dismissively at Olivia, leaving tracers of gold in the air. "And put yourself in the line of fire? Self-sacrifice in a Price? I doubt that highly."

"You don't know what I'd do," she said darkly.

Constantine smiled lazily, deceptively casual once more. "The day a Price sacrifices herself is the day the end of the world begins. You are welcome for the save. It will, of course, never happen again."

He turned away from her and touched my free hand, turning it palm up. "That was truly exceptional, Crown. You should always glow like this." He slid a small envelope along the skin of my palm, gold light trailing in the wake. "Enjoy your birthday present," he whispered.

I mechanically gripped the paper.

He sauntered into the shadows, disappearing moments later. And still I couldn't force myself to move, or tell my fingers to relinquish their choke hold around the button in my other hand.

Olivia stared long and hard at the space he had occupied before whirling to face me. She looked at my closed fist and expressions vied on her face. Pain, irritation, grim determination. "Don't ever let someone use a leech on you again, unless I'm there. Swear it."

I tried to force my mouth to move, my throat to work, air to pass... Nothing emerged.

She pinned me with the look, the one that made even the Excelsine officials sweat. "Swear it."

The smooth edges of the metal dug into my palm; I was gripping the button painfully hard. The thought of letting someone pull thoughts and magic from me was not at the top of my to-do list. "I don't plan," I said, my voice oddly hoarse, "to allow that to happen again."

The lines around her mouth tightened at my wording, and I could see her formulating and discarding arguments in her head, but by mutual unspoken consent, we pivoted and headed back to the car at a quick pace. My limbs shook and I jogged unsteadily. The dome had withheld any magic use inside of it from showing up on the grid—I had gleaned that knowledge from Constantine's thoughts while we had been connected—but there would be evidence of the dome's collapse. The Department would be here any moment.

As our jog became a run, I gripped the circle of metal tighter. "A button?" A barbed fishhook would have been a better representation of the magic contained within.

I had been leeched of magical control and thought. Constantine could have taken whatever he wanted from me, just like Raphael had—turning my magic into...containment domes, and horrible boxes, and weapons that stripped magic.

I pushed the envelope Constantine had given me into my back pocket as our pace increased to a sprint. In light of everything, I didn't want to see what he had given me for my birthday yet.

"A button looks unexceptional," Olivia said in between gasped breaths as we rounded the last corner. "Especially here. Never trust anything people wear."

I thought of Constantine's belt and the battle cloaks with their multiple fastenings, and nodded spasmodically.

We practically dove into the car, and buckled in quickly as I shoved the key in. I didn't relinquish my hold on the button, and my grip on the steering wheel pressed it into my left palm. I pressed far too hard on the accelerator, squealing the tires before they bit into the road and jerked us forward.

"Where is the nearest port?" I only knew the port that was located in the coffee shop in my suburb. Olivia and I had been using it each day to get back and forth between the First and Second Layers. Knowing where other ports were was a critical gap in my knowledge that I hadn't considered. But I knew Olivia had traveled to our house on the first day knowing all of the street names and businesses in our neighborhood. She'd likely mapped out the city as well when she'd found out we were going there.

"One quarter of a mile to the west. In the basement of another club. Leandred probably used it."

"We'll go there."

"No. You are too bright." Olivia's lips tightened. "Leandred was right. Even I can see your edges are glowing. You can't go back to the Second Layer until you are warded again. You step into the Depot like that, and all hell will break loose."

"Okay." I nodded. I had no idea how to fix such a thing. "I'll drop you off."

"No."

"Olivia—"

"Are you going to shove me out of your moving car?" The even tone of her voice indicated that this would be the only way such a result would occur.

"We'll pick up your things at my house, then I'll drop you off at the coffee shop."

Olivia did something on her pad. "I rerouted William and Nephthys to your house. They are on their way and have made appropriate excuses to get Mike and Delia to return to the Second Layer. We will discuss—"

"No! Tell Will and Neph to go back too." I reached for the two-way journal Will and I kept, determined to do just that.

She effortlessly moved the journal out of my reach. "It is far too late to send another note. William just said they are on their way."

"Fine. Then they can escort you back."

"No."

"Those men were after you." I gripped the steering wheel. "And at the library today..." Anguish gripped me, making it hard to speak. "You almost died twice today." And I had been entirely unsuccessful so far in fixing death.

"And yet here I am, alive. In this car, arguing over my welfare with you." There was something off in her voice, an emotion brimming over that she was unused to and unable to suppress.

My hands shook on the wheel. My mouth opened to continue the argument, to say anything, but all that emerged were horrible, broken sounds. I swallowed them down and tried to focus on the car lights in front of us.

The car was tensely silent for long moments.

"You can't die," I managed to say as I jerked onto the highway on-ramp.

"I am staying," she said, almost savagely, her normally steady and dismissive tone completely gone. "You are cementing my decision."

I concentrated on the broken spaces of the lane lines and tried to take deeper breaths. "I don't understand."

"No, you wouldn't." The savagery had leeched from her tone, leaving it distant. But the distance didn't seem to be aimed at me. She was leaning closer to me, if anything.

After a few moments of silence, I looked over to see her staring through the windshield like it held unpleasant secrets. Her gaze turned to me, steady and dark, then dropped to where my hand was still clenching the leech against the steering wheel. "Leandred wouldn't have given you that unless he had future plans for it to be in your possession. You must avoid him from now on."

The round metal bit into my palm. "The magic required my permission. I gave it to him, both times."

"Exactly."

I felt a little lightheaded. I wanted to press a hand to my head, but neither would relinquish their grip on the wheel. "You think I will give him permission again."

"I know you will." Olivia's voice was dark. "What did he give you in that envelope?"

"I don't know." I couldn't think about it right now. My mind was racing with too many questions to properly verbalize. "Why do you think—?"

"Because you give everything when asked...or when you see that someone you care about has a hangnail." She sounded a little hysterical, totally unlike my unflappable roommate.

The sound peeled my right hand away from the wheel, where nothing else had, and I touched her wrist on her lap, trying to soothe her like Christian and I had done for each other a thousand times. Instead of calming her, a higher, crazed sound issued from her mouth at the action. But she didn't peel away. I kept my right hand touching her while I drove with my left, and after a few minutes of silence, she gave a nearly boneless shudder and melted into the seat.

"Do not discount the timing tonight, Ren," Olivia said tiredly, after a few more miles had passed. "Leandred arrived. We were attacked."

Beneath my palm, the metal leech pressed the steering wheel. "You think he was the main target?" The attackers hadn't known my name, but the leader had clearly identified both Olivia and Constantine. Olivia had once told me her mother and Constantine's father were both allies and enemies, so an attack on both of them likely had roots in whatever bound their parents together. "You think he was followed?"

"Or he deliberately led them to us."

I swallowed. Thinking about how Constantine had been willing to sacrifice Olivia was an exercise in tension. "Why? There was no alliance between them. They were going to kill him there at the end. And he would have killed all of them, if you hadn't intervened." Connected as we'd been, I had felt their death in the brittle caramel of Constantine's intentions—as if his emotions had transferred to me to become my own.

"They don't need to be allies to be tools. I know you think of him as a friend," she said, gripping her black skirt, her whole body radiating tension. "But you cannot underestimate Leandred. You need to stop trusting people." Her voice was dark.

My foot pressed harder on the gas pedal as the shadows of the highway thickened around us. "You think he was hoping to gain something by almost dying tonight?"

She looked out her window. "I think that tonight allowed him to use that leech on you." Then more softly she said, without turning, "I think that Origin Magic was actively used in the First Layer tonight."

Chapter Four

RECONNECTION

FORTY MINUTES LATER, Will leaned against the side of my bed, pushing his glasses up his nose and over his gray eyes every few minutes as he examined the containment, container, and leech devices. "I've never held a leech. Wow. Dad said I wasn't allowed to make one in the basement, even for science. No one outside of the Department is allowed to use them, and even then only by special permission from the Tribunal, and even then--"

Neph touched his shoulder and Will stopped speaking, dark head bent while he quietly but enthusiastically investigated the devices, twisting and stroking them while he adjusted the hidden dials in his glasses that allowed him to run a more detailed visual analysis.

Delicately poised on my bed with her legs crossed, Neph was a desert oasis, radiating calming comfort. Olivia, on the other hand, sat rigidly at my desk rifling through one book after another.

A long scratch on Olivia's cheek had been mostly concealed with makeup during the car ride home, but was now red again. Olivia had taken care of non-surface wounds in the car with the small and limited magical first aid kit she had for things that makeup wouldn't cover—enough to pass the inspection of my surprised parents when Olivia and I had breezed in saying that we had changed our minds and gone to an all-ages club in our town for a short while, instead of making the long car ride into the city.

Mom had been so relieved to have us home that she hadn't questioned it. She hadn't even allowed the presence of Will to scare the bejeezus out of her when he and Neph had knocked on the front door. Mom had hit him with a broom the first time they had met, so an awkward reintroduction was a vast improvement.

Neph, on the other hand, had a far different effect. Both of my parents had stared at her long brown hair and warm brown eyes for what felt like ages, then mumbled something about finishing up house projects and getting started on that design they'd been putting off.

Even though the feel of her was muted here, like a veil thrown over the top of her magic, being a muse obviously still held some power in the First Layer.

Still, just like every mage in the First Layer, Will and Neph were cut off from using the living magic of the Earth here. And like Olivia, they were ignoring my distressed directive to return to the Second Layer.

"I'm happy that you are both unharmed," Neph said.

Olivia looked at her, tight-lipped. "The news feeds are silent, but I know you know something about what happened at the library. Alexandria is part of Ahmed Bau's territory."

Will glanced up from his examination and anxiously looked between the two of them.

Neph hesitated for a second—her gaze on me. "Yes."

Will looked even more anxious. Neph touched his shoulder and he relaxed.

"There were a number of devices stolen from the Origin Magic section there. I don't know about the other institutions, but the community conjecture is that the Origin Magic sections were hit at each."

I swallowed.

"We do know there were dolls involved in the attack," Neph said. "No bodies and no blood have been found, and there was nothing to resurrect."

I nodded slowly. "There wasn't any blood inside the library either. Dolls...that makes more sense. I just figured the library, you know..." I made motions with my hands. "Ate the offenders then took a magical napkin to the halls after."

The others stared at me, their grimaces indicating they didn't appreciate such an image.

"Yeah, so." I clapped my hands together to stop the chomping motions of my fingers. "Dolls. Is using them a normal battle tactic?"

Seemed pretty smart to send in expendable forces.

"No." Neph's voice was calm. "Dolls are easily defeated. And golems require extreme magic in their creation and power to control. Constructing unregulated humanoid ones is severely illegal."

"Hard prison sentence." Will piped in unhelpfully. "And soul spells can backfire."

I looked hard at the floor. I had dabbled in dollmaking while trying to resurrect Christian. Legality hadn't made much difference to me. I wondered if there had been trapped souls within the vessels that had been crushed today. I quickly shook the thought away and rubbed my eyes.

"It's not like terrorists are worried about a prison term for illegal doll usage," Olivia said pointedly.

"But how did they get them inside?" Will asked. "The library's scanner would have rejected them."

A memory hit me. "I saw a group carrying long purple boxes—and one of them was the leader of the men who attacked us tonight. Hang on." I grabbed a piece of paper and sketched the scene from the library out quickly, keeping everything to scale—the people lugging the boxes and the boxes themselves.

The boxes weren't human-sized, but they could contain parts. We discussed the mechanics of building the dolls inside the library itself. Of using them as decoys while the terrorists sought their real targets.

Will's gaze turned inward. "Someone tried to grab Olivia and Constantine on the same day the library was attacked. Connected events? How do we protect ourselves?"

My friends had been in danger twice today. And I couldn't get back into the library to complete the protection wards for my parents. I couldn't even return to the Second Layer until I "dimmed"—however that was going to occur. In my present state, I couldn't protect anyone.

Deep breaths, deep breaths! The memory of Christian's voice focused my actions and

I breathed deeply, capping my sudden and imminent freak out.

Everyone was staring at me, and Neph's hand was extended in my direction, as if she was trying to channel magic.

I rubbed a hand across my brow. Panic attacks were always awkward.

I managed to speak again after a minute. "Does your mom have any crossover with the library or a connection to it, Olivia?"

"She is a benefactor, like thousands of others...but otherwise, no. And the events were not connected even if one villain was the same," Olivia said. "I'd bet my entire trust fund that Leandred was behind what happened to us here."

"Liv—"

"He wanted to use your magic, Ren."

Something nonverbal passed between Will, Neph, and Olivia, again. In any other circumstance, I would have been pleased that the three of them were bonding over something. Bonding over shared thoughts on my peculiarities, however, wasn't what I'd had in mind.

"Yes, we all know my magic is weird and wrong. It's noticeable to everyone when I'm not surrounded by thousands of other magical weirdos, like at Excelsine." Or in Alexandria's library. Or the Depot, or Ganymede—all places with so much pulsing magic that I was rendered normal inside.

"Your magic is beautiful," Neph said, her voice sharper than I had heard before.

"Her magic is dangerous and she doesn't know how to stay unnoticed," Olivia said, more pointedly. "Which is—"

Neph's graceful body lines grew taut. "How dare you s—"

Olivia cut her hand through the air, her expression fierce. "The denial of facts is ignorant. Ren will constantly be a danger or in danger for the entirety of her life. She needs to stay unnoticed. And who here thinks that is going to happen?"

"I can see the Layers sometimes," I blurted. "Visibly."

No one looked surprised.

Will rubbed the back of his neck. "Yeah. Ren, Leandred couldn't have messed with the Layer system without being an Origin Mage or connecting through someone who could understand and wield Origin Magic."

I looked quickly at my fingernails, at the charcoal that ghosted underneath. My heart thumped painfully in my chest.

The Layers had been created by three Origin Mages working together. Origin Magic held the entire Layer system together and, as one of the hardest magics to wield, was the only magic that could change it. Which was part of the reason Origin Mages were so feared. The ability to tear through the very fabric of the world was not an ability governments wanted mages running around with.

Will cautiously continued, as if my growing silence was a barrier he needed to carefully surmount. "I've crossed paths with Leandred in classes and on the club's circuit."

The informal delinquent's club...of which I too was a member.

"He is extremely powerful," Will said slowly. "With the kind of intelligence that leads to terminal, dangerous boredom. But even as one of the most powerful mages on campus, he doesn't use magic or see the world the way a mage has to in order to wield Origin Magic. Most people can't actually visualize and manipulate outside of three dimensions."

I cringed and my vision flipped to black-and-white patterns overlaying everything—swirling into each other, one encapsulating another pattern one moment, then being encapsulated the next—then flipped back to stark color. The patterns that had covered my closet door, that had accompanied my Awakening sketch, and that had emerged from the box Raphael Verisetti had taken from that sketch—the same designs that always lurked in my mind when I looked at something for too long—swirled just out of view.

Olivia looked coldly at Will. "I didn't realize you were friends with Leandred."

Will shook his head. "I'm not. We've crossed paths. It's not hard to deduce power levels and intellectual abilities, especially at Excelsine."

"His intentions?" Neph asked.

"Bad?" Will shrugged helplessly. "It's not like his reputation is unearned. But even Delia, who can ferret information out of anyone, says that speaking with Leandred is an exercise in learning nothing of importance. He keeps what he cares about close to his chest while being an open book about everything inconsequential to him. No one ever knows what he is planning or thinking—even on the club circuit, which is a true feat."

Will's attention focused on me.

"I don't know of a single person he calls a friend. Except maybe you, Ren. He gave you that item last term to help us downgrade our offense level when we were going to do the secret ritual—and you hadn't even asked for his help. That was insanely unusual."

Everyone was looking at me, and I could feel Olivia's pointed thoughts about my stupidity in trusting Constantine with anything like friendship. "He felt he owed me. Constantine is very business oriented. He pays debts promptly."

Will's gaze was piercing. "And coming to the non-magical layer to give you a present on your birthday?"

"Hubris?"

Will grinned.

"Stop." I could hear Olivia's teeth grinding together. "I can't stand any more of this. She is not his friend. He plans to use her. That fact is as obvious as the reason why." The pencil in her hand broke in two. "He is giving her things and tending to her like he has never done for anyone else in this world because he knows what she is."

A spark of magic burst from Olivia's fist, a loss of control I had rarely seen from her before.

Will lost his grin, his expression uncomfortable in the extreme. "Which brings us back to the crux of the matter, Ren," he said as my heart thumped in triple time. "There is no way he could have manipulated the Layer System without a seriously rare device or a person at his disposal that had the capability to gain the designation of Origin Mage."

"Okay." My throat closed up and my vision went a little fuzzy around the edges. It was one thing to think about something in the abstract, and another to full out admit I was the monster-in-training of the bedtime stories that mages told their children. "Okay. Yeah. I...I know." No one said anything as they all watched me wrestle with words.

Olivia sat stone-faced in her chair. While we were in the car she had wrestled a vow from me against saying anything to anyone about our trip through Kinsky's painting.

It wasn't like Will or Neph needed another point of data to conclude the matter—I could see from their expressions that both already believed I was on the path to being an Origin Mage—and they were still sitting in my room. But if Neph and Will knew everything—would that make them finally look at me in fear?

I should say nothing more. I should stay absolutely silent.

"Raphael Verisetti stole some of my magic when I Awakened, and he has been using it to do horrible things," I blurted out.

I couldn't take it. Couldn't hold the secrets in any longer. If they were going to leave me, I needed it to be now, not later.

Will was already aware of Raphael's presence at my Awakening—he had been stuck in the man eating sketch Raphael and I had created together, after all. But his eyes went wide at the "still using my magic" part.

Neph's pupils dilated as well, making her soft brown eyes darker. "I...see." She said it calmly, as if I hadn't just told her that I knew the man who was in the top ten most wanted on every Second Layer government list. A man I had seen do terrible things...both physically and emotionally to people.

"He taught my high school art class for six weeks. Before..." I arced a finger helplessly, as if over an invisible timeline in the air.

My once mentor, who had kept me together after my brother died...waiting for my magic to show. Awakenings were powerful magic events, and I still couldn't recreate a fraction of what I had effortlessly created under Raphael's coaxing that one day.

On that day, I could have brought Christian fully back to life, even with him six week's dead. I would have too, even at the high personal cost it would have required. But unbeknownst to me, Raphael had already resurrected Christian to a half-life—a cursed life. After grueling weeks of trying to resurrect him, I had needed to...take care of making sure Christian rested in peace instead.

I ran shaking fingers through my hair and gained strength from the fact that no one had stood up and walked away.

"Have you had other contact with Raphael Verisetti, Ren?" Neph was watching me closely.

I deliberately didn't look at Olivia or Will. "Yes, in Ganymede Circus, during the destruction of the town. And he visited me on campus after the...incident with the bone monster." Incident was a nice way of framing my last necromancy experiment, which had created a monster that had temporarily destroyed a good amount of the mountain near the dormitories.

Olivia made a noise, disapproval of my need to share heavy in her gaze. She thought information should be kept locked tightly and firmly within as few minds as possible. Mostly, just hers.

"He visited? Campus?" Will asked, eyes wide, gaze pulled automatically to Christian's burial sketch which, as always, was situated near my pillow. I would never tell Will why his gaze was always drawn to it. I would let him think it was because of the grand adventure he had had inside its lines.

"He came to our room. Just taunted me a bit." I waved my hand, unwilling to talk about the content of Raphael's taunting—the threats, the stolen research, what he had done to Christian, or the offer he had made. "You know how it goes."

"No, I really don't," Will said frankly. "How could he get on campus? There should be wards against him. Did you tell Dean Marsgrove?" Will's expression was as serious as I had ever seen on his normally mischievous face.

"He knows. He said he would take care of it."

I wouldn't say anything more about the incident—especially not how I could have sacrificed Will to get Christian back. It was bad enough that Olivia had been witness to the conversation with Raphael, but Olivia had needed to blackmail Marsgrove into letting me stay at school for the next term as well. I'd leave that tale to Olivia.

Olivia and Neph weren't paying attention to us, though.

"Are we going to have a problem, Bau?" Olivia said, and with her use of Neph's last name, the tension in the room increased by an entire magnitude.

Neph's warm eyes gathered a layer of frost. "No, we are not, Price."

Will looked between them, biting his lip.

"Who is Ahmed Bau?" I asked, wanting to understand the strained glances and surname references. Olivia had deliberately dropped the name earlier.

"My uncle," Neph said hesitantly. Tension stole into her shoulders. "He has advocated particular plans for forwarding muse rights. I do not share many of my uncle's aims, but I am still part of his commune."

Ah, that kind of issue. "You don't have to agree with your family," I said, giving her an encouraging look. "To still love them and help them."

My Mom and I had disagreed on everything for the last four years.

Neph smiled brightly, and the tension in her body blew free like sand in the final gust of a storm.

Olivia, on the other hand, paused the belligerent note she was writing, and peered up at me with an unreadable expression on her face.

"I've missed you, Ren," Neph said, affection in every syllable. "Even though it has only been three days."

I smiled back, warmth enveloping me. They weren't leaving me.

I thought of six things I could make for Neph to ease her stress or that we could do together when we returned to campus. I started constructing a model for one such project in the back of my mind.

Olivia made a tapping noise on my desk with her pen.

"Do not be concerned, Ren." Neph didn't look at Olivia, she just continued to smile at me in a reassuring way. "Olivia and I are done with our argument."

A ringing noise jolted us from our positions. Will checked a device at his belt. "News reader," he said for my benefit. "On a passive feed. Works like radio in the First Layer."

"Red Re-cap Bravo: Four attacks are currently taking place across the Second Layer. Buda, Pest, Thaican, and Siberiat are all under martial law. All citizens are advised to seek safe lodgings immediately. Any information that could lead to the apprehension of any mages involved should be reported to—"

"Seriously not good. Not counting the libraries and museums today, we've been without a direct attack since Jauvine," Will said while the voice issued standard emergency directions.

Jauvine had been the second town Raphael had destroyed last term using my magic. Using my magic to attack and destroy.

"And it just occurred to me...um, Ren?" Will said.

"Yes?"

Will was examining the walls of my room as if a fully drawn poisonous serpent might leap out at any moment. "Your wards..." He licked his lips nervously. "Who...? I mean, I know you've been working on wards at the library, but who put up the, um, base wards?"

I jolted to my feet, panic running through me, and yanked open the door. "Go. Now. You are in danger here. You need to go."

When no one moved, I strode over and pulled Will upright and tucked a hand underneath Neph's elbow, lifting her to her feet as well, adrenaline giving me strength. "You need to leave for your own safety. Now. Olivia, start packing." I gave Will and Neph a firm push toward the doorway.

Will threw his hands out against the frame of the door, like a cat being forced where it didn't want to go. "What? No. All of us need to go. This is no time to be stubborn. This is not magic we know how to defend against."

My magic.

"I can't leave," I responded. I planted a foot and leaned my shoulder into Neph's back, pushing her against Will and trying to force them through. "Stop catting against the doorframe, Will."

Will gurgled out a few choice expletives. Neph's inarticulate sounds were way more exasperated.

Concentrated on jamming them through the opening, I threw an order over my shoulder, "Olivia, pack."

"No," came the instant reply.

"Ren, you have to come too," Will said, still swearing as I put myself in a less steady, but far stronger, diagonal position that Christian and the football team had used on the practice equipment on the field. I pressed harder, sandwiching the three of us together.

"I can't. Let go, Will. Olivia said I couldn't return to the Second Layer until I 'dimmed' or fixed whatever broke free on me." My wild hand motions were wasted on him as he was entirely focused on setting his feet against the doorframe.

And Olivia never joked.

"You can't stay here," he argued, huffing as he lost an inch of ground and had to lock his elbows again.

"I can. I have enough wards up now to give anyone a nasty surprise, but the ones in place only protect Crowns. And I need to make sure. I have to protect my parents until I fix this. I'll be back soon. Olivia, pack." I attempted to corral her into our shoving sandwich solely through harsh glares over my shoulder.

Olivia's expression was blank and unresponsive to my glowering. "No."

"I need you safe. It's not safe here." I'm not safe.

"No." Her tone brooked no argument.

"Olivia—"

"No." Her gaze was immovable and held mine.

"You know better than anyone what I've been trying to do with the wards." I grunted as Will got a foot in place and started exerting pressure backward. "Raphael placed the original ones. He placed them over a period of a month, and probably while slowly sucking away any pre-Awakening magic that I leaked. He never let me paint before my Awakening but he was always encouraging me to draw totems and other weird things."

Like abstract concept assignments on drawing invisibility. My mouth tightened. I could hear his silky words in my memory: 'Concentrate on making that which is visible invisible. Project the suggestion of invisibility. Of the eye sliding right by.'

God, it sucked. He always knew exactly what to say to get me to create. And how to betray me when I needed help. At the reiterated thought of how his actions had stopped me from resurrecting my brother, I couldn't stop a half-sob from emerging.

Olivia abruptly stood and strode toward us. Finally. I ruthlessly shoved thoughts of Raphael's betrayal and losing my brother into the background. I would never fail again in protecting my loved ones. I could get Olivia to go with Will and Neph back to safety.

Olivia strode up to Will and gave a sideways karate chop against the inside of his elbow. He squawked and his arm buckled, breaking his position. The suddenly unchecked momentum in his direction thrust the three of us through the doorway and into an ungainly sprawled pile in the hall. I blinked at the cream carpeting an inch away from my face. Blood flow slowly made its way down my neck and into my hanging head.

"Ugh. Olivia, why? And Ren, why do I always end up beaten on the floor when I come to your house?" Will's glasses were skewed diagonally across his face, his gaze hampered by the trim board near his nose.

Between us, Neph was pliant, and where the bare skin of our wrists met I could almost feel the calming and healing spirit that always hovered around her. I could almost sense that spirit flowing through Will too. Like we were a sandwich full of homemade ingredients. Already off-center on the pile, I reluctantly pushed myself free of them, making sure not to step on any limbs.

I collapsed against the nearest wall and let my head drop into my hands. "I'm sorry."

Neph's fingers were around my wrist almost immediately, her touch creating warmth that seeped into my skin. I gave her a watery smile. Will was sitting with his knees drawn up on the other side of the hallway, sheepishly running his hand up the back of his head.

"I'm sorry too," Will said. "The first thing is to figure out how to dim you—or whatever." He waved his hand in a vague circling motion toward my head.

His gaze went back to my room and to the devices that he had been playing with earlier. "And with some advanced preparation...there is nothing stopping us from coming back tomorrow with better personal defenses, more information, and a plan. I...I have some thoughts. Let me research some things tonight."

Will was sporting the glint in his eyes that meant serious illegal business would be forthcoming.

Neph cocked her head. "Based on what you've said, you shouldn't leave the wards at all, Ren, if you can help it."

"Can do. Olivia,"—I made a shooing motion at her—"pack."

"No."

"Yes."

"Are you going to eject me from your house and protection, Ren?" She looked at me coldly. "Because I'm not leaving otherwise." She shoved Will's and Neph's things into their hands, addressing them. "The taxi will be here in five minutes to take you to the coffee shop."

I hadn't even heard her calling one.

"Olivia—"

"You don't understand, Ren, I know," she said, her voice was cold, but her body language indicated that she was hanging by a thread. "We discussed this in the car already. And I don't need you to understand anything other than I'm not going."

Will and Neph busied themselves by standing and mindlessly fiddling with their packs—adjusting the straps on each other's shoulders. They judiciously did not look our way.

Five lost arguments and five absurdly short minutes later, I watched the yellow cab disappear from view, then trudged back to the family room where Olivia was being tightly hugged by my mom on the couch.

"Oh, Ren." Mom's expression was distressed, and she pulled me down into their crushing hug as I entered.

I gave her an awkward pat in return. What was going on? I looked over to Olivia for direction, but she was staring wide-eyed at my mom as if my mother was some sort of rare magical creature.

Catching my gaze, Olivia shook off the expression and jerked her head to the left. I followed her gaze to the late night newscast on TV.

The announcer said, "Five men were attacked in gang-related violence in an area of the city usually free of gang activity. Authorities have said this was a random event. All five victims suffered brain related injuries and are currently under watch at St. Mary's. In other news, a tsunami has decimated the western coast of—"

The newscaster enumerated a devastating death toll in some faraway place, but my mind was stuck on the "gang" violence and brain related injuries.

My mom's hug grew more fierce. "That's right near where you were going! You just missed it. My baby. Not again," she whispered almost too low for me to hear. I didn't have to hear it, though, to understand her freak out. Christian and I hadn't been lucky enough to avoid the same type of incident four months ago.

I gave in and returned the embrace fully.

Dad gave me a bear hug with whispered endearments, and Mom hugged the stuffing out of Olivia again. Mom petted her hair in an entirely surreal gesture. One didn't "pet" Olivia Price. Mom was obviously unaware of this.

"I'm going to make popcorn." Mom wiped her eyes and hurried out of the room. I hoped she wasn't going to start scrubbing the kitchen again... Or start crying.

I looked at the new drawings that were pulsing with energy on the walls around us in an artistic blend of the abstract, geometric, and fanciful. I had carefully hung them throughout the house in the last few days. The designs—the very fibers of the paper—were full of magic as powerful and intense as I could manage under the constraints of my brief library time.

Normal people would see them as static pictures, instead of the vibrating forces that they appeared to me.

Without being able to use active magic in the house, hanging them had only been possible for me because of Raphael's base wards.

My lips tightened.

"Ren?"

"S'okay, Dad," I said, without looking at him. "It'll be okay."

I hugged my cuffed arm close to my chest. It had to be.

~*~

I had given Olivia my bed and slept in the trundle beneath since the start of vacation.

Tonight, though, Olivia was lying as stiff as a mummy on the bed, her arms tightly crossed and the side of her body pressed against the wall, leaving a conspicuous amount of empty space next to her.

"Safety sleeping?" I asked as lightly as I could, knowing that I had to take the lead. If someone had told me months ago that I would be leading any social interactions, I would have laughed.

"Fine." She gave a wave, as if long-suffering, but she didn't have to move an inch, already in sharing position.

I pushed in the trundle and climbed in with her, our shoulders touching as I got comfortable. Olivia stiffened, then relaxed. I could feel the low hum of sympathetic magic circulating between us. It wasn't live, active magic, it was just a simple connection. Since I was connected to the wards, and Olivia's innate, natural magic was mixing with mine, the entire ward set would strengthen as a matter of course. Probably not enough to keep Raphael away, should he decide to do something, but enough to enhance the protections already in place.

Enough to fortify the newly wrought wards that I had constructed in Olivia's presence. They had to be enough. Please.

I stared at the ceiling for a long while. "My magic—"

"A rock is just an object until it is picked up and used to bash in someone's skull."

"But—"

"That someone illegally took your magic and chose to use it in such ways is not on you."

I nodded shortly, jerkily. "I'm sorry for throwing you lip over toe through that doorway. And yanking you through the painting."

"Well, you should be sorry for those things." She tried to make it sound like a joke, but it fell flat in the silence of the room. I could feel the comforter tug as she gripped it harder.

"We were going to die," she whispered, looking up at the ceiling. "Had our positions been reversed, I would have let go of you." Her voice was barely audible—a confession in the dark. "I wouldn't have thought otherwise."

I gently nudged her shoulder. "Letting go would have been the smart move."

She didn't respond.

"It would have," I repeated.

"Ren—"

"Liiiiiv," I drawled out, trying to tease her out of the shaken, strange mood that had suddenly overtaken her.

"I don't...I don't know how..." Her voice trailed off miserably.

I turned my head toward her. "You are my friend," I said definitively. "We are friends."

"Okay. Yes." Her voice was even shakier.

I turned back and gave her another light bump with my shoulder, letting it rest there. I could feel some of her tension physically drain away. "Let's get some sleep."

Surprisingly, she dropped off to sleep immediately, which allowed my own tension—forcibly subdued so I could help Olivia—to creep back into existence.

With thoughts of protection—successes and failures—heavy on my mind, my thoughts invariably turned to Christian and his life and death. My brother—who I had always protected, usually from his own hilarious schemes—had pushed me to the side when we'd been attacked by rogue mages four months ago. He had used that single moment to save me instead of using his newly awakened magic to save himself.

I couldn't let that kind of thing happen again.

I thought of Olivia's words of a rock being just a rock. I wrapped the idea around me, but I couldn't reconcile the matter in my head. Once the rock was used as a weapon...it was considered a weapon.

It was a long time before I fell asleep.

Chapter Five

THE ENEMY WITHIN

FIVE BLEARY MORNINGS LATER saw Will, Neph, Olivia, and I huddled in my room watching a looped cycle of news reports, listening to Second Layer gossip, and doing "dimming" work.

The Second Layer had enacted more serious security measures and most of the major cities were locked down. I had seen news feeds of Alexander Dare helping with security on three separate occasions. I could pick him out of a crowd of five thousand combat mages—it was a little sad.

With the new security measures, returning through the checkpoint would be a concern, but I was decidedly grounded, at present. And my magic was "lurching" increasingly beneath my cuff, trying to escape.

Will had the good idea—and sheer balls—to suggest using the leech, Olivia's container, and the four person ritual we had used last term to heal campus, in order to "fix" me. That Olivia had been displeased with the suggestion, was an understatement.

Arguments. So many arguments.

Olivia had been pretty harsh with her thoughts about Will's motivation. One thing about Will's delinquency, though, was that while he misused magic, very frequently, he never misused friends. Constantine, on the other hand...

I rubbed my fingers along the postage-sized stamp of material that Constantine had given me for my birthday. There was nothing remarkable about it in size or shape, but nothing about Constantine or anything he created was unremarkable. I poked the middle and a ripple ran along the tiny fibers. The entire paper lengthened with the motion, more fibers rippling out to accommodate the change in size.

The material kept its innate properties while changing shape and size at my command. It had been created specifically for me to draw upon, then shrink again.

"Ren, are you listening?" Olivia demanded. She and Neph had finally come to a grudging agreement on how to do the ritual piece.

"Yup." I flattened my palm and drew my fingers inward to collapse the material again.

"What is that?" Will leaned closer.

"Leandred's birthday present." Olivia's lip curled. "I recommend against touching it."

Will poked the edge anyway. He swore and stuck his finger in his mouth. "Electrified," he said, his voice, garbled. He shook out his hand. I could see him forcing himself not to reach forward to touch the material again. "And still able to maintain its original attributes regardless of size. Fantastic."

Its protection mode activated by the foreign touch, the material immediately shrunk the rest of the way to its postage-sized shape. Days ago, Olivia had experienced the same misfortune as Will.

"That's unlike anything I've ever seen," Will said, leaning forward, fingers twitching. "He made that for you? I was so right."

"No, you weren't. It's not friendship, it's calculated advancement. Leandred never relinquishes a worthwhile investment," Olivia said irritably. It was only something she had repeated five times already.

"I know, Liv." I stuck the stamp back in its envelope and picked up the leech, giving it a little shake. "Now, what say we give the ritual and this bad boy a try?"

"Yes." Will pumped a fist into the air.

"No," came the other two voices in the room.

If it had been up to Will and me, we would have had a trial under our belts ten minutes after discussing it the first time, and two-dozen trials since. But with Neph and Olivia participating, we weren't allowed to do more than read books and plot.

I exchanged an agonized look with Will. This whole "safety" thing was grueling.

"We've agreed to do it, but there is still something missing, and you both know it," Neph said, never losing her normal, calm facade. She was spreading all the serenity she could muster, as her muse training dictated. "Will and

I won't see you for a few days, but we will be doing research and asking the elders about spell linking. We will have plenty of time to fix things before school starts."

That meant Day Five was also a scratch.

And not being able to do something made the emotional impact of the week surrounding Christmas a thing from which I could not escape. Maintaining a grueling, sunny expression was at an all-time high in the face of the holiday and all the family events surrounding it.

Overly cheerful during the daytime, I pulled Olivia into everything, tried to keep smiles on every face, and forcibly attacked the creeping sadness I could feel in my parents every time they had a moment to think. So I didn't let them have time to think.

I pushed aside my research in favor of keeping everyone as jolly as possible. For my parents, who had lost their son. For Olivia, who couldn't quite understand my family's bond, but felt compelled to participate in every moment she was afforded—playing four-person board games and cards, discussing politics with my dad, cooking with my mom, watching crappy and awesome movies, teaching me how not to be crushed by her at chess.

Everyone was going to be happy and safe, or so help me, I was going to go on the reign of terror that a mage with a proclivity for Origin Magic was expected to muster.

Determination fueled me, even when I failed to fully sleep at night, plagued by fevered dreams I could never quite remember upon waking.

But the itch of my magic had almost started to hurt in the last few days. I missed using magic. I missed Excelsine. What if—?

A tentative hand petted my hair, making me jerk out of my thoughts. Olivia was on the couch next to me, her hazel eyes questioning, her book open on her lap. Across from us, Mom was doing something on her computer and Dad was attempting the crossword in the paper.

I smiled—a real smile at Olivia. She smiled back and gave me another tentative pat, before returning to her book. Foot to leg, magic hummed around us. I took a deep breath. But I couldn't release all of my anxiety.

Neph and Will were taking care of their demands at home and wouldn't return until the twenty-eighth. Add a few days more to that and we'd be looking at the start of school again—possibly with me unable to return.

And Olivia...Olivia was hunkering down, as if she had already started planning the best way we would need to live as hermits in the basement. That thought made my magic itch worse.

Two nights after Christmas, and with increasingly wrenching thoughts on my mind, I fell asleep with one thought in the front of my mind. I had to do something.

~*~

Monsters and beasts lunged and snarled from the walls of my room, wisps of magic and memory swirling them into knights and warriors, then back again, as I stood in the center of the madness.

My walls were once more alive, and the creatures, graphics, and mad things I had painted and drawn, galloped chaotically—knights and warriors, monsters and beasts—amongst twining grasses and mercurial landscapes. There was no more brown, congealed paint on the walls. Colors swirled around me, like crazy, painted fireflies. If only I could catch one... If only I could make everything safe...

"So sad, butterfly?"

I whipped around. Raphael Verisetti stood in the center of a star burst, relaxed and unconcerned, his warm golden skin and eyes in direct opposition to his nature.

Without thinking, I threw a blast of magic at him. Astonishingly, magic surged to my fingers, then shot into a kaleidoscope of riotous colors that swirled around him. A strange, non-magical deflection. He smiled at my shock.

"What...? How...?" I looked at the swirling colors, then quickly checked the bed, to make sure Olivia was okay.

"She's fine. Quite a dark bit of prey, though, isn't she?" He smiled. "I do hope she survives what is coming. She'd make a powerful bishop on my board with a little...motivation."

The colors swirled around Olivia's sleeping form, then moved back to Raphael. I watched the colors tessellate. "I'm dreaming."

"Mmmm." His head cocked to the side. "Such boring and sad dreams, butterfly. Tsk, tsk." He strolled forward. "But you have finally let me come rescue you from them."

Even knowing it was a dream, I backed away. Raphael had powers and knowledge that I did not, and we both knew I was not yet his equal. "I don't require rescuing."

"Ah, then you can rescue me from them. Depressing. Elation and triumph would serve you far better."

The shifting colors brightened his eyes, edging them with a manic tinge. The edge had always been there, but I concentrated on it now. Helping Olivia with her personal-interaction study had made a few things obvious. "Elation can only be followed by decay."

"Don't be boring, butterfly. I detest such consummate inaction that analyzing others begets. Better instead to make people dance to your favorite tune. You were made for the latter. And you know it. That's why you sent for me."

My fingers curled, kaleidoscopic color squeezing from between my knuckles. "I didn't send for you." Not again, not again.

"And yet, here I am." He spread his arms wide. "Squeezing through your explicitly warded wishes and into the absolute prison of a padded cell you have made the place you call home."

I set my mind to undoing whatever I had done to invite him into my dream.

"Butterfly, I can feel that. I'm hurt." He pressed a hand against his heart.

"Did you send those men?" I demanded. "Did you try to kidnap Olivia and Constantine?"

Cities and towns and global destruction, I could barely comprehend the kind of scale at play in Raphael's world. But the fate of my friends...that, I clearly understood.

"You wound me, thinking I would find any excitement in such dull tasks. I have allied myself with witless creatures, unfortunately. Ones who now believe themselves to be stalks of celery." He looked at Olivia's sleeping figure. "Wretched and lovely, that little bit of magic performed by your friend. It made it impossible for me to figure out why they were there. Your entire quadrant should be off the map. An annoyance all the way around, as they lost us something valuable. But do remind me to praise your roommate for her vengeful creativity when next we meet."

I focused on Olivia and the steady rise of her chest. I wasn't going to let that happen.

"You, however..." He grabbed my chin. It felt as real as any touch. "Allowing that boy to use your magic? Don't ever let him do so again."

I yanked away. "Only you?"

He smiled. "At another time, I might cheer our melodramatics, but you have been foolish and require fixing. You do me no good stuck in the non-magical world. And if we linger here too long, you will be unable to accept my glorious proposal."

"I'm not making any deals with you," I said flatly.

"You've already made a deal with me. The tube of lilac paint for a second level magic. A contract that has not yet been fulfilled on your side."

Even in the dream, at his reminder, I could feel the magic of the contract we'd made circulating through my veins. I clawed at my arm and the promise living inside of me.

"You wanted that tube of paint so much. You would have done anything. On a scale that numbers to ten, what is a pitiful second level magic in the scheme of things?"

"Bad, when you are involved." I'd been so stupid. But he was right, I would have done a lot to gain that tube and the promise it had presented to resurrect my brother.

"Hurtful, but true. Alas, for you, not even death will stop you from fulfilling the terms. And if you stay in the non-magical world, that is what will result—in glorious and sanguinary technicolor detail."

He could be lying. I wanted him to be a liar, instead of just being painfully cryptic and demented. But the furious, painful itch under my skin, under my new cuff, said he spoke the truth.

Raphael's brow rose in profound amusement. "A developing Origin Mage who suppresses her magic and its use...is a catastrophe in the making. And deadly to all around her when the devastation unleashes."

I swallowed, deeply unhappy at what he was hinting. A glitter of gold caught my eye. Even here in the dreamscape my subconscious mind conjured the box he always carried.

"Come, come. Let's make this a painless transaction." Raphael smiled, and the box disappeared with a flick of his wrist. But I knew it was still on him somewhere. Since my Awakening, I had never seen him without it.

Made from my magic. My Awakening magic. Thoughts tumbled and my mind pressed hard. My magic. I needed that box.

Raphael's smile turned gentle. "One thing at a time, butterfly."

His finger pulled along the edge of the stars to the left of him, gently slitting the fabric of the dream, and hinting at a world beyond. "A little friendly advice—don't tarry long in the non-magic world once we've finished here."

He stepped one foot through the rip in the dream and I forced my gaze away from what lay beyond.

"You will come with me whether you like it or not." His amusement infuriated me. "However...there are things I can offer for swift cooperation."

No.

"Count yourself fortunate that I need your promise fulfilled now, butterfly. Your merry little band of misfits can't fix the spells you ripped away when you consorted with that boy. Can't fix something that I specifically put into place. You cannot freely return to the Second Layer without my help. And you have bound your lovely companion to you. She won't leave without you, and what do you think will happen to her, trapped here with you, a ticking time bomb with that cuff upon your wrist?"

"I haven't bound Olivia." My anxiety ratcheted higher. "And I'll make her return, eventually."

He smiled. "Binding someone doesn't require force. Someone so bereft of genuine love and affection, once given a taste, will never let it go. But these are paltry matters. Come."

I stared at Olivia's relaxed form. My heart was beating too rapidly for a dream state. "I'll get Marsgrove to fix the spells."

"Didn't you learn from that mistake already?" Raphael's eyes sparked maliciously, but he quickly smoothed his expression into serious lines. "You are allowing yourself to fall behind mentally, butterfly."

The sincere voice he had wielded and the mentor persona he had worn in the weeks following my brother's death and before my Awakening, were as compelling now as they had been then. The sudden absence of madness in his eyes and the momentary glimpse of a long lost friend temporarily muted my hatred.

"You've lost your focus here during this week-long lamentation of death." His gaze was piercing and serious. "But you have no time to grieve. You will stay sharp or I will kill you myself."

The dreamscape started to unravel around us, and I gathered the tangles of dispersing thought. "You are the reason Christian is gone," I said.

"No. Those idiots who didn't realize what they had are the reason. I simply followed the delicious trail left behind and clasped opportunity by the throat. But that's all in the past. If you allow the Department to chain you when you get back to school, I will wipe you free of this Earth. Which would be dearly regrettable. Come. This is your last chance to follow and bargain freely."

He stepped fully through.

Don't follow. I stayed where I was.

"You will come anyway," he said in a singsong manner. "And what might you find, should you follow freely?" His low voice beckoned from the other side of the void, reading my mind in my own scape. "The key to the protection of your family and friends? What sorts of answers live here in the beyond? What sorts of...things?"

Raphael knew me well—had studied me and picked apart my brain when I'd been at my most vulnerable.

Darkness followed the path of the unraveling dream as threads slipped from the sky.

"What might you lose by allowing your anger to override opportunity? Have I not protected your home and family from discovery thus far? I know you want to be able to protect them apart from my machinations. How can you protect anyone if you stay here, neutralized in the non-magical world?"

Brilliant colors and sounds flashed and echoed through the slit.

Don't follow.

A sweeping sound of melody and light pierced through and coiled around me. Thrice damned determination, curiosity, and purpose moved me forward. I felt the promise I had exchanged for the tube of paint urging me onward.

The only way that I would beat Raphael and become more was through knowledge and experience. I touched the edge of the split dream—the sheerest silk in the deepest shades of purpled black.

Don't follow.

"What might you discover, butterfly? How will you finally break our tie?"

I pressed the curled edge inward with my fingers and stepped through.

Chapter Six

HOLY INNOCENTS' DAY

OLIVIA'S NEWS READER beeped incessantly for attention, but she continued to ignore it, watching me through narrowed eyes as I fumbled with my clothes, awkwardly pulling on a new shirt and trying to get out of the stretchy pants I had worn to bed.

"The spell just snapped back into place during the night? That is the explanation you are going with?" she asked.

"Mmmhmm. Sometime during the night, it just whooshed back." I made a swooshing motion with my hand so I didn't have to meet her gaze. "Now we can return to the Second Layer." I chewed on my middle fingernail, my gaze on the floor.

My words weren't false. The spell had whooshed back into place. Raphael had just done the whooshing.

"Ren—"

A shrill noise issued and the needle on Olivia's grid detector registered five marks. A hologram burst up from her news reader as a weird sensation overtook me—like an enormous echo of my own magic pulsing somewhere far away.

"Return now," Olivia's reader slowly and unnaturally articulated. "We repeat—all Second Layer citizens must return to the Second Layer immediately and head to a designated safe zone."

The magical echo gave a final burst as a hologram of a man burst into view. A ruined town smoked in the background of the image.

"Greetings from the once illustrious little town of Sassraf! We citizens of the Third Layer have endured long months of negotiations with your Second Layer politicians, and have offered much to regain what is rightfully ours—to rebuild our glorious and storied empire. Unfortunately, the politicians are without compassion or understanding for those possessing other nationalities, and for the people they serve as well! It is you, the people, who must rise against them."

On the street, a shot of a cowering crowd came into holographic view.

"Your politicians told us to 'do our worst.' Such an interesting turn of phrase." The man smiled, all teeth and sharp edges. "Your authorities can not protect you, not now, even if they want to." The man tapped his lip. "Or perhaps we just haven't found the people they will protect. Nevertheless, these folks' right to defense by their leaders seems to be absent. On today of all days."

Olivia's lips tightened. "It's Holy Innocents' Day," she said to me.

I thought of the painting by Reubens—The Massacre of the Innocents—that immortalized the biblical event.

"No," I said, as if the word could negate my sudden understanding of what was about to take place. "Turn it off, Olivia," I said, as the man grabbed his first victim.

"Hijacked feeds continue until the magic ends. They've done it before by targeting the broadcasting devices of every Second Layer citizen. The hologram can not be turned off." Olivia's gaze didn't falter as the first victim fell forward and the next was pulled into place.

Deliberately killed with magic. Like Christian. My eyes shifted focus as the second body in the hologram jerked and fell.

"Even if you shatter the device, the magic will remain, and the hologram will continue," Olivia said, her expression shuttered. She didn't look away from the man's face.

The leader looked directly into my eyes. It had to be the spell, making it seem like he was looking directly at the viewer. It spiked my stomach, though, as if he was insinuating that I was personally responsible.

"We will grant you the amount of time in seconds that you have withheld from us in years. Give us back our homeland. Cease your greed and the greed of your politicians. Or perhaps next time we will find someone your leaders actually care about."

Like Olivia. Or Constantine. Targeted on the street. Or my parents, ordinary and magicless.

Or like Christian.

I distantly heard screams in my head. I stumbled, and my wrist pressed against the wall as I tried to steady myself.

Sunlight coming through my bedroom window turned laser-scope red, and a massive boom shook the house.

I pulled my hands together and looked down. Crimson. Numbly, I looked at the walls of my room, and the tinted paint made from my Awakening. The dried paint had started dripping again. My cuff...I had pressed it against the wall, inadvertently or not, and the remnants of paint were eating through the metal as I watched. Red lines seared paths from one edge of the metal to the other, then connected out to the paint on the walls, connecting to the tinted brown paint, mixing it to the color of stained blood.

The red lines sank into the wards, sparking crimson...sparking the absence of my magic's control––the complete freedom of any intention that rocketed through my brain, save for freedom and destruction.

I threw myself toward Olivia and we fell to the floor as a second boom rocked the foundation. Something flared in my backyard, and the man in the hologram looked behind him in sudden, virtual terror.

The hologram combusted violently, the hijacked feed ending in whatever destruction had been about to overcome the man. I tucked Olivia under me. I could hear the crackling flames and smell the acrid smoke. The earth made a horrible rending sound beneath us. We were going to die. I was going to kill us and I couldn't stop it.

A man's hand clamped painfully around my half cuffed wrist, excruciatingly pushing the flexible metal strands back together. The sounds, the shaking, the smell of fire...abruptly stilled. The redness sucked into itself, leaving behind brilliant yellow sunlight and a horrible silence.

The clamped hand wrenched the broken cuff up my arm, tearing skin, and snapped a new cuff around my wrist. The flexible metal fused together, tightening fiercely to touch every bit of skin underneath it.

Emptiness ached inside of me as my magic was abruptly consumed and neutralized once more.

The hand squeezed the new cuff painfully, as the broken one was yanked away. A rustling of cloth signaled that the broken one had been shoved into a pocket. My gaze was frozen, though, on the paint drying to brown once more on the wall in front of me, and my thoughts rooted on what had almost occurred.

"Olivia," a rough male voice said.

"I'm fine, cousin." But Olivia, still trapped beneath me, stared at me, her expression unreadable.

"On your feet, Miss Crown." I let Phillip Marsgrove, Dean of Special Projects at Excelsine, yank me up. I didn't care where he had come from so suddenly. Just that he had stopped whatever I had started.

"I didn't mean it," I blurted, tears forming. There were so many things I meant with that statement that I wasn't sure which of them I wanted Marsgrove to hear.

His arctic-gray eyes were cold behind his silver-rimmed glasses. He was wearing a black-and-silver pinstripe suit again, like some sort of First Layer armor. I blinked my eyes dry and focused on the top button—one of the many inconspicuous-looking masculine adornments—on his suit.

"We are returning to campus. Now. Pack your things." His painful grip remained on my wrist.

This time when told to pack, Olivia didn't argue.

Excelsine's dozens of terraced and enchanted mountain levels, and its never ending, stunning views from each, were hard to appreciate as Marsgrove pulled us through the screaming crowds that had collected in thick pockets at the top of campus. The overwhelming magic of campus, with its sensational architecture, strange animals, and dangerously whimsical atmosphere was smothered by a blanket of fear.

The same despair that had been present after the destruction of Ganymede Circus, was tangible, at ten times that strength. Mages were crying hysterically. Accusing gazes darted everywhere. Judgment Magic was being wielded indiscriminately and with severity—attacking people who had told white lies that morning along with those who had an urge to kill.

"Kill them! Kill them all," shrieked a girl who was alternating between sobbing uncontrollably and screaming incoherently. A stray piece of Judgment Magic zapped her, physically punishing her for her ill thoughts, but the punishment only increased the volume of her vengeful cries.

The mage who had cast the magic was also kneeling painfully on the ground. Anyone using Judgment Magic became subject to its backlash, as I had experienced with the Justice Tablets. But in such frenzies, those who felt it their duty to punish wrongdoers, stoically accepted the physical consequences that were returned.

"Seneca needs us to be strong," said a boy who reached down to lift the incoherent girl.

Marsgrove's hand tightened. Olivia's impassive eyes met mine. "Seneca Holmes was in the hijacked feed. In the lineup. She's in the year ahead of us. Lives in Sassraf."

I shuddered. Had I blown her up too? I didn't know what had happened there at the end.

Nor did I know what had caused that initial echo of my magic. Inside of my dream that wasn't a dream, I had given Raphael a cleaning spell wrapped inside a finishing cloth. It had seemed so harmless. It still did. Cleaning spells didn't destroy towns, or dodge government safeguards, or hijack communications.

But the echo... My magic had clearly been used in some way.

Manic, muddled thoughts overwhelmed me and I sought a focus to stop my burgeoning hysteria. My eyes snapped to the powerfully familiar figure standing at the grassy edge of Top Circle.

Likely wishing he was out there fighting something, Alexander Dare's shoulders were tight with tension as he stared down the mountain while speaking to a mage in a dark suit. The man at his side turned slightly, just enough for me to catch a ragged breath. Dare's uncle—the same one who had tried to convince Dare to leave me for dead the night Christian died.

Mages in similar severe, dark suits vigilantly cast dark gazes over everyone passing them by. The Department's enforcers had been highly visible in the Depot as well. With upturned collars and buckled dark chokers secured around each wearer's throat, they were impossible to miss.

They had been here at the end of last term in order to determine what or who had been responsible for the chaos. They hadn't found me yet. But it was only a matter of time until they did. Perhaps minutes, even.

An enchantment popped into my head, then wildly rippled out. The crowd screamed as the ripples grew and distorted the air in crystal waves.

Marsgrove's fingers constricted painfully around my left wrist and a half-sob took me. The enchantment had just slipped out—and it was a spell I didn't remember ever learning—which meant that Raphael had given me the knowledge surreptitiously.

The gazes of the choker-wearers darted everywhere, looking for a target to blast, but their hard stares slipped over me as if I didn't exist.

Alexander Dare's gaze, on the other hand, directly connected with mine.

Marsgrove yanked me down one of the alleys between the Top Circle buildings, as words fell hysterically from my lips. "I didn't... I don't—"

"Shut up," Olivia hissed around Marsgrove, on his other side. "Say nothing."

"I disagree," Marsgrove said, his gaze murderous. "Feel free to expound at will. Loudly."

Then he grimaced, as if suddenly stabbed. That meant the contract spell that Olivia had placed on him had decided that he was attempting to breach the agreement by coercing me into speech. He pressed his lips together and verbalized no more of the assuredly dark thoughts running through his head.

But, as we marched down the mountain and toward the dorm, he never let go of my wrist. He hooked his free arm with Olivia's, providing the illusion of a double-armed escort rather than a jailor transporting his most dangerous criminal.

In my room in the First Layer, Marsgrove had been able to affix the new control cuff—my third—without my permission because of the academic contract I had signed in blood months ago. It chafed my skin and magic worse than the first two cuffs had, but I had to believe it couldn't harm me irrevocably. Olivia had covered all bases in her personal contract with him, so the cuff had to be an administration-approved design.

Even if it was going to do horrible things, though, it was too late at this point for me to do anything other than determine the best path forward. I let the thought bleed through my hysteria and infect the rest of my fears. Lamentation would gain me nothing. Dealing with and fixing things was my only path.

We briskly entered the Magiaduct—the nine-story aqueduct-like stone structure that ran the circumference of the Fifth Circle and housed all of Excelsine's students.

Marsgrove shoved us into our dorm room, and as soon as the door closed he started yelling. "The Department is swarming campus, finally getting their opportunity to implant their devices. They were here last term because of you and your actions. And now, with today's events they have justification for an actual foothold. They are placing "protections" everywhere on campus. And you—you—thought it a good idea to use Origin Magic on the Department while in the midst of a crowd?"

My throat closed up and I could barely hear the expletives he reeled off in my direction.

"Don't leave this room. Don't approach them. Don't do anything," he said, his tone dark and containing no amusement. "You are going to destroy us all. You've already begun to, and my own cousin has made it so I can do nothing. I can't leave you in the First Layer, and I can't allow you anywhere else in this one."

I rubbed my wrist to relieve the deep indentations from his fingers. Numbness was starting to be replaced by anger. "You said you were going to check on us. It's the twenty-eighth. Where were you when we were attacked?" I asked angrily. "I care nothing about what happens to me. But Olivia? How could you—?"

Marsgrove grabbed my arm, this time around the bicep, and gave me a shake. "Attacked when?"

Olivia gave me a tight look as she pried his hand away, then steered her thirty-something-year-old cousin to the side of the room. She drew a clear curtain of magic from one wall to the other, and they began to argue behind the privacy ward.

Their argument meant Olivia hadn't mentioned the First Layer attack or our presence during the Library of Alexandria onslaught to anyone in her family.

I numbly unpacked in the strangely silent room while they argued.

As I was putting my last shirt away, the edges of the privacy spell lifted. Marsgrove turned to leave.

"Are you going to take the paint spell off of me?" I demanded as he grabbed the knob. I needed to learn how to control these abilities. Olivia...my parents...the earth opening... I shuddered involuntarily and stared at Marsgrove. He needed to free me so that I could do better.

"No. God, no. Be very thankful that I can say nothing about you to anyone, or else you'd be on a dissection table already." He barely spared me a look as he slammed the door forcefully behind him.

I started shaking as adrenaline rocketed through me.

Olivia whisked items from her suitcase. Her movements were tight and controlled, but her fingers, too, shook as she placed a pouch on her desk.

Watching her shake caused my magic to thrust upward with unconscious intention, but the new cuff immediately dispersed the force—controlling my uncontrollable urges since I could not.

I shakily touched the flexible metal, momentarily thankful for it. It hadn't stopped the Department spell, however. I needed to figure out if that override had been due to power or Raphael.

"Liv—"

"Phillip said he only found us because he recognized what was happening when a similar type of magic was used in Sassraf," she said, drowning out my question, and calling Marsgrove by his first name.

I nodded slowly. "I felt an echo of my magic being used somewhere far away. It was...strange."

It hadn't been the same as the magic Raphael had used in Ganymede that made the world slow down around me, but rather like an echo of it. The world had slowed for me when the other town—Jauvine—had also been destroyed last term.

Something tickled the edges of my consciousness.

Olivia ripped a coat from her bag. "Phillip also said your house is a dead zone in a community mind-controlled by a terrorist," she said. "Who knows what got sapped from you by us being there. Despite my detector giving off alerts, nothing reported on the grid during our stay. Nothing, Ren. Phillip silently checked on our way here."

My heart never seemed to do anything but pound anymore. "Wha—?"

"Can you feel the connection to the wards on your house?" Olivia asked, her gaze intent and demanding—nearly anxious. "To your parents?"

I felt around my magic, which had been reactivated like a plug stuck into a socket upon entry to the Second Layer. The feeling attached to the house wards was intact and strong. "Yes."

Relief crossed Olivia's face so swiftly that her expression crumpled. "Good. That's g..." Olivia froze, her last word trailing off.

"Olivia?" I moved toward her automatically.

"That crasseetar," Olivia whispered, standing straight, her entire body tightening, her gaze turned inward, betrayed.

"What? Who?" I asked, alarmed, both by her posture, her translated swear word, and my sudden inability to complete more than a one-word sentence.

Her gaze was vicious as she focused on me. "Leave the building. Now. Don't return for at least two hours."

The magic that connected us together shot the severity of her demand straight through my nerve endings. Despite Marsgrove's demand that I do the exact opposite, I scrambled and grabbed my messenger bag—thankfully still packed with my notebooks and reader—then shot out the door.

As I quickly descended the dorm's steps, I passed a statuesque woman calmly ascending. My feet nearly entangled themselves in recognition. I had seen the woman before, featured in the news feed after the Ganymede attack—the woman who had made the comment that anyone displaying talent for Origin Magic would be "dealt with." The posh, icy woman I had thought—at the time—that Olivia would love. My brain sorted features quickly, superimposing posture, features, and regard in overlaid images.

My subconscious had obviously recognized the similarities while watching the news feed, but I had been far too focused on other things at the time to make the conscious connection.

I froze, gripping the rail, as Helen Price turned the corner.

Due to the contract magic he had signed, Marsgrove wasn't able to say anything about me.

He had sold out Olivia instead.

Chapter Seven

CHAOS

OLIVIA'S MOTHER never once looked my way. Whatever enchantment Raphael had forced on me seemed to work, at least temporarily, on everyone Department related.

Olivia's expression had clearly indicated I was unwanted in whatever was about to happen, but my heart thumped wildly, and I stayed rooted to my spot until the people behind me forced me into motion. A steady stream of Dorm Twenty-five mages filed down the stairs and exited through the heavy wooden door at the uphill side of the building, with me in tow.

Outside, I stopped and let the streams cut around me. I felt unnaturally anxious. Olivia's mom was obviously not the warm, caring figure that mine was, but, she wouldn't hurt her own daughter. Mothers didn't do that.

To the right and left, as far as my eyes could see, masses of students were exiting the Magiaduct through the doors that delineated each dorm section.

My unnatural anxiety won out. I turned to head back into the building and upstairs. Olivia had told me to leave the building, but I could slip into one of the open study areas and wait for Helen Price to leave. I could stay nearby. Just in case.

"All students, again, please make your way to Top Circle," a soft, lilting voice said on the air. The sound curled around the crowds, and those students not already heading uphill, began the trek. I didn't realize I was trekking up with them, until I was halfway up the stairs that lead from the Fifth Circle to the Fourth.

Go back! my mind screamed.

But the lilting voice in the air reiterated its command, and I continued climbing. The unaffected portion of my brain said that I shouldn't be ascending the mountain, away from my roommate and back to the madness of Top Circle where Marsgrove was. Magical suggestion was obviously laced through the words drifting on the air, though, because I kept moving forward. I gripped the strap of my bag, focusing on the positive. All students. That meant Olivia would be somewhere behind me. We'd meet up top. Everything would be fine.

I was sweating by the time I reached Second Circle. I hadn't climbed the mountain since my first week at school. I looked around me. Thousands of students were climbing the multitudes of staircases that dotted the steep hillsides between circles. It was an extremely strange sight. All of the on-campus ports must have been closed. Either that, or the administrative enchantment gripping all of us had embedded a sudden will for exercise.

Bottlenecks to the next set of staircases formed with so many of us trying to reach the heart of campus.

A sudden, loud cheer erupted from students on either side of me, startling me. Most of the expressions in the slowly moving crowd turned ecstatic and fierce. But a few displayed annoyance—or even anger—before composing into neutral lines.

"That's right. Don't scarp with us, or this is what you will get!" A boy lifted a fist in victory.

Unlike most of the students around me, I didn't have a magical frequency to deliver news mentally, so I shakily grabbed my news reader from my bag. The holographic faces of two men and one woman popped up, rotating above the screen. There were red "X's" over their faces. Three Third Layer politicians had just been assassinated by vigilantes.

Retaliation. Retaliation in a war I was ignorant of and embroiled within.

A video of the retaliation replaced the still images—masked men exterminating the three Third Layer politicians with horrible, explosive magic. I covered my mouth, trying to keep my breakfast down.

Frequency users saw this mentally? Projected directly in their thoughts? No way was I getting one.

As I fumbled to close my reader, my world turned to sludge. Each movement became painfully, horrifyingly slow—the movements of a nightmare.

No. No.

"Campus lockdown! Repeat, lock any campus portals still open!" thundered a strident adult voice.

People around me screamed. My molasses-slow fingers fumbled over my reader's shut-off switch, missed it, and a second video popped up. Everyone and everything around me continued at normal speed, while I existed outside normal time and space. Black-and-white patterns scrolled over everything in view for one suspended second.

The world cracked and snarled back to real time and my body unfroze as quickly as it had frozen, causing me to stumble uncontrollably. I fell forward with the momentum, taking down three other mages. My limbs splayed out on the grass and my bag and reader flew forward. People were yelling at me, but I couldn't process their words. Gasping deep breaths, I watched the hologram continue to scroll images of absolute devastation and despair.

The Second Layer town of Cadmiat, population five hundred, had just been destroyed.

Like Ganymede. Like Jauvine. The thoughts that had been tickling at my consciousness discharged, fully blown into active awareness as everything connected. The feeling, the magic, the patterns, the pull, Constantine's leech, Raphael...

The box.

My God, the box from my Awakening sketch was a leech. One that didn't require Raphael to press a device against my skin or ask for my permission. The pull was different from Constantine's button, but the horrible feeling of having my control ripped away was the same.

But...if Raphael could pull my magic from a distance whenever he wanted, why wasn't he pulling it all the time? Did it require a visit? A touch? Some sort of actual permission cunningly taken?

My fingers curled painfully around a rock in the grass, as I dragged myself forward toward the reader and its horrible image feed. At the edge of the scorched, cratered vision, holographic men and women in buckled collars shoved two men to the ground and clamped blindingly white cuffs on them. But no smirking, golden-eyed man was caught. I watched the captured men. There was deep fervor in their expressions. Even in hologram form, the light of their magic dimmed under the power of the cuffs, but the fervor in their eyes remained.

I vaguely registered the students yelling and shoving at each other above me.

"She pushed me! What is wrong with her?"

"Maybe she knows someone in Cadmiat. Have some empathy!"

"Ren!"

At the familiar call, I looked up to see Will pushing his way through the crowd.

"Ship those responsible to the labs!" someone hollered behind me—hate and anguish permeating their voice.

"Human rights must be maintained!" someone else shouted, though their voice sounded irritated by the fact.

"They aren't human! I hope they dissect them, drain them, and use their magic to blast the rest of the cockroaches!"

I crawled the last few inches to my reader. A bitter cold feeling spread through me. My magic had been used for this. Raphael had taken that box from the sketch I had created months ago during my Awakening.

Familiar hands lifted my reader, then me, and I rested against Will for a moment.

Administration Magic swirled and morphed around us, locking campus down.

Will shut down the image feed on my reader as the tactics of the Second Layer's enforcement unit turned brutal on the telecast. I numbly shoved the device into my bag, guilt and horror pulsing wildly inside me. People around me continued yelling. I heard Raphael's name mentioned more than once, along with others on the most wanted lists, including the sharp-eyed man who'd been featured in the Sassraf hologram—Vincent Godfrey.

The crowd moved and I stuck to Will's side as we climbed the last staircase, negotiated an alley between the buildings that formed a perimeter around the top level of campus, and stepped onto the crowded grassy field at the center of Top Circle.

Department mages stood in strategic positions around the perimeter and on the cafeteria steps, scanning people in the crowd, rapidly and systematically. Little bits of magic flew from their finger scanners into the crowd, then back—tagging the bleating human sheep in our circular pen.

Will was looking at a device in his hand. "Mike and Neph are almost here."

"How—"

"How did I find you? I stuck a tracker on your bag that activates on campus," he said matter-of-factly, without looking away from the device in his hand. "An arrow shows up in the right corner of my glasses and leads me to you. We should try inserting the tracker in a piece of jewelry, though—something you don't take off. Maybe a ring with a holographic display? Add some extras. Do you think with some paint we could—?"

I stopped listening as I looked frantically at my bag, freaked out that I'd been tracked, even if it was by Will.

No, I'd freak out about it later, I thought, as one of the Department mages aimed his finger our way. Cerulean magic blinked around us, encompassing the twenty people surrounding me.

Little blue dots appeared on each mage's shoulder.

A student with pretty emerald eyes stood straight and tall on the cafeteria steps beside the three Department mages. She smiled at us with a politician's smile, then suddenly narrowed her eyes, her smile dropping as her gaze swept my shoulder. Alarm spiked. I looked down at my shoulder. No dot.

I was terrible with names, but I had sketched the girl's face into my mind months ago—the girl with the lilting voice who I had attempted to sit with on my first visit to the cafeteria. She wore three rings, indicative of a magic user proud of her Second Layer lineage.

She was a student, not a Department employee, and like with Dare, Raphael's spell apparently didn't extend to her, because she looked at my face, then leaned over to read the scan held by a Department mage. I had no idea if I would show up on the scan or not, but the probability was high that something about me would not match up to whatever showed up on that scanner.

I poked Will's sticker, causing him to look at me, then I hurriedly magicked a duplicate on my shoulder. Will's eyes bugged out and he immediately erected a silencing spell around us, and tried, vainly, to hide me. "Dear Magic, take it off!" he hissed, and looked frantically in all directions. "The stickers have tagged magic in them and anyone from the Department who sees you will know you haven't been properly scanned and they—"

"It doesn't matter," I said tightly, thankful for the small space of privacy he had given us. We'd only be able to use it reliably for a minute. More time than that would invite someone in the crowd to break the enchantment. Silencing spells, unlike silencing runes, were notoriously weak, and a favorite target of the members of the delinquent's club. "I'll explain later."

He nodded slowly and I moved so that we were standing shoulder to shoulder again. The girl's green gaze honed in on me immediately and switched between my shoulder and face. I shifted on my feet, but tried to project a calm, law-abiding facade.

She looked at the scanner again. However the magic worked, it must have shown our small quadrant as all tagged. Her gaze reluctantly moved to the next target and I allowed myself a small breath of relief.

Will tapped under his ear, indicating incoming news on his frequency. "They are warding out anyone from the mountain who is not a registered student, faculty member, resident, or in the administration. Residents who live in the lower levels will have to stay below the Eighteenth Circle. All students will be locked into the levels above that. Secured."

Or trapped. Depending on one's definition.

"Excelsine was declared a safe zone," Will whispered. "It always is. My parents pushed me through a port as soon as we could reach one. There was a weird earthquake in the First Layer and a decimating flood in the Fourth around the same time as the Sassraf attack. Muses were told to return to their posts across the layers, so Neph should be here soon."

Top Circle was standing room only already.

"Safe zone," Will said. "That's why everyone wants their kids returning here. Though the Department being here is new. The media mages are making a big deal about it right now on the news feeds, celebrating the increased safety."

No sooner had the words left Will's mouth than a flying monkey decided an untimely trip across the Top Circle skies might be a good idea. It flew overhead for a half second before a jet of black blasted it out of the sky. Immediately, three Department mages tied the monkey's arms behind its back and stuffed it in a cage that was labeled "For Processing."

The magical sweeps continued. Department mages violently put down any animal that wandered near the Administration Building and returned any magic that came close.

A rebound of a weather enchantment blasted one student, and another had to be revived from a banishment hex. Both spells—however innocently intended by the caster—had returned upon them at three times the strength.

Under such swift and brutal repercussions, magic use died off completely around Top Circle.

Alexander Dare stood next to a pillar at the shadowed entrance of the cafeteria, his focused gaze watching the Department mages storm around below. His expression was stony. His left hand twitched the slightest bit and five combat mages smoothly descended the stairs and disappeared into the crowd to the left. A similar gesture sent five more to the right.

No dragons were riding the supernatural winds. No gaudily dressed mages were performing tricks. No enchantments curled and coiled among the grass. People whispered and stood far too still. Even the ever-changing clothes I had become accustomed to seeing remained flat and stagnant. My gut clenched at the completely unnatural environment.

Mages in flowing garments—muses—started forming circles around the flagpoles that edged the grass center of Top Circle where all of us were standing. Will didn't look concerned by the action, but I was getting more freaked out.

Sudden pain burst full blown in the back of my neck, and an immediate urge to get back to the dorm made me bend over, hands on my knees. It was an abrupt and overwhelming desire induced by magic, and forcefully urging me back down the mountain.

"Ren?" Will whispered.

"S'okay. M'fine," I slurred. I straightened just enough to see Neph gliding toward us, past the cages and severe Department mages. She was sporting a soft, beautiful smile, but there was urgency underneath her calm facade.

As soon as her arms enveloped me, most of the tension between my shoulder blades seeped out, but the urge to return to the dorm continued to press against my mind.

"I need both of you to return to the dorms," Neph whispered in my ear. "I can free you from the magic completely, but my influence will fade on Will the farther away he gets and he will try to return. You need to make him keep his forward progress."

"Okay," I whispered back in quick agreement. Everything in me was screaming to return to the dorm. My feet were just unable to move me that way.

I saw Helen Price join a few Department officials who were speaking together in front of the Administration Building, and quickly nodded against Neph's shoulder.

Magic washed through me at every point that touched Neph. I took a startled breath as the enchantment keeping me on the grassy field cracked. Before I even realized we were in motion, Neph was lightly pushing fingers against my back, guiding us through a thin path that magically opened in the crowd. Neph's magical influence caused people to shift one step forward or back, clearing our way.

The muses who were gathered around the flagpoles nearest to us glared at Neph. She steered us past them, down to the edge of Top Circle and one of the many staircases.

"I can't go to the dorms yet, but you must return with Ren, Will." Neph's soft voice was soothing, but again there was a sense of urgency beneath it.

"We should stay," Will said, hearts in his eyes. "We can watch you work."

I shifted, anxiety pulling again, and I circled Will's wrist with my fingers. "We should go back. Neph wants us to."

"But—"

Neph's smile stretched, straining. "I need to drift the magic with the rest of the community. Most of the officials will be gone by dinner, if everything goes as planned. We'll meet then."

I paused my urge to retreat and examined Neph. "Are you going to be okay?"

"Yes. We are expected to form a working enclave around the Joining Rods—the flagpoles—in order to filter out fear and increase obedience, since nearly everyone is gathered together."

That was...very unnerving, but Will was nodding as if it was normal. "You don't need anything?"

Neph smiled. "No. I'll explain what I am able to, later. Where's Olivia, Ren?"

"In our room."

"Good." Neph touched Will's wrist. "Will, you'll get Ren back to the dorms, right?"

"Of course, Neph." Will looked a little vacant, but he was nodding.

"I know you will. Stay safe. I'll see you both soon."

She turned and headed to the nearest group of muses—who were still scowling at us.

"She never lets me watch her group practices," Will said forlornly.

I nodded, then frowned at the chilly looks Neph received as she drew closer to the group. I pushed Will into motion. "I know. I always have to wait outside."

"That's because they would eat you alive. Neph can protect you everywhere except inside one of their warded group sp—"

Bzzzz! Will's tracking device buzzed. I edged away from it automatically and increased our pace down the steps. Will touched his glasses, then pressed a finger beneath his ear, his expression showing surprise. "Mike is on campus and headed to our room, but his frequency is off. Strange."

The urge to check on my own roommate pressed forcefully.

Will looked distracted, like he did when he was working on a particularly difficult problem. As we reached the Third Circle, he finally said, "There's something...wrong. I'm supposed to be on Top Circle, aren't I? Ugh." He closed his eyes for a brief moment. "Now I see the spell. I hate Administration Magic."

I did too. And I didn't like the feel of the wards holding me in—making me itch to unlock them.

We hurried down steps, slopes, fields, and more steps to the Fifth Circle and Dorm Twenty-five as quickly as our feet would take us. I wasn't going to be able to walk for a week after this, but I didn't care.

As we reached the currently empty mountain level known informally as Dormitory Circle, Will frowned. "The spell is getting weaker. Whatever they are doing is almost over."

"Good. I need to talk to Olivia," I said, my feet moving faster. "You find Mike, then we'll meet at dinner later?"

"Yes." He frowned again. "Make sure you stay inside until then."

"Can do." I nodded briskly. "You're okay?"

He nodded. "Yes. The spell just ended. I'll check back with you after I talk to Mike." He pivoted and began the trek to the Magiaduct entrance five down from ours.

I entered the building and sprinted up the hauntingly empty stairwell to the second floor. As I opened the door to our room, relief swept me. Olivia was sitting at her desk.

I closed the door, panting, and tried to move past my crushing relief.

But the itch quickly overtook me again. There was something off in the room. Like too much freshly crushed peppermint in too small a space. All of my warding work had made me increasingly sensitive.

And Olivia was sitting stiffly—too stiffly—at her desk.

I touched the wall, connecting to the wards that were infused by our combined magic. The wards that were directly connected to her brightened—and showed the physical damage on her aura.

It was as if blows had rained down on her magic. I instantly reached out to touch her skin, to soothe the welts that couldn't be seen without magic, but she shoved her chair back, removing herself from my reach. "Don't touch me."

I curled my fingers in. "Your magic—"

"Is my concern."

Olivia looked as detached and cold as she had when I'd first moved in, with none of the ruthless humor and protectiveness she had started to display in the past month.

Unease made my stomach clench. "That was your mom, right?"

"Are you asking if I sold you out?"

"What? No!" But I knew why she was saying it. Helen Price had promised the public on national feed last term that anyone displaying abnormal tendencies would be harshly dealt with. And she was the mother of my roommate, who knew every one of my dirty secrets. "No."

Olivia's gaze was cold. She said nothing.

But her debate tactics worked in the reverse as well. "Don't be stupid," I said, echoing her favorite saying. "If that had been your plan, you wouldn't have ordered me to leave."

"I could have sold you out afterward." Her voice was very clinical.

I took an automatic step toward her. "What did she do to you?"

There was a struggle on her face for a brief moment, before the cold won out. "Nothing." She turned and briskly rearranged her desk.

I let my bag drop on my Guernica comforter for the second time that day. Looking at the Picasso image depicted on my bedspread, horror and guilt re-established themselves quickly in my thoughts. "A town called Cadmiat was—"

"I'm well aware of the news. I'm not the one without a frequency."

I bit my lip. Maybe I'd wait to bombard her with everything I had discovered. "Campus is...weird. Neph said things would be better by dinner. She made us leave Top Circle before the muses did something with the flagpoles."

Olivia's shoulders tightened, but she didn't comment. Being back in our warded room, my magic started to relax and stretch out in relief, connecting to the magic around me. The damage to Olivia was apparent in the sluggish way the wards weren't recharging her. It was as if someone had put a knot in the one that promoted medical rejuvenation and health. I poked the ward, trying to figure out how to unblock it.

Olivia jumped out of her chair and started throwing things into one of her favorite designer bags.

"What are you doing?" I asked. I nearly dropped the magical probe in my alarm. "Where are you going? Don't go out there."

She didn't answer, and I pulled further along the thread of magic that was off, concentrating on it. Right there. A brown spot in the green. I sent a ribbon of turquoise down the thread.

"Stop!"

Startled, I did.

She lifted her bag and started for the door.

I scrambled and grabbed my bag, slinging it around my shoulder even though I really didn't want to go back outside.

"What are you doing?" she demanded.

"Coming with you."

"No."

"I'm not letting you go out there on your own. There is something wrong with you, and weird, horrible things are happening."

"There's nothing wrong with me," she hissed.

I concentrated, using the knowledge I had gained through hard study and nightmares. "Okay, okay. But—" My words cut themselves off.

Olivia's aura fully burst into view. The welts were angry, deep, and salted, as someone might do if they wanted to increase pain and slow healing. Fury boiled deep within me, overtaking all other emotion.

"What did she do to you?" I tried to keep my voice even. I took an aggressive step toward the door. I knew exactly where to find Helen Price.

Olivia threw herself in front of the door, blocking my way. "You aren't leaving."

With Olivia standing in front of the clear door wards, I could see the wound fully—the horrible bruising and jagged tears. It was similar to the damage sustained by Constantine during the attack in the First Layer.

I rested my hand against the wall and set my magic free, anger sharpening everything. I could see the flow of magic filtering through the clear lines on the wall and into the air, connecting to the wards in the room. More importantly, to the blocked spring green one that promoted healing.

Olivia shuddered, and I could see one of the welts looked slightly better, like the magic was healing. She took a hostile step toward me. "Leave it."

"Let me help. Or let me go after her."

"No."

I pulsed another clot of magic to the spring green ward.

Her retaliation was fierce. The air in front of me exploded with color. My shields blocked most of it, so she slammed her hand against the wall and shot a sickly ochre along the same pathway to which I was still connected, splitting the spring green and shooting straight into my hand.

I lurched back, then lunged toward the bathroom, dropping my bag and making it just before I threw up everything in my stomach.

"A stomach virus?" I spit into the toilet again, saliva coming fast as my stomach roiled. "Really, Liv?"

Instead of healing, she had done the exact opposite. She stood in the doorway and her expression was nearly unreadable—not because it was blank, but because there were too many emotions there. I focused on the part I could clearly relate to—the stricken part.

My coolly controlled roommate was wild-eyed and horrified underneath her anger and pain.

"They let roommates poison each other?" Shaking my head made me throw up again. "Seems like a really bad idea."

The upside was that all I could now concentrate on was how physically terrible I felt, putting the psychological effects of the previous few hours on temporary hiatus.

"Don't you want to know what happened to all of the roommates before you? Don't you wonder what happened to them?" Olivia's voice was almost hysterical.

"Yes." I fumbled for an enhanced Kleenex from the rarely used box and wiped my mouth. If I attempted one of the magical functions on the toilet at present, I was going to give myself a swirly, at best—flush myself through to the processing plant, at worst. "But it doesn't matter in the end."

"What do you mean, it doesn't matter?" Her voice had gotten low and dangerous.

Nausea rolled again. I put my forehead on my arm, willing the wave away. "I'm not going to leave you."

"I'll make you leave."

Based on her tone of voice, she was willing to give it a try. I wanted to ask why, but that was not a question to ask a cornered creature. There were a thousand things I could say in response, things that could get me anything from a second bout of stomach flu to missing limbs to a wholly uncertain outcome.

I closed my eyes on another wave of sickness. "I'd rather stay. Here. With you."

"No, you wouldn't. No one does."

"Yes." I held down the remaining contents of my stomach through force of will alone. Throwing up at this moment in the conversation would send the wrong message entirely. "I would."

"I'm not going to sacrifice myself for anyone!" Her voice was high and hysterical again. Alarmingly desperate.

I didn't understand what she was referring to, specifically. But that wasn't important. I flushed the toilet and stared at the water as it swirled into the vortex that would head to the processing complex in the Midlands. It finally cleared to crystal again. "Good. I don't want that," I whispered.

The bathroom door slammed.

Forty minutes later, I felt well enough to crawl across the floor and slowly pull myself up into bed. Olivia was nowhere to be seen. Her usually meticulous desk looked as if a tornado had touched down.

Going after her was out of the equation now—if the building caught fire, about all I was going to be able to do was close my eyes and enjoy the heat.

And if Olivia went straight to her mom, like she had expected me to assume she would, I was going to be dealt with sooner, rather than later. I was too sick to care, and my accessory-to-murder guilt said I would deserve it.

I shakily sent Will and Neph notes on my "status," saying I had caught a minor flu bug and was going to sleep. When Neph wrote that campus was stabilized and that she wanted to come heal me, I lied and said Olivia was taking care of me. I didn't want to deal with the fallout from admitting that Olivia had actually poisoned me instead.

I shut my eyes and willed my stomach to still and the world to be different when I woke.

No. I jerked, causing my stomach to roil again. I would make the world different. And I would take back my magic.

Determination and hope, even grim hope: those traits had gotten me through the painful and horrific experiments I had done last term to revive Christian, and they'd serve me again.

Olivia strode back into our room four hours later. She said nothing. Didn't look in my direction. Just readied for bed, placed two additional wards on the door, and turned off the lights.

Loneliness and despair flashed through the room magic, connecting us for a moment, then there was nothing, as she shut me out.

Olivia had opened up about many things during break, but her home life had not been one of them. Observing her in my own home had only shown me glimpses of what her life was not.

After I was sure she was asleep, I put a lid on my nausea and redirected the room wards designed to refresh my core and heal me, toward Olivia instead.

~*~

Unprotected and drained, as I fell to dreaming,
Raphael's golden eyes and sly grin appeared.

Chapter Eight

FERAL ENHANCEMENTS

I WOKE VIOLENTLY the next afternoon, to harsh sunlight piercing the window above my bed.

Olivia was at her desk and I felt along the thin thread that still clung to her. Her magic was at full strength, her wounds were pink and healing, and she was better emotionally. Less despair, more coolness. She was determined about something.

I backed my protection and refreshing magics out of Olivia's streams and hooked them back into mine. A bit of vigor returned, enough to let me push myself out of bed and into the bathroom.

A ghastly image of crazed reddish brown hair and dark circles stared back at me from the mirror. Bloodshot eyes mimicked jagged dream memories. I had tried—tried so hard—to fight Raphael. To find the stolen box and rip apart his dream facade.

"You'll never find it searching that way, butterfly."

He'd parried my attacks easily—pinning me to the wall of the dream—amused.

"Determined to block me? That won't do. You will force me to come in person to collect all you owe."

I owed him nothing else. He had collected his Second Level Magic in the lost haze of the world beyond my dream two nights ago. Yet, unease slithered down my spine like the serpent Raphael reflected. Deals with devils never truly ended.

He had smiled—smiled—over my anger and questions about Cadmiat, and told me that power was a gift.

I had summoned up enough fury to eject him finally. Finally. But clinging to the edges of the dreamscape, seconds before he had been blown through, he had gotten in one final taunt.

"Choices, butterfly. What will you choose this time? Or rather...whom?"

I splashed my face with water, rubbing my eyelids more aggressively than necessary. I had been too sick to leave last night, and had slept right through the morning. If madness still reigned outside, I was going to risk it for some fresh air.

I was determined that today was the first day of the end of Raphael Verisetti's hold over me.

I dressed manually, still not convinced that my clothes would stay put if I dressed magically. The last thing I wanted was to run around campus naked.

"Good morning," I finally said to my roommate.

If being a "Carrera marble statue" was the most desired state of being, Olivia was in museum-quality shape. I felt like the sticky, gummed floor at the pedestal's base.

"You added protection streams to my side of the room," she said in her professional, clipped voice, without looking up.

"Yes."

"Even after what I did to you and how miserable you felt."

"Yes."

There was a thick knot of tension in her shoulders. "Why?"

"Because you are my friend."

She didn't respond. Her fingers continued working precise magic over her desk.

Pained at the loss of the easy communication we had established, I tossed out an opening. "I'm going to the library." Ask me why. Please.

She moved a piece of paper efficiently from one pile to another. "Crowd-calming magic was forcibly pushed. Clubs have restarted and even though everyone knows we are being manipulated, everyone is stupidly trying to pretend this is just an early start to term. Classes are starting a week ahead of time."

I grimaced.

"And someone from the Justice Squad came by. Said you weren't answering your tablet."

Crap. I fished out Justice Toad from his silencing pocket, and he unhappily croaked three late alerts. A bold message said that squad enforcement was back in effect and that if I didn't answer, I was going to be fined fifteen additional community service hours.

I was half tempted to push the tablet back into the silencing pocket. But because of the contract I had "signed" when Marsgrove had "enrolled" me, the Contract Magic would eventually make me do my community service. And at this point, I needed all the free hours I could get in order to free myself from Raphael and fix...everything. I mechanically signed in and activated myself on the Justice Squad's roster.

Great.

I gathered things into my bag slowly, hoping Olivia would say something—anything. The empty lunch plate on her desk indicated that she had eaten. I was starving, but at the same time, my recovering stomach protested my favorite waking fare of pancakes and sugar.

"Would you like to come to the library? Or...I can stay?" I tentatively asked.

Everything about her stretched tight—from her muscles to her magic. "Neither. I have a meeting."

I ached at her cool tone, but nodded and rubbed my hand along the wall, stroking the spring green ward there. I added a protective pulse to it. Olivia shivered and the muscles in her arms clenched harder.

I stuffed a few plain granola bars into my bag along with the remaining tube of crackers I hadn't upchucked the night before.

As I approached the door, I stole a peek at the new notes around her desk. They were always invaluable glimpses into her mindset, since Olivia implemented plans immediately. Repeated words littered them—sacrifice, death, kidnapping, protection, triumph, consequences.

She sat stiffly in her chair, cold, composed, regal. Poised like a woman who had been reared to rule. To brook no distractions or friends in the path of life, but merely to collect sterling pieces for her chessboard.

I touched the silver knob. "I'll see you in a bit, then?"

She didn't answer. I stepped into the hall, closed the door quietly behind me, and looked at my room key—the one Olivia had given me, officially making me her roommate instead of a stowaway. I curled my fingers around it.

The campus news feed on my reader indicated that all off-campus ports were still closed, but that on-campus ports had reopened.

Students passed by, smiling, waving to each other, and casually chatting about what classes to take. That freaked me out more than if they were running around screaming in despair. There weren't any Department mages about, but a few of their student recruits were easy to spot as they watched and recorded data around campus.

As I walked, the casual atmosphere began seeping into me, loosening my stride.

I sent a note to Neph and Will saying I was on my way to the main library. The old me said to conduct the leech and dream research on my own. The new me was embracing the fact that I had friends, even with Olivia acting the way she was.

Two students stood beside the entrance to the library, looking at each passing student, then clicking their fingers in patterns against their wrists or thighs. As a non-frequency user, I could only guess at what they were doing.

Unease vied with the unnatural calm that had seeped into me.

As I walked into the library, my shoulders immediately loosened and calm swirled through me again. The very air felt soothing and light. A reflection in one of the many glass panels showed a smile on my face and a peaceful expression. My steps felt almost jaunty. What was there to worry about?

I looked at my two-way notebook. Neph and Will had responded that they would meet me in thirty minutes. The first two floors of the library were packed, so I headed to the fourth floor, an area that didn't generate much traffic.

I grabbed a helmet from the entrance bin and entered the papered fray.

Books immediately swooped through the air, diving hungrily toward me—hardcover raptors interspersed with soft, chirping paperbacks. Their pages opened and closed, rippling and fluttering near my head. Unlike the traumatic experience at the Library of Alexandria, this was like being approached by a flock of pigeons looking for hand fed seed.

"No one's been feeding you boys?" I asked, always happy when surrounded by paper and magic.

As I moved through the stacks, seven books followed me, hoping to find an opportunity to swoop in and extract my thoughts and experiences and transfer them onto their pages. Magical Attacks and Kidnappings, Teenage Confusion, Poisoning, Feral Survival, Terrorist Threats... I stopped reading the titles. The rustling of paper and parchment and the comforting little clunk when a book plopped on a table were the only sounds aside from my heavily beating heart.

In the ceiling's dome, a large black-and-white book perched on the circular banister, watching. The edges of its hard cover were tipped forward and little, hard, papered claws gripped the railing.

The books about criminals, and accomplices, and magical siblings trying to raise the dead—those always followed me. The black-and-white one never did. Yet, it always watched me.

Based on the black-and-white patterns flowing around its covers, I could guess at what it contained.

I didn't even need to enhance my senses in order to guess. Though, enhancing my senses would be a great bonus right now. Maybe that would keep me from making stupid decisions—like swallowing whatever emotional magic was filtering through campus and the first floor of the library, or making deals with terrorists.

The black-and-white book's hard left corner edge imperiously gestured to a smaller tome perched near it on the rail. The smaller book, whose cover boasted a shifting kaleidoscope, responded to the directive and dove toward me. Its covers opened wide and I braced myself. While some books were amusing and wonderful, showing history visually on their pages, some were horrifying and activated nightmares.

An open maw of whirling kaleidoscopic colors screamed toward me, and before I could think on what that might mean, the book shocked me by clamping tightly around my right hand. I had never seen a book clamp anything other than a mage's head—hence the helmets.

I immediately shoved at the binding of the rabid book. I should have guessed the books could turn savage!

"Origin Magic," a male voice said. "They won't release the information on what was taken from the libraries, but is there any doubt? And they arrested two more ferals."

I froze at the unfamiliar voice and the topic of conversation. The book's pages rippled around my stilled palm, settling and gripping harder.

"Yes. Working for the terrorist factions. Hardly a surprise." The familiar, deep, smooth voice that answered made my pulse jump to a different staccato. Alexander Dare.

I looked in all directions. Emptiness. Silence, but for the fluttering and chirping of the books. Not good. Dare was someone I never missed seeing. My gaze always zeroed in on him—he got even hotter up close. I took a small, unwilling step in the direction of his voice, toward the circular shelf stacks positioned underneath the cupola.

A flock of books was circling like buzzards above, surveying prey below. I kicked myself for paying too much attention to the silence of the Fourth Floor. The circular stacks created a semi-private meeting space that the combat mages sometimes used. Used, obviously, with silencing runes.

"Can never trust ferals," the first, unknown voice said. "Too easily seduced. They have no national identity, no affiliation."

"What about common sense?" a sarcastic voice added. "Everyone knows the Third Layer isn't going to win. Everyone, except for them, obviously. Not that I don't want to kick your crumps as early as possible in the new year, but I had plans for the first, and they didn't include being stuck on campus bending and scraping before a bunch of buckles. 'Yes, sir. You, what, sir? Want to stick a monitoring device up where, sir?'"

Quietly, I lifted my hand and the book that was secured like a papered lamprey around it. Guide for Enhancing the Senses was printed on its cover in raised prismatic letters. I couldn't feel any knowledge transferring out of me, rather there was something that was pushing into me, speaking to my magic, nudging my senses around—forming a knotted pattern near my right ear, and another beneath my tongue.

"Good thing you keep a stick up there already, Lox."

Laughter, deep and rich with camaraderie—like the taste of chocolate and caramel—came from the other side of the stacks, mixing with the underlying bitter mocha of anger and irritation in the group. I touched my mouth, unused to the physical taste of emotion.

The clamped book pulsed as I drew nearer to the bookshelves hiding the voices. With my free hand, I reached out to touch the spine of a shelved book. Magic bubbled under my skin and inflated behind my eyes. I rubbed the furrowed, leather spine slowly, feeling each ridge and dip under the pads of my fingers—the knobby edges, smooth paths, a scent of spearmint gum. Sudden knowledge bloomed that three people had touched this book in the past two weeks, running their pointer fingers in a similar pattern down its spine. The book to its left had only the slightest smoothed trail traced by a single finger, barely touched with oil.

I nudged the space between the spines, hoping they would move an inch to each side.

The shelved books chattered at the book clamped to my hand, rippling their pages in greeting, then they suddenly turned an indistinct color, allowing me to peer through them.

Through the small, hazy portal, I saw Alexander Dare across the alcove, lounging back casually in a chair, surrounded by other combat mages. He lazily tossed a ball of swirling blue and white light from one hand to the other, a loose smile on his lips, the end of his delicious laughter trailing through my overly sensitized hearing.

I recognized most of the guys by sight, though not by name. Two of them were members of Dare's elite team, while the others I recognized from when the Combat Squad worked with the Justice Squad. Combat mages came in all shapes and sizes, but there was an air of danger about each of them, even the smaller ones. The focus in their gazes was always absolute and overwhelming.

"I hate Olean's classes," one of them said.

"But how will you know about the feral threat, unless you take one of his courses?" Dare asked, sarcasm heavy in his smooth voice.

"Take the course by fast feed. Saves the droning."

Someone snorted. "No one needs his class for news on the feral threat anyway. Daily news feed? Information For The People flyers? Threats to Public Health and Welfare bulletins?"

"The Baileys take their news reporting seriously," Dare said, and the ball of blue and white became a muted hologram showing numerous people shouting, before shifting back into the swirling, chaotic ball he loved to casually wield.

"Mmmm, Bellacia Bailey," another voice said. The expression on the doughy boy's face could only be described as dreamy. "In the midst of this shitstorm, there is no finer specimen of womankind."

"Johnson, I thought you were yearning after Straught?"

"She kicked Johnson's crump sideways," Lox said. He was a large blond who looked like he would be comfortable carrying a broadsword. "Good thing for him she's on shift right now. She'd be booting him here too."

Dare smiled along with a number of the others.

A vibrant picture bloomed in my mind of the statuesque girl with the Athena vibe. I had seen Camille Straught in the heat of battle. I could definitely imagine her kicking the crud out of the doughy boy.

"But you'll need to refocus again, Johnson. Lovely Bellacia has eyes only for Axer these days," Lox said, a little tightly.

Dare's smile turned false. "Pass."

"What?" Johnson blinked out from his enraptured state. "Why would you pass? Bellacia Bailey."

Dare's blue and white ball morphed immediately into a picture of five screaming harpies, and it took a long moment for my enhanced hearing to stop ringing from the pain of hearing it.

The other mage on Dare's team, the deadly and silent mage sitting next to him, shot magic at the image, causing it to explode.

Dare smirked and swirled his fingers, calling back the exploded shards of magic to reform the ball in his hand. "Show her your account numbers and frequency list, Johnson. It's all connections and riches with that group."

"Really?" Johnson cocked his head. "That's all it takes?"

An older boy leaned over and beaned the younger one across the back of the head with the flat of his palm. "Idiot."

"Ow, man! I had two head wounds from Boxing Day."

"Yes, watch his tender rookie flesh. Johnson is looking to woo." Lox seemed to have gotten over whatever had irritated him. "And he thinks his brain is needed."

The outward tension caused by world events was still present, but as talk turned to inconsequential things, there was obvious relief on a number of faces.

"The helmet coming his way will help, then," someone said.

A flurry of groans and curses met that statement.

I touched my helmet with my free hand and cringed. But wearing a helmet was better than letting the books that constantly circled me have their way with my obviously delicious brain.

"I can't believe they are trying to push that law through. No way am I wearing some regulation Department bullshit in competition. I mean, yeah, we all feel bad about the butchery at Shintering, but no way. No way."

"Would do you good, Lox," Dare said, voice far too innocent and casual for the smile curling his lips. "Keep those last few bits of magic and brains inside your skull rather than out."

"Kremp this bit, Dare." Lox tacked on a rude gesture, though it was of the lazy variety that close male friends shared. "Just because your pretty head hasn't been crushed lately doesn't mean you aren't due."

"Still sore about Boxing Day? Get Bailey or one of her giggling minions—like Norrissing—to kiss it better for you."

Lox gave him another rude salute. "You can terminate me a hundred more times like you did on Boxing Day. I'm not wearing their helmet."

A number of other voices agreed.

"They restrict field of view."

"I hate those spectacle guards."

"There is always an interior mirror-effect, no matter how many mages tinker with the materials."

"We'll be narwhal slaughter."

A chorus of negative comments and grumbles echoed.

"We need to stage a revolt. Tell them we won't compete. That we won't patrol."

"Argue material and enchantment pros and cons all you want—I don't care," said a boy in the crowd. "I'm not having an open port to the Department running around my brain."

That grim comment made the rest go silent.

"Me neither," someone else quietly said. "I don't care if it makes me a conspiracist, but 'sending stats' of my health and mental magic to any government or authority via an open port is not happening. I won't compete if it becomes a requirement."

Voices echoed agreement––more subdued agreement this time, but still firm.

"They can't take on all of us. Not even if they send more Department stiffs."

"How can they think this is going to pass?"

"They are banking on Dare, Lox, and Ramirez towing the line." A guy pointed at the first two, then toward the silent, dark and deadly boy slouched next to Dare. "As well as the top contenders at the other schools. And that the rest of us will follow."

Everyone looked at the three for answers. Lox looked as if he'd bitten into something foul. Ramirez slouched silently, staring at the questioner with dark eyes. Dare lazily tossed magic back and forth between his hands.

"Well, Dare?"

"I've been well informed that they are going to enforce it across the board," he said calmly. "The media mages won't let the politicians dismiss it, and certain parties won't let the media mages forget. We need to pick our conflicts...carefully. You know that."

"I don't care! If you can't raise a shield that covers your head first and foremost, and provides death and damage status, you have no business competing or being a combat mage at all. Everyone knows the injury rate is higher for helmeted mages on a true battlefield. You have to use diffused magic to keep them on. This legislation is not for our true benefit."

Dare continued casually tossing his magic ball of light.

"Why are you so scarping chill about this, Axer? You hate regulations."

My translation spell had been letting odd things through ever since I'd returned. I had to do a quick search through the bracelet encyclopedia

Will had given me to translate what "scarping" meant. Ah. I didn't realize three humans were capable of...performing such motions together. "Crasseetar," translated in a likewise manner. "Crump" was pretty obviously the part of the body that...got kicked. I did a quick search on "buckles" and it returned as a slang term for a Department enforcer—likely named for the buckled collars around their throats.

Dare threw the magic up in the air, where it began to spin. "You do realize that they haven't yet specified what a 'helmet' has to be, right? Stop thinking of what is or what could be forced upon us and start thinking of what we can make it. If we are ahead of it, we can control the product."

There was silence.

He smiled slowly and the ball of light twirled out into a very thin, nearly clear magic. A clear field with delineated points of magic rotated in the air.

"Axer, you are a genius," Lox said fervently.

"If only you wore a helmet more, you could say the same."

"A humble, terrible genius." Lox's smile crept upward the way my brother's had when he had been planning some horribly awesome mischief. "But this... Yes. We'll have to talk to the device nerds."

"So, we go with the legislation?" another boy asked.

"The next few years are going to determine the future of this Layer. We capitulate to this legislation, and to what the Department is doing to campus security this term, all while putting...other plans into effect," Dare said, his blue eyes dark.

"You have a plan for security?" the boy said.

"Of course he does." Lox looked almost resigned.

Dare smiled. "There are key assets that are always overlooked. We aren't going to overlook them."

Another book landed on my shelf, edging into place, pushing the semi-invisible books closer together. The books chittered at me as I nudged them again, trying to see what Dare meant.

Ultramarine eyes shifted suddenly, pinning me to the spot—as if he could see through the magic, and see me watching.

Time slowed for a moment—an audible clock in my head began ticking slower, heavier beats.

"Assets and threats," he said, his voice drawn-out with the slowed time, intense gaze still seemingly connected to mine.

A real hand clamped my wrist and I jumped. Enhancing dropped. The book caught itself before hitting the floor, then in a kaleidoscope of swirling color and flapping pages it flew back up to the dome above.

Will's brows rose and his hands reached out, tracers of light tailing each movement. "Whoa!"

With one hand over my pounding heart and the lights tessellating around me, I stumbled, steering Will away from the shelves. The sound of the flapping books was loud—too loud. Dare was going to barge around the stacks at any moment and accuse me—rightly—of eavesdropping. He'd grab my arm like Marsgrove and haul me away.

I stared at the tiny hairs standing on end along my arm. One hair moved, then two, three—

"We're downstairs," Will said, his voice echoing through my skull. "You weren't answering your journal and we were worried."

"Sorry," I whispered, increasing my pace and trying to clear my head. Without the focus of the book, sensory information everywhere vied for attention. Surrounded by a whirlpool of swirling shadows, the black-and-white book watched me with predatory intent as I shakily ditched my helmet at the stairs.

Freed from the weight, my head felt far too light and I grabbed the rail for support.

Neph was waiting for us at the bottom of the stairs—she never visited the fourth floor—and she enveloped me in a long hug as soon as I reached her. Warm, dark brown hair scented with jasmine engulfed me. The area surrounding her was a sauna of comfort with her soothing tendrils of magic cocooning me against the overwhelming stimuli outside. I let some of the tendrils seep in—let the edge of lingering sickness float away—but pulled away before she expended too much energy on me. I could feel her exhaustion too.

As soon as I disengaged myself, sound, touch, and taste blasted from every direction once more. I could see magic connected to me in hundreds of different shades. The golden tendrils frightened me the most. I specifically associated gold with Raphael, and there were hundreds of points of golden light burrowing into me—and not just in my left hand as I had previously observed.

Neph drew a soothing finger down my aura. "What has you scared?"

Everything.

"Nothing. I'm fine." But the lingering feel of Neph's magic made me blurt out, "Bad dreams."

As we walked, light and sound wavered in patterns around me. At first the patterns were hazy and indistinct, then they became sharp and edged. The waves told me that twelve people were walking within thirty feet of us—five maintained a brisk, three-miles-per-hour pace, another four strolled, and three moved at a crawl. Two of the people were calling up magic flavored with ill intentions and my senses flagged them as threats.

"How easy is it to bypass silencing runes, Will?" I tried to keep my voice at a normal volume, uncertain whether I was whispering or shouting.

I didn't look at him, but he was a solid weight of stability at my side. If Neph was warm comfort, Will was a steady rock.

"Depends on the level of protection. The one we always use is Grade Four." I heard the echoes of movement and sound as he tapped his pocket. "Because of the tethering, they aren't weak like silencing spells. You'd need a pretty wicked spell to get through a Grade Four."

"What about a book?"

The feel of Will turned to unconstrained excitement as we headed toward our favorite spot in the south corner. "One was attached to you, wasn't it? I wasn't sure. Those are really rare. Non-head clamps give transfer bursts free of charge. The books usually want payment, though."

I thought of the black-and-white book—I felt it was still watching me, even though the fourth level had a completely opaque floor. An enhanced certainty told me that at some point, the book would demand some form of payment. The same certainty said that it was a supremely dangerous book of magic. Of Origin Magic.

Not good. So not good.

Will pointed to his head and my eyes followed the motion as swirls of cream-colored magic followed his finger. "With head clamps, you give something to get something. And with all clamps, the results only last for a short period of time. Which book attached to you?"

I rubbed my head, then my palm. I could still feel the impression of each papered fiber on its pages. "Guide for Enhancing the Senses."

Will whistled. "Nice. What did you use to bargain with?"

I shook my head and touched one temple. I could still feel where the metallic helmet had been pressed to my skull. I put my canvas bag on the table and the smack echoed, little waves of sound emanating out.

Neph put a hand over Will's, and I could feel the calming magic she released, like aloe vera pressed to a burn. I could see it flowing from her into him.

"Ren is overwhelmed. Give her a moment."

I stared at the magic. Then at the tendrils that were flowing between Neph and me. In, out, in, out. I lifted my right hand, turning it, watching the turquoise, mint, and tan tendrils shift and stretch. The tendrils flowing into Neph were questioning, gentling, asking. The ones back to me were soothing and answering.

Will activated his silencing rune on the table. I could see vivid crimson and navy stitching a net over us.

"Okay." I breathed in deeply, watching the magic that connected us—for there were threads to Will as well, and ones that ran between the three of us. I carefully avoided the gold ones. With senses enhanced I could see everything. Smell, taste, feel. If I could grow accustomed to the overload, then—

"Other than the creep factor, why don't more people use the books?" I asked.

"One mage, Arnold the Crazed, tried to clamp twelve books on at the same time." Will circled a finger around his ear. "Thought he'd be a super-mage, but magic can't force the brain to process unlimited knowledge."

I could buy that. I was having trouble with just one. But that didn't mean I couldn't learn how to do more.

Will was still talking. I tried to focus on him.

"Besides, if you are giving payment at the same time as you are receiving the benefit, it is really hard to concentrate. Kind of belies the task, even if one of the books is a concentration enhancer. You have to figure out how to separate the senses and most people have trouble with that." He shrugged. "As to other reasons why people don't use them, the invasion of privacy can be...detrimental. All kinds of things can end up in the books, if you don't choose correctly. There are always strings attached."

I pictured the black-and-white book with its rigid spine. There would be strings there. Many strings.

"Olivia can tell you all about book contract magic and what you can do to protect yourself."

God, Olivia. I swallowed, and looked at the wards connected to me—gleaming and distinguishable. Olivia's threads were forest green and strong, but a sickly, synthetic brown still swirled underneath—light enough now that I wouldn't have seen it without the enhancement. I tried to pulse magic to it, to nudge it to a redwood brown, but the magic slipped over it like oil on water.

"What is Olivia up to?" Will asked.

"She has a meeting," I answered, trying to fix the sickness again without success.

Will nodded. "My Mechanics United team is meeting tonight too. Everyone is trying to pretend things are back to normal. You missed the real weirdness last night, Ren, when people were simultaneously trying to accept and reject the calm. Things are better today. The muses have been working overtime."

Neph's soft brown eyes were unreadable, but I could see her exhaustion along with something spikier. I pulsed a soothing thread back along the input line to Neph. She gasped, the spikes softened, and her eyes turned glossy as she smiled at me.

"I am happy to be back on campus with you both," Neph said in an unsteady voice. "The last few days of break were...taxing."

I remembered the mages dressed in white who had given her dirty looks yesterday, but had demanded her help regardless of their animosity.

"What happened at Top Circle, Neph?"

She looked away, and her connection thread pulsed. "The community is required to assist in all emotional protection matters that occur on campus. In return, we are granted a continuous way to exercise our skills, the ability to attend school, and a few special privileges."

"But what happened on Top Circle?"

Sickly colors swirled around Neph, almost as if her magic was panicking. "I cannot say. Please, Ren."

Will looked at Neph with wide eyes, then at me, and shook his head frantically.

"Okay, it's okay." I pressed at the threads between us and sent a continual flow of comforting magic toward her. If it drained my reserves, so be it. I had learned how to work at an absolute minimum level of energy last term.

Neph loved to talk about being a muse, but clammed up when talk turned to the community, what they did, or how or why she had been semi-excommunicated. I didn't understand the muse community or their need for so much secrecy.

But when it came to trust in a purely emotional way, Neph was at the top of my list. Will and I had clicked intellectually from the start, and Olivia and I had clicked magically. Neph was pure emotion. She was a cozy, comforting blanket for me, and I hoped the feeling was mutual. We hadn't needed a drawn-out process to be friends. We had met...and that had been that.

My friends were vastly different from each other--in how we connected--but no less important to me.

Neph relaxed completely, as if I had flipped some sort of calming switch within her.

"This is not a question about what specifically happened," I said, picking my words carefully while keeping the steady flow of magic going. "But why are the officials trying to calm us en masse like that? It freaks me out," I admitted.

Will grimaced. "Put a bunch of anxious, overpowered magic users under the age of twenty-two together, and even the control cuffs can't limit the destruction. And this campus is filled with overpowered magic users—some of whom make the Department nervous."

Neph's anxiety level increased, so I switched topics.

They brought me up to speed on the events that I had missed, though they carefully and obviously omitted some things. Through the waning magic of Enhancing, I felt their good intentions, so I let their omissions slip by without comment. I focused on retaining the awareness of the links I had with them, committing all of the colored threads to visual memory along with their relative positions, focusing my warding knowledge to maintain them.

I'd be able to send energy to Olivia even faster now, not having to rely on using the magic in our room to see the connections. Due to my focused effort, as the effects of Enhancing dissipated, the threads didn't disappear from view.

A definite benefit, and perhaps worth the price I might have to pay.

As Neph and Will discussed the classes they planned to sign up for, I simultaneously drew designs for the protection project I wanted to construct for Neph, while monitoring the activity around us. There were lots of mages on the lower floors of the library, actively watching each other and watching us, around the walls and through the glass ceilings.

Some of the combat mages from the fourth floor were now mixed in with other groups around us.

Will and Neph paused their speaking, but I could see something travel the thread between them. Talking via frequency? Knit together as we were, everything that connected us was bright. I swallowed.

I wished Olivia were here.

"So." Will looked at me expectantly. "Dreams?"

"Normal dreams?" Neph added softly, head tilted.

"No." My smile wobbled. "He has been visiting me."

Using Raphael's name in public, even under a silencing ward, was a bad idea. The verbal reactions to Cadmiat's destruction yesterday had made that exquisitely apparent.

"I need to block it from happening again," I said. I would block him. Kick him out. Eject him from this Layer, if I could.

"How can we help?" Neph asked. Her initial look of horror at the revelation that Raphael was visiting me in dreams became one of support and determination. Will nodded, and I could see the connection lines strengthening between the three of us.

Relief and commitment fiercely crushed my other emotions. "What do you know about dream wards?"

Wards first, then I could begin disentangling myself from the rest of Raphael's net. I needed to tell them about Raphael's box—a leech permanently attached to me. But that was a revelation better saved for a more secure location. I shuddered. Speaking the words aloud would make them real.

Will immediately detailed everything he knew about traveling in dreams, and Neph elaborated on how a mage could affect the emotions of them through setting, details, and components. Then they helped me locate texts for further research.

I spent a two-hour maxed session in a reading room—combing over and combining five different texts—then a ten-minute session in the red streaming room. Will and Neph had stayed at the table while I was away.

As I returned to my seat, Justice Toad croaked from my bag to let me know that I was now on the clock for community service duty. Great.

I sat and let my forehead drop onto my folded arms.

Neph laid comforting hands on my shoulders. Her magic soothed the rough edges of mine. "Success?"

"Yes." The streaming room mind spell was incredible, but being bombarded with a thousand pieces of information at once generated a lot of random data. I had funneled as much of the knowledge as I could into a notebook that was connected to a mind enchantment I had created.

I blindly tapped the notebook with one finger, and spoke into my arms. "I have lots of things to try, and thankfully there is a fourth-floor book that should help. It's going to take me all night, but I think I've got a solution. Thanks for staying."

The sensation of being watched washed over me. It felt...familiar. With my forehead positioned as it was, I could see the multitude of connection threads weaving lights along my midsection. I absently examined them, trying to figure out if—

Rip!

I sat straight up and my hand went to my chest as a strange, unconnected rip tore through me. Justice Toad gave two loud croaks. I fished him out of my bag and saw that Two Level Twos had just occurred in the Politics Building next door.

I quickly logged that I was on my way.

Neph and Will continued what they were doing, both of them used to my community service routine. "Leave your stuff," Will said. "We'll be here."

As I walked to the stairs, I could still feel the unidentified, but familiar gaze tracking my movements. I rubbed my chest. The dull ache was still beating there, and I fought a thread of unease as I headed to my first service call.

Chapter Nine

OLIVIA

STRIDING INTO the brick and glass Politics Building next door, I initiated the temporary enchantment I had mastered last term for a quick energy boost, then scrolled the call stats. Two offenders, curses thrown, a debate gone wrong in the debate auditorium.

I'd make sure to tell Olivia all of the unprotected details later. Even if she was still out of sorts, I was certain she'd be amused by a debate duel.

I stopped cold in the auditorium's doorway as I watched my roommate shoot a dart at someone and heard my tablet beep again. The beep meant that the offense had been upgraded. Possibly due to what looked like a poisoned dart. A poisoned dart that my cool, collected roommate had just thrown at someone's throat.

I hastily whipped the tablet forward and pressed a ready-made enchantment. All action stopped, all limbs froze. The girl on the receiving end of the dart, a lanky, brown-haired girl, froze in the act of falling—a violent red curse outstretched on her fingertips. Olivia's face was frozen in a mask of furious, deadly intent.

The debate audience sat at the edges of their auditorium seats, enraptured by the scene playing out in front of them. Cretins.

A tailored boy who looked to be on the upper edge of twenty-two, belatedly hurried up the steps toward the frozen combatants. "Okay, okay. I realize we might all be a little on edge with what has recently happened. Let's take a fifteen-minute break."

People reluctantly began rising from their seats.

I pushed the tablet's re-right button. The magic pulled Olivia and the other girl upright and extinguished any remaining combat magic, shooting the unfulfilled magical components and any half-formed enchantments to the Midlands for modification and dispersal. The girl was vaguely familiar. I racked my image memory as I executed the steps needed to contain two combatants.

The Contract Magic was pretty creepy, as always, in the way it subdued mages. And enrollment contracts were signed in blood.

The tablet's built-in first aid enchantment stabilized the poison, but the girl would still need to go to medical or to the Neutralizer Squad. It was the student's call which avenue to take.

The vaguely familiar image of the girl slotted into place. She was the one I had tried to spell with Justice Toad after she had insulted Olivia last term. Unfortunately, the karmic magic had promptly turned me into a toad.

This was obviously not the first time that she and Olivia had crossed verbal swords, though maybe it had been the first time they had resorted to physical ones.

I looked at her name on the incident log. Inessa Norrissing. Another image connected as my gaze hit the three rings on her right hand. She had been sitting at the magicists' table where I had first placed a cafeteria tray––sitting next to the emerald-eyed girl, who had greatly overshadowed her. Magicists were old magic. That meant she and Olivia probably went way back, and obviously not in a good way.

Great.

I withheld a sigh, then released both girls. "A Level Two and Level Three," I announced. Patterns were important in the justice system. Forms had to be followed.

Inessa was immediately in motion, neutralized fingers pointing at Olivia. "I want her punished!"

I gripped my tablet. "Punishment is the point of me being here, Miss Norrissing."

"Watch how you speak to me." Her finger turned in my direction. "I know who you are, and we are watching you," she hissed.

I looked down at Justice Toad and tried to keep my intentions semi-stable as my body grew both hot and cold. "Looks like cleaning the facilities in the Eighteenth Circle field house is an available punishment."

JT helpfully listed fifty toilets in the scrolling description of the task. Even if the Norrissing girl cleaned with magic, it would still leave her magic feeling like it had cleaned a toilet. Magic was part of a mage and each use left a temporary mirrored mark. Unpleasant, if one used magic for things other than creating rainbows and butterflies, as I knew well.

Her lips snapped shut and sharp spikes of black shot out of her aura. Even if I'd lost the remnants of the enhancement spell, I bet I would have seen those; they were so strong.

Justice Toad scrolled a few other interesting possibilities. "Or, look at that, I could give you animal—"

"I will clean the facilities in the Eighteenth Circle field house tonight, by my magic I so do vow." The black spikes crystallized into a carbon film and small noises of rage worked the passageway from her throat to her nose.

The taste of her wrath was as unpleasant as if I had licked a dirty fireplace.

The spells inherent in the Justice Magic gave me the power to physically remove her from the conflict premises. I pointedly dismissed her, which made her back away from us with stilted, wood-burnt steps. I turned my gaze to Olivia, who coldly looked back.

Her pink-furrowed lips were stretched and tight. I was already highly attuned to her and the extreme emotional and physical responses she couldn't control at the moment nearly made me forget my own name.

Justice Toad vibrated in my hand. I wiped a finger across the smooth skin of my forehead, feeling the pounding in my skull underneath.

"Well?" Olivia demanded. "What am I cleaning? Or am I going to run pointlessly for three days?"

To my knowledge, Olivia had never been in trouble, though she had seen enough service workers give me punishments to know how the system worked.

A thought wiggled around insidiously, my senses clinging to it from multiple directions. "Do you...? Do you want to shadow me for fifteen hours? It would increase your punishment hours, since you wouldn't be doing the penalty alone, but you could use this as an opportunity to get a first-hand observation of the system and meet future clients."

Her expression went flat and unreadable. "You would sacrifice your time?"

I would be required to put in twice the hours, in order to compensate for the justice aspect of the parceled magic—which was a crushing sacrifice in the wake of all of the research I needed to do—but Olivia was worth it, and I needed to let her know that. We could share in this.

"Yes. It will be fun, doing this with you."

Something broke in her eyes and a ripple of smothering tightness gripped me even though she physically turned away. A second later, I felt the ripple ease, and when she turned back she was composed once more. "By my magic, I so do vow."

She turned and strode quickly away. I let the contract magic wash over me, then made to follow.

"Ren."

I turned to see Delia standing behind me. I hadn't seen her in the crowd, and I wondered how long she had been standing there. I had programmed Justice Toad's default setting to silence proceedings from strangers' ears, but I hadn't thought to add a shield against friends too. And Delia, in particular among my friends, was prone to mischief. Our first meeting had resulted in me almost getting eaten by a swamp monster due to her deliberate deception. I was really hoping she hadn't heard the entire conversation.

"Hey. How are you?" A stupid thing to ask when the world was going to Hell. I awkwardly gripped my tablet.

"You shouldn't have done that." Her expression and eyeliner darkened. Her clothing, too, grew more severe with her emotion—lengthening and growing sharp edges. "You shouldn't give Price more than she deserves."

"What do you mean, Delia?" I asked carefully.

"Your personal loyalty is one of your best qualities. It is not one of hers."

"That's not true." I thought of all the secrets Olivia knew and had kept hidden for me.

"Give it time," she said bitterly. "You forget that I have known her longer. Magicists are loyal to their governments, not to their fellow mages."

I wondered what had produced the bitterness underscoring her words, since Delia was friends with numerous magicists.

"Olivia isn't a magicist."

"No, but if you investigate her mom, you will see she is something even worse." Delia stepped away as the club was called to order again. Her eyes were now completely rimmed in coal, and her charcoal eye shadow was extending upward. "Protect yourself."

~*~

I quickly retrieved my items from the library, reassured Neph and Will that everything was okay, then set off in search of Olivia.

She was sitting on the west face of the mountain, the setting rays of the sun igniting her face with light almost too brilliant to focus upon.

"Hey." I sat down on the grass next to her. A balmy breeze blew over us, in stark contrast to the winter snow and bundled up skiers, snowboarders, and sledders three levels down. Weather magic was a beautiful thing, especially in the midst of emotional turmoil.

Olivia and I sat silently for a long time, watching the sun sink beneath the peaks of the distant hills. The waning sense enhancement gently pulsed with conflicting feelings from her.

"Do you want to talk about it?" I asked quietly.

"Norrissing said—" Olivia cut herself off and smoothed the hair above her forehead, straightening the already perfectly straight locks. "Well...what she said is hardly relevant."

"It's relevant to me."

Olivia looked off into the distance. The view was stunning here—at five thousand feet in the air, we had an uninterrupted vista for miles around, with zero altitude effects—but I had a feeling she wasn't seeing any of it. Her gaze was far off, but inwardly focused.

"My path has become hazy," she said.

I weighed my response carefully. Olivia had never deviated from the path she had been born to—that had been obvious from our first meeting, and Delia's words had strengthened that observation.

"I think that happens to a lot of people our age. All those self-help books say so."

"It doesn't happen to me."

"Perhaps your path is becoming clear? Maybe you are only seeing the haze you have been in as the path clears before you now," I said.

She didn't reply and we watched the last rays disappear.

"What did that girl, Inessa Norrissing, say to get you so angry?"

"It matters not." Her voice was strange—half-revelatory and half-bemused. "My path. Yes, you are right. I am in charge of my own destiny."

She rose and brushed off her tailored skirt. "And she is an ant beneath my shoe. Come. Let's sign up for classes, like the rest of the lemmings. Then we can go to the cafeteria. I'm hungry, and you haven't eaten enough in the past two days."

Startled, I nearly lost my grip on my bag's straps. Olivia willingly wanted to go to the cafeteria? "Really? Great!"

Her gaze held mine. It was painful, the anguish and uncertainty that resided beneath her cool facade.

I wanted our friendship, and our group camaraderie, to be the new normal for her. I wanted to envelop her into my family.

As the winter sun faded and the magicked lamps on campus brightened, we fell into step and I nudged her. Some of the tension eased from her shoulders. A pained look stole across her face.

"Thank you," she said.

I nudged her again. "Hey. At least your bad days don't come with jumbo-sized monsters."

"Not all monsters are large," she said quietly. She straightened her shoulders. "Now. Service. Let's discuss how we are going to bring miscreants to justice and help my clients stay out of trouble."

That sounded like my roommate, which was a huge relief.

But as Olivia continued ticking off points on her fingers, the hair on the back of my neck prickled.

I surreptitiously looked around. I couldn't see anyone, but there were eyes focused on us.

Watching.

Chapter Ten

CLOSE ENCOUNTERS OF THE GOOD AND WORSE KIND

THE RELIEF OF BEING UNITED again was strong when Olivia and I finally sat down at the cafeteria table we had inhabited at the end of last term. Mike and Neph were already seated. Neph smiled at me and floated over a scratch paper that I had forgotten in my mad scramble to reach Olivia.

I watched her easy use of magic wistfully. I could do some extraordinary things, but because I hadn't been brought up with magic, the easy, everyday magics still eluded me.

"You are the best, Neph. Thanks." The paper had a list of possible classes on it, along with animated doodles I had made around the ones I liked best. "We just signed up for classes."

That made me sound normal. Normal mages signed up for classes. Normal mages didn't worry about how their magic might be used to destroy civilization.

Normal!

The calming magic that was actively pushed throughout the cafeteria touched me. Everyone else was allowing it to blanket them—even Olivia—and Neph wasn't doing anything to make it stop like she had at Top Campus, so I drank the calm down too, wanting to be chipper and not paranoid for my friends.

Positive thoughts—cross-layer peace would be achieved, magicists from all layers would clasp hands together and sing a united anthem, and Raphael would retire from evil, then gift my magic to an orphanage.

"Hated to miss your birthday, Ren. We are totally rescheduling that celebration," Mike said, pointing at me. He looked tanned and healthy, and not at all like the corpse he could have been if he had been part of our First Layer parking lot adventure.

"You didn't miss much. Rescheduling sounds good." I grinned.

He returned my smile. "Good. What classes did you sign up for?"

I relaxed into calm thoughts and smiled at him. "Individualized Architecture and Design, Layer Politics 101, and Engineering Concepts in Warding. I'm also continuing Personal Study with Stevens."

I needed to know more about the world around me, and Neph and Will had said they would take politics too, so it would hopefully be a solid combination of time, course requirements, and interest.

Engineering Concepts in Warding, taught by the ever-awesome Professor Mbozi, would provide me with the extra tools I needed to ward my dreams, increase my protections, and keep the people around me safe.

Since Marsgrove hadn't removed my art restrictions, I couldn't get into any of the regular art buildings. So I had to take art classes remotely—hence the individualized study.

Someday, maybe I would be able to take the art classes I wanted, like a normal student.

"What about you, Mike?" I asked, breathing in more calming magic.

"Cloud Formation and Placement, Ice Manipulation, and Rain Dancing."

Neph looked at him in interest. "Rain Dancing is a difficult field of study."

Mike grimaced. "I suck at rain. My adviser demanded I take at least two courses in it this year."

He brightened. "But my snow manipulation has undergone a recent dramatic increase and I should pass out of it after this term. Will told me you three were thinking about taking Layer Politics, so I took it as an elective. Should be an interesting class with the current worldwide mess."

"I'm happy you're taking it with us," I said, relieved. I could easily hide my ignorance in the midst of a bigger group.

Delia pressed her tray down and lightly dropped into the seat next to Mike, her black bob swaying as she did. "Add one more to the tally. I signed up for politics too. They increased the cap and brought in more assistants because of the overwhelming student interest."

Olivia violently poked her tiny, blue asparagus stalks, and Delia ignored her as if she wasn't present.

Mike shook his head as he looked between them. "What are the rest of you taking?"

Neph lifted her hand gracefully, and the every-spice shaker lifted into the air. "Dancing in Teams of Five. Movement with Ten. Spectacles and Spectaculars. Layer Politics with you four, and Medical Field Magic."

Olivia glanced up sharply at Neph. Intensity I didn't understand still simmered between them, but Olivia's gaze was less harsh. "Medical Magic? Good."

Suspicion rose in me. Was Neph taking the class because I had temporarily lost body parts and been repeatedly maimed last term? She had patched me up more than once.

"Do you have lab hours with the class?" Mike asked Neph.

She nodded. "Two a week in the field."

"Great! You'll probably be working Winter Wonderland as a lifeguard then." He pulled up a holographic image of the Seventh Circle runs that ran the circumference of the mountain level. Arches at the bottom of the level seamlessly ported the skiers back to different arches at the top, making the runs infinite and varied. In the image, a lifeguard exited a chair and used a red rod to tap the leg of one downed skier and the wrist of another.

"On campus anything short of death is taken care of by students studying Medical Magic," Mike informed me. "They rotate weather mages daily to keep the snow and conditions fresh, so we might be on duty together, Nephthys."

Delia tapped a holographic skier with her fork. "The runs are excellent this year. And the snow is perfect. I did the runs yesterday and today—no complaints."

Mike's chest puffed out and I felt fierce warmth in mine at the normal nature of the conversation.

"Glad to hear it. Spent half my holiday doing credit work for the snow hours. There were twenty of us working on the weather, five working the ports, and two on the controls," Mike said, ticking off the numbers on his fingers. "We were supposed to be working this week too—lots of stuff still left to do—but they activated the system anyway to get things 'back to normal.' Glad you are enjoying the runs, D. The challenge course on January twentieth is my design. As is the one on February seventh. Thought the Department was going to close the campus-port system permanently there for a bit, like they did with off-campus arches."

Uneasiness spiked around the table. The table threads that connected to Neph suddenly pulsed harder, lessening the disquiet.

Mike cleared his throat and carried on the conversation. "So, what are you taking, D?" As far as I knew, Mike was the only one allowed to call Delia that.

"Politics with you ruffians, Stitch-by-Stitch Magic, Threading 220, and Medieval Fashions through the Layers."

The middle two sounded unbearably interesting. And timely. I made a mental note to talk to Delia about interlaced clothing wards. Sleeping in warded pajamas seemed like a fantastic idea.

Mike looked at Olivia. "What about you, Price?"

"Legal Matters between Layers One and Two, Legal Matters between Layers Two and Three, Defense Defensibles, Corruption and Gain, Punishment and Guilt, Sacrifice and Glory, and Magical Lie Detection."

The entire table blinked.

"You going to sleep this term, Price?" Mike asked.

"I sleep as needed. William?" Olivia asked in her clipped way.

Will rallied quickly. "Devices in the Age of Mysticism, Magical Engineering Mechanics 310, Architecture with Ren, and politics with nearly the lot of you."

"Architecture?" Delia asked. "Not quite explode-y enough for you, is it?" Delia had known Will casually from the delinquent circuit before we'd become a united table.

Will pulled out a sheet of paper I had created with pulp and magic under Professor Stevens' guidance, and a magical pencil, also of my design. He sketched a device on the page. The sketched device exploded into a starburst on the paper, burning to the edges in flames that strained against containment.

"Architecture and Design. Model sketching and animation. Stupidly useful for advanced models and pre-testing, but the Engineering Department doesn't utilize it the way they should. Yet." He grinned. "But I'm sure Ren and I can blow up all sorts of things in the project portion."

More than one person rolled their eyes, but Delia smirked and stroked her alert bracelet. The bracelet automatically shut down the suggestion enchantments she loved to abuse so much.

Funny, that. Other types of mages were allowed free reign to use such skills, but try and stitch them into clothing and people panicked. Something about wearing a rogue enchantment in one's favorite sweater terrified people in a way that government-issued control cuffs didn't.

Will was grinning madly. "And, maybe we can get the professor to buy future class supplies from 'Renwill Enterprises' when she sees how awesome our completed assignments are."

Mike flicked his empty spoon at Will.

I opened my mouth to add something, but the hair on the back of my neck lifted. I immediately rubbed the area, freaked out that I could feel each hair extended. The most concentrated batch of hair was stretching in one particular direction. I waited thirty seconds, then as casually as I could, let my gaze sweep that way.

The girl with the emerald eyes met my gaze head-on, not even bothering to look away. She cocked her head in a contemplative way, while next to her Inessa Norrissing angrily jabbed her finger against the table top. Little darts of crimson magic sparked from the contact.

Not good.

~*~

After dinner, I trudged back to the library alone. Will had his Mechanics United club meeting, Mike was on snow patrol, Delia had Fashion Guild, and Neph was on muse duty. Olivia had another debate meeting, but she had assured me with a fierce, concerning look, that the outcome of this meeting would be different from her last. That could mean one of two things—that she wouldn't get in a fight again, or that she wouldn't get caught, if she did.

The minute I entered the fourth floor, the black-and-white book's cover tilted toward me. The spell from Enhancing had worn off, but my ability to see my own connections remained. A long thin dollar-green cord ran from my chest to the book. A debt to be repaid.

Great.

I painstakingly cleared my mind of random desires, in case the book read and acted on another of my thoughts, then got to work.

It took fifteen minutes, but I finally succeeded in calling Vivid Dreams in Transition to me using its card catalog spell. It certainly would have saved me a lot of time last term, if I had known these tricks from the start, instead of having to stubbornly figure out everything from scratch.

The book flew toward me in a haphazard flight path of swirling colors. As opposed to the more dour tomes, the books that found joy in their own existence were glorious to watch. Unfortunately, dealing with them directly was usually aggravating. They tended to be prone to mercurial fits of emotion and theatricality.

Helmet in place, I let the book nuzzle my shoulder before I activated the cooperation spell. It gave an audible papered sigh as it plopped on its back cover and opened to page one.

As I leafed through, its blue bookmark tongue waved in the air like a cobra, repeatedly trying to lick my hand.

I transferred data quickly between the book, Justice Toad, and my reader, using my fingers as bridges. Justice Toad ticked another two community service hours onto my total as the tablet disapprovingly did the work I asked of it.

Getting punished for misusing the tablet's magic was well worth the amount of time I saved, though. Adding Olivia's hours to my tab was kind of a blow, but these two extra hours would be easily offset. Frankly, I was a little immune to adding one or two hours here or there after racking up two hundred plus community service hours last term.

Exhausted, but relieved that I had some actual tactics to try before going to sleep again, I released my finger bridge and shut the book.

Approaching its designated shelf space, I thrust the book toward the open slot between two other tomes. But Vivid opened its covers and pushed against the spines of the two books—like a cat refusing to get into its carrier.

"Come on, just go in there." I wiggled its spine and pushed harder, exhaustion starting to overtake my higher brain functions. The streaming room visit earlier had taken a lot out of me.

"You'll be released from the card catalog spell." I tried coaxing. "Doesn't that sound great?"

Lick.

Ack. I rubbed the back of my hand against my jeans again. Who knew what else that bookmark had licked today? I was going to need some magical disinfectant.

"Pardon me," a husky voice said.

I shivered. Every time a lick made contact, it caused vivid hallucinations. Such a dangerous book, dealing in dreams and fevered imaginings. It had been whispering things to me post-licks for the past half hour. And Vivid's dream-induced whispers were getting downright eerie. My mind was even substituting Alexander Dare's voice now.

A stringed light of pure ultramarine pulsed from my chest in response.

A dangerous book. Especially when I was running on fumes.

Vivid pushed back against my hand, hard.

"Come on, buddy, just go in." I tried to clasp Vivid's covers together and shove it into place. I got hit with another blue-bookmark-tongued lick.

"I was wondering if you could help me with something."

"Yeah, yeah. I'll help you with something," I said in a dark tone, suddenly irritated with the book's taunting and the blue string's pulsing.

I gave an extra-firm shove, and finally, finally, the book seated into place, tongue firmly wedged in too. It wiggled a bit, so I pushed against the spine with a finger. If I was quick, I'd be able to make it to the stairs before it tracked me down for another taste.

"You make it sound painful."

I realized that someone was standing next to me at the same time that I realized that a real, live person—and not the mischievous book—had been the one talking.

"What did you say?" My voice went weirdly high pitched as I looked up into unnaturally blue eyes. He was leaning one shoulder against the bookshelf, so close to me that we were nearly touching.

Alexander Dare and I hadn't had much to say to each other since I had died for him. Well that wasn't entirely true; he had tried to talk to me, but I was stupidly incoherent around him and conflicted––wanting him to recognize me from the night of Christian's Awakening and subsequent death, yet not wanting him to recognize me from the same.

His eyes were still the color of ultramarine paint straight from Michelangelo's brush.

My hand dropped and Vivid thrust itself backward, licked the side of my face in one long blue bookmarked pass—whispering dirty thoughts as it did—then ruffled its pages in supreme amusement and self-satisfaction as it flew away in a triple-looped pattern.

Dare gave the fleeing book an unreadable glance, then gazed at my ink-slobbered cheek.

Nothing brilliant or witty lit in my head. I stared blankly at him, wiped my cheek, and wished I had a portal to Hell.

The skin around his blue eyes creased under the windswept, dark hair brushing his brow. Irritation was a pretty normal expression for me to see on his face.

Still hot.

"I saw you exiting the streaming room earlier," he said in a horribly casual voice, as if he was trying—and failing—to be anything other than irritated with me. "The librarian said you are in there frequently."

I swallowed. I really needed to be more careful. "It's a useful room."

He tilted his head. "And yet I pulled you out of a regular reading room when you got lost to the information, what, three months ago? The first time you stepped into one."

I gave a queasy laugh at the thought of what he wasn't saying. "They made me nervous before, so I had never tried one. I got over it." Olivia had hated the rooms before I helped her through the process. Surely he'd buy that excuse from me.

Lies! Feral alert! Right in front of you!

"You must use an indexing spell in the streaming room, if you emerge without looking like total death."

I didn't respond, keeping my lips clearly shut on the urge to ask, "How do I look?"

"Many mages hate all of the rooms and rely on the first management spell they find," he said.

"Okay." One word answers seemed safe.

He hesitated strangely for a moment. "I saw your notebook. You bridge the information, don't you?" His eyes were piercing.

Combat mages had such focused gazes, but his was unmasking—like he had already searched and found what he needed and was simply guiding his opponent, me, into the carefully laid trap he fully controlled.

I gave a nervous laugh. "Yes, I use a bridged indexeting spell."

Indexeting wasn't a word—in any language.

His focused gaze never wavered, but either irritation or amusement briefly flitted across his expression. "Which indexing spell do you use? I'm looking for a better one."

If I didn't know any better, I would think he was attempting to make small talk with me. But there was no way that could be true. Which meant he was digging for information for nefarious purposes.

Panic and adrenaline surged and combined with the one effect I had managed to maintain from the Enhancing enchantment. The ultramarine string attached to his chest twanged into luminous view, spanning the space between us. Linking us quite clearly.

My hand went to my earlobe and I tugged it, desperately casting about for anything not completely insane to say as my mind spiraled out of my control and I tried not to stare at the connection. Indexing spells, indexing spells… "There are a dozen good indexeterering…in-dex-ing," I said slowly and stupidly, "spells for the reading rooms."

Die, die!

But my mouth decided it needed to make up for all mental shortcomings. "For average searches, I like Mueller's. I read that combat mages usually like Calaveri's, but that's shortsighted, don't you think, as it is exactly the same search order your magic would already perform. And the streaming room is like a reading room on crack."

The words spewed out faster as my panic increased. "Or you could get a book on them. I know where those are." You know, right here. In front of us. "Or, wait, what do you want to stream? I should probably ask that first. I think it would be pertinential."

Pertinential? Panic overlaid panic and my brain shorted to survival blips. The kind of blips that were flaring neon signs that said—Escape! Escape as quickly as possible!

"Pertinent, I meant pertinent. But wait, you asked about mine," I said, steamrolling on, unwilling to listen to an undoubtedly agonizing response questioning my fitness as a member of the human race—magical or otherwise. "It combines Mueller's, Calaveri's, Winslop's, and Ng's, with some extras. It's in beta stage with a recording spell that locks in your head for an hour afterward—I based it on magic locks, crazy things, yeah?" Oh, my God. "And it downloads in crazy bits to an enchanted notebook using Perry's code, but the lock works well and gives you an extra hour, and our magic is very sympathetic and connected—"

His brows shot upward at that and I started stuttering worse. My gaze was drawn again to the ward connecting us—the one that was now pulsing weirdly.

Escape! "So it should work for you, and here!"

I laid my hand on his wrist, and the ultramarine connection immediately reformed along the completed circuit of skin-to-skin contact, running from chest to arm and up the opposite path. Blue light flared brilliantly. I shoved the magic through the connection, and the blaring neon mental signs suddenly read—Holy-Dragon-Fire!—at the thought that I had just thrust magic into Alexander Dare without asking first. His face could only be described as a mirror of my thoughts—filled with astonishment, and a dawning "smite her immediately!" vibe.

Neither of us moved for a full second, full on shock overtaking everything else as the warm sienna of the spell transferred. No colored spell ball had formed in either of our hands, as one might politely pass a spell to someone else. No, the spell had gone directly through and into him––bypassing any shield.

I tore my hand away and the floor wavered in my view. I quickly and mechanically grabbed a blank piece of library memo from the floating tub that was always zooming around. My fingers were still warm from touching him.

He needed instructions. I was going to be dead after he killed me and he wouldn't be able to use the recording spell.

I force-shoved my magic to scribble the directions for the spell's use—panic and horror making my magic sharp and crazed and available for mass personal destruction of the social kind.

Vivid dove out of a looping spiral, and a blue bookmarked tongue reached out and swiped my cheek. Its spine curved into a smirk. I jerked, elbowed Dare in the chest, and sent my shouldered bag careening into the shelf to the right. A piece of paper from my bag fell to the floor. But grabbing it would take 1.5 extra seconds that I needed for running.

"Here." I shoved the papered directions against his chest. His hand automatically curled around it.

Then I ran as if the hounds of Hell were nipping at my heels.

Chapter Eleven

ALWAYS BACK TO YOU

IMMEDIATELY ACTIVATED the spell I had created last term that specifically allowed me to avoid Alexander Dare. But by the next morning, I discovered there was something weirdly off about it.

So I avoided the library like it was a plague-infested ship of rats. I avoided the cafeteria. I even avoided a Draeger visit in the Battle Building, just in case. To top it off, I entered the Midlands on the south side of the Ninth Circle, far from the paths normal mages took.

My paranoia stretched high. Eluding the Junior Department, as I had taken to calling the students who seemed to consider it their duty to register and report campus threats, was nothing in comparison to my desire to avoid Alexander

Dare. The Department was a shadowy threat. Alexander Dare, on the other hand, was real and ridiculously godlike—likely with all the gorgeous, smiting vengeance associated with the divine.

Thankfully, upon entering the Midlands, the Okai building appeared immediately, welcoming me inside. Both of my animated rocks were doing well, though Guard Rock communicated with his gestures and pencil strikes that they had been staying inside for the past two days. Relieved, I gave Guard Rock and Guard Friend pats and talked to them while I painted on a magical canvas I had purchased at an Expressionists' meeting. Painting soothed the edge of my magic, though nothing could cure my mortification or underlying unease.

Still, seeing Guard Rock and Guard Friend whole and hale was a huge weight off my mind. They counted in the category of "beings I needed to keep safe."

In the forefront of a farmhouse scene, I inserted images of the rocks in a parody of Grant Woods's American Gothic. Guard Rock touched the paint of the pitchfork his counterpart held, then thumped his pencil down in approval. Not wanting to risk my Awakening paint on frivolity, I was still able to use one of the better batches of paint I had made with Stevens, resulting in the costumed rocks slowly and theatrically moving inside the world of the picture. It made me smile and Guard Friend clap.

Because Okai appeared immediately upon my entry into the Midlands, and deposited me on the edge of the Midlands when I exited through the front door again, there was little need for me to be concerned anymore in the otherwise deadly territory. But even taking the few steps from the edge of the Ninth Circle to Okai's door, I could feel the foreign magics filtering through—and the junior stooges stalking the deadly mists.

I had to admire their fortitude, even if their creepy gazes unnerved me. Talented mages died in the Midlands every day and even stooges weren't exempt from mortal danger.

Upon exiting Okai, I checked the door to make sure the lock engaged. The building never stayed in one place long enough for a normal mage to approach it—but better safe than sorry.

A good amount of my research—including the golem and empty dolls I had made to house my brother's soul—had been stolen by Raphael last term.

I had felt Raphael poking at the dream wards last night, laughing, but the wards had been a success. Hopefully, the wards I planned to raise tonight would prevent even his pokes, and maybe deal him some damage.

Five watchdog stooges stood just outside the mist when I exited. I let a few stray calming vibes that were floating around campus attach to me, but no amount of pressing or calming magic could diminish my tension completely. One of the boys stared hard at me, took a note, then went back to speaking with the other four.

Justice Toad alerted me halfway back to my dorm that an immediate all-hands meeting had been called for the Justice Squad, so I wove over to another port, and triple-hopped the mountain—fifth level south, third level northeast, fourth level west—to minimize walking distance, then trudged to the break room. Since all external forms of magical transportation, like portal pads and carpets, were banned on campus, it was a campus-wide game finding the best port paths or naturally occurring transfers to get from point A to B.

Isaiah Gellis, the head of the Justice Squad, stood in the front of the room as everyone filed past and took seats.

I nervously glanced around, but no one was looking at me strangely. Good. No one on the squad usually paid me much attention. Currently, I was the only community service member assigned to the squad—the token delinquent in a room full of do-gooders. The Justice Squad was made up of students who were dedicated to making campus a safer and more orderly place. The community service folks who got roped in never quite fit that mold. And most of the mages who were forced into community service on the squad, only did it for a night or two.

Not for two hundred hours, like I'd initially been assigned. My excessive amount of hours meant I was considered a semi-permanent member, and had to attend meetings.

"Folks," Isaiah said, "I have just been informed that for the next month we will be increasing patrols and sanctions on campus, per new security stipulations. Effective immediately, Level Four Offenses will require board review."

I grimaced, and my least favorite member of the squad, Joseph Aldwin Peters, smiled, his back unnaturally straight due to the metaphorical pole stuck up his...spine.

Board review on Level Fours would put a serious dent in the lives of many of my cohorts in magical crime. Olivia was about to get a lot of new business as a defense attorney.

"I'm sending the new information to your tablets, but this might be a good time to shore up punishments. Let people know that the noose is tightening and that the administration will be watching."

The administration. Right. The back of my neck itched, and I could already feel the cold stares of Department eyes. Thankfully, the campus's forcefully calming magic continued to keep my very real panic mostly contained. I could see the blue mists seeping in through the vents.

"Also, keep in mind that the Second Layer Combat Competition is coming up in six weeks.

We usually work with Excelsine graduates to provide security on campus while the combat mages are competing, but this year...the Department and Excelsine officials have made...an agreement. The Department is dropping their review into the craziness that happened last term, and the much revered Peacekeepers' Troop will provide security for campus during the competition week."

Most of the others, including Peters, nodded grimly. I sat up straight, alarmed by their response, and elated that the Department wasn't going to interrogate all of us after all.

A promotional video for the Peacekeepers' Troop appeared on the wall. Men and women bent their knees in succession, then took aim, firing spells. Like some sort of cheer squad doing battle drills.

The video zeroed in on capable, determined faces and well-practiced maneuvers. "Your magical security is our magical business!" The video feed exploded in a shower of lights. Showy and empty.

Isaiah continued through his agenda, but I stared at the finished feed, mystified, a little horrified, and a lot intrigued.

I waited a few minutes after the others had cleared out of the room then approached Isaiah.

"Security? But that doesn't include me, right?"

He looked amused. "Since your community service period extends past Winter Term, you're an official part of the squad for whatever happens during the winter." His dark brown eyes sparkled with humor. "Congratulations."

"Great." I sighed. "What does security entail?"

The Justice Squad dealt with the contractual magic that each student on campus was bound to. Usually we didn't have to chase people down or fight them. The Combat Squad dealt with those types of things—escaped Midlands magic, intruders, monsters—and the Neutralizer Squad was called in to put mages and magic back to rights. But now Isaiah was saying...

"When the combat mages leave campus en masse to attend the Second Layer Combat Competition, it leaves campus without security.

So every year our squad works with an outside group—usually made up of combat mage alumni—to provide campus security. But with the way the Department is reacting to Layer events, the higher-ups pushed for the Peacekeepers' Troop."

Isaiah shook his head, frowning. "Usually we just partner up to provide eyes, ears, and aid to the alumni, nothing exciting happens, and the Combat Squad ribs them about being too old to fire spells. This year... Well, no one wants the Department getting a toehold into Excelsine, but the public is currently terrified and crazed and they've convinced the people in power—many of whom have kids who attend here."

I stared at him, no response forthcoming from my brain.

He gave me an encouraging look. "Politics. But Selmarie and I will take care of everything. Don't worry about it much, okay?"

Dare might be the unofficial leader of the combat mages, due to his outright badassery, but Selmarie Senthuss was the twenty-two-year-old head of the Combat Squad.

A no-nonsense mage who answered to the administration on the Combat Squad's behalf, created their patrol schedules, handled their crazy personality clashes, and who was a fierce fighter herself.

I rubbed my cuffed wrist. "I, uh, don't know how to fight." I wanted to protect my friends, with certainty. But protecting campus as a magical bouncer? I had almost ended campus last term. I wasn't sure it could survive me running around blasting monsters every day.

He waved a hand. "Don't worry. Most of the squad is in the same boat. We're dealers of justice, not combat. That's why we will partner up and why the combat mages will help us prepare. Just get some rest and wait out your assignment."

Okay. Maybe... Maybe I could do great things. Protect campus and reduce my guilt and make it safe enough that the miniature dragons returned to the jet streams.

Maybe they would assign me to casing the Midlands. Guard Rock with his zombie radar, and me with some quick-drawn traps... We could take them. The randomness of nature and magic was far easier to understand than people, most of the time.

This assignment... It could be great. It could be my ticket to my magic helping instead of hurting.

If only I had realized then what Isaiah meant by "assignment."

I made the trip back to the dorm to check on Olivia. Thankfully, she was in her chair and her magic was back to full strength. It had only been three days since we'd happily played board games at home in the First Layer—though it felt far longer. But we'd get back to that state. I'd make sure of that.

"Nephthys told me that Verisetti is visiting you in your dreams," she said as soon as I shut the door.

I nodded, chucking my bag onto my desk and collapsing on my bed, exhausted. I was always exhausted in the magical world, though. "I put up wards when I returned from the library last night, but you were already asleep. He poked and prodded last night, but didn't get through."

I had been forced to dream instead of my two feet repeatedly jabbing my open mouth while Alexander Dare watched on.

"Nephthys said you had the dreams while in the First Layer too." Olivia's voice took on a distinct chill. "You never said anything."

"It was that last night. The spell snapping into place?" I ran fingers through my ponytail. "I let him 'dim me' so we could come back. I was trying to figure out how to tell you without you yelling at me. Speaking to him at all was a mistake, I know. He took me by surprise, and he knows what buttons to push."

I had been making a lot of mistakes lately, which was off-putting. I had been so careful in the past. But I was working with a lot of new variables instead of the ones I had always relied upon.

"Did he connect through the wards? Are the wards not enough to keep your parents safe?" she demanded.

"No, it was me. I did something that night. Invited him in by accident. I was drained. The holidays..." I shook my head. "I wasn't sure if seeing him wasn't really just the crazy, all manifesting in my mind."

At Olivia's immediate physical withdrawal, I straightened my posture. "Not drained because of anything to do with you," I said quickly, trying to minimize my inadvertent damage. "Being without Christian." I hunched in my shoulders. "First birthday, first Christmas."

Her withdrawal warmed back to a dissecting regard. "Emotional involvement. The consequences of making, then losing an attachment."

I was pretty sure she was talking to herself, but I responded anyway. "Worth it." My voice sounded strained. "Worth it," I whispered again.

"You put up these protections last night?" She pointed at a few colorful ward strings that were concentrated over her side of the room. I had put far more on her side of the room.

I cleared my throat. "Yes. I wanted to make sure they would protect you."

She moved something on her desk, one of her emotional delaying tactics. "I wish to add to the rooms' wards too."

I smiled, and gave a small, relieved laugh. It would protect her even better if we built them together. "That would be great, Olivia."

~*~

After extensive consultation with Olivia that lasted through dinner, I went to the fourth floor of the library to look up the double spell that would allow us to increase the dream wards to triple-powered strength. Raphael would be very sorry tonight when he came knocking.

Because of my experience with Dare, the library was one of the last places I wished to be, but I was better equipped to deal with Vivid than Olivia was. Olivia would rip out its tongue.

I checked to see if Alexander Dare was near, then double-checked that the avoidance spell was still in place. The spell still felt weird, but that was probably because any associated thought I had of him caused a jump in the attached ultramarine line I was now very aware of.

Having a connection to Alexander Dare wasn't new, but seeing the very bright thread was. It vibrated, taunting me. I could have done without the visual reminder. Ignorance really was bliss sometimes.

The Book of Time signaled midnight as it flew through the air, sounding out twenty-four pulped chirps. I had been working for five hours straight—two of those in a reading room—but I still hadn't determined the correct order of steps for the enchantment we needed to try before going to bed.

The words moved on Vivid's page, a result of bleary eyes and foggy thoughts. I needed to sleep or get a mused-up recharge from Neph. We had to get this enchantment right. I couldn't risk letting Olivia be sucked into some sort of horrorfest with Raphael, if we screwed up.

"I can't let anyone else I care about die," I said to Vivid's pages. Its tongue waved in a consoling fashion, then jerked suddenly in an upwardly pointing manner. I had no idea what it was trying to say—that loved ones were in Heaven?

I shook my head. "That's not... Look, I know. He's fine. He's at peace. He's probably rocking things up there. But I can't let anyone else I care about die."

Vivid's bookmark jerked more aggravatingly. Pointing, yes; but to Heaven, no.

I lifted my gaze...and saw Alexander Dare standing in front of me, arms crossed, head tilted so he was looking down at me with dissecting regard. I might have to rethink my hotness scale. He kind of defied it.

My stomach sank. In the afterlife, I'd consider it, certainly. And it would be in the afterlife, because he was looking right at me.

He had always been on the edge of destroying the avoidance spell. I had barely been able to maintain the illusion in the Midlands without detection last term. It was a tricky and draining spell to hold. If I lived through this confrontation, I'd have to try something new. Maybe a permanent invisibility spell. Only a few people would miss me.

"Hi," I said, resigned to my fate. Too tired to argue.

Something indecipherable shifted in his expression, then smoothed out. I got the feeling he was mentally shifting tactics based on my response. "It worked," he said.

What worked? My social destruction? He was obviously not referencing my avoidance spell. "Do I need to pack now or later?"

His brows drew sharply together. "What?"

I put my forehead on my crossed arms, which awkwardly and painfully strained my helmet upward, the strap pulling on the underside of my chin. Wearing a helmet because I couldn't fend off the enchanted books on my own didn't even rank in the top three worst parts of this moment.

"Come back tomorrow," I said into my sleeve. "Brain functions, starry-eyed awkwardness, and my will to live will all be operational again sometime in the morning."

Vivid, sensing an opening, tried to weasel between my arm and cheek, hoping to push the helmet from my head. Its blue bookmarked tongue lapped the hair at my neck excitedly.

Whatever. Do your worst.

The book was pushed to the side, along with my hair, and long, warm fingers touched the back of my neck. A triple-shot of adrenaline and white light surged through me, electrocuting my spine, and firing all neurons in my body.

"Whoa." My torso snapped straight. Everything was sharp, crisp, and overwhelming—hyper-stimulated by whatever magic Dare had just shot into my skin.

His arms crossed again, his gaze unapologetic, looking like he had stepped out of a magical GQ spread. "Consider us even now. Your indexing spell worked, but you shouldn't use magic on someone without their permission," he said pointedly.

I saw people doing magic on other people every minute of the day. What he meant was—don't use it on me without my permission or I will squash you. I had seen his magic used for squashing. It wasn't pretty.

But as the magic surged within me, that fact barely registered. I looked at my arms, dazed as each tired cell revitalized in a long magical stream. "Sorry about magicking you yesterday. That was a mistake. But you can feel free to do this to me anytime. Permission granted."

I caught the hint of a smile on his face before he wiped it away. "Why did you say our magic was sympathetic and connected?" he asked.

I waved a hand, feeling my own adrenaline course. It nearly overrode my panic—like a drug that encouraged life-risking behaviors. What would I have done for a restoration like this last term? Given at least a rib. Maybe two. "It seems like we are?"

"No."

I was pretty darn certain of our sympathy and connection, but I was perfectly happy to pretend otherwise. I nodded and the energy coursed through my neck, making me shiver. "Yes, I think I see that I was mistaken."

"My 'no' was a rejection of your vague answer. Try another," he said, the last word overly pronounced.

"Er..." Careful, careful, no mistakes. "We are all connected?" That seemed appropriately batty and in character—I was absolutely never coherent around him. I waved my hand in his direction, watching the traces of light it left in the air, trying to convey to him wordlessly that I was too flighty to hold a conversation.

He didn't answer and his eyes dissected me like a puzzle box he was determined to destroy.

Don't speak! Say nothing more! The risk-taking adrenaline he had sent surging through my blood and magic made me want to take a chance and blurt out everything, but my mind was screaming not to fall prey to that piercing gaze. I rolled my shoulders and the magic blazed a path along both blades, converging in the middle and shooting down my sternum. The ultramarine thread pulsed from my chest to his with jeweled brightness.

I stared at it for long moments, truly mesmerized. "What spell is this?"

I stretched my right leg, feeling the tingle travel all the way down. I repeated the motions with my left. "This is insane. I've been sitting here all night, yet I feel like I could run a marathon—without a Justice Tablet forcing me to do it, and believe me, I've been on the other end of that."

A smile curved one edge of his mouth. "Family trade secret," he said, finally.

"You should bottle and sell it. You could give the muses a run for their money."

"It's better," he said, with certainty that bypassed arrogance. "The only way you would get such a benefit from a muse is if you had a personal one, and no one risks that."

I didn't know why not. Neph was awesome. I couldn't stop rolling the magic around my limbs. "You'd make millions."

He spun a ball of blue magic in his right hand. Hopefully it was a reflexive motion. It seemed unlikely that he would have given me the energy boost if he planned to throw a spell of doom at me.

"You haven't answered my question," he said.

I didn't want to answer his question. "How did I get through your shields anyway?" Perhaps skin-to-skin contact combined with the sheer element of surprise had done it? I'd have to look into that. I needed every edge when I saw Raphael next time.

Dare's expression turned unreadable. "We are toeing around the same answer."

"It's because we are sympathetic?" I asked, surprised.

"No. You can't get through a shield simply by being sympathetic with the mage who holds it. If that was how it worked, the shield would be useless. There are probably a thousand mages at this school who you are sympathetic with at various levels."

"Oh." That made sense. My eyes automatically moved to the bright blue cord between us. There was sympathy and there was connection, and they didn't have to go together.

His ever-present ball of magic moved with his almost unconscious hand motions. "Poor memory?" he asked casually. "They drill that information into everyone in primary. Then again in secondary school."

My adrenaline surged into a riotous whirlwind, whipping along my veins.

"Right." I tried nodding at him, as if I was confirming memory problems, but the motion was stilted.

He knew. Alexander Dare knew I was feral. I could hear it in his unspoken words, though I could read nothing in his expression as to what he thought of my feral state.

I stopped nodding, stilling all motion completely. "What are you going to do?"

"Why do you think I'm going to do anything?"

"You wouldn't be here discussing it with me otherwise."

His lips pulled into a half smile, increasing his hotness past the scale. But then his expression tightened. "An interesting comment, since you are surprised that I am here discussing anything with you right now."

"What do you mean?" I licked my lips, alarm of a different nature taking hold.

He tossed the blue ball of light onto the table in front of me. The light puffed out in misty blue swirls, leaving a piece of paper behind.

His unnaturally blue eyes were cool. "You dropped that yesterday."

I gingerly lifted the note—ice freezing my veins at the words on the sheet. My other hand reached immediately for my bag. The note that tethered the avoidance spell should have been in there, not in my hand.

But written on the paper in my hand, in my handwriting, was Avoidance Spell – Ex Repellant and Protection. Scripted beneath my words, in someone else's handwriting, was Alexander Dare. Someone had cast a spell to reveal who I'd been avoiding with the ex-boyfriend spell, and it was pretty obvious said spell caster was standing in front of me.

Oh, shit.

He touched the skin under his ear, tuning into whatever his frequency was alerting him to. For a moment, I thought I was saved—some eight-headed monster was tearing up lower campus, or maybe a freak storm consisting of man-eating breakfast sandwiches was swooping through the skies—he'd stride off to do battle and forget me completely. But his finger dropped and his expression smoothed again into a dissecting stare. A stare totally focused on me.

"A curiously strong avoidance casting," he said. "And yet I found you anyway. Think on that."

He turned on his heel, then strode away, battle cloak and gear magically forming and flaring around him.

Double shit.

Chapter Twelve

THE LIGHTNING FESTIVAL

I LEANED MY WEIGHT against the magical microwave in our room, eyes barely open, and put my hand in the personalization square that would allow me to influence what I wanted to happen inside it. I tried to concentrate on telling the box to add powdered sugar, chocolate chips, butter, and cinnamon to my Magi Mart waffles in the perfectly coordinated way it did when I wasn't exhausted.

It would be the perfect start to my morning if I ended up with rock hard ultramarine-colored waffles because I was still fretting over stupid Alexander Dare. Fretting had kept me awake even after finally linking in the last room ward with Olivia six hours ago.

Dare's parting words had been anything but reassuring. But I had to admit that Olivia and

I wouldn't have been able to do the wards without the energy recharge he had given me. With a free finger, I touched the beam of ultramarine attached to my chest. It vibrated in the midst of my grateful thought. Weird.

I rubbed my eyes, then yawned into my hand as Olivia emerged from the bathroom. Despite our mutual exhaustion, we were far more relaxed than we had been before the wards had gone up six hours ago. Protection and unity of purpose. United and strong.

In addition, I had a feeling that the calming magic on campus had kicked into our room, finally. But Olivia didn't seem concerned, so it had to be fine.

"Do you want me to—" I yawned again, and pointed to the microwave, "—put something in for you?"

Olivia was already dressed, all in sharp black. "And have it turn me into a reptile as soon as I eat it? No, thank you."

I examined the box through bleary eyes. "Reptiles? Can it do that?"

Olivia's outfit changed into sleek gray threads as she re-examined the lethal pair of boots she had magicked on. "Who knows what your magic would do," Olivia said, apparently satisfied with her boots and matching deadly apparel.

I wondered if I could get a bunch of small, talking reptiles to dress me as if I were Snow White. That would be useful, and a fun way to start the morning.

The box dinged. My waffles looked great. But I grimaced at the arboreal salamanders staring up at me from both sides of the heating box. I knew what they were—last term I had zapped twelve offenders into different types of salamanders courtesy of Justice Toad's amphibian magic. But shouldn't I have gotten, at least, a tiny mutant crocodile here? Stupid magic. Stupid thoughts.

I carefully scooted my plate away from contamination, then scooped up the salamanders, opened the window, and waited for them to stick to the stones. They scampered down the outer wall of the Magiaduct toward freedom.

They hadn't even tried to braid my hair or sing lovely songs. I closed the window, sighed, then washed my hands.

Five hours was an eternity of sleep for me these days, but we had used a lot of room magic and drained some of the strings that normally rejuvenated us while we slept. Olivia's deadly apparel matched the dark circles under her eyes.

But Raphael hadn't tapped into my dream bubble last night. And not even a blip of a nightmare had threatened other than continual, mortifying dreams of Dare. Better not to think about those—who knew what my magic would do.

Satisfied with her outfit choice to wear later in the day, Olivia changed back into the comfortable, loose fitting garments I had gotten her to wear in the First Layer when it was just family hanging out. In order to completely set the wards we had constructed, we couldn't leave our room for sixteen hours.

Which meant I didn't have to risk running into Dare until dinner—an added bonus.

Lunch came and went with us eating Magi Mart fare and chatting companionably.

Ding.

I wrapped a section of hair around my finger and flipped pages on top of my reader, looking for anything interesting to add to the wards, or anything we might have missed. I loved being able to have electronic books magically pop up into real books. And wow, but that calming magic was working overtime. I barely even remembered what to be concerned about.

Ding.

"Something is in there for you." Olivia waved a hand toward the black delivery box.

I blinked at the studded metal box, and indeed, a small orange light was blinking at the top. Orange indicated a delivery for me, purple for Olivia.

But I hadn't ordered anything and no one I knew on campus ever sent me mail. Most people I dealt with were serial rule breakers, and wouldn't risk exposure to identification spells.

I opened the heavy, wrought-iron door. A brown, wrapped package sat inside. I stared at it, thinking hard on what it might be. It gave a sudden hop and I took a hasty step back, breaking through the shell of calming magic. Trepidation sank in.

It was possible for someone to send me something through campus post simply by knowing my name—campus magic worked with the blood and magic enrolled students gave, connecting it to the personal magic in rooms.

"Liv, how do you check mail?"

Her pen stopped scratching her page. "What do you mean?"

The package gave another hop. "For bombs and things."

Olivia heaved a sigh and started writing again. "The postal magic won't let anything harmful go through."

Two hops.

I tapped the magic of my leather bracelet's encyclopedia and started mentally scrolling through information on postal spells. Will had made the bracelet for me to replace Christian's leather band, which had burned to ashes when I had saved Will from my Awakening sketch. The package started jumping up and down in agitation. I scrolled faster.

"Now that you've acknowledged the package, the magic will pester you until you accept it. It doesn't like uncompleted tasks." Olivia flipped a page in her book.

The interior of the delivery box started to emit heat. Postal topics flipped from one to the next in my head. Acknowledging, accepting, addressing…

When the warmth from the box approached combustible levels, I grabbed the furiously hopping parcel. The package went immediately dormant in my hand, cool to the touch. I shut the door and leaned against it, eying the parcel warily.

Nothing happened. "Can you choose not to open a delivery?"

Olivia shrugged, still not looking my way. "As long as it is out of the delivery system, you can do whatever you want. Spells can be attached to attract your notice and encourage you to open something, but they are easy to uncover."

There was no address information of any kind on the package. "Nothing harmful can be delivered?"

"Not through the box. Through other means, yes." Olivia's shoulders stiffened strangely.

"But not through the box."

"Yes, Ren." Exasperation.

I scratched the back of my neck, turning the package in my hands. It was neatly wrapped. Precise.

"Oh, for—" Olivia shoved out of her seat and held out her hand.

I looked between the package and her hand, then sighed and began unwrapping it.

Olivia's hands went to her hips. "I thought you weren't going to open it."

"Yeah, well, if it is dangerous, I don't want you to open it and get hurt instead."

Something unreadable passed through Olivia's eyes. Her arms crossed over her chest.

Beneath the brown paper was a wooden box containing a glass orb. Gold and white light drifted inside the orb like gentle lightning trapped in a container. My fingertips stroked it automatically. It was beautiful.

Olivia's arms uncrossed as she stepped nearer, seemingly drawn to it as well. "A lightning blast. A very expensive one."

She must have read my blank expression, because she continued. "A firework core. For the Lightning Festival. Haven't you heard anyone talk about it?"

Something vague tugged at my memory, but I had been pretty busy thinking about other things in the past few days. "Maybe?"

"We were supposed to be in the First Layer tonight with your parents." Her gaze turned slightly wistful. "I guess I hadn't given it much thought what we'd do in the First Layer on the eve of the new year. But here the eve is used as the night to remember and reflect upon the past year." Her voice softened. "To remember those you've lost."

Our gazes held, then she carefully lifted the firework and examined it. "Traditionally, it is an internal reflection of releasing the souls of the departed. Mages also use the Lightning Festival as a time to cast hopeful wishes for the new year."

"That sounds..." I cleared my throat. "I like that."

She nodded, still looking at the swirling lightning. "This is a very fine core. Craftsman grade. Expensive." She set the firework back in my hand. "And it is made to be personalized. We are stuck here for another three hours and I can see your brain is starting to seep from your ears. Look up enchantments on your reader. You can put as little or as much of yourself into the firework as you wish."

"Do you know who sent it?"

Her eyes narrowed and she picked up the wooden box, turning it in her hand. "No. Didn't it say?"

I shook my head. The list of people who knew I had lost someone was short, though, and didn't require anonymity. My thoughts must have been obvious, because Olivia regarded the firework even more closely.

"You think Verisetti sent it?" she asked.

"Maybe." Especially after blocking him successfully—the timing of the gift was suspect.

She didn't bother to say that he couldn't get anything through the mail system—the man had shown up in our room, despite being on a blood-and-magic list of people who should have no access to campus. Olivia immediately started casting spells. A revelation spell and origination spell failed to reveal anything. But a dozen others proclaimed the intentions around the firework to be good and well-intended.

Unfortunately, Raphael frequently thought his intentions for me were good, and that pain was beautiful.

Olivia shook her head, lips pinched. "Someone took pains to remain anonymous. Not very like Verisetti, I think. If he sent it, though, then he truly means no harm by it. Not even of the emotional kind."

"Probably not him then." I smiled tightly.

"Are you going to use it?"

I looked at the firework. A remembrance of those lost? A litany of images of Christian formed. The firework brightened in my hand seeking to automatically absorb the trapped memories yearning for freedom. "Yes," I whispered.

I had let Christian go. I had done the right thing and he was at peace. I knew this. But that didn't mean I didn't miss him. I thought on Olivia's words—an internal reflection of releasing the souls of the departed. Grief and Grieving would approve. And I vaguely remembered seeing a section on festivals in the index.

I hugged the firework to my chest. Regardless of who had sent it...it was mine now. I set to work.

After the sixteenth hour, the wards were fully bound and Olivia went to speak to her adviser. I finished up my firework configurations a little before sundown. Luckily, the firework's core was supposed to do most of the work.

Holding the beautiful orb to my chest, I walked among the mass of bodies heading to different sections of the mountain. After exhaustively reading up on the festival, I was beyond ready to experience it. The sheer number of fireworks was bound to be astonishing—wishes, hopes, and remembrances waiting to be released.

Emotion choked me in anticipation, and I hugged my firework a little tighter. A celebration of Christian's life and a remembrance. I could do this.

More than one narrowed gaze hesitated on me as I passed. How much more time did I have as a free woman? One month? Two?

The calming magic whispered at me not to worry. I embraced it, because worry wasn't going to motivate me any more than my determination already did.

I hiked down from Dormitory Circle. There would be no bad viewing area, but there was a small area filled with jagged boulders above the ski slopes that was rarely populated. That would be a perfect place to watch and reflect.

Alexander Dare was with a group carrying an arsenal up the hillside. Two boys lugged a large slate-gray box and were joking about dropping it and lighting the mountain on fire.

Dare's gaze met mine, then dropped to the singular object clutched to my chest. I wasn't the only one carrying a single firework, but I realized there was something very telling about having only one and traveling alone. I looked away before I could see his reaction.

A few steps down, I stopped. Why was I separating myself? I looked around. It was a personal event to many—there were mages holding vigil on the running track on top of the Magiaduct, their legs crossed, eyes closed, and lips moving in the wind. They had probably been there all day—yet there was a sense of sharing. The promise of lightening a load. The magic in the air was growing so thick that it was almost tangible.

Turning, I hiked past the combat mages again, who appeared unable to take their arsenal through any arches. My magic led me to the large Third Circle field where I easily found Neph, Will, and Mike. I tugged on the thread that connected to Olivia. She arrived minutes later, as if she had been waiting for me to call—as if this connection had always existed as a way to contact each other.

I couldn't put into words any of my thoughts, but when our shoulders touched, I realized words weren't needed on such a night.

The magic running through the crowd tapped me politely. In the mood that I was in, I didn't question it or let it concern me, I just opened myself and let it sift through me, connecting Mike to Will, Will to Neph, Neph to me, me to Olivia, then from Olivia to the next person in the crowd, then on and on, connecting our entire community for this one night.

Just as the sun's rays dripped the last bit of red onto the horizon, bursts of blue and white lightning split the sky. Fireworks lit the air, one boom after another. Every color and shape was alive, breathing around me. The blooms lit the landscape for miles around as the bangs echoed over the countryside, and reverberated around the circumference of the mountain, enveloping all of us within the bursts of light.

The opening fanfare released one last burst. A pause. Then a single flare lit the air. Emotion seared through the communal connection—fear, beauty, acceptance...and for a moment I saw a face and the intense love that the person who released the firework held for that person. The light twinkled out, and another took to the air—regret, surprise, denial. This one held no image and was tinged with undiminished sorrow. Another was of pure joy. An embrace of having had their person in their life for even a moment.

Each blast held personal significance, making every eruption different as we shared the emotions. Sadness, affection, despondence, hopefulness. It choked me. Being a mage—when it wasn't terrifying—was wonderful.

The maker and enchanter of each firework left their mark on the crowd in an all-encompassing net of beauty, celebration, and memorial. A slight pressure pushed upon me, an indicator that it was my turn.

I released my sphere and it lifted. Lifted with my sadness and longing, my love for my twin and my devastation at his passing. Connected to my magic, the firework dipped at each of my internal sorrows and lifted at the loving memories that passed through my mind. The communal connection would only experience the color, flavor, and spirit of my remembrance, but the memories played like a movie montage for me, ending with Christian throwing a football to me in the backyard, laughing as I tumbled into the garden plants, then cheering as I held the ball high, flat on my back. Always catching what the other threw, always supporting each other, always pushing each other to greater heights.

At that moment it didn't matter who had sent me the core, or for what purpose it had been sent. It was my firework, my remembrances, and I ached as I watched.

It bloomed white, then gold. Then burst in a thousand points of beautiful glitter and dust.

After returning to our room, I picked up the journal that connected to one my parents had in the First Layer. The journal was filled with careful observations and anecdotes of magical life and humorous bits and stories I picked up. Nothing emotional or revealing.

I had needed to hide so many things last term. And still, this term I had secrets I couldn't share with them, but I could share my emotions. My fears and hopes.

Tonight...tonight had reminded me that even when things were strained or painful...I was not alone.

I picked up my pen.

Dear Mom and Dad, tonight the magical world held a celebration called The Lightning Festival. A celebration of the coming year and a reflection of the year past. A time to remember those we love and those who have passed. It was both lightning and lightening.

I took a deep breath.

I miss Christian. I sometimes wake up with a dream to tell him on my lips. And a little piece of me dies each time I realize the emptiness of that reality. And yet I continue to awaken. I continue to dream. And I try each day to fill my new reality. Not to fill my emptiness randomly and meaninglessly, but to choose a positive, meaningful path.

I thought of Christian's parting words to me. That we would see each other again. And after tonight I believed them once more. The feeling strengthened within me, healing another piece of my broken soul.

And it reinforced my resolve.

It took me awhile to fall asleep with my thoughts and emotions running rampant. But when I woke, I felt clearheaded for the first time since being back on campus, and I knew what I needed to do.

Chapter Thirteen
FRIENDS AND FOES

DORM ONE was not my favorite place, but it was past time I paid it a visit.

I stood in front of the door, debating what I was going to do and say. He might not even be awake yet, but I could almost feel a presence on the other side of the solid barrier, waiting to see what I decided.

Down the hall, a dark-haired girl exited a room and pretty emerald eyes immediately zeroed in on me, narrowing. I had sketched her face into my mind many times—the girl who had watched me the other day, the girl to whom Inessa Norrissing had been ranting, the girl with the lilting voice who I had attempted to sit with on my first visit to the cafeteria.

Dorm One was fraught with old-money magic users. Dare probably lived around here somewhere. But I couldn't let that matter.

The girl continued her narrow stare, raking me over from head to toe. I turned my attention away, uneasily deciding to ignore her and focus on my task.

It would be stupid not to be leery of the man on the other side of the door. Constantine was very, very dangerous. I had known that from the beginning. But I fingered the expandable stamp he had given to me for my birthday, and thought of all the time he must have spent creating it. Of all the late nights we had spent on different experiments. Of the serious, concentrated look that overtook his features when no one else was there to witness it, the delight when one of his experiments worked, and the helpful hand he automatically extended in the workroom. That was the Constantine I was friends with. And the one I sought.

I gave three raps in quick succession.

I was not alone, and my friends wouldn't be either.

The door opened as my knuckles hit the third time and the movement pulled my hand forward.

"Crown." His customary seductive smile was in place, but the confidence that usually underscored his direct gaze was tempered, as if he thought he needed to monitor what he said to me. The expressions in his eyes and smiles rarely matched, but the caution I sensed in him, was something new. "Something you need?" he asked smoothly.

For someone as narcissistic as Constantine, even a slight deviation toward a normal emotional response was worrying. I knew the concern showed on my face, so I discarded the verbal script I had prepared. "Are you okay?"

"Are you?" he asked in a lazy voice.

This was my fifth day back on campus and even though I hadn't seen him, he assuredly knew I had been on campus this whole time—he always seemed to know what I was up to.

I wondered if he really had been standing on the other side of the door for the past two minutes, wondering if I would knock. With all of the other indications, that was entirely possible.

I looked down. The violet and bronze threads that spanned the space between our elbows pulsed with guarded, yet hungry, bursts. The feeling in them was so similar to Olivia's.

My shoulders drooped with remorse. "I'm sorry it took me so long to visit. Can we talk?"

His expression grew less readable, but the threads gave a jolt and he opened the door fully.

I swallowed. "I wanted—"

"Stop." He tapped the jamb in a pointed manner, indicating caution, and his eyes narrowed as the change in his position allowed him to see down the hall.

I cast a quick glance that way and saw the girl was still there. The concentrated look on her face said she was talking to someone internally via frequency, but her gaze was still locked on me.

Constantine's hand gently wrapped around my back and he pulled me past him. I quickly stepped with the motion, almost missing the look of physical agony that suddenly overcame the green-eyed girl's features as she buckled over, clutching her stomach. And then she was out of view completely and Constantine was locking the door behind me.

Smirking, he slipped something into his back pocket. "Now, what did you wish to discuss?" he asked, as he sat in his favorite wing-backed chair.

I blinked. "What just happened?"

"I invited you inside," he said blandly.

"No, with that girl."

"What girl?"

I shook my head, still standing. "Fine. I want to talk about the leech."

The violet and bronze connections twanged, but he laughed and pulled his fingers along the black ribbon that he always kept near. It had been strangely absent when he was in the First Layer. "You are too direct, darling. You've been living with Price for too long. Evasiveness and prevarication make good allies. The longer and more diabolical the truths, the better. You need to try to trick me into a revelation. Now, what did you wish to speak about?"

"Can we just talk about the button?"

"No," he said.

"There once was a mage from Old Crow, who had a leech used on her elbow. Her friend said, here try this! It's something easy to dismiss. Oh, that too-trusting mage from Old Crow."

"Limericks aren't evasive, darling."

"You waited for Olivia to be taken down, knowing I would give you permission to use that leech on me to save her," I said.

He hadn't counted on being hit with the horribly damaging purple spell, though, and I wondered if he would have fought differently had he known it was coming.

He gazed at me with hooded eyes. "Of course."

There were many questions that could follow that statement. Why, being the topmost of them.

"Did you accomplish what you set out to do?" I asked instead.

"Yes."

"Are you going to tell me your plans?"

"No."

"Are you going to do it again?"

His ribbon stilled. "Will you let me?"

I sighed and sat on the seat across from him, pulling my legs beneath me.

The black silk remained motionless. "You trust too easily."

I met his gaze without break. "Only the first time."

He smiled, and the lines of his body and face relaxed into their normal positions—or at least the ones I only saw when we were alone. Palpable relief pulsed both ways along the connection threads.

"Thanks for the stamp. It's brilliant." I held it up, shaking it into a palm-sized sheet. "It must have taken you days to make it."

"Weeks," he said, with false humility.

"The envelope spell to allow this to travel between the layers is extraordinary. Good thing, as no one could help me bring it back here." I looked at him pointedly, referencing the protection spells that had shocked Olivia and Will.

Even if he usually used it for evil, Constantine knew a lot about mind and protection magic, which was another thing I was eager to discuss.

"The material is only for you, Ren," he said, his voice lazy. "Why would I want anyone else to have something—or know about something—so brilliant?"

"And here I figured that you would want everyone to know how magnificent you are. To be the most renowned materials maker in the land."

Constantine's smile was casually superior, but his eyes told a different story. "Fame makes fools of us all."

Fame, notoriety, Raphael... Those were things that I could do without. Just thinking about Raphael made me take a deep breath and reach for calm, but as I did so I was not gripped by any of the eager spells laced through campus. It was as if the calming magic was thwarted here.

Constantine's ribbon moved more quickly between his fingers. "That explains the thin, jagged layer of peace overlaying your horrible mass of anxiety. You aren't drinking in any of that rot with the calming spells are you? Don't you listen to the conspiracy mages?"

His tone was teasing and derisive, but his gaze was not.

"Er...no?"

He raised a brow.

I looked at the connection threads. They now hummed with dark fondness and light derision. A checkered pattern wove between us. "But that's not important right now," I said.

Later, everything else later.

"Con, I—" I swallowed, suddenly unable to get the words out. His black ribbon went as still as his body. "I need to know about the leech."

His ribbon stayed still. "A trick-worthy line of questioning finally, even if the trick is emotional extortion." His tone was considering, but his body positioning was not. "Didn't you ask Price about the device? I'm surprised she even let you visit me."

"She doesn't know."

"Slipped your metaphorical leash, darling?"

"Con…"

"I can't control who you befriend either, more's the pity."

"Constantine."

"Didn't you look up the information in the dark library? I'm surprised at you," he said.

"I looked up four-dozen books in Main. It was all rot—ethical concerns and arguments. Nothing about construction."

Just like information on Origin Magic; either I had to register myself on a list somewhere in order to access the good stuff—something I couldn't afford to do at present—or I had to figure it out through long, intricate, devious study.

"And you are stalling," I said, giving him a look I hoped expressed that I was unimpressed. "You said you've been studying up on...things. Where did you get the leech? How do you make one?"

Heavy pulses waved along the threads connecting us. Desire and anger, anticipation and fear. I tried to examine the emotions individually, but just as they separated, they were brutally crushed, stilling and suddenly empty. I blinked before looking up at him in astonishment. How had he done that?

His gaze was narrowed on mine, tension crinkling the edges of his eyes. "You are so full of surprises. How did you tether an enhancement spell?" he asked.

"Death? And a strange book?"

A bark of laughter issued. He released whatever knot he had created in the threads connecting us, but there was an absence of something in them now, something Constantine. His gaze remained piercing. "You can see a connection between us."

I looked down automatically. "Yes."

"Colors?" he asked tightly.

I looked at the waving lines. My parents' deep, strong shades of rose coupled together, and the ones that connected me to Olivia, Will, Neph, and Dare were all vibrant. Each of them had engaged in powerful, personal magic shares with me. Some threads defied characterization, comprised of my own magic—to Rock Guard, Guard Friend, Okai. Others existed in various degrees of brightness that had yet to be labeled. Raphael's, unfortunately, shone brightest, like sunlit gold.

The other sense enhancements from the book had ended. But the one highlighting the people I was connected to remained. Determination, coupled with all of my weird experiences with wards—especially with my first death—had allowed me to keep the connecting threads in view, once I was made aware of their existence.

Constantine's had been strong like the others, but now his were dull. Masked.

"Yours were a strong violet and bronze," I said pointedly. "And somewhat informative. What are you afraid of?"

"I'm afraid of nothing. Don't be silly." He unfolded from his chair, his gaze already on the door to his workroom, his connection threads still absent of anything I could read. His voice frequently lied, but his eyes rarely did. He was hiding both his gaze and the threads.

"Come, Crown. I'll show you what I have."

I didn't know which part of our conversation had made him stop playing games, but I felt no small amount of relief as I rose to follow him. "Thanks."

He waved a negligent hand over his shoulder as he unlocked his workroom, but there was an air of disquiet about him.

"No, seriously... Thank you, Con."

His hand paused on the knob. "I know, darling," he said softly. "I feel your gratitude and unnecessary concern. Thread connections work both ways, if one knows they are there and how to find them." He pushed the door open.

They did? I looked anxiously at the pulsing gold one that I feared the most. "How do you stop them? How did you stop ours?"

He didn't respond for a moment. Something told me that he was seriously unused to hearing himself included as part of an "ours."

"Your naïve openness is part of your charm. Why would you want to be dead like the rest of us?" Amusement laced his voice. Only a darkening in the connection let me know that it was forced.

I touched his back as I passed him, and pushed comforting vibes down the completed connection circuit. He was so like Olivia sometimes.

He didn't move for a moment. "Gathering us all together like lambs?" he asked lightly.

"Friends," I said, putting my bag down, very used to him somehow reading my mind even without a known connection. "I'd never mistake you for a lamb."

"It would be a deadly error," he said, just as lightly.

"Did you come to the First Layer with the intention of using that leech?"

His gaze met mine as he pushed aside some of the papers on his workspace. "No."

"With the hope?" I knew better than most that phrasing was important in the magic world.

"Hope is a diabolical and stupid emotion," he said. "And yet it continues to exist."

"You wanted to use it."

"Of course I did. I knew it would be magnificent—viewing the world and magic in the way only you can see it." He hesitated a moment, then gathered a few books together, and stacked them on the table in front of the chair I had yet to sit in. "What did you do with the button?"

"I hid it." In the small secret hollow in the bricks of the basement that Christian and I had used for things we didn't want our parents to find. Olivia and I had hidden all of the things taken from the terrorists there too.

"You didn't destroy it?"

"No." I had thought about it. Briefly.

Something pained, hungry, and desperate slipped through his shield, and an unreadable smile curved the edges of his lips. "I am unaccustomed to being forgiven. But then I'm never sorry." He leaned over the table and curved a finger under my chin. "I'd do it again," he whispered.

"I know," I said, not allowing the charged silence following that statement to settle.

He smiled and sat in his work chair, tapping the top book on the stack in front of him. The scholarly attention he usually hid was on full display now that we were in his work room, and his eyes narrowed in academic focus, flirtation gone. This was the Constantine who was easy to be friends with--the Constantine who never appeared outside of this inner room. I sat.

"With that particular leech, in order to use it, I had to receive permission from you—that is true with any of the lesser forms of leeches. All forms are hard to create, but as with anything, there are rising levels of difficulty. Leeches that do not require a mage's permission are true works of magical art."

He laughed lightly at my grimace. "Fortunately for you, they are extremely rare, and using one will get a mage a life sentence in prison. Which neatly brings us to law enforcement."

He flipped a few pages in the book and tapped on a picture.

"The cuffs used by law enforcement remove casting ability completely, and require no permission, but they don't allow the enforcer to use the magic therein either. You can think of law enforcement cuffs more like inhibitors—they do leech small amounts of magic in order to keep the mage alive, but they don't give magic to someone else. Of course, the legislators continuously toy with the idea of taking and using the magic of imprisoned mages in some productive way for society, but they haven't yet won over public opinion and personal fear. So, as it stands, law enforcement cuffs are the least compelling of the leech forms."

He leaned back and I started flipping through the book he had opened—titled Leeches, Leashes, Collars, Cuffs, and Control.

"Leashes and the internal collars they connect to..." He stretched his ribbon. "Combine the properties of both a cuff and a remote leech. They are truly the thing to fear and to learn to guard against. Like law enforcement cuffs, debate continuously rages over them. Currently, leashes are banned, except in extreme circumstances, and deep within hidden facilities that the government doesn't discuss." His gaze met mine pointedly.

"Can I take these?" I touched the stack of books, thankful they were simply made of paper. This was one of the rare cases where I wouldn't want to experience the Library of Alexandria's books or halls on a topic.

"Of course. They should fit in one of your storage papers for safe transport." I heard his implicit warning not to be caught with anything written on the subject matter.

I did as he suggested, letting the books sink into one of the storage papers visible on his rectangular work table. As I folded the paper, my gaze took in a mathematical sketch on a paper beneath it. I touched the sketch, then moved it so I could study the one stacked beneath. A complicated pattern of pentagons interconnected in a two-dimensional rendering of a far more complex structure. "A dodecaplex?"

He smiled through the strands of hair that fell into his face as he leaned forward on his elbows. He looked down at the sketches as well.

"A project I'm considering roping you into. Courtesy of your storage papers and the delightful firsthand peek into the way you can manipulate dimensions greater than three. Visualizations I can only grasp like a lost dream or drug-fueled haze—that showed me the secrets of the universe for a single moment in time. So tantalizing and frustrating. So perfectly you."

I shook my head, amused, and shuffled through more papers, then stilled.

"That is exactly what you think it is," he whispered, our bent heads nearly touching. He was far too close for such a diabolical revelation.

Rudimentary plans for creating both a leech and a leash were laid out in fine detail on the papers touching my fingertips.

"You knew I would come to ask you about the leech."

"Such is the stupidity of hope," he said, sounding too amused for the emotion to be real. "But I felt it there when I was controlling your magic. Something...else...with a claim on you. That is what you truly seek, is it not? A way out from someone's leash?"

There was something very off in his voice. He usually kept things close to his chest, but there was an intensity, a need he wasn't able to hide.

"Yes," I said, somewhat numb, my mind already going down the path he had laid forth on the paper—easily following the path because it had already been fluttering around my thoughts. It was one of the reasons I was here.

Constantine knew my working mind well. I usually sought to build or create in order to understand a concept before I flipped it on end.

He leaned back, his hair sweeping to the side, a smug smile muting the anxiety that still trickled beneath his facade. "Then I'm at your disposal."

Olivia...was going to be furious with me.

Chapter Fourteen

WE'RE DOING WHAT?

"HEY, Olivia?" I asked as I shut the door to our room and batted at the calming spell trying to attach to me.

She inclined her chin to show me she was listening. Best to lead with something besides 'I visited Constantine and we are going to make a leech that will rob me of magic! Yay!'

"Why haven't you shut off the calming spell to our room?" I asked.

She turned her full attention my way. "Why are you asking?"

"Well, it's a little weird, right? Having that pump through? We didn't have a calming spell last term and we did fine." Mostly fine.

"You are addicted to the cafeteria. What kind of magic do you think always blasts through there?"

"But the cafeteria recharges us and balances magic levels, right?" I chewed a fingernail, then went searching through the heaping pile of books, paper, art supplies, and random hair bands on my desk, looking for one of my specialty pen tops to chomp on.

"And we only spend an hour at a time there, tops." I motioned in the vague direction of the cafeteria, then around our room, as I sat down. "We are in here a lot more than an hour or two every day. The spell has been on all day. It will even be on while we sleep."

The thought of it made me itchy. I scratched my neck.

"You've required the extra calm," she said. "Everyone has."

I shuddered at the remembrance of what campus had been like before the crowd-calming magic had kicked into place.

Grief and Grieving made a big deal out of dealing and accepting, rather than denial, though. "True. But I'm ready to go cold turkey now."

Her shrewd gaze narrowed on me. "Calmness provides rationality and limits unreasonable behavior." Her gaze was far too pointed for me to escape her meaning. "I'm willing to go along with the herd for a few days."

"Camille Straught and her lot are always going on about how control cuffs regulate ferals because they can't regulate themselves. And yet you're telling me they are sucking down calming spells?"

The edges of Olivia's mouth turned up into a smile. "You are calling the Second Layer Magicists hypocrites?"

"Yes."

"People create the truths they desire."

"Constantine and his roommate shut off the spells in their rooms."

"Of course they did." Her gaze pinned me completely. "Why were you there?"

"Getting help."

"From Leandred?" she asked in a tone that indicated the only way he could help someone was through death or dismemberment.

"Yes."

Constantine was my friend, but I was his business partner. I didn't delude myself on that score. But that didn't mean the score couldn't change. It had taken a lot for me to change that same mismatched status with Olivia. A lot of patient, galling moments where I had just steadfastly refused to budge from my friendship course.

Her fingers tightened, then loosened on her chair, as she tried vainly to maintain her calm. "He leeched you not quite two weeks ago."

"I know," I said. The excitement in my voice had to be overly obvious, because she recoiled from me.

I scooted forward. "The experience made me aware that Raphael has some sort of permanent leash on me. And knowing that problem means I can fix it."

Olivia's eyes narrowed, and I could see her quick brain working. "Verisetti said something last term about you 'tugging' him."

"Yes, he said I tugged his thread." I looked down at my hand. "I am connected to him," I whispered, feeling nauseous. My magic vibrated discordantly with the feeling.

"Of course you are." Olivia's voice was brisk. "Breathe."

"No, you don't understand. Not just a connection. Cadmiat. He used my magic. Ganymede Circus. Jauvine. All of them. I felt him draw on my magic and I could do nothing."

"I thought he was just using your captured Awakening magic." Her gaze turned inward. "Verisetti having a leash on you... I should have seen that."

"It freezes me each time. Makes me useless. My magic killed all those people," I whispered.

"Don't be foolish." Her voice was hard. "And this is exactly why we still have a calming spell. Suck in more of it before you completely hyperventilate."

I steadied myself and shook my head. "We need to get rid of the calming spell." Every time I said it, I felt more and more certain. And now that I knew Olivia was keeping the spell going for my benefit, the belief was absolute.

"Liv, I know you, of all people, don't want a spell dictating how you feel."

The edges of her mouth tightened. "Perhaps it's better than the alternative."

Oh. Oh, Olivia. Anger at Helen Price overwhelmed me and I struggled to suppress the feeling.

I closed my eyes and touched the wall, sending comforting pulses through the room. This time, Olivia's threads tentatively reached out in return, and I embraced them.

It was stunning to realize that Olivia had just confided a weakness, even if it was a momentary one.

"Let's return to Leandred's part in all of this," she said briskly, piecing back together her powerful facade. "And the thoroughly stupid things you are already planning to do with him."

If I didn't embrace the subject change, I was going to say something unforgivable about her mother, so I grabbed my storage paper and retrieved the books. "Constantine gave me these. We're going to start working on constructing different types of leeches and a leash too."

"Absolutely not."

"We don't need to complete them. I just need to understand the characteristics of each design, and what the different parasitic magics feels like at a core level. So that I can identify which leech and leash are attached to me."

"Absolutely not."

Her reaction was anticipated. I looked down at my fingers and let the bright colors that continuously flashed around them slip into view. "Raphael came to me. In the dream I had in the First Layer. Don't you think that was...weird?"

"Weird? Your connection with him is downright disturbing, Ren."

"Well, yes. But he visited because he needed something. It wasn't to help me." I shook my head slowly. "Sometimes Raphael celebrates chaos for its own sake, but this time? No. He needed a Second Level magic, or the excuse of claiming it from me. He needed to lay that magic on me. Either to get me back into the Second Layer or for something else. Maybe for multiple reasons."

Olivia folded her arms and tipped her head, nodding. "Okay. What other reasons?"

I frowned. "He yelled at me for letting Constantine leech me. But how did he know? Those men couldn't have told him. Not in the state he confirmed that they were in."

Olivia frowned back. "He felt Leandred use the leech through you?"

"What if...what if using Constantine's leech corrupted some of the power from Raphael's? And he needed to fix it? The Second Level magic he got from me? It was a cleaning spell—one that people use to fix things already in place—like circuits that have been disturbed and need to be reformed. A spell made from my magic."

She nodded slowly. "Powerful magics sometimes clash and consume. A small disturbance could have made the magic unstable for him to use."

The theory would be easy enough to test if the button leech wasn't hidden deep in my parent's house.

"So if we build another leech...?" I asked in a leading voice.

"Verisetti would have shored up the links. Made it so that the same break couldn't occur twice," she said.

"So if we build a better, more specific leech...?"

"No."

"There seems to be some sort of limit on what Raphael can do—some recharge timer—or else he would just be leeching me left and right. I don't know how long I have, but I won't be used without my permission again," I said harshly. "I won't be." My words came out as a vow.

"I understand, Ren," Olivia said, her tone uncharacteristically soft. "But Leandred is not the answer. He wants to use you. He is using you."

"Yes, I know," I said tiredly. I was well aware of Constantine's faults. And that no one trusted me to see them. But Constantine made choices, just like the rest of us.

Olivia looked at me as if I'd grown two heads.

Justice Toad beeped.

"We are not finished with this conversation, Ren," she said in a tone that clearly indicated she would deal with my idiotic notions after community service was completed. She rose and promptly readied to leave.

I looked longingly at the refrigerator and thought of the burritos nestled inside. It was eleven a.m., and I always started to get hungry before noon. But we had chosen to do service today when we both had time—and for Olivia, that meant now. I placed my new books in the secured spot under my bed, then grabbed a few energy bars and my tablet.

"Where to first?" Olivia asked as she passed a hand over JT's screen to register that she was also on duty.

"Looks like the Performing Arts Center," I said as I locked the door behind us.

There were thousands of places—and clubs—on campus I had yet to explore. What would be happening at the Performing Arts Center? I pictured a chorus line gone wrong. Or two members of a modern dance trio offing their third.

"They are rehearsing Mardyk and the Eight Dragonslayers currently," Olivia said. "So someone in the cast probably exploded over how poorly their fellow actors practiced during break, then 'exploded' something for real. Lots of pyromagics are used in the production. Mardyk is a cross-layer legendary character. Whoever plays the role always has access to way too much dragon fire. They leech it from willing dragons, then use it for displays. Or for items like your lightning core."

I blinked. "Really?

She nodded. "Contract magic with willing dragons. A little like Leandred's toy; you gave him permission to use your magic for the period that it rested against your skin." Her lips tightened. "William informed me that I need to bring you up to speed on contract magic in general, and library contracts specifically. We'll do that Tuesday night." She made a note on her pad.

Our winter schedules were filling up quickly and completely. I wondered what normal students did. Partying and playing video games and happily imbibing serenity spells, no doubt.

Best to shift such wistful thoughts. "How did you know what was being rehearsed?"

Olivia pointed at her head as we walked. "Frequency app. Campus schedule scroll. I loaded it for this week, figuring it would be useful while on duty with you."

Very useful, as frequencies often were. But the idea of seeing the media's pushed images in my head was still too unsettling. "How many apps can you load?"

"Depends on how many connections each requires. Ten on average. I substituted this one for my Historical Figures and Strategies app." She grimaced. "I'm looking forward to swapping back."

I quizzed her on historical figures and strategies all the way to the Performing Arts Center to see if she could recall them without her app giving her the knowledge automatically. As expected, she did pretty well.

At the Performing Arts Center, someone had indeed used dragon fire to scorch everything in sight. I noticed that the offender had a starred note on his justice file labeled "pyromaniac." And yet, they had still given him dragon fire to play with. Sometimes this school rocked so hard.

Once things were sorted out and punishments dispensed, we were on to our next call. It was proving to be a busy day on the circuit.

Doing community service with Olivia was awesome though. I fielded the social aspects of the calls, while she took copious notes—mental and physical. She always had an intriguing perspective to add, and her concise, all-encompassing reports were far better than my rambling ones. We talked about the infractions and the ways they could be legally defended or prevented.

She lit up—animated and happy—when talking about such things, and no matter how many hours I'd have to make up due to sharing service with her, I held not a shred of doubt that I'd made the right choice.

~*~

After accompanying Olivia back to our room, dismantling the calming spell, then scarfing down a burrito, I trudged to the joint Justice Squad and Combat Squad meeting.

I was determined to hide out in the back of the room. I was tired, my stomach now hurt, I had books to read—so, so many books—a billion hours of service to fulfill, a roommate still to convince, a terrorist to get rid of, and a world to fix.

This whole guarding campus thing the squads were about to discuss had lost its appeal at about the same time I had kicked the calming spell to the curb twenty minutes ago. Me protect campus? I was like the flame at the edge of a dry forest—a forest whose inhabitants were going to learn, sooner or later, of the danger simmering at their door.

And speaking of dangers... Dare was sitting in the very back row of the room, absently rolling teal magic, ringed with sapphire, in his palm. I immediately averted my gaze and took the farthest empty seat from him. The position, unfortunately, put me a few chairs over from Camille Straught's laser gaze, but at this point she was the lesser of two evils.

The head of the Combat Squad, Selmarie Senthuss, a smartly dressed girl who looked a decade—not four years—older than I did, started addressing what would be happening during the term. I doodled anxiously in my notebook as she talked, connecting talking points together with magic.

I rubbed my neck, magic prickling. I could feel people watching me. To relax, I set a sketched gopher running along the magic connecting the points on my paper.

~ We would each be assigned a mentor on the Combat Squad.

~ We would each be assigned a partner from the Peacekeepers' Troop when they arrived.

~ We were required to do an elephant-sized amount of reading and practicing.

My gopher sat on the last point and crossed his stubby arms in protest. My previous euphoria on using my magic to help instead of hurt campus was now completely buried in bureaucratic drivel and pedantic homework. Homework and time I couldn't afford.

"That is it for today." Isaiah's voice prompted my gaze upward. He was staring at me in slight reproach. I gave him a weak smile and closed my notebook. "Assignments were just sent via frequency, so everyone should have the complete pairings list. See me if you have concerns."

Peters shot me a look full of venom. Two others did the same—a far change from the dismissive looks they had given me when I entered the room. I fiddled nervously with my pencil, not understanding what had changed between then and now. I had only been doodling! Not setting anything on fire.

Since I didn't have a frequency, I was going to have to ask Isaiah for my assignment. I waited in my seat as everyone filed out. A group of mages that included Peters engaged in a furiously whispered argument with Isaiah, then shot me looks ranging from unfriendly to downright hostile. It took fifteen excruciating minutes, before Isaiah and I were the only two left in the room.

Isaiah looked at me and sighed.

Not good.

"Ren."

"I was listening, I promise." I held up my notebook. "I took copious notes. I think better when my pencil is moving." I chose not to add that it also helped me stay awake. "I'm sorry that it looked like I wasn't paying attention."

He shook his head. "It's not that. You are a reliable member of the squad. I'm sure you will be a reliable member for the next four years." He couldn't stop a sly tilt to his mouth, as he liked to tease me about how I was sure to "earn" service for the rest of my tenure here.

If past behavior was any indicator, I probably would.

"Oh." Then what had those looks been about? "Everything okay with Olivia temporarily helping me out? The punishment was accepted. And no magic forced her here tonight."

"Actually, the provost loves that one student convinced another to help. He's already talking about rotating regular students through the squad on a five-hour-a-term basis."

My jaw dropped, aghast.

Isaiah laughed, and the tension dropped from him completely for a moment, making his dark, good-looking features stand out. He was like Will, he got even better looking the more one got to know him. "Kidding. Kidding. But this isn't about that. It's about the assignment."

"You decided against assigning me?" I asked hopefully. I released tension from my shoulders that I hadn't realized I had been holding. "I can see why people would be envious I got out of it, but I think campus as a whole will be relieved."

"You misunderstand me. You have been assigned, but there has been an...uproar...over your assignment."

I looked at him, blankly. "I'm a community service worker. I don't belong here as it is."

He smiled. "Time to change that tune, Ren. You are going to be in a key position on the roster. Your combat mentor already requested extra hours from you—ones in addition to your current load—straight off. You are supposed to meet immediately." He looked at his screen and frowned. "Well, five minutes ago now."

I pictured Camille Straught working me over, then pummeling me into feral submission three hours a day. "Great," I said, resigned. "Where do I need to be late to?"

Isaiah tapped his screen, not looking at me. "There is a bit of a...competition each year when it comes to who gets assigned to whom. I've already had five complaints about your assignment."

I could see Peters and a few of the other guys killing each other to get pummeled by Camille Straught.

"Just switch me out then." I'd be thrilled to get happy-go-lucky Johnson, who was always getting tricks played on him at their cafeteria table, and always bore them in good humor.

Isaiah shook his head. "No can do. You were asked for specifically, and your combat mage gets what he wants."

My palm went clammy around the shoulder strap of my bag as another option became painfully obvious. "Who is my mentor, Isaiah?" I asked, my voice going high.

He sighed. "Alexander Dare."

Chapter Fifteen

TRAINING

MY FEET WOULDN'T move any faster than a forced slog as I approached the Ninth Circle of the mountain—they knew there was a guillotine at the end of the journey.

Dressed all in black, with a shirt that hinted at all the perfection beneath, Dare's arms were crossed as I walked the unbearable distance across the grass between the last arch and his position. His blue eyes were flat and unreadable. "You're late."

"Yup." What else was there to say, except, "Why am I here?"

"Because I asked for you. Let's go." He turned and headed toward the Midlands, no battle cloak in sight.

I lagged behind for a moment, then hurried to catch up. "Listen, if this is in retaliation for that spell—"

"Why would I retaliate? The search spell worked just fine." He kept walking. "Very useful."

His smooth voice didn't give me anything to work with, but there was something overly controlled in the way that he walked. As if, even though he had asked for it, he was uneasy in our pairing as well.

"Um, good... But I meant..." I let my voice trail off as I clutched my bag. The revealed spell paper containing his name was still inside.

"What? The other spell? Am I supposed to care that you were avoiding me? Other than a few scant meetings across campus and fighting the beast last term, I don't know you." Without breaking his long strides, his gaze met mine. "Do I?"

Yes. "No."

I followed him over the boundary line and into the Midlands proper, and the usual spark of joy lit inside of me as Okai immediately appeared at the side of the path. Guard Rock opened the door, pencil stick at attention. He saluted. At his side, Guard Friend waved. Their multi-colored threads rippled against my chest with welcome.

Dare's gaze followed mine. Used to strange things, though, he turned his attention back to the path spanning the distance before us. I flicked my fingers at my side as I walked past. Guard Rock tilted his rock quizzically, then nudged Guard Friend back inside Okai.

The door closed and the building flashed away in a tile slide.

I thought about lagging behind Dare just enough to lose him in a slide too, but that would hardly endear me to him and it looked like we were stuck together, at least until we got the initial information transfer out of the way. We tile slid together into an open field and I cleared my throat. "Are we meeting the others?"

"No. It's just the two of us."

"So...you are going to teach me how to be a combat mage?" I prepared myself for a walloping. I had accidentally connected to him several times in the Battle Building's simulation matrix. I knew my fate in such circumstances.

He frowned. "No."

My confusion must have shown.

"It takes years of diligent practice and study to become a combat mage." His frown turned darker. "You can't just flip a switch, perform a montage, and become one."

I lifted my hands in submission. Way to go, Ren!

Isaiah hadn't specified what we would be doing. I had just assumed combat training would be part of it.

"I have no idea what I'm doing here. Didn't they tell you that I'm..." I licked my lips. This sucked. "Sort of on parole?"

His ultramarine gaze was flat. "I don't care why you are on the Justice Squad. Just that you are on it and have to follow my command."

That didn't sound at all foreboding.

"Great!" Total terror. "So, er, what am I supposed to do, if not fight for campus freedom?"

"Defense encompasses more than fighting. Watching. Precautions. Containment. Flexibility in strategy and problem solving. Coming up with unusual solutions. Like your search spell. And...other things you've shown an affinity for."

Other things, like the patterned rocks that had killed the bone monster. Tension tightened my shoulders again. Everything with Dare came back to that and the questions that I hadn't answered. That I never planned to answer.

"Just because I accidentally got something right—"

"The tricorn?"

An image of the tricorn-turned-toad with its three wart-horns popped into my head.

"Justice Toad—my, er, tablet—did that."

"Tablets read and interpret the magic and intentions of their mages."

I didn't want to talk about that either. "You know what else is a good defense? Knowing who to call when there's a problem."

"You don't have a frequency." It was a statement, not a question.

"I am sure I can call you via your tablet." By definition, the alert system necessitated that the ability was there, somewhere. Will probably knew how to do it.

Dare's gaze didn't break away from mine as he snapped his fingers and a piece of paper appeared between his forefinger and middle finger. I took it from him, automatically.

It was warm. Warm from his skin. Written on the paper was his name exactly as it had been scripted in the revelation spell.

"Have your tablet absorb it or secure it to a journal," he said. "And you will have your contact."

I felt a little strange as I secured the paper deeply in the front pocket along my upper thigh. I almost asked something stupid to break the tension, but held onto my words at the last moment.

"You should contact me, if there's a problem." His gaze turned acute and businesslike. "But the tablet magic already contacts me, so what do I need you for?"

I thought this was an excellent question and patiently waited for an answer. He was not amused by my strategy.

"Prevention, observation, analytics. How do you tell me in helpful, concise terms what the team is walking into so that we can be prepared? How do you anticipate the problem before it gets out of control with the Peacekeepers' Troop?"

"The Troop will be doing all of the campus guarding and you will return if there is a problem? I will be a glorified assistant?" Relief spread through me.

"The Troop." Dare laughed without humor. "Is little more than a band of political mercenaries, who do as little as possible, and are quite skilled at taking credit for any successes while making sure others are blamed for any failures. Don't trust the Troop."

"What?" My relief immediately became alarm again. "Why were they hired then?"

"They usually aren't. We normally work with retired combat mages who once attended Excelsine. But the Troop has political clout. They are seen as the best. And the politicians want to say they assigned the best. It doesn't matter whether they are actually competent as long as they come across as professional and orderly in the political arena. And they will. Nothing that has gone wrong on a job has ever, ever been judged their fault in the aftermath."

I thought of their promotional video. They had appeared as a well-formed group of skilled cadets who trained at every hour. But marketing and sales tactics were something that Christian had naturally understood and utilized. We hadn't fought or competed for attention often, but I had learned some hard lessons when sibling rivalry did rear its head—that behavior and the appearance of behavior were two very different things.

"Why don't you complain to the administration?" Total terror seemed to be doing a decent job of making me converse with him like a semi-normal person for once.

Darkness lit in his eyes. "I have. Contrary to public opinion, I don't always get what I want, especially when politics are involved. And because of what happened last term, the Department had bargaining power." One extended finger pointed at my nose. "You are going to make campus safe and contain any threats."

388

Anxiety lit and twigs snapped around me. The ultramarine thread that connected us brightened, and all of my senses sharpened and switched into survival mode.

He pointed to the side where a number of large saplings were tearing into one another. "Tell me what you see." His voice was pure steel and command.

My anxiety increased tenfold at the immediate test. "Fighting trees."

"Do better."

I started to sweat. I touched my leather bracelet, accessing information from its magical encyclopedia as quickly as I could. "Fighting gorondiers battling for territory."

"Do better."

Magic answered my anxiety, and I had to use precious seconds wrangling it into my control so that I could use it and not have it repressed by my cuff. I barely, painfully, managed control as I looked at the warring trees and withdrew the map I had created last term. The map constantly redrew itself as my four paper dragons soared and gathered information from the ever-shifting Midlands.

"Fighting gorondiers battling for territory on tile 43562, which is currently on what would be the eleventh circle, fifty-eight degrees west." I had initially numbered the map tiles as they were identified, for ease of identification and memory use, but using them for anything other than identification often tripped up my spell. Such was the Midlands' magic, and the sheer expanse of territory involved.

Tiles shifted around us, and the trees disappeared. Sweat broke across my brow. The magic involved in accessing the dragons, the map, keeping a lock on the gorondiers, and piecing everything together required extraordinary effort.

I swallowed and forced the spatial information patterns to bloom again. "Now they are on the twelfth circle, two hundred fourteen degrees east."

He stared at me, his gaze piercing, a strange expression on his features. "Do better."

Unwilling to set my bag on the ground and risk it getting whisked away in a slide, I juggled it, the map, and my magic connections to my paper constructs. Dragon One was rapidly losing juice under its new constraints.

Creating another cartography set would cost me paint. My lips pressed painfully together. Because the dragons had been created—unknowingly—using permanently allocated magic in the mountain, I had thought that they would maintain themselves forever. Using space permanently was how I had gotten into trouble last term.

Normal mages used temporarily allocated magical space for everyday enchantments such as clothing swaps as well as enormous, complicated creations. Permanent enchantments—rooting an enchantment for all time without shifting—was a far different can of worms.

My mind immediately sought to retain the parameters of the magic while my concentration burned through the energy keeping the paper aloft. The space parameters lit in my mind like a magical grid and I held onto the spatial thought of them as the contents of the allocated space began to sizzle. If I could keep hold of the permanently allocated magic, I could use it again without repercussion or guilt.

Dragon One plummeted to the ground in flames. Two of the remaining three dragons started to sear as well, thinning their corresponding position lines on the map as they lost their power. I had less than a minute left before I lost all of them.

I grabbed a pencil from the bottom of my bag and let the tip move across the map paper. It was one of my better pencils, and the magic seeped out of me and through it. A messy, moving image of the trees and a wobbling, compass-like direction and locator emerged from my charcoal tip. I shakily handed the paper to Dare.

His gaze held mine for a long moment, then he took the paper and moved in a slow circle, watching as the paper wobbled on its shaking axis, pointing an arrow in bright green toward an area to the left.

"Stay within three feet of my back." He didn't look at me as he said it, clearly expecting me to follow the instruction.

He followed the indicator and I blindly followed him, so closely that I could almost feel his body heat, nearly tripping along the path as I tried to hold the arrhythmic magic streams.

Unable to concentrate on anything other than holding the different streams, I put my fate firmly in his hands. Regardless of anything else, in matters of safety and protection I trusted him completely. Because of how I first met him, I probably always would.

The remaining dragons were flapping vainly, trying to maintain their altitude, as the allocated space that signified their existence tried to refit itself as part of the enormous, temporary well that everyone on the mountain used.

The world around me broke into a kaleidoscope as I tried to hold it all together. The landscape shifted again, and new colors burst in prismatic waves.

Dare, the only clearly defined thing in my otherworldly view, followed the new path on the map in his hand without saying anything, and easily dispatched anything savage that came across our path—monsters from zombie cities, lakeside and arboreal dwellers, forest beasts, sky giants. With a flick of his wrist, he sent the magical beasts that were surging up, swooping down, galloping by, or lunging in for a kill flying to the side. Using mostly long-range artillery magic, he never moved more than three feet away from me.

Dragon Two fell in my mind, its paper burned through to ash. The drawing Dare held thinned more and I could feel myself two steps from falling over. Dragon Three fell. Dare turned toward me and two fingers touched under my chin. I zinged upright. The adrenaline overload made everything in me stand straight. Dragon Four, which had started to sizzle, gained altitude and reproduced a thin, but strong, five-millimeter line on the page.

I looked at Dare, dizzily.

"You gave me permission to do that," he said. It was hard to focus as my magic sucked in the extra jolts, but his tone was smooth and almost casual. "You said any time."

I really did have to remember to phrase my words carefully at all times. But the juiced-up state snapped my magic into one last blaze.

The gorondiers came into view, as if their tile had been called to us, and Dare stepped onto the tile, tugging me along with him. He stared at the drawing for long moments as it flickered.

The last dragon fell, ashes drifted over my head, and the drawing in Dare's hands stilled. The map lines turned a light, pasty gray.

I was running on hyped-up overdrive due to the magic injection, but as soon as the buzz left me, I was going to be dead on my feet.

His gaze was unreadable as he looked at the gorondiers, the empty map, then back at me. "I'm tempted to ask you to do better."

"You want me to port you directly to them next time?" Will and I might be able to do something with his pad technology, and school permission. Will was good at getting permission for his testing. He knew exactly who to ask and how the academic system worked. Obviously, so did Dare.

But if Dare confirmed right now that he wanted me to do it, I wouldn't be able to, and that would mean disappointing him. The sudden curl of anxiety wasn't pleasant. "I can work on it?"

I couldn't see his expression, as he had turned to run his hands along the bark of the carnivorous trees, calming them. The magic he left behind was clear, but the feel of a soothing camel shade tickled the edges of my consciousness as it spread from his hands, then blanketed the trunks. The fighting trees relaxed, lethargic. Dare moved between them, motioning for me to follow.

"This is going to work out just fine," he said, as I hurriedly caught up. It sounded like a threat and a promise.

The tiles shifted around us and Dare turned left, modifying his path. I stayed close at his heels through twelve more slides, only able to do so because of the energy he had given me. His body language was confident as he moved, easily adjusting his path as he moved toward something.

"You know where things are here," I said abruptly. "Without a map."

"I stroll these levels every day, and have done so for the past two-and-a-half years. Even the chaos mages don't get in here as often as we do. They like their classroom theory far too much."

"So, what? You use some recognition of the magic?"

"The chaos mages would be out a thesis each year if a known pattern existed. But certain tiles—as you deem them—seek to attract. They are always striving to be reunited. Naturally magnetic." His gaze pinned me. "The path of that magnetism leaves a trace. A tension. A winding path to follow. The bigger tiles that group together to form large landscapes or cities are the easiest to work with. If you can get to one of those, you have a good chance to eventually find another."

Eventually was really the keyword. "There are gazillions of tiles."

"Well, I haven't numbered them. Unbelievable," he muttered. His back was tight, as he came to a stop near a red stream under the current, unnaturally lime sky of the Midlands.

"It seemed to be the best way of keeping track," I said, feeling the need to defend myself. "I come here sometimes. I find it comforting." I looked over to see a gnarled shrub on the bank eating the remnants of its neighbor.

Dare seemed to be looking for something in the shrubs. "Comforting?" His attention focused on the cannibalistic plant that was now licking and cleaning its thorny chops with a leafed branch. "Most mages are terrified here. And the ones who do frequent these levels like to think them full of spiritual chaos."

I had been unafraid of dying when I began traversing the chaotic, gorgeous, and terrifying levels last term, and by the time I had stopped chasing my brother into death, I had already hooked myself into Okai. If I bypassed Okai for some reason, I had enough experience to know what to expect in the Midlands, but I was walking meat here and I knew it.

I never just strolled the Midlands—skipping through brilliantly flowering meadows and frolicking in the sun. I ducked, dove, climbed, ran, and crept with Guard Rock and his super guardian senses at my back.

Dare had taken care of at least twenty beasts that would have eaten me when I was concentrating on the map dragons' magic.

He was still looking at me for a response on why I wasn't terrified. "Well, at your side is the best place to be, right? Wouldn't being afraid question your manliness or something?"

He stared at me for a long moment, and I could feel the heat creeping up my body. Stupid mouth. Stupid crush.

Thankfully, he concentrated on the area around us again. I could feel hidden eyes tracking and watching us—there was always something watching in the Midlands. Dare crouched down near the feral bush and nudged it to the side. His fingers grazed the dirt beneath and dug inside. When he pulled them out, a singed wing of a paper dragon was cradled in his palm. Crouched on the ground, he looked up through the dark hair falling across one eye, and extended it toward me.

I numbly took it from him. Fear finally crept into my emotions.

Doing magic around Dare was dangerous. It would have taken me a vast amount of effort to find the remnants of the dragons—and they were mine—but he had tracked this one in less than twenty minutes.

"How...?"

"Traces. Everything leaves them."

He had found us the night of Christian's death because I had broadcast some sort of trace with my not-yet-Awakened magic. He had tracked me even in the non-magic world.

I edged away from him before I consciously realized what I was doing.

The corners of his eyes tightened and he rose abruptly. "You will need to figure out how to follow traces in order to be effective at this job." He pointed at the dragon and the stilled map. "Can you do that anywhere?"

"The tracking? Not for a sustained amount of time. And setting up a map requires...sacrifice."

"What kind of sacrifice?"

Precious paint drops. "Magical sacrifice."

Sarcasm overcame his features and he opened his mouth. "Specif—"

"Axer." Lox strode out of a tile slide, Peters trailing him like a spooked Chihuahua. I stuffed the dragon wing into my pocket. "It's Pisces Rising. We still on for the factory hunt and processor check?" Lox asked.

"Yes. As soon as the shadows are out."

With the way Lox immediately looked at me, I realized that Peters and I were the "shadows." Lox examined me slowly, then dismissed me and nodded to Dare. The two combat mages started forward, and Peters followed immediately behind them. I trailed, gripping the paper remnant in my pocket and wondering how I was going to keep the secrets I needed to keep.

A sudden shot of tangerine jarred me from my thoughts, and a crash followed. Dare and Lox were still walking, as if nothing had happened, though Dare was lowering his hand.

Looking to my side, I was dully surprised to see a small trollish creature splayed on the ground.

A tangerine mist floated away from its body. I checked all of my limbs and sighed.

"Thanks," I muttered, not bothering to yell it up to Dare. He probably had freaky magical hearing in addition to his other supercharged powers.

Peters was wide-eyed, his eyes darting everywhere. I had been in the Midlands briefly with Peters and Dare just before the bone monster had appeared last term, and though Peters had been uncomfortable then too, he looked far beyond that now. I wondered what had happened to him in his first shadow session with Lox to make the usually irritating boy look this spooked.

He had to have done this before. Peters' birth had probably been recorded on the Justice Squad's roster, he was so into his duty. I snorted.

Peters jumped at the sound.

I frowned. "What's with you?"

"This is nothing like last year. Nothing like I signed up for. Twenty squad members have died and been resurrected at least once in the last hour alone."

Peters and I weren't friends. At all. But he now had my undivided interest. "Why is that different from last year?"

But Peters clammed up and said nothing further.

We finally reached a tile containing Midlands' mist. The mist clung to the edges of the Midlands and always signified an exit. Stepping through the mist, I was surprised to see a crowd had formed on the edges of the Ninth Circle.

The emerald-eyed girl from Dorm One was in one group, along with a few mages who were not part of either squad. Her gaze took in the four of us, then narrowed in on me. She smiled—a social smile that didn't reach her eyes.

Without even a simple farewell to anyone, Peters made a beeline for an arch that would take him to Top Circle, obviously eager to get as far from the Midlands as quickly as possible. The girl stepped into his path and said something. Peters immediately stood straighter and answered, though his face lost none of the strain.

He was freaking me out now. Justice Squad members never went into the Midlands on calls alone, but we did enter sometimes in groups. What was different about today?

"Squad training tomorrow."

At the smoothly voiced statement, I jumped and whipped around, imitating Peters' jitters.

Dare's brow rose sardonically at the action. "Then meet me here the day after. Perhaps, get more sleep before you do. Aries Rising in two days. I have your class schedule, so I know you are free."

He turned and strode back into the Midlands with Lox and the other combat mages.

It wasn't until they had all fully disappeared from view that I realized two things: In my tired and hyper-aware state working so much magic, I had stopped stuttering around him.

And, in the same state, I had offered to figure out how to port him through the Midlands. Something no normal mage could do.

~*~

At dinner, I glumly told Will, Neph, Mike, and Olivia of my fate.

"You are working with whom? Where?" Mike's jaw was someone near his plate of steak. "You have the worst luck."

"Yeah," I said morosely.

Olivia's gaze was less sympathetic. "Working with Axer Dare is power. Learn from him. He doesn't give anyone other than his immediate group the time of day." She meticulously forked her salad. "Power."

I frowned. "I've seen him help people. He helps all the time." He helped lots of people. Like me, and me, and more me, all in different, unknowable incarnations.

"Yeah, he helps everyone," Mike said. "He's a campus protector, the campus protector. But he doesn't give those he helps the time of day. Doesn't talk to anyone more than he has to. Saves you, then he's off. Like Bautermann."

I did a quick lookup on that. Bautermann was this layer's version of a magic-wielding Superman. But a colder, more ruthless type of Superman.

Dare had helped me beyond rote duty, though. Off campus. A whispered sympathy to a bloody, unrecognizable, ordinary girl.

"Bautermann slaughters anyone who gets in his way, Mike," Will said, half-laughing. "Dare hardly has that sort of need for vengeance."

Mike pointed his spoon. "Bautermann's motto is that individually caring for strangers is a liability."

Olivia stabbed a green. "Vengeance is bred in his bones. He is the grandson of Benedict Dare."

"Bautermann?" I asked, trying to scroll information on my leather bracelet and listen at the same time.

Will and Mike both laughed until they were holding their sides. Finally, Will looked around, then leaned in. "No. The Dare family owns and lives on the island that holds the lost archives. Very valuable. Waged a full-on war three decades ago against the combined military forces of a number of nations in the Second Layer who were trying to take them. The Dares won. Bloodily. They picked off an entire quarter of the forces like ants in a line, and kept them under an anti-resurrection bubble until the first retreat was called."

I poked at my bracelet without absorbing more information from it, and thought of Dare's statements to his team in the library. About defending Excelsine against all threats, about maintaining its independence from government supervision. A core family value, obviously.

"They destabilized two perfectly adequate governments and completely ruined a third as a result of those battles," Olivia said. "Not to mention the economic and social impact on the others."

Mike pointed his spoon at her. "If a government is unstable enough to be overthrown, it shouldn't be attacking nations offshore."

"Provocation breeds stupidity," Olivia said dismissively. "The archives should be shared, but they were simply the excuse. It was obvious what was going to happen when Maximilian Dare married Sera McEllian. A choice that all knew would provoke war. And no matter how quietly they stick to their island or try to put forth their scion as a protector of the realm, the danger to society will always exist. They will never be able to hide the warlord he could be."

I blinked. A conversation long ago between Dare and his uncle drifted through my head—'You play too many team sports. We should have raised you as an assassin instead.'

"They made reparations, entirely of their own volition. They didn't have to." Mike pointed out.

"Benedict and Maximilian Dare understand politics and manipulation. They destroy everything around them in defense of anything they consider theirs, then helpfully hand service to the realm. Make no mistake, anything a Dare does is plotted meticulously."

I poked at my potatoes and decided against eye contact of any sort.

"And anyone with access to the family scion needs to take it." Olivia's voice forced my eyes upward and she gave me a look that brooked no opposition. "Caring for strangers individually is a liability for a warrior. Make yourself not a stranger."

Mike shook his head. "Become a target instead."

"Many muse groups practice a similar philosophy," Neph said, nearly out of the blue. She looked and sounded tired. "For the group, the good of all. Never get attached to anything, or anyone, outside of that."

An uneasy silence stole over the table like a broken link in the chain, combating the calming and re-energizing magic that floated freely in the air.

Will shifted in his chair. "Er, Neph—"

"And other groups teach members to attach," Neph said, forced calm in her voice again. "Every group is different."

"And some groups are quite split, are they not?" Olivia said, her voice clipped. "Attaching to treasonous causes within?"

Olivia and Neph held a silent battle of wills, one that discouraged outside participation.

Mike forcefully changed the subject to class schedules that went into effect tomorrow, but I watched Neph's graceful form continue to move wearily and automatically through dinner motions.

As we all cleared up to leave, I touched Neph's arm. "Can I come by?"

I had finally figured out how to use our connection to recharge her, and she had never looked so in need of some energy.

She smiled tiredly and magically dumped her dinner remnants into the trash vault. "I do so wish you could. But I have practice and procedures all night. And they—" Her gaze caught something over my head and her expression closed off. "We are implementing a large-scale project to automatically reset unbalanced emotions on campus and to reinitialize a more balanced atmosphere hourly in order to reassure the elders and unseat the need for any outside presence." She looked down. "Don't come by tonight. Tomorrow?"

"Of course."

Now that we had limited our room's calming spells, the forced calming of the masses sounded far more...nefarious again. But I trusted Neph. And even if I didn't, the threads that connected us were pure and reassuring.

I watched her gracefully walk to join the other muses, slightly apart, but grudgingly included as they exited en masse.

I felt Will come up to my side. "Will?"

"Ren?" He answered in a cheeky voice, but his voice contained a subdued note beneath it as he too watched Neph leave.

"New project," I said, watching Neph disappear from view. "Three to four hours. Do you have time?"

I needed to read all of those leech books as quickly as I could, but Neph needed me now and I had something particular in mind to help her.

Will nodded, and I knew that his quick mind understood the minimum of what I was asking, and for whom the project was intended. We had worked together far too frequently—and the essence of my bond with my brother still bound us—for him not to extrapolate from the angle of my gaze and the tone of my voice.

"Of course. Lead the way."

We skirted by the watchdogs carefully, entering the Midlands by way of a long, stony section of the Ninth Circle that frequently slid into the chaos. Because of the rockslides and ease of injury when entering a place where injured mages could get eaten, it was beyond stupid to enter the Midlands in any part of said section. That made it perfect for us.

Okai and the rocks immediately welcomed us. Guard Rock poked Will's shoe twice with his stick in competitive banter.

I quickly located base materials and pulled up the relevant documents on my reader while Will opened his engineering notebook and started asking questions. Dare's magic recharge had given me the idea. I didn't know what he had used, but creating a small bit of container magic for Neph couldn't hurt. A little bit of us to reinvigorate her when she needed a charge. She was always helping us.

"Muses run on the vibes that they send out," Will said as we tinkered in the creepy, but relaxing atmosphere of Okai. "So the seriously large task of calming campus should be keeping them energized. I don't know why Neph has been so drained. But maybe it's something 'muse-y' that doesn't get publicized."

Guard Rock stood at attention by the door while Guard Friend groomed him. They had hung their farmhouse portrait on the wall, above where they liked to stand. For a second, I contemplated how they had hung it. One rock standing on the other?

I focused back on Will, who was looking at me critically. "You okay?" he asked. "You are not as freaked out as I'd expect with everything going on."

"Calming spell in our room," I said. "We just got rid of it, but I've still got the remnants partially riding me."

Will frowned, then nodded. "And Neph is your muse. Maybe that's it."

"What? Me being calmed affects Neph?"

He shrugged. "If it's preventing her feedback loop from kicking in, maybe? I'll look it up. She looked tired, but not in danger of detonation. We turned off the spells in our room right away. Mike hates them, and they lessen my desire to create. For most people it is easier to control magic when they are focused and calm. Maybe Mike and I need stress and chaos in order to get things done." He shrugged again. "But Mike does have a 'tracker' on the campus system so that he can tell at what level they are dousing us. He is adamant about keeping track. Says it tells you a lot about the administration's emotional state."

"But...Neph?"

He frowned. "The relaxing vibes that muses exude work on them in the same way. The release of the magic relaxes their system. If she is helping to calm campus, she should be experiencing a strong Zen kickback. But you are her most important component. If she's not getting feedback from you, that might be the problem."

"Wait. Hold it. Rewind. Are you saying that if muses hold energy in instead of releasing it, they overload on stress, and poof?" I motioned a blast outward with my fingers. "Muse bombs?"

"Yup."

I looked at him in horror.

He chuckled. "With the campus effort, there is no way any of them are holding anything in, including Neph. And it's why they have a community—to take care of all the muses and to make sure each one stays on the level. They regulate some things in a pretty draconian way. Lots of the internal regulations benefit the muses. But some of them…" He shook his head. "She doesn't complain to me either and the community keeps information locked in each muse with magic."

More determined to succeed, an hour later I examined our half-finished prototype. Will had had the great idea to make the container into a sachet, encompassing the magic in a bundle of comforting smells.

"Maybe we should infuse a little of Neph too?" I asked, turning the soft fabric in my hands. Delia had shown me how to make crudely magicked hook and loop fastenings that when pressed would each activate a little burst of the magic within. "Make it so that she feels the feedback loop of helping us, even if it is a false feeling? Or maybe rather than false, it is better to say that it would be a memory of the feeling—feeling like she is helping us, even when we aren't near?"

Will nodded decisively. "Yes. Add that to the list."

We worked on it together, using Neph's lingering magic on both of us to bind bits of ours inside. My magic was naturally neutral to Will's, but the resonance from his time in my sketch and the use of the sketch sword brimming with Christian's magic combined with mine, had set up a good degree of affinity. And we continually worked to figure out better ways of combining our magic. Will was of the opinion that relying on natural sympathy was lazy and laziness should not be rewarded. Will relished challenges.

But sympathy had bound Olivia to me—we would never have become friends if not for that initial tie that had stopped her from expelling me from the room. Sympathy was merely another component of a relationship.

Talking and creating was easy with Will, and we caught up on recent events while we worked.

"You are certain you want to work with Leandred on developing a leech?" Will asked, voice calm, as we put the finishing touches on the sachet just after midnight. Dangerous projects never fazed Will, but there was something strange in his voice.

"Yes. Olivia is livid about it."

"You'll be fine," he said, his tone switching to a reassuring one. "And I'm happy to help, if you need it."

"Thanks."

He nodded. "You going to tell him about this place?" And there was that strange note again as his voice suddenly shifted to too calm.

I examined him as he concentrated on the pouch in his hands. His gaze didn't rise to meet mine. I looked at the workspace around him. Will's solo projects—like his portal technology—were mostly kept in the room he shared with Mike. No matter Will's scoffing, he reaped rewards doing magic near his highly sympathetic roommate. But the projects that Will and I were working on together that required less...legal...means and ingredients, had all migrated here.

I looked over to the rocks. Guard Friend had finished buffing Guard Rock and they were sitting together near the door, keeping watch. Keeping Okai, which Guard Rock and I had found together, safe and private.

"Well?" Will's voice was calm and his eyes were focused on the magic seeping into the sachet. Neither fooled me.

I bumped his shoulder. "No. It's our secret lab, right? With Neph and Olivia keeping an occasional eye on us so we don't Frankenstein out?"

His fingers relaxed around the pouch. "Okay. Yeah. You sure?"

"I'm sure. And Constantine is a home turf kind of guy. He loves playing host." Spinning webs from his velveteen chair. "If we need to go somewhere else to do the magic, we will find another location."

I removed the pouch from Will's fingers and placed it in a fiber bag before giving it back to him. "This needs some absorption time. And I have something else for us to work on. Something occurred to me during the time I spent with Alexander Dare today. What do you think about using chaos magic for skipping portal pads across space?"

Will brightened, his eyes behind his glasses reflecting his feverish creative thinking along these new lines, and we discussed seriously geeky things all the way back to the dorms.

~*~

I brought Olivia up to date on everything as we carefully scanned for any newly placed calming spells in the room, strengthened our dream wards, and readied for bed.

"You spent four hours on that pouch?" She asked grimly.

I dimmed the lights on her equally grim expression.

"Ren, you worry too much about other people and too little about yourself."

"Oh, hush. You love me." I feathered a hand over the ward threads connecting to her. They bloomed brightly in the darkness for a moment before fading to their normal luminescence. I hadn't yet convinced Olivia about adding a glowing night sky canvas to the ceiling, but in the meantime, I could brighten our room in other ways.

Olivia sighed—a resigned sound in the softly lit night—ending her heavy momentary silence. "Good night, Ren."

Protection of friends: +2

Failures: 0

Chapter Sixteen
THE POLITICS OF CLASS

OLIVIA ANSWERED a knock at our door the next morning while I scrolled news reports.

Whoever was on the other side said nothing and the door clicked back shut. I forked a piece of pancake absently and looked up to see why Olivia was still standing. She stared stone-faced at a letter in her hand.

"First day of class pep talk? You getting a security detail? What is it?" I popped the pancake piece into my mouth and stabbed another.

There was an expression on her face that I couldn't immediately interpret.

"A response to my name in the campus news feeds," she said. Tight-lipped, she slit the seal on the note, but hesitated before opening it.

I shuffled my reader with the hand that wasn't holding a fork full of pancake, and my magic flowed into the news feeds, using Olivia's name as my search term. News articles folded up and out into spread-out holograms that mimicked splayed newspaper pages.

Olivia Price, who has had five roommates already in her short time at Excelsine, was severely punished for engaging in a magical duel with upstanding legal student Inessa Norrissing. Receiving a Level Three Offense, Price was the first to fire an enchantment. When questioned about the incident, Norrissing confirmed that she had been acting in self-defense and stated, "Price is a danger to fair-minded students and should be—"

I swept the articles together, then slammed them back into the reader and turned it off. "The nerve of her. Don't give it a second thought."

Olivia didn't answer, so I looked up. Mist was rising from the open note in her hand. Before I could even formulate a question, the mist dropped, coating her skin and sinking inside. Thin veins of magic pushed outward, then suddenly constricted, choking her throat and squeezing her sides. I threw myself forward—my reader and fork clattering on the ground—grabbed her arm, and pushed her toward her bed before her legs gave out. Olivia sat hard on the mattress, the paper naught but ash in her hand.

With quick fingers, I swiped the ashes from her hand, fully expecting to be hit by the same malicious magic just by touching it. But whatever curse had been used, it had either passed, or was specifically made to strike Olivia. "What was that?" I demanded.

"A warning."

"From whom?" The administration? That was what the Justice Magic was for.

She didn't answer, so while I sent healing vibes—again—through the room wards and our skin contact, I broke down what I knew.

One, Olivia wasn't darkly threatening anyone with vicious retribution. Two, Olivia had hesitated in opening the letter, but had done so nonetheless. Something so foul could not have made it through the delivery system, according to what she had said before, so a letter sent by courier should have made Olivia at least cast basic spells to check the contents. But, three, she had accepted the letter, and four, judging by her facial expression immediately before she had opened it, she had known something of what it contained.

She had known who sent it.

I replayed her strange expression in my mind. It had been halfway between broken and resigned.

My hand involuntarily gripped her arm harder. "Your mother sent that to you?"

"I was warned."

"Warned?" White-hot fury scorched me and I released her before any of it transferred accidentally. "I'll show her warned." I marched over to my dropped reader. "We are going to—"

"Ren."

"—put up a three-powered ward on anything crossing the threshold to—"

"I need to respond."

"—reflect Armageddon back on anyone who dares—"

"I need you to leave, Ren."

"—to try something like that again. In fact—"

"Go."

"What?" I asked, derailed. "Go?"

She took a deep breath. "I need to respond."

"Fantastic," I said with relish. With a flick of my wrist, I flipped my reader to display Juleston's warding tome in all its humongous glory and started to flick pertinent pages and illustrations out into the air in front of me and to my sides, gathering a series of thick images and text around me that I could work with and combine. "Just give me a second to devise an appropriate response."

There were some very edge-of-legal wards I could work with. I flipped to the next page. Like this one. I snapped it out to join the others and let a trickle of magic paint the air with a note from my mind on how I could enhance it. Manipulating wards was firmly in my skill set at this point, and Helen Price was going to regret her actions when I was finished. Olivia was my roommate.

"You can't do anything, Ren. And you can't be in here while I respond. The magic will know."

"Good." I flicked out another image.

"No. Not good. She doesn't know about you. She didn't even ask any questions about my roommate when she was here. Verisetti's magic works that well. But if you put something deliberate on the returned magic—"

"Oh, I'll give her deliberate." I smiled at my reader and flicked a power graph a foot out from its top and combined it with two of the images already in that space.

"No. You don't understand. She'll get rid of you. She'll really get rid of you."

"She can tr—"

"Please."

I froze. Surrounded by a collage of potential vengeance, my hands shook as I choked on unsatisfied fury. Olivia never begged.

I gave a short, tense nod. "I'll go." But that didn't mean I'd do nothing. I carefully saved my research cloud and magical mind map, and folded them back into my reader.

She was silent as I cleaned up my dropped pancakes, gathered my things together, then ran my fingers along the healing ward—draining part of my magic in order to power hers faster.

"I have politics at ten, then a squad thing at one. Lunch in between?"

"Yes."

"Write if you need anything," I said, deliberately softening my tone. "I'll skip politics."

"Thank you." There was fierce warmth to her tight words.

But the tension that had coiled within me wouldn't leave.

Protection of friends: -1

Failures: +1

I didn't like the new scoreboard.

I headed directly to the Midlands. I had an hour before class, and I was going to use it well.

The rocks greeted me happily and I told them what a good job they were doing. Their bellies protruded proudly.

"You are good protectors," I whispered, patting them.

I looked around the workshop, not gazing at anything in particular as concept and design formed in my head. I released the research and mind map into the air over my work bench. My hands and magic gathered supplies—paper that I had made with pulp and mixed magic, a pencil I had created while concentrating on warding and protecting my brother's soul, and the lavender paint that had been produced in my Awakening event. Then I focused on the exact enchantments I needed to wield, and to will, into existence.

First I sketched an egg—drawn inside a caterpillar, inside a pupa, in the wing of a butterfly—and layered wards and screens throughout in intricate designs that whirled along the edges of the embedded designs.

Four drops of precious paint activated it. The life stages slowly bent, morphed, and furled together as they rolled into the three-dimensional egg that would incubate the magic inside until it was provoked.

I very carefully made sure not to get any of the paint near my brand new cuff. I'd been doing well at keeping my magic usage deliberately conscious and controlled, and I couldn't afford for anyone with enhanced sight to see a ratty half-eaten cuff on my wrist.

Guard Rock and Guard Friend watched attentively from their post, their rocks tipped toward me, ultra-focused like they always were when I used Awakening paint. The lavender paint had been used in their conception, and they seemed to be connected to the magic of creation.

I was shaking by the end, but finally, balanced in my palm, was a small paper egg that would be indestructible until its magic was called forth. I slipped it into my bag and took a deep breath, surveying my dwindling supplies.

The lavender paint tube was nearly empty. I still had the garish orange tube, but it had been created under the mindset of unease and betrayal. Raphael actively wanted me using it.

Outside of applying it for destructive purposes, using that tube was out of the question.

With regret, I thought of the ultramarine paint that I had wantonly wasted months ago. Powerful, protective paint mixed to match the color of Alexander Dare's eyes.

I needed to do something about my paint situation soon. Somehow, I needed to convince Stevens to help me make another batch in the vault. I still required a guide to tweak my mixing and magical induction, in order to focus the power I needed.

Professor Stevens...who knew Raphael.

An evil Stevens in league with Raphael would be just my luck.

I popped an energy mint from a tin Delia had given me last term. I'd given her a fabric pen I had made especially for her, and she'd been so giddy that she had pressed the tin into my hand the very next moment. The mints didn't replace the naturally beneficial alternatives that sleep and direct magic-sharing provided, but the small energy boost tricked my overexerted magic into thinking it wasn't quite as depleted.

I chewed the mint and tried not to think about my paint supply options as I walked toward my first real class at Excelsine. The first class in which I was truly and legally enrolled.

Layer politics was sure to be...interesting. And in a class of a thousand students, I wouldn't stick out. I pasted a smile onto my face and thought cheerful thoughts.

Upon entering the enormous indoor amphitheater and lecture hall, I stuttered to a stop. The green-eyed girl from Dorm One was standing near the podium and her gaze immediately narrowed on me.

Right.

As I carefully navigated the huge auditorium to get to the open seat next to Neph, I learned the green-eyed girl's name and background from the whisperings of the mages milling in the aisles.

The infamous Bellacia Bailey was leader of the Second Layer Magicists on campus, the daughter of a press mogul, and an all-around intolerant individual. Her eyes followed my movements, even after I sat down. Lovely.

Beauty mark on her left cheek. Long hair, styled in a multitude of braids and wavy sections. Tasteful, but form-fitting clothing that swirled dramatically between black, green, and gray. It wasn't hard to see why Johnson, the combat mage, was mooning after her—her facial features were perfect and her assets plentiful on a fit, but not-too-thin, frame. Christian would have already been forming a game plan.

Mike, Delia, and Will were trading quips, and I tried to listen to them instead of awkwardly staring back at the girl whose narrowed gaze was focused on me.

The rest of our thousand classmates quickly filled the seats and an energetic, medium-sized man strode into the pit of the lecture hall. His cream shirt had one swirling white button loose at the neck and his arms were relaxed and resting in the pockets of his twelve-buckle trousers. "I'm Professor Harrow. And you are in for a ride this season as we observe and discuss what is happening across the layers and how the different policies and politics will drastically affect the lives of many."

He introduced the five teaching assistants, of whom Bellacia Bailey was one. Each assistant looked over the audience with a sharp smile.

"Let's start with our syllabus and an outline of the current conflict." And with that, opening salvos into the tenseness that would be our term began.

I took copious and agonizing notes as each bullet point made me slip down further and further in my seat.

Seventy years ago, an Origin Mage named Flavel Valeris had accidentally blown the majority of the Third Layer to bits along with irreversibly killing the brightest scientific and magithetical minds who had been experimenting with him.

Every Third Layer citizen in the surrounding one thousand miles—which contained the most populous and enlightened cities in the layer—had also been irreversibly destroyed.

The blown layer magic had been thrust unequally into the Second and Fourth Layers, with smaller amounts blasting through to the First and Fifth. There had been no one capable of fixing it.

The Second and Fourth Layer citizens and politicians had steadily appropriated the extra magic surrounding them—taking a little here, a little there. Decades later, when a new Origin Mage Awakened, returning the layers to how they had previously been arranged was no longer...desired by all parties.

Due to all of the factors above, the new Origin Mage, Sergei Kinsky, had been leashed immediately upon discovery by the Second Layer government and hidden from public and inter-layer knowledge.

When Kinsky's existence was discovered by the public at large, the people of the Second Layer needed little convincing that their government had done the right thing. The Third Layer's cataclysmic devastation—and new propaganda—had justified Kinsky's leashing. He had been considered a danger to society.

But politicians in the Third Layer had been up in arms and had immediately shouted about broken treaties. Here was someone who could restore their homeland, and yet the Second Layer was storing up Kinsky's Origin Magic for their own use instead of for equitable magic redistribution.

At this point a number of students in class began to look mutinous, and disagreeable murmurs traveled through the room.

The professor sliced his hand through the air to silence the crowd, and I noticed that more swirling buttons appeared on his shirt the more animated he became.

"We will explore both sides of the conflict this term. If that bothers you or threatens your family's values, you are in the wrong class. Feel free to exit at the back."

No one rose.

Bellacia Bailey's expression remained calm—a politician's smile plastered on her lips. I nervously turned my attention back to the professor.

"Here in the Second Layer, we have built entrenched infrastructure for the last sixty years using that extra magic...infrastructure that, if lost, would cripple our magical functioning." Harrow was a man much given to gesturing and he used both his voice and energy to fill the space and keep student attention. "And in the Fourth Layer, creature transformations rely completely on the bubbled spaces that were 'given' to them seventy years ago. Illicitly gained or freely taken, no matter how anyone thinks about it, those living in the two surrounding layers now require that space to continue their way of life. And yet, should the magic space not be returned, as the layer creators designated, and as treaties state? Exploring this very real problem will be one of our challenges this season."

He rubbed his hands together and the sleeves of his arms rolled half up his arms. It was obvious he found this all very exciting.

I, on the other hand, was panicking.

"Over the term we will discuss Origin Magic and the Origin Mages, the gods and villains of our system."

My panic experienced a sharp spike. I skimmed the expanded syllabus, heart pounding.

"How can we utilize the magic that was leeched from Sergei Kinsky, the last Origin Mage? How do we use the next Origin Mage? Should the

Second Layer give its leeched magic to the Third? Should the Third Layer be responsible for dealing with its own mess? Seventy years after the detonation in the Third Layer, which side of the endless debate will you be on?"

I swallowed.

Harrow smiled. "If you want to talk about the political system and checks and balances, take Government. This course is titled Layer Politics. We will be exploring political philosophy, ideals, triumphs, and mistakes between and among Layers, with an emphasis on what is happening in the world right now—the failed negotiations, the progress, the terror campaign, the next steps, and possible consequences. If 'might makes right,' should the broken Third Layer be collapsed completely and the immensely valuable remaining space be integrated into the others? Do we look to the First Layer to re-distribute that which has been lost? Do we have an intrinsic responsibility to protect the non-magical world? Throughout the course, there will be many ideas and implications for you to consider. Let's begin with free discussion!"

Free discussion? My seat suddenly shifted, whirling me through space as the humongous lecture hall re-formed into a giant room containing circular discussion tables. Mike, Delia, Will, and I had, thankfully, magically slipped into the same table unit. Neph's seat had gotten separated from us, though. I took stock of the two strangers at our table. We'd need to pinpoint how the room's magic broke us into groups, so that next time we wouldn't be separated. Will nodded at me, obviously thinking the same thing.

A chair appeared to my right and a figure sat down, legs folded gracefully to the side, a picture of womanly confidence. Out of the hundreds of tables she could have chosen, Bellacia Bailey had chosen ours first.

"Delia."

Delia tilted her head. "Bella."

"I'm surprised to see you here." Her voice was warm and lovely—gracious—but something about it set me on edge. It was practiced and perfect. The perfect tone and volume, just like Olivia at her most polite, but whereas Olivia naturally pushed people away, this girl drew listeners closer. To ensnare them.

My overactive and completely alarmed imagination was getting away from me again.

"Satisfies a requirement." Delia's facial expression was friendly enough, but her eyeliner grew heavier, tapering to sharper points. "Our surprise is mutual—I thought your schedule precluded assistantships."

"Triple focuses are a trial, but due to what is happening, I couldn't let current events be moderated by someone with less intensity and passion."

Intensity? She certainly had that. For sure. I wondered what her three majors were. Politics, obviously. Communications, likely, with her family being in the media business. Business maybe?

"Speaking of moderation..." Her eyes focused on the rest of us. "My name is Bellacia Bailey. I'm a third-year student with a focus in politics, and I'll be one of your teaching assistants this term. And you are?"

We introduced ourselves in turn, but her eyes lingered on me. "I don't believe that I've seen you around campus before this year."

Delia's lips pursed, Mike's gaze narrowed, Will's eyes widened, and the two unknown students in our group seemed mystified, as their gazes flipped between us.

"I'm not very noticeable." I laughed uncomfortably. "I transferred this year."

"Mmmm. Don't be unkind to yourself, dear. You are fairly lit from the inside." Her smile was friendly and welcoming, and her words flowed graciously over me. I could tell her anything. I couldn't look away from her mouth as she formed her words. "From where did you transfer?" she asked.

I transferred from nowhere, I wanted to confide.

A sharp stab to my leg registered, and the sudden pain made me look down. Will's pencil tip retreated to a notebook open in his lap. A box sketch—my design—was detailed on the page. My mind sharpened on it.

"Four Corners," I said, blinking at the design.

"Oh! I have a very good friend there." Bellacia's voice made me look back up at her. Her smile was kind. "Charlotte Gregorferi. Do you know her?"

The image of the box sketch rotated in my mind, pushing against...something. "No."

"What about Beresil Abutnot?"

"No."

When I had chosen Four Corners Academy from Marsgrove's administrative packet as my first-year alibi, I had done so deliberately. Student population was thirty thousand. Located on top of the western United States, I had a better feel for the general vibe of the changed world there. And students—even the sixteen-year-olds—were able to live off campus, if they chose, as long as they were inside the perimeter ley lines that existed around the town.

"Mmmm. Alas. But their news frequency is a wonderful thing. Do you enjoy the Sounding Patrons or Cipri Cataclysm more?" A graceful hand waved through the air and I could hear a thread of magic like the tinkling of a bell.

Mike briskly leaned his arms on the table. "Do we need to sureifeit a cresching sheet?"

I stared at Mike, whose language was suddenly riddled with foreign words. Crap. I had forgotten to tell Will about my faulty translation spell. I subtly tapped Will's chair and motioned to my wrist. His eyes widened, and a second later, his fingers crept around my bracelet and wrist under the table. Mike's words rearranged in my head—'Do we need to download a discussion sheet?'

"Oh, dear. Have I extended introductions too long? I am always so pleased to meet transfer students. Please do forgive me. To business then." She smiled at Mike and he relaxed a measure. "A discussion packet will be pushed to your student panel, along with class notes. Professor Harrow believes in full disclosure—in everything it seems, even when there is no need." She laughed pleasantly. "So every detail of lecture and discussion will be included, using the Recording Enchantment. That includes any student whispering as well, so do remember to keep entertainments outside. We will be having an exciting term discussing the current political landscape and how each of us can be a model citizen."

She rose. "And with that, I bid you farewell for the morning. My contact information and assistant frequency are all included in the push."

I looked to the far corner to see Neph looking upset and concerned as she watched us over her shoulder. She obviously felt the tension, even from far across the room.

There were many reasons for concern. Like the idea that anything I said would be recorded for anyone in the class to see or hear. That terrified me so much that my lips didn't unseal during the group "discussion" where we were supposed to express our current positions.

"What happened in there?" I hissed to Will, when we were well away from the building, my lingering fear preventing me from raising my voice. I waved to the others, who had gotten separated by the crowd behind us.

"Bailey spread an enchantment. Two actually. You threw off the first when you concentrated on the sketch. The second only affected mages who hadn't completely integrated a translation spell."

I closed my eyes. "She knows I'm feral."

"Definitely," he said.

After all of that Origin Mage talk by Professor Harrow, there wasn't a calming spell in existence that could work on me now.

"But think of her like Olivia, just a year older," Will said. "She doesn't randomly make claims. She gathers facts. She is a journalist. And even though the Baileys skate the edge of sensationalism in some of their rags, they are still bound to certain standards. She will have to gather proof, if she's going to reveal your circumstance or do anything about it."

It wouldn't be hard for her to collect proof. I tended to do magic loudly without realizing it.

Will frowned. "And being feral isn't a crime. People are just scared of those who have power they might not be able to control. But you wear a cuff. And feral magic bursts settle within three years of one's Awakening, then you are just an underage mage like everyone else here."

Except I wasn't a mage like everyone else.

"Most of the magicist fears revolve around ferals being easily indoctrinated into the wrong set of political beliefs," Will said. "People are dumb."

"Why aren't there any other ferals here?" I kept my voice low as my gaze swept the moving crowd.

"Most get placed in small, private institutions—the better to indoctrinate them with traditional Second Layer standards and beliefs, and to keep their magic under control. Then they slowly matriculate elsewhere when their feral status has passed. So there are likely older students here who were once feral," he said. "They just don't advertise it."

"Okay." I took a deep breath. That made me feel better. Sort of. I wouldn't be here at Excelsine either if Marsgrove hadn't made the mistake of bringing me to campus, then locking me up in his home at the base of the mountain where the professors lived.

"But back to Bailey. I didn't see either of the enchantments she cast." I had gotten pretty used to seeing and anticipating magic and it unnerved me to have that confidence dented.

"You didn't see them. You heard them. She's a popular, talented vocalist. Sirenic focus. She uses her words and voice."

Great. Business wasn't her third major, and I was a sailor without cotton balls. "Politics, communications, and freaky Siren abilities—she's going to rule the world."

I'd have to inform Olivia.

Will laughed. "Probably. Who cares. As with any other mental head-gamer, make her think she has you pegged, then do your own thing. She can rule, as long as she doesn't take away our grants or nitpick our experiments. Midlands tonight?" he asked hopefully, nudging me.

"Yeah." I could use some stress relief. And... "Let's work on your portal pad tech."

Will brightened.

We needed an expedited way to get off campus and out of this layer, if or when we had to.

Delia had another class, but Mike and Neph finally caught up to us when the crowds thinned.

We headed to lunch, whispering furiously about what Neph had missed and what we could do about securing discussion seats together. Neph, because she was a muse, had been put into a group that contained only muses.

The whole muse thing was weird. Before we'd met, Neph had been a ghost on campus. But I had somehow attached myself to her in a burst of magic, and now anyone whose attention I directed to Neph could see and interact with her—and to some extent could see the rest of the community.

It wasn't like muses were physically transparent. Mages knew the muses were there—but I had seen their gazes glossing over them, like looking over unremarkable people in a crowd—even if there was only a single mage and a single muse in a room, the mage wouldn't pay attention to the muse as an individual. There was some weird thing people were always trying to tell me about magic sharing and controlling ties and the rewards of having one muse or access to all muses.

So the majority of mages took what the muses yielded, then ignored them, and the muse communities reaped whatever their own benefits were, and that was that.

And since the magic that hid the muses from normal view on campus apparently worked in classrooms in the same way—in a class discussion, the magic assigned muses together, so they'd be able to actually discuss concepts.

But Neph didn't want to be in the muse discussion group, and we wanted her to be with us. We just needed to overcome the magic the administration had put in place for the muses.

Will had explained it in a little more detail to me during our "Neph project" discussion.

"But we should be able to change the summoning and assignment magic by linking Neph to you, Ren," Will said adamantly. "We just need to figure out the right administrative thread."

As if talking about muse-y things made the rest of the muse community notice, as we entered the enchanted, glass cafeteria, Neph was summarily called over to one of their tables. I couldn't hear what was being said, but I didn't like the way they were pointing fingers and scolding her like an errant child.

Olivia arrived and pinned the remaining three of us with a probing glare as she regarded the uneasy silence at our table. "What happened? Michael? William? Ren?"

"Class." I slouched over my tray. "Muses. Stupid magic world."

Olivia looked over at the muse table where Neph was still being berated. There was an unreadable expression on Olivia's face. "They have control over her until she graduates." She briskly whipped her napkin onto her lap. "But that is for later discussion. Tell me what happened in class."

Mike shook his head and gave me a pitying look. "Bailey is one of the teaching assistants. Harrow didn't look pleased with Bailey when I saw him talking to the assistants at the end of class. Bet she got 'assigned' by someone higher up. The professor didn't pick her, that's for sure."

A calming spell tried to wrap around my pinkie finger. I shook my hand, throwing the spell off.

Olivia smoothly opened her magically sealed glass of mixed vegetable and fruit juice. "And?"

"In a sea of a thousand, Bailey spent fifteen discussion minutes—the first fifteen minutes—with our group," Mike said.

Olivia gripped her glass tightly before finally taking a drink. "She knows, or at least suspects, that Ren is a new mage."

I forced myself to take deep breaths and smile. Not only new, not only feral...

"Diseased and deadly." I joked, making light of my predicament. "Question, though—why didn't Bailey get charged for spreading an enchantment to influence me?" I was used to being brought up on Justice charges fairly quickly.

Olivia looked sharply at Mike and Will. "What enchantment?"

Mike shook his head. "Light influence and compliance charm, then she disrupted new translation charms within a twenty-foot radius. With a little assistance, Ren weathered both."

Olivia's finger tapped her glass. "Mages are expected to be able to repel spells at a certain level. If she didn't get charged, the enchantments she cast were below the legal proficiency requirement for students entering Excelsine. No one else was affected?"

Olivia looked to Mike for confirmation. He shook his head.

She looked back to me. "You need to work on repelling auditory magic, Ren. Immediately."

For all of my powerful explosions of magic, Bellacia's light enchantments were a reminder of how vulnerable I still was.

"I'll run some simulations with Draeger in the Battle Building," I said. Even though Draeger was a simulation himself—purchased my first week here so that I could practice and learn the basics of magic without outing myself as feral—he was a hard taskmaster. Needing to lighten the atmosphere, I added, "He'll probably get me to stuff my ears with magic by simulating squirrel tail earplugs or something."

I was used to altering Christian's moods by badgering him back to happiness, and Mike easily took the bait and bantered with me about rabid magical varmints taking over the school one eardrum at a time.

Neph appeared, finally. She looked exhausted. As she sat down next to me, a little of the exhaustion faded, though dark circles still ringed her eyes.

Will was nearly vibrating as he leaned across the table. "Ren and I have something for you! We didn't get a chance before class to give it to you."

She gave him a fond look. "How are you, Will?"

"I am excellent. And you are going to be excellent too, in but two minutes." He shoved his hand into his bag, rooting around for the item he sought.

"I feel better already," she said softly, smiling at me. The circles were loosening, shade by shade.

"Rough night of practice?" Mike asked Neph, the echo of 'and rough run-in with your community five minutes ago?' also implicit in his words.

"Yes. But necessary training, so they claim." Her expression tightened.

"Can you tell us about it?" I gently shifted some magic her way. The dark circles under her eyes faded.

She shook her head, an apologetic and somewhat lost expression gracing her features. "Muses take an oath every time we leave our communes. Especially in a scholastic environment, our elders worry over what might be revealed."

"The muse conspiracy," Will whispered conspiratorially to me with a wink.

Neph looked sad. "Yes." Her eyes drifted toward specific tables dotted around the tiers. Tables full of energy that was flowing outward to the normal tables surrounding them. Tables full of muses chatting serenely with each other. Each day I saw the energy a little more fully—likely a by-product of being near Neph so often.

The muse tables were epicenters of magical energy. The muse community was closed to outsiders and they banded together as a force—mostly overlooked and unseen. But when I had met Neph, she had been sitting alone. She had been sitting alone every meal that I had seen her. At that point, I had just thought it was because she was new to campus like I was.

"Well, Neph, this product, made especially for you by the geniuses at this table, will help," Will said, and offered her a box in a hodgepodge mix of movements combining professional showmanship and amateur jazz hands.

Mike and I exchanged glances, both trying not to laugh. Olivia gave a full-bodied sigh and continued to methodically eat her salad, though she watched keenly to see what Will and I had made.

Neph carefully took the pouch from Will, her eyes shifting between us. "What have you two created?"

I gestured for her to open it. Christian had always taken an agonizingly long time to open things I made for him, knowing I found the waiting torturous.

Neph gracefully opened the box and lifted the sachet nestled within.

Mike leaned toward her and whistled. "Nice. Now I know why you were rifling through my atmospheric compendium, Will. A keepsake spell to keep the elements from fading?"

Will nodded and he and Mike started talking weather enchantments and the ways in which they could be used outside of their most obvious aspects.

Neph, on the other hand, remained silent. Her fingers moved over the silk bag. A waterfall of dark hair hid most of her expression, but one finger shook slightly as she pulled it along the outside of the silk. The threads that connected to her touched the bag, then pulsed out toward both of us.

"Thank you," she said softly, clutching the sachet to her chest, her expression still hidden from view.

"It was our pleasure," I said, my tone deliberately casual. Will piped in his supportive response as well.

Neph looked like she needed another minute to compose herself, so I engaged Mike on weather-related enchantments as well, keeping the talk easy and casual. Neph tucked the sachet into the inside crook of her elbow as she ate with her other hand, and even Olivia joined the easy conversation.

Oddly, by the end of lunch, I felt strangely euphoric. Will looked almost high too as he and Mike waved good-bye and headed to their next classes and labs.

Neph gave me a long hug powered with the smell of the sachet. When she pulled back, the smile on her face was happier than I had seen since our return to campus. My euphoria increased.

As soon as Neph left, though, Olivia stared at me with a look that said she was going to pierce said euphoria with a verbal knife. Even though she had participated in the conversations, she wasn't as easily swayed by conversational turns. And she had definitely not been swayed by the one I had used to divert the subject of my feral unveiling. She pinned me with a look that said as much.

I quickly reached into my bag. "I have something for you too."

I put the paper egg on the table between us.

She narrowed her eyes at my obvious diversion. "Your gift to Nephthys was not what I was going to discuss first." But her fingers automatically reached for the egg and its embedded magic. She stopped herself just shy of grabbing it, her training deeply ingrained. Olivia didn't usually touch magic from others without weaving ten different revelation spells first.

I said nothing as she hesitated, but when she lifted it into her hand a moment later, it was all I could do to withhold the fierce smile that threatened to overtake me at her implicit statement of trust.

She moved the egg around her palm, examining it carefully. I could see the magic thrumming through the paper's surface and attaching to her as she touched it.

I knew she felt the magic, and the connection, and that she likely guessed at some of what I had done. "Ren?"

"It's a small protection." I tried for a light, slightly dismissive tone.

"You used paint."

"Yes."

Her fingers curled possessively around the egg. "You shouldn't waste paint on me."

"It's anything but a waste."

She didn't respond; her gaze focused on the gently curved paper.

"Just keep it on you. Please?" I said softly.

After a moment, she gave a stiff nod.

"Great," I said, relieved. "Thanks."

She pinned me with a dissecting gaze as she tucked the egg carefully into her shoulder bag. "Is this why your magic felt exhausted at the beginning of lunch?"

I waved a hand. "It's always exhausted." That was usually a good thing for other people, as it drained me from doing anything accidental and destructive. "But I feel great now."

"That's Nephthys' doing. She—" Olivia hesitated, and her fingers dipped into her bag, touching the egg again. She shook her head. "Nothing. I'm happy you are recharged."

As we dumped our trays, she still looked hesitant, so I badgered her into talking about her morning class, encouraging her to dissect all of the ways in which her classmates were idiots.

She accompanied me to a henge of five arches. One arch in the cluster would send me to the squad's meeting point, and another would get her close to the main law building. I waved. I wouldn't see her until late. She wouldn't be at dinner, due to her class load, and I was on duty alone for community service tonight.

She glanced at her bag, and at the egg inside, then she returned my wave with focused attention—she was still unused to such casual gestures of friendship—and stepped through the arch.

Stay safe, Olivia.

I couldn't trail her everywhere on campus. She had the egg for protection now. It had to be enough.

Chapter Seventeen

CRIMINALLY YOURS

THE SQUAD GROUP meeting was...lengthy. The entire Justice Squad and six members of the Combat Squad, tromped around the far corners of the mountain and examined ley line positions and tested protection points. We received checklists of what to search for and what to record on our rounds...a rotation list to follow, blah, blah, blah. It was a good thing we'd only be responsible for protecting and monitoring campus for the single week when the combat mages were gone. This was so not me.

There was no way Dare painstakingly filled out forms every day, so the Combat Squad had to have some system that eliminated the busywork—maybe some sort of mental frequency recording at point of observation.

But Justice Squad members weren't given that privilege. Fighting monsters wasn't my thing, but filling out the horribly long and detailed forms they were handing out to us now as examples of what we would have to do really wasn't.

Dare wasn't part of the inter-squad group training, but I had the horrible feeling that he would quiz me on all of this information tomorrow. With that in mind, I paid extra, careful, painful attention.

Mike poked at his food at dinner. Mike, Delia, and I were the only ones currently occupying our dinner table, and I was pretty sure Delia had only joined us because Olivia was absent. Olivia and Delia had been avoiding each other like the plague due to what Mike deemed "grade school conflict."

"I still think the administrators should have waited to start school," Mike said.

Delia smirked. "Rain class sucked, huh?"

"I am a horrible, horrible rain dancer. It was like watching a frost chicken run on two feet instead of three."

I quickly accessed an image of a frost chicken on my bracelet encyclopedia. It was a colossus cow/chicken hybrid that had a large extra limb for stability, and that achieved a frozen internal temperature perfect for food preservation. Right. Someday I was going to have to make a trip to the Fourth Layer.

Bellacia Bailey passed our second-tier table and smiled. "Good afternoon."

Delia and Mike both stopped speaking for a moment, and smiled thinly back, echoing her greeting. I didn't bother; I was too busy watching the way the air vibrated with the sound waves of her magic.

Magic flowed through the air around her with every warm and rich word that emerged. Fascinating.

When she was finally out of sight, Mike nudged me. "So, how was architecture?" he asked.

"Great!" I made an effort to form my potatoes into a careful pyramid, so as to avoid their gazes.

"You didn't go," Mike said, obviously not fooled by this tactic.

"Nope."

Instead, I had visited Constantine after squad practice and we had fiddled with a vortex he was constructing, skating the thin edge of a write-up once again. What was with him and vortexes anyway? It was like he was constantly trying to get expelled. But at least we had re-established our normal relationship as partners in crime and I had been able to help him with something.

When I finally looked up, Delia laughed and winked at me. "Already slaffing? And on your first day?" she teased. I frowned for a moment, before slaffing translated with great effort into skipping. Great, Bailey had set my translator on the fritz again. I rapped the bracelet Will had given me—as if I could fix the bad reception signal—then tasked my magic to fix the "circuits" on its own. Some magic attached to the leather and some washed right over the top. The bracelet gave a half-ping, as if rebooting.

Grimacing, I just put my mind to paying better attention.

"Individualized study guidelines say I can attend anytime," I said, pointing my fork at Delia. "Will and I rescheduled the feed to sometime tonight."

"Sure you will." She smirked. "Right after you find something unbearably interesting to work on."

Before I could respond, my magic gave a sudden tug and my gaze shifted upward. Dare sat down in his customary seat at the table in the corner of the first tier, his back to the rest of the room.

"We'll see how rescheduling works out." Delia leaned back in her chair, bangs brushing her eyebrows. "When you stop by during service duty tonight." She tapped her lip with one lacquered fingernail and tipped her head to the side as if thinking hard. "How did you get community service again? Following rules? Hmmm."

I poked my potatoes. "Very funny."

"It is, but I love your two-hour shifts." She withdrew a small weaving she'd been working on from her bag and pulled five of the end threads together in a complicated series of knots that she made look easy. "I'm planning something amazing and diabolical tonight that should only ring as an itsy Level One. You'll love it. Make sure you grab the call. But in the likely event you happen to miss it, I'll show you when you come by for help on some other new project you rope yourself into."

"I will get it all done," I protested.

Delia examined me through her bangs in a way that indicated she thought my self-awareness deserved a setback. Her fingers kept manipulating the magical strings steadily. "Did you use the fastening I showed you? The one that took thirty minutes of your nonexistent time a few nights back to learn?"

I put my hand to my forehead. She was right, I'd probably end up with ten more projects tonight. That was just how my life worked. "Yes, it was great. Will and I used it on something we designed for Neph. Thanks again."

She smirked and addressed Mike without taking her gaze from me. "Ten munits says Ren doesn't do the class feed tonight. And that Will plunges her headfirst into something else instead."

"Twenty. They are both insane. They'll plunge, but then still manage to shove in the class feed when all rational people are in bed."

"Bet."

Magic circled around them, then settled.

"Thanks a lot, guys." I speared a ravioli. "Feeling the love."

"You would be feeling it if you stop looking like a vagabond once in a while," Delia said, then added something extra-saucy about how hard I could feel it that made Mike choke on his food.

Delia smirked at him, then refocused on me. I quickly hid my grin. I chewed my pasta and quirked a brow, waiting to hear today's "Aggrieved Fairy Godmother" report.

"Ratty ponytails and random streaks of charcoal and magic on your cheeks and clothes, Ren, are not really selling the availability of a nubile, young mage in need of some serious—"

"Manticore!" an angry voice yelled.

I jerked my head toward the voice, expecting to see the monster of the day, but the cafeteria was blessedly monster free.

"I'm telling you, we should do the manticore," the same unfamiliar voice said, liberal curse words punctuating the statement.

The table of gamers five tables over from ours started arguing loudly, drawing attention from the rest of the second tier.

"No, a one-horned beast first. Then the manticore on Level Two."

"Don't be a jally-bot, ladtoe," said a redheaded boy to a boy with hair that defied gravity.

"Conceptual shalley planning. If you don't start out smaller, Trick, you have nowhere to go."

None of the unfamiliar words translated into anything G-rated.

They started arguing more vociferously until the redhead threatened, "I'll give you a one-horned beast."

Magic swirled and shot from his hand. The other boy ducked to the side, saving himself and his hair. The bolt swept up toward the corner of the first cafeteria tier, directly at Dare, whose back was still incongruously presented to the rest of the tables. It seemed an even stranger position now that magic was flying toward him.

I waited for Dare to spring out of his chair, whirl around, and counter the attack.

He didn't do anything of the sort. Leaning back, he played with something on his plate and was likely smirking at the raucous conversation that always enveloped the most popular combat table. But I saw Ramirez—the dark and deadly boy sitting next to him—turn slightly.

A combat mage sitting across from them who had a clear view of the room said something, but it was far too late. I watched in morbid fascination, wondering what Dare was going to look like with a unicorn horn.

He never moved. The spell hit, then ricocheted violently—blasting the redhead who had cast the spell clear out of his seat and against the railed edge of the second tier. My translation spell took that moment to fix itself completely, ringing loudly and clearly in my head as the boy furiously swore.

Three horns emerged from the redhead's face—one from his forehead and one from each of his cheeks.

Dare never bothered to turn in his seat. A few mages at his table who could see the results laughed, and I could hear, "Do that in practice today," and, "Cast that at Johnson on Friday."

Either Dare had countered the redhead's spell without movement or visible care—very possible—or one of Dare's natural shields had a three-power force—three times the effect, reflected back at the caster.

Mike shook his head. "Never shoot anything in the direction of that table, or toward any of the other combat tables...especially now. The combat mages go a little batty during competition season while practicing for the combat qualifier and games. They hold full defenses and shields in place for stupidly insane amounts of time. And some of them always hold them."

I looked at the boy trying to stem the growth of his three new pointy additions.

"Noted," I said, a little awed at the horns.

"Brilliant," the redhead's companion said as he helped him stand. "Add a horn geometrically at each level until the final beast has ten of them shooting out magic in a whirlwind of directions."

"For sure, lad! For sure!" agreed the redhead, excitement in his voice as they put their drastically dissimilar heads together to hash out their new plan.

"Idiots," Delia said, though her tone was fond, indicating that she knew the two boys. But her next few words required active translation making me frown down at my bracelet.

The translation spell was likely on the fritz again because of Bailey.

Mike shook his head, still watching the gamers wildly plot their games and the combat table discuss battle spells. "Wait until you see the combat qualifier. It's insane."

I absently wiped my cheeks, hoping I'd get the charcoal off without having to be active about it. I had seen enough of Dare's fighting tactics. When it did come time to practice defensive maneuvers with him, I was going to be frost chicken feed.

~*~

"We are aiming to rid you of the leash completely, and I know that you want to try a temporary leech solution to see if you can break some links, but if we go right for multiple leeches with increased power, you could subvert things far faster," Constantine said later that night, his finger tracing a diagram in one of the books we were sharing.

I nodded. "Sounds like a horrible plan. We should try it."

His expression turned sincerely amused. "You should be shocked and appalled and calling me all sorts of names over the threat to your health and independence."

"Self-preservation is for losers."

He leaned forward, spreading his fingers over the pages. "You are my finest entertainment."

I patted his hand and looked at the particularly horrifying illustration he had been tracing. "I know. Now tell me about this design."

"The button used between us required skin contact on both sides to conduct the permission and leeching aspects. This one does as well, but in a more, shall we say...alarming...way. You preset the permission. An additional device or holding magic is required to"—His fingers made a looping pattern—"keep the permission safe."

Like the box, but still not quite enough power or terror. "What about a controller of some kind? Something that allows magic to be leeched over a distance...maybe by pinching space? Tricking the leech into thinking it is skin-to-skin even when there are miles of actual distance between leech and leechee?"

He inclined his head. "That would be possible, especially if you are speaking of a single layer design. Port mages bend space inside a single layer every time they work. Poking a hole between layers is harder, but not impossible. Especially for someone who can wield Origin Magic. Using Origin Magic is like sticking the master key into the unbreakable lock that is the Layer System." His long fingers mimed breaking a lock in two.

I nodded, pulse picking up as it always did when the subject arose.

"Well, we don't need to try anything between layers yet," I said. So far, I was reasonably sure that Raphael had always been in the same layer when he had used the box on me. The destruction in Sassraf hadn't been the same. The magic I had felt on Holy Innocents Day in the First Layer had been an echo, not a pull. "If we are going to try pinches, we should bring in Will."

Constantine wrapped his ribbon around his pointer finger. "I prefer working with you alone."

"I know. But Will knows travel and transportation magic better than anyone I know. He's trustworthy, not afraid to get his hands dirty, and has a lot of experience dealing with my messes. Like serious experience trapped inside my messes," I said ruefully.

Something sparked in Constantine's eyes before being banked back to their normal fire. "That's an interesting choice of phrase. Fine. Bring him with you next time, and we shall see."

"You won't regret it."

He gave me a long-suffering look, and I flicked a finger at his shoulder, sending out the magical equivalent of a nudge, just as Justice Toad rang to let me know I was now on call and had an active alert. "Service duties. Next two hours. Gotta go."

"See you in thirty then, Crown. Don't do anything less than I would."

"Right. No." Constantine with a service tablet would be the worst idea ever. Hopefully Provost Johnson never got it into his head to give him one. I looked at the call stats. Dorm Five. "Give me at least thirty-five minutes unless you want me to zap you extra hard or ignore the call completely."

"Depends on how you plan to zap me," he called as I exited.

I rolled my eyes because I could hear his active amusement underlying the false suggestiveness of his words. We both knew I'd respond as soon as he hit the active offense log. Like Delia and Will, Constantine made sure to do any testing that would get him in real trouble while I was on duty.

It was just another way the club of misusing-magic users worked the system. If anyone on the club circuit learned when a two-hour time window commenced for a community service worker, they tested like mad during that period. Since multiple justice mages were on duty at the same time, there were no guarantees that the community service worker would show up at the offender's door, but the increased opportunity that the person might respond to a call mitigated some of the risk and opened up an avenue for quality punishments—like cleaning buildings where offenders could simultaneously rifle through cutting-edge research, or patching up magics that forwarded their own aims.

As I walked on top of the Magiaduct from Dorm One to Five, I shook my head and hoped Provost Johnson never figured it out. Professor Wellingham, who was in charge of the Justice Squad, totally knew, but I was pretty sure he had already given up on humanity, in general.

I knocked on the appropriate door in Dorm Five ten minutes after the call registered. My tablet had already fully labeled the villainy—a Level Two "artifact control restriction" registered to an Asafa Frey.

The door was opened promptly by a boy with bright red hair and green eyes. I almost blurted out something about his face missing three horns, but managed to hold my tongue.

"Well, damn," the boy from the cafeteria said, running a hand through his short hair. "It registered." He sighed. "Who took the hit, sweet justice lass? Asafa or Patrick?"

"Asafa Frey," I answered, amused.

He sighed and addressed a pair of dark legs sticking out from under a behemoth of a desk. "Sorry, Saf. Was supposed to be my turn." He turned back to me. "Could you give us but a moment, dear lady, to finish our testing log?"

He looked resigned, as if he expected me to object. But always interested in the goings-on around the rule-breaking circuit, I nodded. "Sure. Mind if I come in?"

Justice Toad would either heat up if we overextended the appropriate preliminary call time or turn someone into an amphibian. My tablet had a quick draw, but at this point, I was pretty used to catching rogue hoppers and turning them back into people.

Clover-green eyes examined me, then lit up. "The new gal! Lucky day for us, Saf. Come in, my gal. Name's Patrick, or Trick, if you are going to be around a lot. Asafa's over there. We're almost finished."

It never took long for anyone to identify me as a community service worker. Something about me obviously screamed my illegitimacy as a policewoman.

"Gaming system test run. You don't mind if we finish copying down the notes and schematics on how we put it together, do you?"

I furrowed my brow and looked at Justice Toad. "Gaming systems are legal," I said, scrolling down the log to find information on the offense.

"Er, yes. But ones that use compulsive magic, not so much."

"You make people want to continue gaming? Are you finding that people are playing too little?" I asked in astonishment, unable to comprehend such a thing. There were more or less permanent gaming tables set up on the main floor of the library—tables with elaborate holograms and students with magical sensors at their temples and palms playing the games at all hours of the night. I saw them every visit I made to the library. And I was in the library a lot.

The cafeteria boy with the truly spectacular, height-defying hair emerged from underneath the large desk in the center of the room. "Just testing human limits. All done, Trick, but it's going to take increased power, a better art render, and the implementation of our upgraded controller specs."

I looked at the game controller in his hand—a thin headband that wrapped horizontally around the user's head—and all sorts of ideas jumped fully formed into my mind. A controller that used compulsion and could work at a distance...

I couldn't stop a smile as I cocked my head to look at the controller from another angle. The club worked insanely well on the barter system. "What kind of art rendering?"

Both boys looked at me, looked down at the doodle-covered notebook peeking out of my bag, then grinned.

Chapter Eighteen

HIDDEN SIDES

I WON MIKE TWENTY munits when Will and I jammed in the architecture class feed before midnight. It was mostly syllabus and intro, but exciting nevertheless. Class was going to be fantastic.

Will and I had also gotten in a quick visit to Constantine together, who'd smiled at the hologram of the controller in my palm, then interrogated Will to within an inch of his life. I was just happy Constantine had stopped his questioning before Will admitted who it was who held the other side of the leash we were fighting against. I could see in Constantine's calculating gaze that he knew Will was aware of the leash holder's identity, but, strangely, Constantine never pressed. Then again, it wouldn't shock me if he already knew.

Constantine could assemble a thousand piece emotional puzzle from the tiniest social and emotional clues.

With Constantine's consent to include Will in the project, the three of us brainstormed past the edge of sanity. One thing the three of us had in common was an absence of imaginative limitations.

Despite the many shadowy threats surrounding me, and an uncertain clock ticking down to when Raphael could use my magic again, studying at Excelsine was awesome. If there was one thing that I had learned in the last six months, it was that I had to balance uncertainty and fear with other, more positive actions and thoughts in order to maintain a creative peak.

So I let a grin pull to my face whenever I thought about the gaming specs Asafa and Patrick had shown me. Christian would have loved so many things in this world. I loved so many things in this world.

Keeping a mental balance was a continuous struggle that I was determined to win. And when I defeated Raphael, I could... I would be able to do anything.

At four in the morning, I tripped into my room and face-planted on my bed.

~*~

Olivia was gone when I woke to rising sunlight, a slowly lifting mattress, and the heavy, rising beat of the room's alarm clock spell.

I rolled out of bed and hurried to the shower. Warding class with Mbozi was at ten and I didn't want to miss a word.

Two and a half hours later, I was brimming with awesome ideas for shoring up the dream wards even further. Class was going to be great. I had a serious professor crush on Mbozi. A crush that withstood every strange look and resigned sigh he cast my way. Last term I'd helped him rebuild the art vault, art complex, and protection wards I'd destroyed and I had been overjoyed to do the work, pestering him relentlessly with questions.

Normal people probably weren't usually so giddy over speculative engineering, but the work with Mbozi had been key to setting the wards in Okai—the only place other than the vault where I could safely use paint on campus.

I was finally in one of his classes legitimately, and out of an intro class of two hundred, Mbozi had spotted me in the crowd almost immediately. Awesome! I pretended the small sigh he had given immediately after recognizing me was because he was just as excited to do some magical science as I was.

I didn't have time to go to the cafeteria, so I grabbed a hot Magi Mart burrito from our food box—which held individual temperature spells for each food item inside—and plugged the small chip I had gotten from Patrick and Asafa into my reader. I scrolled their game specs as I munched my food. Robots and monsters dominated. No problems there. I had been drawing robots and sword and sorcery imagery for Christian since pre-school, and through the years the designs had only gotten more complicated.

Once I got something set in my mind, it would be easy to repeat the work. But doing quality work on new projects took time. Setting to mind was the time consuming part.

My two-hour work session with Stevens started in thirty minutes and I had to meet Dare immediately thereafter, so I quickly ran to the Midlands to sketch out a dragon for Dare and a small Midlands' map projection. I wasn't going to be able to tie a map to him in the same way I had tied one to me—not without touching him with Awakening paint, which was a giant no—but I could make something he could use.

Unlike the new designs for Asafa and Patrick, it took me barely any time to sketch a repeat of a previous design. And repeating magic was easy as well. If I had done it once, my memory logged it in a physical way. I activated the dragon with a drop of glorious paint, and fought the ever present urge to use more, more, more.

The dragon curled around my palm. I had told Dare that making them required magical sacrifice. The sacrifice was not the effort or my personal magic; the sacrifice was the drop of paint. The dwindling Awakening paint in my last non-orange tube.

As I entered the all-glass interior of the building that housed the offices and labs for the Material Magics and Sciences professors, a yawn overtook me before I could stifle it. Constantine was working in a lab off to the side and raised a perfect, mocking brow at my drooping eyes and post-lunch-without-enough-sleep stupor.

I gave him a wave and pushed into Stevens' work office. In her kickass magical stilettos and designer skirt, Stevens was moving her hands in the air, as if she was writing equations on the wind, using magic that was invisible to my eyes, even now.

"Pulp pressing," she said before I'd even stepped fully in the door. "Ten perfect iterations on my desk before the end of the day."

She didn't take her eyes off the air she was manipulating in front of her.

How do you know Raphael, Professor Stevens? I wanted to ask, but instead my lips said, "We are making paper?"

"Didn't I just say so?"

Before I could stop the words I blurted out, "I'd like to focus fully on paint-making this term."

Stevens' fingers stilled in the air, glued there momentarily. "I don't remember asking for your opinion on what I would teach you when I took you on."

"You didn't. You also weren't completely upfront as to why you were taking me on." That last bit was uttered without conscious determination, and I immediately knew it was a mistake.

She turned. Her gaze upon me was cool and impersonal as her hands dropped to her sides. "Are you challenging me?" She was studying me as if examining a bad slide sample.

"I'm challenging our syllabus."

"Independent study parameters are at the sole discretion of the professor. You are challenging me."

Professor Stevens was a magical and intellectual giant. She was the top of her field, a scientist I highly respected, and a mentor—but I didn't know if I could trust her outside the classroom.

How do you know Raphael Verisetti, professor?

But asking questions aloud about one of the most dangerous terrorists in the world would be stupid.

The question didn't form on my lips, but it hovered in the air between us. It had hovered ever since she had taken a look at the shield set around me—a complete stranger—then initiated a devious introduction between us, trapped me inside of a truth spell, and interrogated me about my loyalties.

That I had forced her to give me a session of her time—and that she had taken me on as a student thereafter—still left the unasked and unanswered question between us: Why had she gone to such lengths to interrogate me in the first place?

Screw it. "How do you—?"

"Your stupid combination of personality traits raises its head again," she cut over me, voice hard as steel. "Intuitive, determined, loyal, chaotic, and reckless. I'd advise a little less of the last, Miss Crown. Learn better as to what questions you should ask, and where to ask them."

My gaze sought out Constantine through the series of large windows that made up the independent labs in the professors' personal territory. He was not looking our way, ignoring us in a too deliberate manner, locks of hair falling over his face, half hiding his expression. But as his gaze finally rose to meet mine through all the layers of glass, his eyes were narrowed and speculative.

Stevens, a strict and demanding professor, mentored only five students from a population of fifteen thousand. I didn't know the other three students personally, but Constantine was her prized pupil. Stevens had previously given me her spiel on the qualities that attracted her attention, and had muttered some of what she thought of Constantine and his extreme brilliance wrapped in an immensely troublesome package. Loyalty wasn't likely one of the qualities she would attribute to him, but it was well known that she had taken him on as a student almost immediately upon his entrance to Excelsine at sixteen.

Stevens was used to managing brilliant and difficult people. I twisted that thought in my head. Raphael could easily be included in the same mathematical set. How did she know him?

"May I meet with you somewhere else to speak then?" I asked, forcing my voice to be polite. "The vault, perhaps?"

Stevens raised her hands to the air in front of her, visually ignoring me again. "No. And reckless questions or those unrelated to your lab work will be met with consequences that you will not enjoy. Your request to focus solely on making paint is faulty and is denied. Systematic steps in different mediums will gain you the experience you need to progress in other mediums. The schedule is set. "

"I'll put in extra hours."

"No. The schedule you need to be on is set." Her jaw clenched, as if she had said too much. "Or you can remove yourself from my lab. Understood?" Her fingers moved in the air.

I needed Stevens, and she knew it. I couldn't produce the quality of materials I needed on my own, not yet, and I didn't have independent access to the art vault and its inimitable equipment. Furthermore, Stevens was a resource I needed to keep in my corner. Even Constantine, who had a reputation for being an absolute horror in class if he found the professor "dull," was careful never to truly alienate Stevens.

I clenched my jaw. "Understood."

I started ripping paper with my fingers and magic, dunking the pieces in the solution that Stevens and I had created previously, and infusing each piece as I assembled them. I pressed them into something new and mine that would key automatically to additional magic of the same type when the magic touched the surface of the page. When one of my pencils touched this paper, the magic in both would more than double in strength.

But the problem of paint remained a blockage in my mind, and I shot thoughts in ten directions, wrapping around the unmoving rock in my mind, seeking paths and alternatives. There had to be another solution for me—one that didn't rely on Stevens or on revealing my nature to someone else—and I'd find it.

~*~

Sprinting across an entire quarter of the Ninth Circle, I arrived at Dare's meeting point in front of the Kratos Battle Building with one minute to spare. Dare stared at me, clearly unimpressed by my dashing arrival.

I bent over, hands on my knees, breathing hard. Damn mountain. I sent the Battle Building a longing glance and touched the mentor chip in my pocket. My Tuesday had been brutal already, and I still hadn't had my chat with Draeger.

My plan was to finish with Dare, then complete the game conceptualizations for Asafa and Patrick in a simulation room while visiting with my simulated mentor. I just needed to get through the next two hours.

"Hi," I said to Dare, when I was finally capable of speech. I wiped my brow, and tried not to think about warlords and undiplomatic marriages as I cataloged his charcoal and black clothing.

Dare lifted his chin in a brief greeting. "Earlier next time."

"I'm on time," I said. "I still have, like, a whole twenty seconds before I'm late."

"Earlier."

"You got it, commander." Wow, working resentfully alongside Stevens for two hours had made me mouthy. "I'll tell Professor Stevens that you said I have to leave ahead of time in order to be earlier for you."

"You left there twenty minutes ago." His highly attractive eyes narrowed. "Perhaps Stevens will draw you a map instead."

Okay, so I had made a small detour to the library to blitz the fourth floor looking for a book on paint mentorship, instead of coming straight here. My mind sucked when it came to ignoring to-do tasks actively pressing against my thoughts.

"I detoured. In the future, you should probably schedule me five minutes earlier than you want me. I'm terminally on time. Early is a five letter word—which is far worse than a four."

A brief flicker of amusement flashed on his face, but a spike of magic from the direction of the Battle Building redirected my attention to a student near the front door. A reedy boy, who looked out of place in front of a building dedicated to physical combat was scribbling something on his thigh, his gaze piercing me as he did. My heart picked up speed. He was one of the boys who orbited Bellacia Bailey and her triple-ring-wearing group—mages who hunted people like me. The ones I had taken to calling the Junior Department in my mind.

Dare narrowed his gaze on the boy, then turned and strode through the foggy barrier that separated the Midlands from the Ninth Circle. I followed quickly behind.

"Ignore them," he said brusquely over his shoulder while navigating the fog. "Their lives hold so little interest, that in order to survive they are forced to try and absorb the spark of others."

I didn't know how to respond to that unanticipated bit of reassurance. Warmth curled in my midsection.

We stepped into a flatland that stretched as far as my eye could see. The sky and grounds gave no indication that we were on a mountain anymore, but I was used to that with the Midlands. Nothing was normal in these levels.

I fit right in.

The familiar spark lit, having barely been extinguished from my visit a few hours past. Okai slid into view with Guard Rock welcoming me back. With a shaky wave of my hand and a push against the thread, its tile slid away. Magic was always bright and effortless in the hours after I worked with even the tiniest drop of Awakening paint.

Dare was staring hard at the space where Okai had been. Not good. Its appearance the first time we'd been here probably meant nothing to him. Appearing twice in a row in this level of chaos?

He looked at me, his expression unreadable. I flashed my most brilliant smile, one that strained my lips.

He stared at me silently for another long moment. "What did you see, when we were in here last term?"

Of all the questions I could have anticipated, that was not one of them.

I thought of the mirror shard. Seeing my reflection and knowing that I was the one who had been slowly, unwittingly destroying campus.

"I saw green mist." Truth, just not all of it.

His gaze was even, but I could almost feel disappointment pulsing through the thread that connected us. My stomach tightened in response. A sliver of the craziness that had infected me last term did so again. I had to work harder. Raphael, the Department, leeches, protection, Olivia, Helen Price, Neph, Constantine, Dare, Origin Mages, weapons...

I had to work harder.

His eyes narrowed and the feel of his disappointment muted to something less readable. I really, really hoped he didn't possess Constantine's alarming ability to read my mind.

"I have something for you," I blurted out.

One brow lifted, but an anticipatory tenseness gripped his body—a tension that hadn't been there before.

I pulled the new dragon and map out of my bag, and held them out to him. As they touched both of us, I transferred ownership to him.

He looked at me sharply, obviously not expecting such a transfer. His gaze shifted back to his palm as he carefully lifted the dragon, gently touching a delicate, thin, papered wing. Black lines drew on the accompanying paper, mimicking the topography of the twenty feet surrounding us.

"It's, uh, limited in range for now," I said. "I don't know how to power one for the entire space of the Midlands and transfer it to someone else yet. I will learn, though." I'd figure out everything. Of that I was certain. "But he'll—" I waved my hands at the dragon sinuously sliding along his palm and between his fingers. "He'll give you a visual snapshot of what he sees wherever he is flying."

I busied myself, hooking my bag back over my shoulder so that I didn't have to look at Dare.

"You made this in two days?" he asked.

"I made it earlier this afternoon." Thoughts wildly pinged against emotion in my suddenly scattered brain, and I was too nervous to be able to understand his tone. So I did what came naturally to me with Dare—I spoke quickly and without thought. "Sorry. I'll try harder next time?"

His expression was completely unreadable, so I excessively concentrated on securing my shoulder strap in the perfect position on my shoulder, one repetitive motion at a time.

"But you can send him a little ahead of you," I said. "If you think you are walking into trouble. Or let him trail a bit behind you, if you are being followed. I mean, it, I guess, not he. But he can develop personality, so..."

Stop talking!

I cleared my throat. "You seem to know how to keep us together so we don't get separated in tile slides. I don't. So he will be subject to slides unless you change that. You shouldn't rely on him completely, though—not that you will anyway—but maybe, he might give you an advantage sometime? And I'm sure you will figure out how to use him your own way. He should take limited commands. Maybe you'll find him useful?"

I cringed. Stop talking!

I wanted to pretend that I didn't wish to impress Dare. I wanted to believe that I didn't have a horribly embarrassing crush on him. I wanted to ignore the fact that even though I barely knew him, due to our initial interaction, he ranked pretty darned high on the list of people I would do anything to protect. But...well, I wasn't all that good at pretending.

Dying for him at the end of last term was a hard data point to ignore.

"Mages aren't supposed to place permanent magic in the Midlands," he said finally, casually, as the dragon coiled in his palm.

Oh. No. Now that he said it, a visual image generated in my mind's eye... Page fifty-four of the Midlands guide in the library, in the small diagram on the right side of the page—"Only defensive, transparent, or temporary spells are allowed, with penalty of..."

Heat rushed up and out through my limbs, and sweat broke over my brow.

I hadn't cared last term. I had been willing to do anything. And I had temporarily forgotten that I couldn't afford to show what I was capable of.

"It's...small? And only works when you activate it? You can tote it in and out?" I let my shoulders drop. The four dragons he had already observed had very obviously been permanent residents. "Are you going to report me?"

He looked at me, examining my expression, then his gaze became far more charged, as he threw the dragon in the air and it caught on a breeze and swept around us. "You attract attention."

I swallowed. I didn't know why I had lost the ability to blend into the shadows. No, that was untrue. It was because I didn't have Christian—my larger than life sibling—to hide behind anymore. Without him I was entirely too exposed.

"I am unfit for this," I said tiredly. "I tried telling you that. You shouldn't work with someone who attracts negative attention." There. My public service warning—a community service necessity—had been issued. He could ditch me now, and I could keep my nice long-distance crush intact and inviolate.

His tablet and Justice Toad both rang an alert.

He watched me a moment more, his gorgeous features arranged in a remote expression. Then he tapped under his ear, silently contacting someone while politely allowing me to observe the action. His finger dropped and he continued his silent assessment as I shifted on my feet. Then he smiled.

"Instead of meeting with the others to fight the rabid Pegasus that just started rampaging Six, we are going to check on something else. Come."

That sounded dire. And Alexander Dare smiling at me? Super dire. And not going to the Sixth Circle to fight a rabid, flying horse that was destroying campus? End of the world dire. But I followed him into a field regardless. Wheatgrass grew taller as we walked and started winding about my legs. I could see the grass swaying against Dare's legs too, but it appeared to be caressing him instead of twining to hold.

He stopped for a moment, and the paper dragon swooped back and looped around his head before continuing its flight path. Dear lord. Made from my mind and activated by my magic, it was already fond of him. My mortification was complete.

Dare's open palm caressed the tops of the stalks that now reached his waist. The stalks twining around my legs immediately unraveled, freeing me.

Dare continued forward and I followed in his path, unsettled. I had seen his abilities here last term, but hadn't realized the true depth of affinity. The stalks weren't caressing and releasing me like they were him, but now they were...tasting, for lack of a better word. Testing and weighing. Sentient life in the Midlands was not always apparent on first glance.

What was apparent was that he had just communicated with the wheatgrass, and either asked or forced it to allow my passage.

Tendrils of fog appeared, swirling inward, signifying that we were once more in a tile at the edge of the Midlands. Likely a tile close to the ninth level, as the swirling fog tended to be erratic when streaming in from the upper levels as opposed to the more controlled nature of the lower third of the mountain where the adults lived. The chaos, experimentation, and magically generated backlashes on the top third of the mountain were enormously high.

Dare moved in a small circle, around a green box that blended with the grass.

Guard Rock had been adamant that I avoid the green boxes that the Department had placed sometime during the night I had been throwing up my guts. He had pantomimed a whole dramatic reenactment of mayhem, destruction, and a throat clenching ending as he had pretended to expire on the floor.

As Dare crouched next to it, I stepped forward to warn him. His head tilted toward me, and he motioned to a tree a few feet over. I stared at him for a second, wondering if he was actually indicating to me that I should climb a tree, but he put a quick finger to his lips, then motioned harder.

Okay. I secured my pack and caught a branch, swinging myself up. Every time I stopped at a branch, he motioned me higher. When I was halfway up, he looked back down at the green box and slipped something carefully underneath.

Straightening, he swung up the tree easily, in less than a third of the time it had taken me. Magic swirled through the small clearing and a boom resonated, shocking me so hard I almost lost my grip. Dare motioned me to follow as he climbed twenty feet higher.

I settled like an awkward leopard, mirroring his more natural pose on the long branch next to me. It was beyond unsettling to be in such a position with him—I had used the treetops here many times to observe and avoid him last term before I had successfully anchored Okai.

Glancing nervously in his direction, I really hoped he hadn't put any past data points together and guessed at that in relation to the avoidance spell. But his gaze was turned downward, his expression one tick shy of smug, as he looked at the crater surrounding the still-intact box.

Two minutes later, a small group that included the reedy mage who had been watching us before ran into view and knelt next to the crater. A hologram rose from the box and images flashed rapidly.

That was a Department box, which made my guess of these students being the "Junior Department" seem more than hypothetically accurate. Department minions in training.

Sweat trailed down my spine. I grabbed for my bag, but Dare's hand stilled mine, his gaze never leaving the mages below.

The images from the box came faster and faster, then exploded. The magical kickback knocked the reedy boy off his feet, and he slid across the ground, hitting a tree on the other side.

The boy swore aloud and two of the others ran to help him. He shook off their hands and rose, shouting. A girl removed another box from her bag, and fiddled with it.

While the girl was fiddling, a slip of green floated up toward us like a leaf swept up by the wind. Dare released my hand and caught it, then slipped the leaf into his pocket.

I tucked my tingling fingers against my branch and stared between Dare and the group on the ground.

The girl completed her tinkering and put the new device in place, then she and the others ran after the reedy boy who was stomping through the mist.

I was bursting with questions. I held them in with difficulty as Dare stared at something, waiting. We stayed silently perched until the tiles slid apart, taking us through the middle of the mountain—always a trippy ride—and clear to the other side.

As soon as I caught my breath, I furiously whispered, "You blew up that device."

He lifted a brow in response and started climbing down. "No." He dismounted confidently, landing easily on the ground. "I baited them into checking the device, then recorded what happened when they did."

I climbed down less gracefully and straightened my clothes. He held the leaf in his palm and it bloomed into a holographic recording. The captured images showed a stream of haphazard broken happenings—creatures running past, magic swirling, spooked mages stalking. Nothing was seamless and little was understandable. But neither of our faces showed at all, even though Dare had been crouched in front of the device there at the end. The last image showed the device blowing up and the stooge's feet being propelled off the ground.

"They still haven't figured out how to stabilize a recording of the Chaos Magic here." He looked darkly pleased. "The chaos professors have been trying forever; I don't know why the

Department thought they could breeze in and do so in a few weeks."

"They haven't tried before?" That seemed odd, though it jibed with a thousand other pieces of data haphazardly collected.

"Campus is closed to anyone who isn't enrolled or actively affiliated. That's the way it has always been. Only the directives in the last month have altered that."

"But the Department—"

"Is an agency without provincial interest. The Department serves the security of the Second Layer as a whole and those in the Department are an entity with and without boundaries. Excelsine is its own municipality—its own small nation nestled within greater Europa. The Department is not part of Excelsine, Europa, or any other nation in the Second Layer. They serve all and none. Command all and none. Their influence is dependent on the length and sharpness of each hook they are able to place."

Shady.

And he was telling me simple facts that I should already know as a magic user. I swallowed at the implication and the potential consequences. We hadn't addressed the topic directly, but this pretty well confirmed that he knew I was feral. Anyone who spent extended time with me eventually guessed that I was new to this world. I was an alien sucking up knowledge as fast as I could, but still deficient in the things most mages took for granted.

I shrugged, making a last ditch effort to play off my ignorance like I was an inept teenager who couldn't name the President of the United States. "I sleep during class a lot."

Perhaps I needed to cultivate the mad scientist stereotype a little more—not caring about anything except the project I was working on at the moment. I was pretty sure I could carry that off with little effort.

"Mmmmm." He closed up the leaf and looked at me. His eyes were heavy-lidded, but the gaze beneath was piercing. "Do you plan to report me?"

I startled. "For what?"

"For baiting them into blowing the device."

"No, of course not."

His expression was jaded, but there was far too much confidence in his posture for him to be truly threatened by the idea of me tattling. The dichotomy put me on guard and I silently watched him for clues as to what I needed to do.

He lifted a perfect brow. "You could blackmail me into doing something for you in exchange for keeping the information secret. It is in your best interest."

Clearly, a test. And one that might be won with an answer either way. Constantine and Olivia would know how to use this to their advantage by asking for a favor or feigning trustworthiness. But I was not the girl who moved chess pieces in this world. I was the defective piece that shot around the board without realizing I shouldn't be able to move in those directions.

I shook my head. "Why aren't you threatening me about the dragons?"

The piercing look softened and a small, devastating smile worked his lips as he rose. "Why indeed? Come."

But...he'd already possessed the knowledge of the dragons. He hadn't needed to show me a secret in return.

I hurried to keep up with his far longer legs, my mind working. Warlords and plans... "You want someone shadowing you who can stay quiet and isn't afraid of getting her hands dirty. That is why you picked the community service girl."

He didn't say anything, just kept walking.

"I can see why you wouldn't want someone like Peters. He sucks. He sucks by the book. But Isaiah is great—trustworthy, and there's a bit of the joker in him. And he's experienced and doesn't attract unwanted attention. I say this without an ounce of feigned humility—he'd be a far better choice."

"Choice? It was an absolute gift, you being stuck on the squad this term."

I didn't possess a response that wasn't potentially embarrassing, so I stayed quiet for a moment, thinking hard. He had wanted me to help last term after the Bone Beast. But he was under the misapprehension that I had done something special rather than the fact that I was the person who had caused the problem in the first place and then figured out how to reverse it.

"Um, I have to repeat. I am a lot of trouble."

"Yes."

I blinked at his response, not expecting him to agree quite so readily.

He glanced at me, amused. "I don't think you realize quite how much."

There was something noticeably more relaxed about him. It was a little unnerving. I wondered if I had passed some other, unknown test.

The Midlands were quieter today, and I noticed that many animals and objects that we passed didn't attack. Lots of things still did—and Dare quickly and ruthlessly took them down—but several beasts that I was used to seeing attack, held their ground. They all watched Dare as we walked.

I thought of the grasses that stroked him instead of fighting.

"We passed two giant centipedes." Giant centipedes. "One attacked, and the other didn't. Why?"

"There are two kinds of beasts here," he said. "Those that live here permanently and those created in the magic or absorbed from somewhere else for a period of time. The permanent creatures recognize frequent visitors and react accordingly. The temporary beasts are usually ripped from their homes or created from chaos, so they treat everything as a threat. If there were only permanent creatures here, the Midlands would have been tamed long ago. The temporary beasts and chaotic magic will make it so that the Midlands are never tamed."

"Chaos mages can't tame Chaos Magic?"

"The nature of a chaos mage is to swirl with the magic, not control it."

"So the devices that are being planted? They just have recording enchantments?"

"For now. But never assume anything is as it appears with the Department or those trying to gain their favor." His voice was dark.

"You don't like the Department? Doesn't your uncle work for them?"

"What do you know of my uncle?" His tone became unreadable.

"Nothing? He's some kind of hunter?"

Dare laughed.

My uncertainty increased.

He held up a hand and the paper dragon landed in his palm. With a twist of his wrist, the dragon disappeared from view. A half-smile remained on his face as he tucked his empty hands into his pockets. The dark silver of his control cuff flirted with the edge of the black pocket. "Thank you for him."

"You're welcome," I said softly, slightly embarrassed still. I liked making things for friends and watching their resulting smiles. But before this I had never given something to someone who made my heart race.

As we emerged from the Midlands, the group of Junior Department stooges were standing near Kratos. Ever since I had identified the posture and watchful gazes of the group, I had noticed at least one "watcher" near the Battle Building. It made it harder to practice in the simulation rooms with Draeger. Anything that made me noticeable at this point could have grave repercussions.

But this time, all their gazes focused on a single point, all on Dare. One stooge nodded to another with no words exchanged. They weren't the open, companion-like gazes of people hoping to recruit an extremely powerful mage when he graduated. They were sharklike—circling.

I gripped my bag tensely. Warlords and plans. "They watch you."

"Always." He looked at me, and there was something devilish in his gaze, inviting me in. "That's part of the fun. Meet here at sunup." He walked toward the Battle Building with all of the Junior Department gazes following his every step.

Floored, I watched him too, and the carefully constructed view of Alexander Dare that I had carried with me last term shattered.

Chapter Nineteen

RUMBLINGS

MEETING AT SUNRISE was not my forte, but my anticipation for rounds with Dare took on a new edge, and a different sort of excitement.

Dare's personal group of five—Dare, Lox, Ramirez, Straught, and Greene—and each of the five of us shadowing them, spent two hours at sunrise tromping around campus, examining everything from the perimeter wards the Department had placed on the Eighteenth Circle to the popular henges on Top Campus. Whereas Dare had assigned me to watching ports and paying attention to how the magic activated, the others were placed in charge of different tasks.

We were then to teach our assigned task to the group.

That went a little less well. Peters, in particular, was irritating about the whole thing, trying his best not to address me at all, or to patronizingly offer me his information on reporting protocol. In return, I tried not to feel satisfaction when he jumped at every small movement in his peripheral vision.

Junior Department eyes focused intently upon our group whenever we passed an enclave. They keenly tracked the movements of every combat mage—even Camille Straught, who was firmly part of the magicists' social set.

Camille Straught, in turn, watched me.

Information imparted by Dare in the group session was without the dimensional edge that his instructions in our solo sessions held—and I listened more attentively to what he was not saying to the group. Aloof and superior, he offered none of the personal anecdotes or tricks that he had shared with me.

That made a strange impression on me, and I questioned my interpretation of the events. It seemed as if Dare didn't care about the other four Justice Squad members in the group, even though he kept firmly demanding that I practice and pay attention to how to impart information to a group at large.

After the two hours were up, the combat mages went off to raid, pillage, practice, or protect something—they hadn't specified which—and the five of us trudged back up the mountain, thoroughly bedraggled.

"The Troop arrives in a few weeks, thank Magic," one of the Justice Squad members said.

"Then we can stop going along with this madness," another grouched. "The combat mages are insane this year. I didn't sign up for this."

"And some of us certainly shouldn't be here," Peters said.

I rolled my eyes and continued following after them, all of us heading to the dorms as the rest of campus rose to begin the day.

There was something special about sunrise. I just preferred to experience it behind closed eyelids.

The thought suspended as the world slowed around me.

No.

Shouting broke out across the grounds, jarringly, and three mages who had been watching us just moments before sprinted past and into the henge we had all been heading toward. They disappeared through an arch, and the other squad members hurried after them.

Returned to motion more quickly this time, I fished my reader from my bag and debated whether I should run after them while I read. I had turned my hologram setting off after the horrific, looping images of Cadmiat, so only stark text greeted me now—"Secret Department installation obliterated!"

Raphael had been silent for too long.

"Thunderstorm of pain," Mike muttered five minutes into Layer Politics.

I tried to keep my shaking unnoticeable in the midst of a thousand people sitting on the edges of their seats in order to hear our professor enthusiastically share the latest on what was happening.

Professor Harrow put forth all of the rumors and theories about the destruction of the secret Department installation. Fresh news with fevered hypotheses of "open war!" and fearful whispers of "Origin Magic!" liberally spread through the uncertain and on-edge audience.

Fueling the fear, a series of unseasonal tornadoes had wiped through a section of the Midwest United States in the First Layer as a direct result. That news just exacerbated my shaking, but at least other people looked equally as unsteady as I felt.

The pictures of the destruction were full-on crazy. A before picture contained a normal looking town that must have been hiding the installation underground. The after picture showed an entire five-mile cube of space...gone. As if a giant monster had taken a humungous, square bite, then swallowed the evidence.

Time to reset the leash clock. But I had very few data points, and I was working against time.

"Discuss the repercussions of the installation's destruction. How will a regulatory body, without a body, respond? How do you think they should respond? What about the responsibilities of other nations? Who do we look to? Do you side with more security or more freedom? Do we look all the way back to the disaster that happened at Salietrex? Discuss."

He clapped his hands and our seats whirled, and Neph was lost again, even though she'd been sandwiched between us. Her seat zipped out and whirled to a muse cluster.

Will's shoulders drooped with mine as we watched her seat fling itself far from ours. My gaze caught Asafa's at a table near to Neph's and he gave me a wide grin as we both realized we were in class together. I gave him a thumbs-up and the signal for "tonight" that I had seen others use on campus—a circle and upward motion. He signaled back in the affirmative before his attention was grabbed by his group's moderator.

I needed to get my hands on that controller, now more than ever. I would end this madness. Full steam ahead.

"Ferals are the reason. And what happened at Salietrex is a prime example."

My attention snapped back to my group, which unfortunately, included the reedy stooge from the Midlands, a second boy who frequently followed me, and Bellacia, who was seated next to me. She gave the reedy boy an encouraging smile.

"Go ahead, Keiren. Elaborate," Bellacia said to him. "Salietrex happened eight years ago and escalated the current conflict."

"Verisetti used three ferals to wreak the destruction. Killed five thousand mages that day, mostly civilians."

My heart beat like a hammer in my chest.

"The Third Layer bastards can't do it on their own. Sure, we all know there are second and third generation mages in the Second Layer who pretend to have immigrated fully, ones who still ally secretly with the Third." Keiren shrugged, a vindictive little smirk on his face. "But they are always tracked. Right, Peoples?" He turned to Delia.

Delia looked a little scary as she silently observed Keiren and picked deliberately at her blue-and-brown scarf with her sharply lacquered fingertips.

I stared at her. Delia kept up with the Second Layer Magicist crowd. I'd thought that was because they were friends. But maybe it was because she had to.

Keiren smirked at Delia. "Tracked and neutered nicely."

"Now, Keiren—" Bellacia started to say in a tone of parental disappointment.

"You should watch yourself," Mike said, sounding bored, even though I could tell that he was clearly angry. "Some of the families you are referring to are quite powerful and have proved their loyalty to the Second Layer twenty times over."

Keiren smiled, falsely. "It's the new, unknown entities we need to fear anyway. The ones who slip by."

"Sure, all eight of them." Mike sounded bored, "What happened at Salietrex was a tragedy. But ferals don't automatically become terrorists."

"There are far more than eight," Keiren said, and the other stooge nodded in agreement like an irritating shadow.

"Scary, different, new! Help!" Mike gave a fake shiver. It earned him a scowl from Keiren and a burst of affection from me.

"Ferals are new."

"Everyone is new at some point—mages awaken at different ages," Mike said pointedly.

"But the young get trained early. They become part of our society legally and acceptably. Their edge gets cleansed away and their views conform to society's."

Essentially, he was saying acceptable mages got brainwashed. Why had I taken this class?

"And yet you don't believe the Third Layer refugees who came here decades ago have conformed," Mike said casually.

"I'm questioning their conformity," Keiren bit out.

Mike nodded. "Of course. It's a lot easier to pinpoint who needs to disappear during secondary school when everyone is loaded down with aptitude tests."

Get me out of here!

"That is what the conspiracists would have you believe." Keiren sneered. "Before sixteen, one's magic is containable and still trainable. After sixteen—"

"After sixteen, what? You're a monster automatically? Can't be taught?" Mike's arms crossed in clearly dismissive body language.

Keiren smoothed his sneer into a cracked smile. "Statistically, ferals are more likely to become rare mage types. I dislike most of their magic because it is dangerous and explosive. And ferals come in thinking they don't need a cuff or require restrictions. They feel they can do great things, change things. But we don't need change. We are already the best just the way we are."

Bellacia nodded regally to that, not interjecting her verbal opinion into an advancing discussion, but clearly stating her beliefs.

I exchanged a quick glance with Will. Individuals who were anti-progress; always lovely.

"That's quite an opinion," Mike said, obviously willing to field the discussion for the rest of us.

Delia examined her nails and looked bored. But I could see the way the edges of her eyes were tightly creased under the fall of her dark bangs.

"Keiren's points have validity. The older a feral awakens, the more likely that said mage will possess an unusual set of skills," Bellacia said lightly. "And that they will be less inculcated in our ways. Their control is always quite poor at the beginning too. They blow themselves up rather easily." She waved a graceful hand through the air. "But a feral who manages to assume control and become part of our society, is welcomed, of course. We don't turn away our own." She gave a beautiful smile.

"You register and track them instead," Mike said.

She speared him with a smile. "Registration is for the good of all. What harm does it do to set to paper one's skills and background? I proudly list each of mine."

"That's because everything you do, and are, is at the top of the list," Mike said easily, with an affable, returned smile.

Delia looked like she'd swallowed a lemon. Whole.

"You are too kind," Bellacia said demurely. "But Sirenic mages give others pause. No one likes to have someone around who can unduly influence them. The same as the muses, who are regulated through their communities and bound to the quality standards they must meet. All of which make the registry valuable. I registered freely and happily. Everyone should."

"Not everyone wants to be tagged and followed," Mike said pointedly.

She tilted her head like an exquisite bird. "What is your focus?"

"Weather."

"A celebrated discipline. We rely on your skills to keep us safe, happy, and provided for. Don't you wish others to engage in the same practices?"

Mike smiled. Some of his teeth showed. "I rely on people to make good decisions, just as I rely on our governments to do the same."

"Then you must see that equality for everyone, knowing what everyone is—their threats and potential—is a grand decision."

"We must agree to disagree."

"Oh, but no, I don't think that we need disagree at all." She gave him a brilliant smile. "Let's discuss it further."

"You would shackle all those who don't support your views. Anyone out of the norm."

I saw Delia touch her bracelet—the one that stopped her from dealing out suggestion enchantments. Except... Tracked and neutered, Keiren had said. I stared at Delia's bracelet, and something appallingly close to rage replaced my urge to flee.

"Unusual mages are to be celebrated," Bellacia said to Mike, their conversation continuing without input from the rest of us.

"And collared."

"Only if necessary," she said demurely.

I looked at Bellacia closely, trying to see through the haze of anger that was enveloping me. There was a distinct possibility that she believed her own words.

"I have no collar. And I am unusual and registered," she said.

My haze grew and I felt my cuff contract as magic sparked unconsciously, seeking a target. Delia looked sharply at me and dug her fingernails into my wrist. The sudden intense pain abruptly made all of my thoughts—subconsciously and consciously—switch to OW!

"And rich and protected. And charming." Mike's smile was wide at Bellacia.

She laughed. "So kind of you. Why—"

"We are supposed to be talking about the destruction of the installation, are we not?" Delia asked harshly. Her fingernails were still painfully digging into my skin, but our hands were hidden from view by the table top.

Bellacia looked at her in censure. "Delia."

Delia smiled tightly. "I don't want to be penalized when we have to do a write-up on our class discussion and haven't covered any of the assigned topics."

Bellacia's smile was perfectly polite, but her gaze hardened. "Of course. Let us discuss the Third Layer terrorists who are trying to end our way of life and take our lives."

An hour later, I pushed out of the room, horrified and drained.

Delia smiled tightly at me and started down campus.

"Wait!"

She turned. Her expression was carefully blank. "Yes, Ren?"

I reached out a finger to touch her bracelet. "I will figure out how to get rid of this," I whispered. It was a vow and my mind was already whirling with possibilities from the leech books I had been devouring.

"No." She pulled her bound wrist against her chest, her expression both pained and fierce. "No. I chose it. It...it keeps me safe. I couldn't attend here otherwise. It's only for a few more years. You have no idea—" She shook her head.

"It doesn't matter what my family has done for this layer over the past seventy years. We will always be suspect. I play the game, though." Her expression took on an edged smile. "And sometimes I flatten the game."

"But—"

"No." She grabbed my wrist and a tendril of magic wound over my skin. "You will do nothing. I want this. But know that you wanting to help means everything to me."

She walked away, and, bereft of direction, I let her.

"Can I just not go back?" I asked wearily as Will and Mike drew beside me. "To class, ever?"

Will nodded vigorously, his expression the one he wore when he was considering how to implement a tricky solution.

Mike shook his head. "It would be worse if you dropped. We'll figure out how to pull you through. If you get past those crasseetars, you're free."

One thing was for sure—there was nothing we could do about Bellacia, but we needed to keep

Keiren and the other boy out of our group. And we needed Neph back in.

Chapter Twenty

CATERPILLAR FRIENDSHIPS

DRAEGER PUT ME through my paces in the simulation room, then I uploaded an anatomy chip to his programming in order to finish sketching and testing the designs for Asafa and Patrick's game. I had spent a hilarious previous session grappling with the game characters' physical viability. My first mistakes in creating monsters with magic had produced ones unable to move without tripping over too-long claws or that couldn't maintain balance with their monstrous beaks.

"Squirrel tips, Cadet," Draeger barked. "You can't make a tiger with that large of a forked tail!"

Those had made for some amusing iterations. Creating monsters while making Draeger swear relieved a lot of pent up stress.

With the three dimensional abilities of the room, I manipulated the last beast, then sketched my changes onto the paper. The simulation rooms were awesome, but didn't save true creation. It was more like dreaming—I still had to get the images on paper and into life.

Saf and Trick had been pretty particular in what they wanted and had given me skeletal sketches for much of it. But the art had been missing that vital component of life. Breathing it into the designs was pure pleasure. I couldn't wait to show them the results.

As I packed up the papers, Draeger barked at me to give him another recounting of what had happened today.

By the time I was finished, my left sleeve was rolled up to my elbow, and I was staring at my cuff as I leaned against the wall. I was thinking of Delia and the choice she made to be tagged and tracked, I was thinking of the weight of freedom and fear.

"There's a thing somewhere within me. Pulling on me," I said, shaking my head. "I'm scared." It wasn't something I had acknowledged to anyone else. The word sounded foreign in my mouth.

"Raccoon paws, Cadet! You are not trying hard enough." His crisp projection paced angrily around the simulation room. Draeger didn't respond well to fear. He beat fear into submission with anger and action.

The image of his shaved head and barrel chest was comforting, even while his overly large muscles flexed as if he were going to pummel me. When I'd purchased a mentor simulation, my subconscious had picked characteristics that it had thought I needed at the time.

The real Draeger, on whom he was based, had been a soldier in life. Now that I had Dare too, it became very clear I seemed to be collecting drill sergeants.

The thought and sense of Dare connected suddenly to the wall. No! Thinking only, no connection! I snatched back my hand. A ribbon of rich brown to match the room's default color pulled from the wall and attached to my palm.

Panicked, I tried to peel the ribbon away. I should have made Draeger practice auditory defense with me instead of mooning around and complaining. At the auditory thought, another wall ribbon immediately launched toward me, combining with the first.

"Stop poking at Axer, Bella," a familiar female voice said.

I looked wildly around, but no one was in the room with me other than Draeger, whose anger had morphed into half amusement, half exasperation. "You connected to another room, Cadet." Draeger shook his head and muttered one of his many weird animal curses. "You aren't keeping your thoughts straight, but at least this is more entertaining."

I had accidentally connected to Dare in the simulation rooms a few times last term, and Dare had always demolished me and cut the connection in two seconds flat. But that hadn't been Dare's voice.

"But Cami, he's going to win the Combat Games again," another familiar female voice said into the ether of my room. "And he will look lovely on my arm."

Instead of connecting to Dare, I had somehow connected to Bellacia and Camille talking about him. Wow. Seriously, time to exit. I tugged at the strip of magic stuck to the wall. It stubbornly refused to part.

"That tack won't work. He isn't interested in you." Camille Straught's voice was no-nonsense. "He doesn't date. You know that. And he'll flatten you socially, even with your influence, if you continue nagging him this way."

"How unflattering that sounds."

"Agreed," Camille said in a deadpan voice.

I tugged harder, putting one foot against the wall, literally and metaphorically.

"He can't be allowed to run loose. You know that, despite your worrisome fondness for him. You know he needs to be watched." Bellacia's voice was far too light. "They are setting up campus so they will be able to do so. He requires a firm hand and a watchful eye. For his own good, of course."

"Secure him another way then. You aren't going to get him on your arm, and your face is far too lovely to be irreparably scarred trying and failing to use mind control on Sera McEllian's son."

Bellacia laughed, a tinkling sound. "You will always be my favorite. I do so love my skin. I only use the finest of Tinctly's creams on it. Fine. Lox is looking exceptionally well formed this year, and he'll likely win the swords and sorcery part of the competition. He'll make a lovely adornment at Father's ball."

"A far more promising prospect. Especially since he was talking about you the other day."

"There's always Ramirez too." Bellacia's voice was too idle... Wow, she really wielded that thing like a weapon. No response issued from Camille. "Unattached and deadly. He would lend me an air of mystery."

"He doesn't date either," Camille's voice was tight. Their background noise rose in volume from whatever magic they were doing. "Watch that second blast, Bella," Camille called, sounding slightly smug.

I got my panic under control and started unwinding the magic in the attached ribbon—as I should have done from the beginning. It was as if I hadn't learned anything from destroying the entire Shangwei Art Complex last term when I had yanked wards from the walls in my panic.

At the same time, I wondered what Bellacia and Camille were doing in there that they hadn't noticed an intruder. It had to be Bellacia's magic holding the room. Camille would have noticed and squashed me by now, I was pretty sure.

"Someone ought to change Ramirez's dating status," Bellacia said in a singsong way. "Perhaps I should tell Inessa to—"

The ribbon broke free. Whew. Okay, no more thoughts of Dare. The ribbon, looking for completion, wildly shot toward another wall, connecting to a second room with a snap.

No!

The panic had only one moment to form, then I was flat on the ground, cheek pressed to the tiles, arms and legs splayed. The connection had been harshly severed by the person on the other side. I had obviously found the real Dare this time.

I groaned. Draeger chuckled above me in his gruff, holographic way.

"Always amusing, Cadet, when you accidentally connect to a real mage."

Why had my brain picked a mentor simulation that had been a combat mage? "Art mages rule, old man."

"Yes, you are doing a nice impression of a flattened squirrel, art mage. Very dignified."

"I'll end you. Pull out your coding, erase your upgrades, choose the Zen Master guy instead. Just you wait." I pushed slowly upward. "Ow. Bruising." I huffed a short laugh at myself, feeling better. Pity party over. "And I'm the personification of dignity. I will not be convinced otherwise."

A shot of magic swirled around my head, then abruptly poked me in the side.

I gave a high-pitched scream, landed on my rear, then shot a bolt of magic wildly toward an unknown shadow on the wall. Before the spell could hit, the walls turned into dense forest and the shadow slipped behind trees, easily evading the blast.

Someone had connected to my room.

Draeger's voice boomed in laughter as my mind made him invisible in order to free up visual space. I could walk or shoot through Draeger, but in a fighting simulation, unless he was actively an opponent or obstacle, he would unnecessarily draw some of my attention.

My room's connection capabilities were obviously wide open in the wake of my mistake with Camille and Bellacia. Either that or I had left a ribbon open to one specific person.

I looked at where the shadow had first shown itself. The magic of the entry point was fading, but the connection was still visible. Stunning ultramarine. I groaned. Alexander Dare had connected with my room, perhaps recognizing my magic after flattening me.

Magic poked me in the side again, almost mischievously. I stumbled back a step and looked around. The simulation rooms were incredible and somehow the floor either ceased to exist or became an omnidirectional mover, allowing me to walk in any direction without actually getting closer to a wall. I could—and had, under Draeger's command—run for miles without hitting anything.

Another poke made me swear. But this time I followed the magic. Traces, indeed. I focused and Dare popped into view, grinning down at me from up on a branch.

"You called?" Dare said, his voice almost lazy—completely different from how he had been before baiting the stooges and blowing the Department's device.

"No. I most certainly did not."

The dirt beneath my feet moved abruptly, and I fell back on my rear. I could see the shadow of a small dragon flying through the simulated jungle sky. I blinked at it, mind connecting the image to my thoughts. The change in Dare's attitude had occurred before the blown device. It had been when I'd given him the dragon.

"What kind of sorry civilian accidentally attaches to a combat mage in a battle simulation room?" Dare said.

Combat mages obviously had the same sense of humor, because I could feel Draeger's answering amusement surrounding me.

"One prone to accidents," I muttered. Magic poked me again.

"I usually don't bother to check the identity of accidental intruders, but imagine my surprise when after feeling a vague echo of the trespasser, I checked and found you."

His magic poked me a fourth time as I tried to stand, then a fifth as I stumbled.

"Okay, that's it," I muttered, finally on my feet.

I twisted my hands and the forest turned into a three dimensional black-and-white block sketch that completely surrounded us. I didn't allow him time to react to the change before I whipped my hand down, redrawing the black line that he was perched upon, and yanking it down like a trap door.

He fell to the floor, but landed in a crouch, one hand on the black and white tiles. His grin turned into something far more delighted and bloodthirsty.

"All of those doodles are good for something after all, Crown?" A twirling staff appeared in his hands and he drove it sharply into the floor, breaking the tiles beneath me and sending me into an abyss.

In free fall, I quickly redrew lines beneath me into a tunnel, then dropped myself Escher-style from the ceiling. I landed back on the floor, which was once more intact, and crouched with my virtual pencil in hand.

Magic blasted toward me and I drew a shield, making the magic bounce. He caught the ricochet and twisted it, sending it back in ten streams. I channeled everything I remembered from the sketch world I had accidentally trapped Will within, and then began drawing in broad strokes, changing the environment around both of us and making the streams hit and ricochet back toward him.

He laughed and let me change the environment, sidestepping my attacks or catching my thrown magic in his palm. His eyes keenly tracked me, watching my movements as he defended against them, then with one swipe, he shattered the line of magic I was using to draw.

The backlash threw me back a step. He had watched, then pinched my advantage at the root. "Oh, it's on," I said.

I launched myself into a box on the floor, collapsed the box into a flat plane around me, then rotated it through empty space to form on a different wall. He turned just in time to catch the dart I threw, transformed it into a glowing ball of sapphire, then tossed it at the ground, falling deliberately into the resulting hole in mimicked manipulation. Crap, he learned fast.

I pulled the wall around me, trapping myself in the white space.

I was so out of my depth. I had never deliberately connected to someone else in one of the other rooms. I had accidentally connected to other rooms—mostly Dare's—a handful of times, but had always been kicked out instantaneously. I had never explored the vast awesomeness that could be produced from one's own head in simulation. Whether any of this was possible in the real world or not didn't matter. Adrenaline and excitement collided in an overwhelming surge.

Hiding within my own manipulation, I tried to silence my quick breathing. After a moment, a small chewing noise registered. Paper tore above me, and the black-and-white head of a papered dragon poked through. Using a projection of my own creation to track me... Oh, it was truly on.

Black fire blew from its mouth and I barely twisted and wrung myself from the paper in time. I landed flat on the floor. A booted foot pressed down on my back.

Okay, not so much on as over.

A dangerous smile smirked down at me. "Again."

After an hour of getting flattened by Dare in increasingly crazy manipulations, I had come to the distinct realization that even while he laughed, Dare was deadlier than I'd seen before or been led to believe. If I thought on it too long, the question of how he had not killed the Bone Beast immediately last term became quite a frightening memory. My subconscious magic and black magic experiments had created something that formidable? Kind of terrifying.

Dare watched everything I did, then used it against me in the next second. So quickly did he convert strategy and moves into counter attack, that I was left wondering how. Ugh. He would have been thick as thieves with Christian in the non-magic world—or in this one, if we'd grown up here.

He requisitioned my hour directly afterward—which had been my free time—and dragged me, limping, around campus with him on his patrol before healing me with a smirk and taking off to God knew where.

I shook off the weirdness of the possible revelation that we might be forming a friendship and dragged myself back to the dorm. A stupid grin painted my face and I couldn't get it off.

Before I could throw myself on my bed, close my eyes, and think up something witty with which to amuse Olivia, I noticed movement on her desk.

A paper caterpillar was inching its way along. A caterpillar, not an egg.

I stared at it for a long moment, stricken, then touched the wards. There was a slight tingle of sickly brown attached to Olivia's health thread, but far lighter than what it had been after the previous attack.

"It ate the magic," Olivia said, without looking up, but obviously aware of the direction of my thoughts. "I opened my mother's note and the egg flew right out of my bag, swallowed the note's magic, then burst into that." She pointed at the inching insect.

"Did it? How strange," I said innocently, trying to hide my concern.

"Ren."

"Yes?"

Olivia was still looking at her desk, her gaze blank and unseeing. "Thank you."

"Absolutely my pleasure." I walked to my bed and changed out items from my bag, giving her some privacy. "You ready to do some serious justice-mongering tonight?"

She cleared her throat. "Yes." Her voice was strong. Good.

"Awesome. Dinner first?" I needed the calories and the renewal energy of the cafeteria.

She nodded.

"And I, uh, was thinking we might make a stop after service?" I shifted on my feet, hoping she wouldn't change moods and kill me.

"To see Leandred?" She looked darkly resigned.

"Uh, no. I wouldn't do that to you."

"Well, where to, then?" she said, motioning for me to hurry up. "My sense of disapproval is awaiting activation."

I grinned at her dry tone and hurried to the door. Maybe I'd survive after all.

She slipped the caterpillar carefully into her bag and I adjusted my wavering tally.

Protection of friends: Restarting from 0

We were both exhausted at the end of our two hours of service, but it had been an invigorating and productive service session. New clients for Olivia and several new contacts for me—a communications mage who could hack any frequency, an alchemist who could exchange one metal for another, and a music conductor who could change the fabric of the air using sound!

There had been a few dull calls, of course. A girl casting a restricted love spell, a few people imbibing things they weren't supposed to be imbibing, two benign room explosions, and the relocation of an entire school of wild grouper to one of the science labs.

Cleaning up enormous, flopping fish had turned tedious after the first few fun zaps with Justice Toad. Lab accidents were normally under the dominion of the class professor, and not in our jurisdiction. But sneaking in after hours to use equipment in order to enchant the entire female population of Excelsine? That fell to us. That they had produced a school of groupers instead of a school of groupies...well, such subpar spellcasting deserved special punishment...a firesnake-skin-collecting sort of punishment.

Testing Olivia's patience near the end, we made a Level Three call to Constantine, who had invoked savage retribution on the girl who had cast the restricted love spell earlier. Why was it always Constantine they were trying to enchant? He might be the king of all that was sensually dark and brooding, but he was the emperor of revenge. I knew for a fact he had a device that downgraded his offense level, which meant he had enacted some serious Level Four vengeance.

The Neutralizer Squad had been called for the girl, so we hadn't seen the results of Constantine's revenge, but I had a mind to go find her again, then shake her with a few "Seriously? What were you thinking?" types of statements thrown in.

Our final service call was to Delia, who had successfully created a weaving pattern capable of hypnotizing the wearer into doing her bidding for a period of five minutes after donning the woven fabric.

Not really a problem—until she had tested it on an unknown subject and made the girl do her laundry.

For someone so determined to rule the world one day, Olivia was capable of a pretty deep well of disapproval, and Delia seemed to enjoy stepping on all of her buttons. I thought of Delia's words about Olivia and Olivia's mom. I wondered if they'd had some magicist war against each other in their previous school. I'd ask later.

Olivia left the punishment to me and I gave Delia laundry duty at the Fashion Design Center. I was pretty sure Delia had sought the punishment, after all—she got the best ideas when she went through the laundry at the Design Center and mentally mixed enchantments together as she sorted items.

Because if Delia had been trying to do something nefarious, it would have been far worse than making someone do her laundry—tracking bracelet or not.

Delia winked at me as we left, looking completely revitalized, as if the fiasco of Politics hadn't happened.

Olivia and I logged out of service and headed toward Dorm Five.

"So tell me finally, what is the purpose of this visit we are undertaking?" Olivia asked, tiredly and reluctantly following me.

"I need you to make sure I don't sign a faulty contract."

She frowned. "A contract? Why didn't you give me a copy to review?"

"Because it is going to be verbal."

Olivia gave me a look deep from her disapproval well. "I'm not going to like this."

"Not in the least." I fished out the sketches I had made and hastily stuck them into a folder.

Olivia looked at the drawings as I moved them. "Art Expressionists Club?" She looked puzzled.

"Gamers. Fun guys."

Patrick opened the door, his eyes bright. "Welcome!" He swept his hands through the air, inviting us inside. "Please, enter our humble abode."

I whistled at the interior of their room. It currently looked like something straight out of a sci-fi dream—projections and holographic images danced on every surface, tests ran, and code scrawled. "Nice." I handed Trick the folder then poked at one of the images in the air.

In the midst of the chaos and equipment, Olivia held herself stiffly and regally, coolly waiting for an explanation.

"We got in a few tests tonight," Patrick said. "No alerts issued, but thanks for telling us about your service time, Ren. Fantastically useful."

Olivia gave me a deeply unimpressed look.

"We'll be just a minute," Asafa said. He smiled out at us from where he was situated under a large worktable hooking up wires with magic pliers. "Have a seat. Trick forgets his courtesies when excited."

"I do no such thing." Trick hastily cleared off space on the small couch in the midst of the chaos.

Dorm Five was laid out in a slightly different fashion from Twenty-five. Larger rooms accommodated a communal work area for the two students sharing the space, but the bathroom was shared with a room of students on the other side. I was a fan of our personal bathroom, but extra workspace was always a good thing. Saf and Trick had chosen to convert their extra living space into a gaming area—with a couch, two reclining chairs, a coffee table, and numerous screens and projector devices—to the surprise of pretty much no one, I'd bet.

The space was currently drowning in magic and tech.

Olivia looked dubiously at the couch, but sat down regally with her legs crossed at the ankles and to the side. I energetically dropped next to her, right foot tucked under my left thigh. We both looked over the back of the couch while Patrick opened the folder. Asafa finished his machinations under the large table, his hair sticking out from his head without a single drooping spike.

"These are..." Patrick trailed off, flipping through my pages. "Saf, wait until you see these."

He put his hand on the manticore-like beast that was snarling and pacing on the page, and pulled a visual duplicate of the animated drawing into the air. His other hand circled the creature, pulling a string of code from one of the displays and making it encircle the image.

The string of aerial code bloomed into a suspended three-dimensional scene with a jungle landscape. Several associated animals populated the landscape.

My beast moved in jerky motions within the new setting, but each movement grew more fluid as Patrick tweaked the circling code.

I wanted to try my hand at that. Desperately.

A whistle sounded from under the table. "Look at the movement. It's learning every time you poke the scene. Sentience, in a completely new construct." Asafa's gaze turned to me. "You did that in two days?"

"They are just drawings with a bit of imagination." I had done enough monster artwork in my lifetime—and Christian and I had always created a backstory for each design—that it was second nature now to mentally assign complete stories to my creations.

And now my magic made those imaginings real. Like Guard Rock... I hadn't consciously chosen his personality—my magic had made it happen and given him free will by pulling on the imaginative practice I had used for years, consciously and subconsciously.

Asafa didn't say anything, but his pliers tapped thoughtfully on his chest. Olivia stiffened next to me, and I automatically sent out a pulse of reassurance along her thread.

We all watched Patrick work for a moment as he pulled one of the robot designs into the air. The monster and robot started fighting under Patrick's manipulations.

"Will would love this," I said to Olivia, trying to distract her from whatever was aggravating her. "Only his love of physical machines must have stopped him from being a twenty-four-hour gamer."

"Will Tasky?" Asafa cocked his head, pliers working steadily again and emitting little sparks of magic. "I saw you sitting with him in politics. Had a mech class with him last year and we got into a bit of quality control trouble. Haven't seen much of him this year. Tell him to stop by any time. Could always use more testers." He gave me a wide grin and a wink.

I grinned back. Having Christian as a brother had made me adore charmers.

Asafa's fingers flashed and energy surged along the wires and connections under the table, then everything disappeared from view with a pop.

Olivia huffed a breath, but relaxed a bit. "Do you have any written terms I can look over?"

Asafa, still on his back, sent a considering glance Olivia's way, charming grin turning into something more serious. Patrick's eyes brightened as he looked at her while his fingers still danced in the images. "The legal gal! We've heard many tales of your wit and prowess."

"Trick is practicing lines for the game. Ignore him." Asafa twirled his tool and pushed out from under the table, his eyes never leaving Olivia as he rose. "Olivia Price?"

"Present," Olivia said crisply.

He passed the pliers from right hand to left and back again, considering.

"Is that a problem?" There was a dark undercurrent in her voice.

He looked between us for a moment, then smiled slowly at her. "No."

If I didn't know Olivia so well, I might have missed the momentarily taken aback expression that crossed her features before her cool facade was once more in place. "Then shall we get started?" she asked crisply.

I wanted to continue watching Patrick work, but I couldn't use Olivia's time indiscriminately, so I nodded.

Patrick pulled a string of code from a red box on the worktable and encompassed the aerial display, then threw the entire thing at the box. It swept inside and emitted a little chirping noise, saving his progress.

Patrick and Asafa looked at each other for a long moment, holding a silent conversation, then both nodded.

The initial terms were easily laid out. "This folder of Ren Crown's art in exchange for Asafa Frey and Patrick O'Leary's latest and greatest compulsive game controller." Patrick held up both items, one in each hand, to allow contractual magic to circle and assign them as the contract's properties. Asafa stood next to him, passing his pliers between his hands.

The contractual magic hovered in the air, awaiting my response.

Olivia's fingers clamped around my wrist, halting me from agreeing to the terms.

Trick's mouth curled and his eyes lit joyously. "Ah, excellent. Saf, you ready?" Trick waved a hand so that the couch turned ninety degrees and two chairs popped into existence across from us with a table in the middle.

Asafa sat in the chair next to his excited roommate. "Yes. Go."

"Negotiation in progress," Patrick said. The contractual magic spread over our four heads, hovering a few feet above, waiting.

"No decisions until the agreed upon words are uttered by each participant—name first, then the word agrees," Olivia said briskly.

"Agreed."

"Agreed."

Olivia's fingers pressed briefly and I repeated the word, "Agreed."

Olivia held out her hand for the controller and Patrick handed it to her. Spells of all sorts twisted out from her fingers and fell over the device, feeling for its secrets. I could tell when she got to the compulsion aspects, because she shot me a look that said we would be having a "talk" later.

"This is your best design?" she asked them.

"Newest and brightest!"

Then, like a switch had been flipped, terms flew back-and-forth in machine-gun fashion.

"The controller, four hours of personal command, upgrades for anything you produce on a controller of any sort in the next six months, and a seven percent stake," Olivia said.

"The controller as is and a fanlee," Patrick replied. I wondered what a fanlee was, but didn't take the time to translate it, as Olivia's facial expression said she already knew.

"Trite. The controller, upgrades as previously described, and a ten percent stake."

"The art, plus fifteen more pieces in the next month in exchange for the controller, any upgrades on it specifically, and a three percent stake."

"My previous terms modified to a seven percent stake," Olivia said.

"Three and a half."

"Bump back to ten, then."

"You wound me terribly. Four."

"You shouldn't play at using a sword, then. Nine, and the four hours back on the table."

"My heart. Battered, fair lady. Twenty instead of fifteen, the four hours back, five percent."

A small smile hovered on Asafa's lips as the two batted terms in increasingly quick fashion. Patrick looked as if Christmas had come twice in as many weeks.

They started speaking faster and it took great effort for me to keep track of "previous terms" and "modifications" as they morphed and changed into nothing that resembled the initial transaction. Anything that wasn't expressly addressed got rolled in automatically to the next sally. Contractual magic was wildly outside of my experience and skill set. If called upon to say anything at the moment, I'd be dead meat.

Asafa said nothing, but every once in a while when Patrick paused, I saw Asafa tip his head. They were talking to each other via frequency, then.

"Eight," Olivia said.

"Six."

"Seven," she said.

"Patrick O'Leary agrees."

"Asafa Frey agrees."

Olivia tipped her head to me, but never looked away from her opponents.

"Uh, Ren Crown agrees," I said.

The contract magic fell, as if the strings holding it up had been cut. It settled over the four of us.

Patrick handed me the controller and kept the folder. Olivia rose and nodded sharply, then strode toward the door, her heels clicking on the floor.

"Great." I smiled, a little uncertain as to what I had actually agreed to, but the controller was now in my hand, so at least I had gotten that. "Talk to you guys soon?"

Patrick's smile was blinding and Asafa nodded with a charming grin.

"Yes. And bring her back any time, art mage."

Art mage was infinitely better than the alternative. And their expressions spoke truth. They wanted Olivia to return. I already liked them both—they embodied my kind of mischief—but their acceptance of Olivia made a huge impact on my emotions. I felt the beginnings of connection tendrils wrap out toward them.

"Great. We'll be on service duty tomorrow for two hours as well."

Both of their gazes narrowed, their smiles widening. Plotting. "Good to know."

Olivia gave me a dark look at the door as I hurried through. We headed up the stairs to the top track of the Magiaduct.

"It's not a secret we have to keep, as to when we are on duty," I said, trying to reassure her. "It's a club thing, helping out other members, and you are becoming an honorary member now, you know," I said cheerfully, as her expression turned pained. "Patron defender of mischief makers."

"We will be discussing this entire venture, Ren," Olivia said as she looked at the controller in my hand. "What was that idiotic brain of yours thinking?"

"Hey, you loved that." We strolled along the track, under the early, star-filled night sky. "I saw your face. I know you."

Something odd and yearning passed over her expression, then firmed back up. "It was an adequate transaction. I shudder to think what would have happened if you hadn't had the sense to bring me along. Honestly, Ren, an O'Leary. They'll lure you with a rainbow and promises of gold, then fleece you blind while you search."

Patrick wasn't short, but he had mischievous eyes that lent themselves to the appearance of puckish deviltry. "Are you telling me Patrick's some sort of leprechaun?"

She snorted. "Don't be silly."

I hadn't really been joking. Not in this world.

Olivia's stride shortened, allowing me to keep up more easily. "The negotiation, while briefly invigorating, was to our favor. O'Leary let his admiration show verbally before the negotiations began. They both made positive comments when they could easily have kept any positives silent via frequency. Frequencies are easy to hack except when under room wards shared between the two frequency users that are connecting. Insults are the normal gambit when first looking at a bargaining chip. Neither was willing to offer any offense to your product, which means they'll want more of your designs and are willing to let you know you have some power."

"Great! I like them and I want to make more. I'm totally going to play those games when I get some free time." I'd have free time. Some day.

Olivia rolled her eyes, but she said nothing further until we reached our room.

"That." She pointed at the controller as soon as we were under the security of our own room's wards. "Explain. Now."

"I can," I said, nodding.

"Good. Go."

"I have an explanation."

"And I'm waiting for it."

I tried to give her a winning smile. It came out as a cringe instead. "Constantine and I are going to use it. To compel magic, not a faceless victim, I swear." I was not faceless. And we were going to put in safeguards.

"Ren…"

"Olivia," I said brightly.

Her lips pressed together. "How?"

I rubbed the back of my neck. I knew how poorly this would go over—anything to do with Constantine went over poorly—but it was better for all of us to be on the same page. Sharing the knowledge would make it safer for everyone—a lesson I'd learned well last term. "We are going to make a series of leeches, trying them out on me one-by-one, then we will attempt one that works from afar," I said into my fist, speaking quickly, "in order to reverse engineer or undercut the existing one."

"No."

"I'm serious. That's truly the plan."

"That's not what I'm saying no to, Ren!"

"Yeah." I tightened my ponytail and didn't look at her. The "try each one on me" and "from afar" parts hadn't been part of my last presentation to her on the topic.

"You are not invincible."

"I know." No matter what I was capable of, or how much better I became from training, there was always, always, danger. Terrible danger, to me and to others. It was impossible to forget the feeling of my magic caged beneath my skin. Or of it being ripped away, out of my control.

"But I have very little time, Liv," I said quietly. "The installation that was destroyed today—I don't know how fast Raphael can recharge, and what might be next? I have to do this."

She said nothing for long moments, and I wished I could read her mind in that moment. She shook her head. "There is nothing I can say to dissuade you from this course of action. You have made up your mind to trust Leandred. You trust too easily." The corners of her eyes tightened.

"Constantine says that too."

She zapped me through the room's wards.

I rubbed my arm, and couldn't stop the smile that was tugging my lips. "That just tickles now, you know."

She sent another, but I avoided the second zap with my sweet new magic dodgeball moves, courtesy of Dare and the simulation room.

I saw a small smile tugging her lips too.

"But seriously, thanks for worrying, Liv. Will is working with us and he'll tell you about it as soon as he gets here. You don't need to imagine horrible, sketchy things happening in Constantine's lair."

"Too late," she said darkly.

Will and Neph took that moment to arrive. Neph looked between the two of us, taking in Olivia's tight expression and my eager one. Neph sighed.

Will leaped onto my desk chair and started spinning. Neph gracefully sat in lotus position on the end of my bed. And Olivia...Olivia outlined what we had just been talking about and worked herself back up to a rant.

"Does no one else think this is a bad idea?" Olivia demanded, looking specifically at Neph. "This project, and the three of them working together? Where is Givens when I actually need him? He'd never allow this."

She was probably right. Mike was pretty protective of Will. However, he was outside of this set of secrets that only Olivia, Will, Neph, Constantine, Raphael, and I knew.

"Leandred trusts no one, but he obviously treats Ren differently," Neph said soothingly.

"That's the problem," Olivia said darkly.

"And Will is perfectly capable of spotting deception," Neph said, however, her voice wasn't quite as strong on that point.

"I'm in the room, you know," Will said as he whirled in my chair. He managed to get in an eye roll exchange with me. "I do have some self-control not to get caught up in a project completely."

Neph and Olivia stared at him without response.

He sighed and stopped the chair's rotation. "Ren, tell them we'll give them nightly updates."

"Full updates," I said reassuringly. "With graphs and charts and popcorn."

"Fine. After you agree to a few things. With magic," Olivia said.

Eyes wide, I listened as she outlined a number of rules that started with the phrase, "When with Leandred, I will not…"

Compiling that list took all night.

Chapter Twenty-One
REMINDERS AND PERSUASIONS

THE NEXT AFTERNOON, I strode purposefully to the art vault to meet with Stevens for our Thursday session.

Olivia and I had spent half an hour in our room after my engineering class rehearsing arguments and debate tactics to convince Stevens to increase my paint practice and production schedule. The vault was one of two places on campus that allowed me to touch paint—even store-bought paint—without adding hours to my community service total, and I hoped that presenting my argument in the heart of the vault would make it more compelling.

My overall paint supply was dwindling steadily, and there were three forces actively working against its replenishment. First, in order to produce extraordinary things, I required magical and personal input in my painting supplies—store bought paint was useless to me.

Secondly, because of Marsgrove's restriction on me, I could only make paint in the vault. Although I could use paint in the Midlands, weird things happened when I tried to make it there. The bad kind of weird things—I had nearly blown up both Guard Rock and myself in one attempt. Something about the enveloping chaos of the Midlands sucked contaminated intentions into the mixture. So, I needed the vault, and the vault meant Stevens.

And thirdly, I needed someone with a high degree of materials or creative knowledge to supervise my mixing—Stevens or Raphael.

I had to convince Stevens. And to do so, I needed to let go of caring about how she knew Raphael. I could do that. I could separate.

With renewed vigor and determination, I turned the corner. Stevens was standing in the small clearing in front of the vault door. Her back was to me and she was talking to someone I couldn't yet see.

Debate lines scrolled through my head in a steady litany. I had practiced perfectly reasonable arguments without allowing a hint of emotional turmoil to seep through. I had memorized the kind of arguments that should work on rational, cooler-headed individuals like Stevens and Olivia—arguments presented with logic and thought, and completely alien to my natural inclination to jump in feet first when my brain said that something needed doing.

Taking a moment to listen to the What-Would-Olivia-Do side of my brain was my gift to the world.

I would focus on the paint issue in clear, concise, rational terms. I was prepared. I could do this.

Professor Stevens stepped to the side, and in that split second every nuance, argument, and justification unraveled as the person she was speaking to was revealed.

Helen Price.

Kill.

Horrifying offensive magic swirled inside me. My cuff pulsed painfully. Uncontrolled magic combined with bad intentions viciously activated the latent control properties in the metal. I clutched at it and gritted my teeth. Deep breaths. I struggled to keep my violent thoughts in check.

Olivia's mother was on campus. Chatting with Professor Stevens like old friends.

The media had reported that the Department had called in all free hands to deal with the destruction they had suffered so personally. If their focus had been to find and eradicate the terrorists before, it was at an all-time high now.

So Helen Price was on campus discussing...what?

Whatever it was, she'd no doubt leave a little present for her daughter on her way out.

I stumbled into the copse of trees that circled a series of benches and tables and shakily removed the paper wasp I had created before Engineering. Using it would mess up my plans for the day, but I struck "Pleasing Dare with Magical Prowess" off my list and held the wasp close. The amount of constrained magic wishing to wreak vengeance leaped and morphed into a new, consciously directed command. The wasp had been created specifically to use its senses for close reconnaissance and recording. I had been planning to give it to Dare to use on the Department devices.

But now it was going to recon something else.

The wasp lifted into the air and banked around the copse. I closed my eyes and concentrated on the thread of magic connecting me to my creation. I focused its auditory sense, which I had been practicing with Draeger.

"Yes, Helen." Stevens's voice reflected a combination of irritation and placation. "I do know how to implement a simple spell set."

"If he has contacted you—"

"Then you will be the first to know of it."

"I worry over you, of course." Helen Price's voice was cultured and sharp. A politician's voice. "And only want to make sure you are safe."

"Don't." Stevens's voice went from firmly polite to one of veiled fury. "We both know why you are here."

"Very well, dearest. But I am here for two reasons, actually. I have to send another message to my daughter. She doesn't seem to be receiving them correctly."

Pain burst beneath my cuff as my magic responded to her comment. I grabbed it reflexively, fingers circling the flexible metal manacle.

It was getting harder for me to concentrate on their voices over my need to destroy. I couldn't hear my professor's response. I called my pyramid construct to mind and struggled with my control.

"Nothing that a few gentle reminders won't fix," Helen answered, as if talking about how to deal with an errant caterer. "Campus is now sealed in completely. The Troop will take care of the rest. I will be back after the Games are finished. I expect a better report then."

At the thought of Helen Price's "gentle reminders," the pain in my cuff buckled my knees. I staggered to the nearest bench and stared at my wrist through painfully watering eyes. Deep breaths. Pyramids building. Flowers blooming. Paper wasps and dragons lifting and flying.

When I finally looked up, the little wasp was perched on my knee, lifeless, his purpose exhausted. The alteration in purpose had used up his magic.

The twinge that affected me every time one of my creations ceased to exist, clenched, and I carefully placed the paper body in my bag. I would resurrect him later with a drop of paint. Paint that I would make.

Rounding the corner, I could see that Helen was gone and so was Stevens.

I jogged to the edge of the mountain and looked at the immensity of Dormitory Circle two levels below. No silky blonde head was walking the staircases toward the Fifth Circle. Looking up a level, however, brought visual success. Helen Price was moving toward an arch that led to Top Circle and the Administration Building. I'd have to sprint to beat her to her port. But...this wasn't merely a battle. This was a war. Olivia's responses to the magic assaults confirmed that the "gentle reminders" had been going on for a long time.

I sent a violent burst of warmth down the thread that connected to my roommate. The cord pulsed brightly in my mind. Sending and sharing magic was getting easier and easier each time I did it.

The caterpillar would be a cocoon when I returned. I was sure of that. But it wasn't enough of a protection. Olivia's forest green magic would still be tinged brown.

I touched the controller in my bag, thoughts streaming around the situation and possibilities.

I could...give Olivia more magic when she needed it.

Paint was my medium—paint allowed me to make things live. And there was a drop of paint connecting me to the protection I had given Olivia. But in order to be enough, it would require applying the results from a combination of the projects I was working on.

When I finally entered the vault and looked at Stevens, the gulf between us dripped with tension and anger.

"You are late. Get to your station, now," she said.

Making magical clay, an otherwise interesting task, might as well have been ditch digging today. We could have at least compromised on glaze.

Whether it had been due to her interaction with Helen or my tardiness, Stevens was short tempered, and took it out on me. I held my tongue, and while I magically pugged clays together—some with the pugmill and some with pure magic—I mentally scrolled through concise statements and accusations I was brimming with the need to unleash.

What are you up to with Helen Price?

How do you know Raphael?

Why did you take me on as a student?

What—and whose—schedule am I on?

Why can't I make paint?

It always came back to paint. Raphael had pushed me to mix it during my Awakening. Marsgrove had cast a spell on me so that I couldn't use it freely on campus. Stevens was controlling my ability to create it.

Paint was the force that had accomplished results in nearly all of the most difficult tasks I had set for myself. I was at a distinct disadvantage in this world, working my way up a steep learning slope—except when it came to using paint. Paint I created.

It was my ace in the hole, as had just been proven by my eavesdropping wasp, which contained a half-drop of the substance.

But, I still needed help making it—making powerful paint. Raphael had guided me through the process during my Awakening. Stevens had subtly tweaked my mixing last term.

Similar to when I watched Will get so far into a spiral of thought that he forgot some of the outside criteria that still needed to be satisfied, having a supervisor limited my otherwise limitless tangents.

With Marsgrove's restrictions, and with campus currently sealed, Stevens held the key to so many things that I needed. But I could not rely on her. And I wouldn't even ask now.

I needed another option.

The magic I was imbuing sparked onto the table as I abruptly stopped kneading. I had another option. An option packaged in a tall and dangerous form, wrapped in a black ribbon.

I simply had to offer him a few secrets first.

Olivia was going to be really furious.

After fiercely wiping two hours' worth of dried clay from my hands, I strode down the mountain and away from Stevens' terse reminder to be on time next session. Instead of going to the Midlands as I'd previously planned to do, I went to see Constantine.

A current of pure dark delight underpinned Constantine's expression. "So that's it," he said, pulling his ribbon around his fingers. "That is how you activate the storage boxes and designate the pulled space. Paint. Of course it is." He said the last in an almost husky murmur.

I closed my eyes. I had told him nearly everything, leaving out only Raphael's name and direct manipulations. Constantine was now completely tangled up in my fate. Olivia was going to be so angry.

"For now that is how I work the magic," I said, opening my eyes. "There might be a better way. I don't know. But paint lets me do things I otherwise cannot. Exceptional things." I looked at him. "Will you help?"

"Of course, darling. Anything for you."

"Constantine…"

He smiled darkly. "Dean Marsgrove will never remotely approach my list of favorite mages. And Stevens is the master I am destined to surpass and defeat."

I rubbed my forehead. "That makes you sound like a supervillain. That is not comforting."

His smile grew, and was no less dark for its magnificence. "You knew that I would want to work on this, otherwise you wouldn't have asked. We can prep right now." He uncrossed his long legs.

I checked the time and sighed. Dare expected me in thirty minutes. "I can't. I have a service commitment I can't get out of."

He paused. "I thought you were on duty at nine tonight?"

"I am. A different service commitment."

He re-crossed his legs and waved me off. "Well, go off and do ill deeds with your service power, then come back after. And send your revised schedule so I can find an appropriate slot in which to schedule vault access," he said, as easily as if I had asked him to loan me a pencil instead of asking him to do something nigh on impossible. "You should have asked last term."

We both knew why I hadn't. Constantine hadn't even tried to seem trustworthy. Even now, in my head, Olivia's voice was screaming her list of "When with Leandred, you will not..." invectives.

But Constantine had kept all of my secrets so far. The secrets I was sharing now shed light on how I used magic, but the knowledge that I could occasionally manipulate Origin Magic was what would actually get me locked up—and he had guessed that secret during our first conversation.

Irrational choice or not, I did trust him. He was firmly entrenched in my fate already, and his leech usage and First Layer manipulation would earn him the cell next to mine. And there was a degree of fondness between us that he didn't hide.

Likely it was a trap that women fell into with him all the time—thinking they were special. But as work colleagues, we had a concrete basis for working together successfully. Constantine was all about what interested him. At present, I fell into that category. I wasn't fooled about my future.

His smile thinned, and he waved me away again. "Go. Shoo."

I sighed at his mind reading. "Sorry. I'm a realist. And you are kind of a dick. But you know I value you."

His expression turned to amusement. "And that you don't place value on yourself. Yes. You are easily manipulated into thinking that you need to offer more than you receive. You should correct that mistake with everyone except me," he said smoothly, stroking his ribbon.

"Very funny. Oh, before I go…" I fished Asafa and Patrick's controller out of my bag and handed it to him.

Constantine examined the device, a sliver of a smile on his lips. "I do so enjoy how your mind works. And I recognize the work. Adding another few hapless souls to your gravitational pull?"

"I think they bounced right into Olivia's actually." I smiled thinking of the glint in their eyes as we'd left.

He grimaced. "Speak nothing more of it."

I nicked the device from his hands. "Be nice and I'll bring dinner with me. Magi Mart?"

"Horrid."

I grinned at his vocal resignation and waved backward over my head as I pushed through the door.

Chapter Twenty-Two
NEW DESIGNS

OLIVIA'S CATERPILLAR had indeed morphed into a cocoon in response to Helen Price's "message." And once again, it hadn't been quite enough to stop Olivia from being hit with some of the magic.

It took me two days of intensive searching and a few extremely shady bargains with members of the delinquents' club, but I tracked down and modified an enchantment that would require some karmic pain from me. Still, darkly pleased with my vigilante effort, I slipped a pre-made spell and a drop of burnt-orange Awakening paint into Olivia's cocoon. Since she always carried it with her now, any spell that touched Olivia would also pass through the cocoon.

And since the cocoon had already been hit by Helen Price's magic, it was easy enough to code it so that any malevolent spell containing the same magical signature would hit the cocoon, then be sent back at the caster at threefold strength.

Olivia would barely feel a tickle as the magic traveled over her, and the returned threefold magic wouldn't register as hers. Olivia would be completely in the dark, so if questioned, her answers would be truthful.

She wasn't going to hurt her mother. I was.

The added enchantment I placed on the cocoon required black magic. Splayed on the floor in Okai while the rocks hovered around me, I healed slowly from the agonizing backlash with a smile on my face.

Neph said nothing about the livid, striped wounds on my skin when I went to see her afterward. She merely healed me and gave me a long hug.

Protection of friends: +1 again

Helen Price's health if she sent another "care package" or "message:" -1 billion

~*~

With the Department taking care of the super-spy threats to national security all over the news feeds, the student watch groups on campus stepped up their watches as well. I took extra care to look ordinary and cheerful whenever I passed one.

I began meeting with Dare multiple times a day to case the trouble spots on campus—hello again, firesnakes!—and to deal with the strange magic or monster-of-the-day issues that always cropped up.

Even with trekking all over campus, the privacy of the Midlands continued to be the place we spent most of our discussion time. My perception of him constantly evolved, as he did a lot of things that were unexpected. He analyzed dirt and magic samples as often as he battled monsters, and he quizzed me and encouraged me to come up with new containment solutions that didn't include fighting.

I did know some things about him fairly well though. The first time I tossed him what he needed without him asking, he looked surprised.

The second time, his eyes had focused on me in an uncomfortable way.

What could I say? "Oh don't mind me, I used to watch you from up in the trees. I think you were stalking me, though. Unknowingly. You know, because we somehow got magically attached."

No.

But he became used to me knowing what he needed most of the time and would simply hold out his hand without looking or asking for an item.

We met frequently at the library. The one time I asked if I should drop by his room, he looked so annoyed that I switched the subject and never asked again. Some mages apparently didn't like others in their personal spaces. I tried not to take it personally. There was a good chance that Dare's room was his oasis. Somewhere he didn't have to be on guard all the time.

Classes, research, leech work, Dare, campus security, and special projects filled my already full schedule.

And I added paint creation happily to my calendar with a coded doodle of a pointy Hieronymous Bosch Garden of Delights plant. Because Constantine, with an elegant snap of his long fingers, had been granted permission to use the art vault.

"I don't understand how you, the bane of the Justice Squad, secure whatever you want from the powers that be," I said, shaking my head as I walked with Constantine through the high gardens near the vault. "Not that I'm complaining, mind you. Just baffled."

Constantine smirked. His strides were long and languid in contrast to my more energetic ones. "It's all in how you are regarded by those with true power, darling, not in how you are regarded by the hoi polloi."

I checked my translation spell. "Did you really just say hoi polloi like a First Layer Brit instead of riffraff or rabble or common folk?"

"I'm versed in many ways for referring to those beneath me."

I rolled my eyes, but darted a glance around the copse to make sure we were alone as he activated the vault door. "Three times a week, an hour each, starting at four p.m.?"

That would be enough. Using paint outside the vault and the Midlands racked up extra hours of community service for me each time I tried it. They were still listed as substance abuse charges, but at least I didn't have Justice Squad members looking at me disapprovingly anymore.

Because I had community service already, additional hours were simply added to Justice Toad's tally. But it was a little like having a magical credit card—at some point I was going to have to pay some severe interest.

"Aries Rising, Ren, not four p.m."

"You just used hoi polloi," I said as we entered the vault. The space brightened with the abnormal, magical lighting that originated from no discernible source, as there were no windows and no light fixtures. "And I've heard you use First Layer times. If someone wants the time translated, their translation spell converts it. Will said there are lots of people who've only been mages since puberty and they still use First

Layer sayings, especially for time. Laziness is universal."

"But it is something that provokes further poking into your background. Something that matters not, in regards to me."

"Fine." I thought about Bellacia Bailey who always seemed to be hovering somewhere near. "You have a point."

"I always do," he said silkily, as he set up a workstation. I chewed my thumbnail and stared at the closing vault door. "Relax, Crown. No one can enter until our time is up. And I will have you out of here ten minutes early every time to make sure no one sees."

I looked around me. "No one ever enters when Stevens and I work here, but I figured that was just Stevens being a ball buster."

"The vault can only be entered through permission of the magic holder who controls the time slot. They changed procedures after someone entered without permission last term." He smirked at me.

I sighed. I had paid for that in thousands of community service hours. I was still paying. "What did you have to do to get permission?"

Constantine's long fingers paused over the scales, then continued their actions. "Nothing to worry yourself about."

That was not good. I knew that from the many bargains I had gone through in order to secure the karmic enchantment for Olivia.

"Con," I said warningly. "I don't want you indebted for me."

"Do not worry. I'm just indebting you to me." He smiled. "Besides, I'd freely give someone else's soul—maybe even two of them—to take part in this."

"Great." I sighed, and slung my bag onto its regular hook.

We only had an hour—fifty minutes, if Constantine was serious about leaving ten minutes early—and neither of us ever dallied when we wanted something done.

Our first session produced three mixtures we fully tossed in the vent that would send them to the Midlands toxic recycling plant.

Constantine watched me carefully, cataloging every moment and measuring my reaction to each new item placed on the scale or in the mixtures. Slight variations in emotional and magical reaction were dealt with swiftly and deftly—at times he was faster than I was at realizing the internal changes in my magical response.

Constantine noticed everything.

No wonder girls were knocking down his door all the time. If he was so focused and responsive with every mark, they didn't stand a chance. It was equal to what I imagined it might feel like to be handled by a pinpointed storm.

Of course, afterward, every girl got tossed from his tornado, to fall broken and discarded to the ground. The storm never cared about the destruction left behind. It only thrived on the churning it did.

"Stop that line of thought, darling. Try thirty milliliters and an emotional shot of remorseless victory instead."

I did as he said, only further convinced that his superpower was that his perceptual skills were lightning fast and ironclad in their accuracy.

If Dare and Constantine ever worked together, they'd be unbeatable.

I looked at our fifty-minutes' worth of progress—all complete failures, but each with a high degree of knowledge gained. Messes made logically. The promise of success in future work sessions was extraordinarily high.

This was going to work out just fine.

While I was on call alone, Patrick and Asafa got into a Level Four situation, which mandated an administrative review. They rubbed their hands together, looked straight at me and said, "Send over your negotiator."

Olivia had them out an hour later, after they had promised to assist two design professors and work some gaming expo in the Spring helping—aka corrupting—tweens in the greater Second Layer community.

Constantine, Will, and I were making significant progress on our leeches and were just starting to dabble with the remote activation of Patrick and Asafa's controller. But we needed to secure another bit of tech from the tricksters, so I sent Olivia to negotiate with them again several days later.

She slammed into the room three hours after departing.

"It didn't go well?" I cocked my head to the side. Since my implementation of the karmic spell, Olivia's health had been at the highest levels I had ever witnessed—take that, Helen!—but her cheeks were abnormally red right now. "Did they wrangle an extra boon? It's okay, if so. Working with them is always fun."

Olivia drew up to her full height. "Of course they did not. What do you take me for? A hornless tricorn? I nailed down every term we wanted."

"Then—"

"They are ruffians!"

Ah. I coughed, holding my hand over my mouth to hide my smile. "Did they flirt with you again, Liv?"

"I will not discuss such absurdities." She began shuffling things around on her desk, obviously flustered.

Awesome.

"We should head down there for tournament night next weekend," I said casually, lounging on my bed with my tablet while pretending to be completely oblivious. "They hold them every Sunday."

"Absolutely not."

Oh yeah. We were so going. I gave her my most earnest look. "We need to check out the console in action, so we can keep adapting our controller correctly."

"You can take William."

I nodded and looked back at my tablet. "Sure. We'll probably be there all day. I'm sure they won't try to acquire any more tech from us while we are playing and having fun. And if—"

"Fine, fine."

Protection of friends and promotion of their happiness: +5

~*~

After the addition of Asafa and Patrick to Olivia's defense roster, her client list bloomed out of control. Asafa and Patrick knew everyone on the troublemaking circuit. And their word was golden. With her crazy class schedule, our project work, her fancy, tedious legal clubs, and her daily or even twice-daily defense litigation, she looked as exhausted as I did every night.

But underlying the fatigue was a deep and fierce satisfaction that I hadn't previously seen Olivia display before. She was enjoying every minute of this term.

"So, Saf and Trick—"

"Cretins," she said without looking up.

"—invited us over tonight instead of waiting for game night."

"Cretins."

"To talk about how the controller slides through mental magic versus holding it. We were approaching it all wrong."

"Cretins."

"And they have a new box of your favorite éclairs in their fridge."

"Cretins." But her frown and the way she started to pack up her bag immediately to visit them indicated that they were starting to be her cretins.

I couldn't withhold my delight.

Dare hadn't even tried to be evasive in his comment concerning Okai the fourth time the building had popped up when we entered the Midlands. Ultramarine eyes had taken in all of the symbols around the doorway and the rocks standing at attention, then his too-blue gaze had turned to me, and he'd said, "Friends of yours?"

We had visited the Midlands many times since—Dare had now claimed every free space in my calendar, no matter how small, so I saw him at least three or four times each day—and he'd said nothing concerning the building or rocks since. But he fully examined Okai's structure, the rocks, and surrounding landscape each time we entered, and I was pretty sure it was all committed to memory. Dare would be able to find me in the Midlands any time he wanted, I had no doubt of that. My secret lair was getting less and less secret. I hoped that didn't come back to bite me.

Why he had let me get away with a panicked affirmative to the "friends" comment then let the subject drop, I didn't know.

Puzzling reasons scrolled through my mind as Will, Neph, and I headed to Okai to work on one of Will's projects. Olivia was busy with Asafa, Patrick, and club business, so it was a good time to nerd out with Will, celebrate our latest successes, and impress Neph.

Will eagerly showed Neph the intricacies of his latest prototyping designs. He had taken our joint projects in our Architecture and Design class, pieces of my previous model sketching and my monster animation for Asafa and Patrick, and our work with the mind magic side of the leeches, then picked out all of the individual "Ren" or "Will" components and added connections common for any mage to use.

After talking extensively to Asafa and Patrick about game design, Will had pulled it all together into a project that was pretty extraordinary. The simulation rooms were incredible, but didn't allow creation to be captured as it was formed. What Will was trying to do was to capture creation specifically in a pinpointed modeling design that any mage could learn. A way of shaping, forming, and capturing from the mind and putting it into a direct framework.

Will, Asafa, Patrick, and Kita, a female gamer in Asafa and Patrick's inner circle who had a business focus, were now actively working on how to use Will's tools—and gaming designs, in general—to revolutionize modeling in engineering. Olivia was looking into the legal and business aspects with Kita for setting up a company to take the product to market. They had been working on it extensively over the past few days

While Will dazzled Neph, I presented a new pencil—full of protection magic and a tiny drop of the winning paint Constantine and I had made earlier that day—to Guard Rock, and a set of smaller, magically enhanced sticks for Guard Friend.

Guard Rock examined and tested his new weapon, and Guard Friend jumped around whipping her sticks in the air. "Awesome, yeah?" I said, warmth filling my cheeks and chest. "We are getting better at this, aren't we?"

"Paint session went well today?" Will asked, watching the rocks work their new treasures.

"Constantine and I completely owned it," I said in satisfaction. In addition to the presents for the rocks, I had made Delia a set of stretchable clay dressing dolls that would "malfunction" and bite anyone who insulted her in their presence. They also came programmed with insults. They weren't sentient like the rocks, but maybe in a few weeks... "We are going to be making Awakening level paint in no time."

Will and Neph exchanged glances.

I put my hand up. "I hear it nightly from Olivia."

Will and Constantine were working well together on the leech project, as I had figured they would. Will didn't have the kind of conceit that would rub Constantine the wrong way, and Constantine was a focused and brilliant mage in a lab setting, which more than satisfied Will. But even though we were zipping along working together as a trio, there was still a formality between them. They wouldn't naturally gravitate to working together on their own after we finished the project.

"We just worry." Will shrugged helplessly. Neph bent to speak softly with the rocks, leaving the conversation to the two of us. "The leech project is really interesting, and I can't wait to start the dodecaplex next week...but Leandred being unnaturally professional behind closed doors doesn't make him any less shady other times. Are you sure you know what you are doing?"

"I think Constantine would argue that he is completely shady all of the time," I said. "But I appreciate you looking out for me."

I bumped Will. He picked up a set of calipers, but I could see him smile.

"And, yes, I'm sure," I said.

Will nodded, letting it go, like he did with so many things that freaked out other people.

After all, he had thought being stuck inside a man-eating sketch had been a grand adventure.

I looked over at Neph, who had drawn Guard Rock and Guard Friend away from the door and was teaching them to dance on their little rock legs, a ribbon of lavender magic wrapping around them like the ribbons that gymnasts used.

Her sachet was attached to her soft belt sash. She never went anywhere without the sachet we had made.

She smiled fondly at both of us.

Warmth gripped me.

Protection of campus: Neutral

Protection of friends: +7

Chapter Twenty-Three
COMBAT QUALIFICATIONS

EXCITEMENT AND ANTICIPATION lit all of campus going into the combat qualifier. Campus safety and traveling restrictions were still in full force, but there were more people buzzing around Excelsine than there had been in the six weeks since classes had started. Alumni, media, and VIP's had been given temporary permission to be on campus after a strict vetting by the Department. Unfamiliar adults interspersed with students on every level of the mountain.

I stayed away from anyone who looked like they had lived longer than twenty-five years.

"An especially auspicious field," a gushing girl said as we walked amongst the excited masses. "The media mages have been listing the biographies, skills, and charts for the competitors at Excelsine and the other schools. I have all of their stats memorized. Isn't Alexander Dare the dreamiest? He's ranked first overall. You should see how each mage ranks compared to—"

The girl was separated from us by the surging crowd.

The section of the Seventeenth Circle that made up the base of the stadium was level, and the field extended inward toward the mountain until it jutted straight up. Carved into the mountainside, the stands rose all the way to the Fifteenth Circle.

Mike and Delia made a beeline for a particular section, dragging the rest of us in their wake. Will and Mike fiddled and debated over which privacy spell to use and where to anchor it. Olivia and Delia argued about who was going to sit where. Neph layered comfort spells onto the seats, and I stared around in awe. Decisions finally made, we raised the wards and sat in a tightly knit formation. I was sandwiched between Neph and Olivia, with Will, Delia, and Mike in the seats directly behind us.

Almost immediately upon me sitting, a guy, shaped liked a redwood, bounded into position in the seat directly in front, forcing me to crane my neck from side to side to look around him. I could catch glimpses of people warming up on the field using staffs, boomerangs, swords, wands, forks, crystals, and other gizmos, but I wanted to be able to see everything.

Olivia looked over at my increased fidgeting. "An ocular magic spell will drift through in a moment. Stop moving."

A minute later, a gong sounded three times throughout the stands, then a trail of magic wound up from the wooden seat and into me. It misted over my eyes and through my ears. Then it bloomed out toward Neph, on my left side, and Olivia on my right. The giant head in front of me started to shrink. The field grew closer, as if pulled forward in a camera zoom.

I blinked and looked at the boy in front of me. He appeared in full form. Looking back to the field, the boy disappeared, leaving the scene beyond clear and near. The boy hadn't actually disappeared; magic had simply accommodated my preferred view.

I could see the mist connecting everyone in the stands, performing the same enhancing ocular and auditory magic on everyone. The mist then shot down—rooting into the mountain, and down into the earth.

My view was now fantastic. Front row, unimpeded view, while still well above the action. The perfect box seat. But when I looked away from the field directly, I could see how far away I truly was, and how close the crowd was that surrounded me. The disparate perceptions were dizzying.

Everyone around me was avidly checking the field, eyes moving in strange perceptual fashions, and fingers manipulating the air in front of them.

"A little bit of battle, a lot of blood. Campus life is good," Mike said, rubbing his hands together over my shoulder.

"Campus is still closed, the Peacekeepers' Troop arrives Monday, and you are making it sleet tomorrow in our usual practice spot," I said.

"Meh."

"Meh, nothing. The combat mages are completely crazed, trying to neuter the Troop before they even get to campus. What do you think I've been doing during the entirety of my spare time?"

"Mad projects?"

"Those aren't spare," Will piped in.

Mike grinned and turned to Delia. "These two. Who are you rooting for?"

"Out of a bunch of hyped-up testosterone junkies spilling blood and battling it out for world domination?"

"You obviously have a favorite then," Mike said, a little dryly.

"Whoever looks hottest in his outfit, of course," Delia said, deflecting a true answer, her attention turned back to actively scan competitors who fit that description.

"Lovely," Olivia said, crossing her arms.

Delia smirked. "What about you, Mikey?"

"There was an all right guy I partnered with last term in my wind metrics class. Ben Franks. Talented. I put down ten on him for the weather events."

"Oh, I heard he was quite good."

"Yeah. Won't dent the big three, though. Dare, Lox, and Ramirez have a lock in the betting magic. They take your munits and backslap you, if you bet outside of them in the big categories." He mimicked the motion with his hand.

"That's what happens when you win the Second Layer Combat Games at seventeen."

"Almost eighteen," Mike said.

"Two months to go or not, Axer Dare was still seventeen last year," Delia said. "Against all the twenty-one- and twenty-two-year-olds. A very big deal. Hot." She winked at me.

I could see him warming up on the field. Five seconds of staring pulled his image closer, as if he stood only five feet away. I panicked, looking to my left and right.

Neph cocked her head at me, her gaze questioning.

"Can anyone see what I see?" I whispered.

"No, it is all individual."

Thank God. I took a deep breath, then watched to my heart's content. I watched him do a particularly complicated maneuver and thought how nice it would be to see it again in slow motion, when suddenly up popped an instant replay with four different, angles to swap between. That explained the eye and hand motions in the crowd. I gave the magic a whirl, swapping images and angles. Wow. There were some nice body angle options. I was coming to these events as often as possible from now on.

Working with the guy three or four times a day, every day, had expunged my crush on him. However, it had left me with something far trickier to label. Such trickiness had been evident when I had finally given him a working paper wasp with which to annoy the Junior Department—the wicked smile he had gifted me with had stunned me stupid.

The warmth I was accustomed to feeling when I gave things to friends and family had been present, but there had been something else there too.

I felt all eyes on me suddenly and for a terrifying moment I thought I might have said all that aloud or projected my view to everyone. Maybe Neph meant it was individual for normal mages.

"Ren? Who are you rooting for?" Mike prodded.

Oh, thank God. "Whoever uses device magic best, of course."

Will gave me a thumbs up.

Mike rolled his eyes. "Nerds. Both of you."

"Nerds with style," Will emphasized.

Delia snorted. "Ren's rooting for Axer. Don't let her fool you."

"Partners have to stick together," I said in a too-serious tone, just to make Delia snort again.

Everyone seemed to accept that answer, though, so I went back to watching the field. Even if I didn't recognize many of the competitors by face or physical reputation, I'd have been able to pick out skill levels just by the way the competitors carried themselves. Strolling, striding, or hunching—arrogant, assured, or scared as hell.

Olivia sniffed. "Uncivilized."

"He's a barbarian really," Delia said. "The kind that would have knocked you over the head and dragged you off to his cave—"

"Never," Olivia hissed.

"Except you are a witch," Delia said. "With or without magic."

Delia jumped and rubbed her leg, laughing at the magical pinch someone had just delivered to her.

I grinned to see Neph looking far too innocent. Olivia's gaze followed mine, and her expression was difficult to read as she realized Neph had defended her.

She had gotten used to me standing up for her, but proving to Olivia that there were other people who wanted to be her friend was far harder. And Delia was actually trying, in Delia's own weird way, to be inclusive to Olivia by including her in her insults instead of ignoring her. I sent everyone the magical and virtual equivalent of a hug, feeling stupidly giddy all of a sudden.

Watching Asafa and Patrick as they bent over something on the sideline near us, fiddling with a console, made me grin harder.

Wait, what? I blinked. What were they doing on the field?

In fact, why were there so many people on the field? I had thought there were eighty combat mages, but there were like a thousand people warming up.

"How many combat mages are there?" And why weren't they all doing campus protection drills with us?

Delia grinned. "No, those aren't all combat mages."

Mike leaned over. "Lots of mages specialize and only compete in one area of the games. Like in devices, you'll see many of Will's irritating classmates. And some mages just want to test their mettle. You don't have to be part of the Combat Squad in order to compete. You could compete." Mike winked.

"No way." I gave a firm negative shake of my head. "After training with one for weeks now I can firmly say, never. I'd be crushed like a bug."

"You're training with Axer Dare. That's like a portrait painter training with Kinsky. It's a little different than taking lessons with an average mage." He pointed to competitors warming up on the sidelines. "See?"

There were a number of mages who were practicing fighting forms, but their movements had a far more exact feel to them—a practiced feel—versus the fluidity possessed by the combat mages I had witnessed and worked with.

Mike pointed along the line. "Those are form competitors. A lot of mages compete in form and scoff over the barbarity of the actual fights."

I watched them for a moment. These were mages who didn't fight to the death, who never used their practiced movements outside of a contained environment.

"Their forms are nice to watch, though." Delia winked at me and I returned her knee bump to my shoulder with a bump in the reverse, extremely amused.

Olivia's lips pursed. "But useless."

With a smile, Delia jerked her head toward a hot guy stretching near us. "Useful," she said, as he bent forward, touching his toes.

Neph cracked a smile. "While I don't disagree that form competitions are interesting, it is the intent the mage adds to the motions that truly makes it an art." She pointed to two mages, sparring. "A dance."

Camille and Ramirez were the sparring mages, and they moved through the same forms that the others were practicing, but with an obvious purpose to their movements as they parried and countered. each other's moves. Neph was right. It was exactly like a dance.

Ramirez moved with deadly grace. Fluid was the only description for the way his body changed positions constantly. The silent boy's lips were turned up in a slightly rakish way. Camille's actions were far more deliberate—each action seeming to be part of a continuously evolving ten-step plan of action she had implemented nine steps ago—her expression was set in dark, determined lines, but there was a nearly palpable energy vibrating from her. Enjoyment.

They changed directions and forms, and I could see that though their dominant styles were those I had already cataloged, there was also a resolute focus to Ramirez and fluidity to Camille in their smaller interchanges. The silent boy and deliberate girl were totally alive in the dance.

"They are beautiful," I said softly. Camille's words, tone, and evasiveness concerning Ramirez that I'd overheard in the accidental eavesdropping debacle took on an entirely brighter light as I watched them.

"They are two of the best. 'Daggers' has lethal aim. Wait until you see how she gained that nickname." Delia sounded far more fond of Camille Straught than she did Bellacia Bailey.

I watched the dance grow more daring. "They both fight in Dare's personal group. Will they fight each other in competition?" I asked.

"Yup. Depends on what they signed up for, of course. And there are team events where they might partner together or split and do on their own. Each event qualifies five mages for the Combat Games. Points are tallied from first to twentieth in each event, and those are cumulatively added to determine an overall winner. And the best will fight in Freespar. Freespar and Game Champion are the glory wins."

The announcer was suddenly surrounded by white light, drawing all attention. "Annnnnnnnnd, it's time to begin!"

The mages all trotted out to the field and stood in a group around a staff. Cobalt magic arced from each mage into the staff, then a turquoise shade arced back to the mage. I recognized the exchange as some form of contract magic.

The group broke up as the participants went to different tents and sections at the edges of the field.

"Let the combat qualifier begin!"

~*~

Most of my focus stayed on Dare's team for the next seven hours. The entire team was ruthless and deadly, and individually they were good at everything, but each member had a specialty.

Camille ruled the physical throwing competitions; projectiles of all sorts zoomed from her fingers and the environment around her. Lox edged out the rest in swords. Ramirez dominated with a rod and wand. Greene, the one I was least familiar with, used exploding devices as if he breathed them. And Dare kicked the absolute living crap out of the entire field in the staff events, barely even needing to trip his competitors in the opening rounds.

The mages on his team gathered multiple wins under their belts, and took second or third to teammates in others.

The field was littered with heats for the hundred different events, many taking place simultaneously across competitions like some huge, blood-spattered track meet.

Neph was called to assist the medical teams a few times, and it was interesting to watch the teams dart in and out, fixing and reviving people.

One of the strangest moments in the competition was when Dare's sixteen-year-old cousin Nicholas won "Extreme Distance Targets," picking off a target three miles away with a pair of thick wraparound glasses and a simple tap to his neck to activate an ocular beam. With the weather enchantments and environmental conditions in play, the competitor who'd won second place had hit the 2.9 mile target in his third attempt, but hadn't come close in any of his three mile attempts. Nicholas Dare had hit the three mile target on his first attempt.

With no other competitors left, his distance limit was left to the imagination.

The flurry of unsettled whispers in the crowd concerning it seemed strange, and the whispers grew when he won "Obstacle Distance"—which involved a non-linear path to the targets, forcing each mage to wrap, bend, and swirl the magic around whatever was in its path first.

The first device competition began in another part of the field and with Will catching me up in his babbling excitement, I forgot to ask about the strange crowd response to the distance events.

The device magic competitions were awesome, but brought back uncomfortable memories of our fight in the First Layer. Constantine would be able to hold his own in this, if he cared. If he was attending the competition at all, though, I hadn't seen him. I wondered what sorts of horrible things Will and Constantine could construct together.

Like our first leech, which was so close to completion.

I rubbed my palm along my neck as another flash of gold taunted me.

Spectators and food passed in and out of the stands all day, but the crowd steadily swelled again as the last heats and finals of the regular events wrapped. The last event would take place alone on the field. There were no qualifications and no heats involved in Freespar.

By the time Freespar arrived, day had darkened to night. I was buzzed on the surreal mayhem and exhausted from watching the all-day competition. The combat mages were good. And watching them compete against each other was more incredible than the very best movie battle scenes.

The announcer appeared on the field. "And now for...Freeeeeespaaaaaaaaar!"

The crowd roared. Fighters on the sidelines dropped towels and lifted weapons, then strode out to assemble. They shifted and moved into their desired starting positions—which was any position they desired as long as they weren't touching anyone else. Unlike the other competitions, there were no rules besides that one. I leaned forward, even though it was unnecessary to do so.

"They all just stand there, then when the bell rings, they start fighting?" I asked.

"Yup. High bets have been placed for your boy going down in the initial charge."

I looked back at Mike, mystified.

"You can plan the initial charge," he said. "It's the only time where anything other than moment-to-moment battle planning can be affected. What happens after the initial charge is out of direct control." He pointed to the field where Dare stood, absolutely still. Most of the bodies on the field were angled toward him, their body positions telltale to the direction they planned to run or cast. They were giving away any advantage for their first strike, but in a field of hundreds, maybe that wasn't the worry.

Five mages decided to get within arm's reach of him for the start. All five angled toward him. Dare didn't move, his gaze focused on a spot a few feet in front of him.

Even if he got two of those five mages, he was going to be gutted three times before he could turn. My stomach clenched at the thought. Madness.

The starting bell suddenly rang, a long shrill sound that made me jump—it was too early, I wasn't ready to see this—but everyone was already moving, and half of the mages on the field charged Dare's position.

In the time that it took for the bell to stop ringing and my gaze to catalog the surge of the field, the five mages surrounding Dare were crumpled on the ground and Dare still looked as if he hadn't moved a muscle.

He stood there, staring almost sightlessly for a full, agonizing second as the rest of the field charged. I gripped my arms tightly across my chest, feeling utter panic. Madness.

Then crystal magic whirled like a prismatic Matador's cape at a hundred charging bulls, and he flung the magic up and down around him as he twisted. A good portion of the charging mages went down, but a dozen of them ducked or flipped as the magic approached their position. Those mages kept coming, and some of them were throwing explosives and thrusting swords forward.

I had seen this before, in Will's hologram before coming to campus. I would bet a thousand munits that Will's hologram had been a replay of last year's battle qualifier.

"Using a similar opening tactic as last year and he's still going to win." Mike's voice was stunned.

"You never show your best in qualifiers," Delia said, bloodthirsty delight in her voice as she started yelling praise and curses at several combatants.

I never took my eyes away from Dare. He seemed to know where each opponent and attack were coming from before they came within five feet, and any magic that wasn't deflected, was caught, converted, and used as his own.

It was true, he wasn't using some of the craziest moves I had seen him perform, and he held no weapon at the moment, but even so, my jaw was still residing somewhere along the floor of the stands.

After our first fight in the battle rooms, he had continued connecting to me whenever I was in there. But, wow, I could now see his toying with me in the rooms for what it was.

The field thinned extremely fast, the carnage of an all-out melee far too severe for long and complex individual battles. When Mike had said it would be over in ten minutes, he hadn't been joking. Bodies piled up into a circle with Dare at the center, which impeded all but aerial attacks until the medical mages on the sidelines magically pulled the bodies away.

As the body count rose, smaller groups worked together to attack him. There were also multiple sneak attacks by competent combat mages fighting in the midst of the charges. But soon enough, it came down to three of his personal force along with only a handful of others.
All of the remaining mages, including Dare, had significant injuries—arms that wouldn't lift,

legs that were broken, bone alignments that simply weren't right. Dare had summoned his staff, finally, and Ramirez fought one-handed alongside him. They took out Lox together. The back of Dare's staff snapped in the air behind him and Camille went down as well.

Dare's gaze was steady and focused as the remaining combatants chose their moves. An uproar shook the stands when only two competitors remained.

Dare twisted to face Ramirez. His fingers curled lightly around the staff. Their battle cloaks had lost much of their finery—the buckles and other ornamental devices already having been used for attack, defense, healing, or whatever effects they had been designed to accomplish.

Ramirez and Dare circled each other, the last ones standing. The faintest hint of an upward curl was evident on the edges of their bloody lips. Each time they had fought in the individual competitions their actions had shown that they knew each other personally and tactically very, very well.

The stands rippled with excitement, bodies pressing forward, people yelling and cheering.

Gold rippled in my view, severely enough this time that my gaze moved away from the engrossing spectacle to search out the source of the glimmer.

Gold wasn't a good portent for me.

A huge roar sounded, then people were jumping wildly and magic was hurtling everywhere in the stands. I hurriedly looked back to the field. Ramirez was on the ground and Dare's staff was pressed to his chest.

Ramirez grinned as Dare helped him stand. The crowd roared as Dare was announced the winner of Freespar, and with his combined points, he was also the overall winner of the competition.

I craned my head back to the crowd, trying to trace any spark of gold as people moved in front of and around me, exiting the stands, chattering and exchanging money.

Hands pulled me around and Delia bounced into view. "Party in Dorm Twelve! Alumni included!"

I blinked away the gilded unease that had enveloped me and focused on her words. The last time I had been to a party in Dorm Twelve, I had accidentally thrown my drink all over the person who had just won the competition. Not a great memory.

"Um, I don't think—"

"Mandatory. Let's go." Delia pushed me sideways through the stands.

I appealed to Neph, but she shook her head with a smile. "It's a good idea."

Will nodded. "Yes, I must speak with Elias Greene about that last device he used. Brilliant."

Mike was already ahead of us on a direct route to Dorm Twelve—no help there. I looked to Olivia, but she was looking into the crowd with an odd expression on her face. "One hour won't hurt," she said gently.

My shoulders drooped and Delia cackled, pushing me into the crowd.

~*~

The surge of people moving toward Dorm Twelve made it hard to feel conspicuous, yet there were people near the entrance closely watching the crowd. One of these days, I was going to reach my "watched" limit and my magic was going to blow.

Once we got past the bottleneck, though, the mass of humanity inside swallowed us whole.

Dorm Twelve was more of a frat house than a dorm. It consisted of an immense gathering room two stories high, with balconies and halls to the personal rooms shooting up and off to each side. Unlike last time, there was no furniture in the room except for a tiered table in the center.

A large glass bowl full of Ambrosia stood on the table. Little glass cupids shot rosy liquid into the center, automatically refilling the container as each cup was magically served. I was handed a full glass, but I discreetly tipped half of the contents into a trash chute on my way past. Half a glass would make it look like I was drinking without actually having to. I still hadn't recovered from the last time I'd tried Ambrosia.

Olivia didn't even bother to grab a glass. In the press of the crowd, our group was quickly split in multiple directions. It seemed as if everyone on campus had come to celebrate. Last time, the party had been large, but this, this was huge.

Olivia and I stayed together in the surge, but got mired in a section of cramped humanity discussing the social commentary and politics of the brutal competition. I nodded where necessary to support Olivia and otherwise zoned out, glass in hand, trying not to draw attention to myself while running project schematics through my head. Mike was working on a magical weather vane, and from the number of mealtime complaints about it, the project was giving him grief. It had been a long time since I had done something for Mike, so I set my mind running with a few ideas that might help with his project.

Olivia's voice grew increasingly contemptuous as she argued with a group of people wearing bright orange. I patted her arm absently and agreed with her statement—whatever it was. The orange people responded in outrage.

Maybe the design of the vane was the problem. Maybe a slightly different shape would adequately express the magic the way he desired?

Neph's soothing magic swept through me and I turned to locate her. She and Will were clear on the other side of the room, up on one of the balconies. Will motioned to me with his hand, then toward the staircase in the corner.

I elbowed Olivia and pointed. She gave a decisive nod, sneered at the people in orange, and strode in Neph and Will's direction with purpose, cleaving the crowd as she went. Trying not to spill my cup on anyone, I cursed that I'd taken a glass at all, and tried to move with the shifting crowd in her wake. Soon enough, Olivia was on the other side of the room, while I was clenched in the crowd's armpit.

A group in front of me started juggling flaming knives overhead. I edged nervously around them, watching as they manipulated the air around the steel, keeping the flames level and the movements steady.

I turned to move forward again, but Dare appeared suddenly in front of me. I jumped and my fingers automatically pushed my cup toward him, the arc of liquid sloshing forward. His fingers wrapped around my cup, steadying it, his magic creating an invisible barrier over the top to keep the liquid from leaving. His eyes crinkled at the corners and the edges of his lips lifted.

Devastating.

"You destroyed my track record for painting you pink at parties," I somehow quipped as his fingers let go, brushing against mine as they released their grip. "And ruined a perfectly good celebratory dousing."

"I'm going to start getting a complex that you just want me to take off my shirt."

I stared at him, heart beating abnormally in my chest. "Uh, no, we wouldn't want that to happen."

Everyone with a pulse wanted that to happen.

I cleared my throat. "So, congratulations on kicking the crap out of everyone."

"Thanks." He looked amused, studying me with his hands now in his pockets. Unlike the mass of people jamming into my back, personal space surrounded him. Even with people calling out congratulatory remarks left and right, no one infringed in his bubble of territory.

I scanned him from head to toe while trying to hide the color that was undoubtedly accompanying the increasing warmth in my face. "You look surprisingly healthy." Broken bones and long gashes had been healed, and he looked as fresh and non-bloody as if he'd stepped off the magazine page I always imagined he rested upon when he wasn't in view.

"Medical. The qualifier counts as part of the exam grade for the graduating class, so they put in extra effort to revive us."

I looked around, trying to see if the rest of the combat mages had arrived as well. I could see Lox and Greene near the Ambrosia table, laughing with each other as they took glasses.

"Thank you for your crap kicking display, by the way," I said, looking back at him. "I feel way better about my own lackluster performance against you after seeing what you did to some of the others."

He smiled. It was a personal smile of a shared joke. And it was possible I was having a heart attack.

"I'll remember to make things worse for you tomorrow."

"Yeah, how about we skip that? Take a day?"

"I don't think so."

"Uh-huh."

It struck me suddenly. Right now there was no assignment, no monster, no strategy to think about. This right now...this was almost like we were hanging out.

As if we were friends.

And I realized that I already clearly thought of him that way. He'd never be merely a friend—not with my tangled emotions surrounding Christian's death—but the ties were all there. And if there were perhaps far warmer notions in my thoughts around the word friend in relation to him, well, I was a girl with working eyes, after all. Not under a stranger-crush any longer, but clearly as susceptible as the next red-blooded eighteen-year-old to the epitome of male magnificence that he represented.

He opened his mouth to speak, then closed it and looked to his left a split second before an arm circled his shoulder. Unlike me, Dare was never surprised.

"Axer, drinks! Countdown! Shot tally! Now!" Lox said, pulling Dare's head and neck in roughly and intruding on his space as only one of his close comrades would dare. Two more combat mages grabbed them both, wrestling off and carving a large swath through the crowd, shouting about what they were going to do.

I breathed a sigh of relief, saved from the entirely unexpected revelation that I might actually be friends with Axer Dare.

"Good evening, Miss Crown."

I swallowed, my relief suddenly tasting like rancid meat. "Miss Bailey." I turned and smiled with effort. "Good evening to you."

"Of all the people that our school champion stops to speak to, it is you." Her voice was melodious. "Congratulations."

Lovely. "I was mostly just in his path, I think."

"But you are here at the side of the room. Not in a path to anywhere of note," she mused, still so deviously pleasant. "No, I don't think you were simply in his path."

Tell me, tell me why. I could hear her voice whisper the words, though her lips didn't move.

I took a nervous sip of Ambrosia before I could remember not to. But better that than to focus on what the echo of her voice was compelling me to do.

"You are working with him, I hear." She looked at the backs of the combat mages who were gathering in the center of the space, getting even louder and rowdier. "Camille said you were partnered with Alexander." She smoothly hooked her arm with mine and started to lead me toward the front door.

"Um, yes, to help the Troop protect campus when the combat mages are at the competition."

"That is so generous of you to help with campus safety. The Troop is a marvelous resource for our campus security."

"Um, yup. I'm sure they will be great. We will all be very safe."

She leaned conspiratorially toward me as we walked, her voice near my ear. "Why don't you tell me your plans?"

Despite tireless hours of defensive practice with Draeger, my lips started to form the words.

Olivia stepped directly into our path, which focused my gaze. The tinkling shards of Bellacia's broken enchantment echoed, and I shuddered with relief.

"Bailey," Olivia said, smoothly disengaging our arms.

Bellacia still had a lovely smile in place, but there was a dark edge to it now. "Price. I was just speaking to your lovely roommate. She is a dedicated student with such interesting friends."

Inessa Norrissing suddenly popped up like a creepy jack-in-the-box.

"Oh, look who it is," Inessa said. "Everyone's favorite symchastersy."

Symchaster-what?

Olivia steadily looked at me, trying to communicate something, but her voice was aimed at the other girls. "Look who it isn't. Come, Ren."

"Do let her decide," Bellacia said in her lilting voice. "I'm sure Miss Crown will benefit from many different points of view."

Olivia's smile was a small, poisonous thing. "I've never put much stock in the notion that every opinion contains value."

"You wouldn't, would you?" Inessa snarked.

Olivia looked at Inessa in disdain before addressing Bellacia again. "Neither does the Free Press. A little trouble with the security of your feeds lately, Bailey? Having a little trouble with hijackers?"

Bellacia's smile spoke of death. "If someone would do their job in keeping our Layer safe, then perhaps it wouldn't be an issue."

I put my free hand to my forehead, my mind trying to muddle out what was going on. "If you guys start snapping your fingers and dancing with switchblades, I'm out of here."

Bellacia's head tilted toward me, her gaze keen. "What do you mean?" Her gaze moved quickly to my hand pressing my forehead, then down my raised arm.

"West Si..." I trailed off. What if they didn't know West Side Story? Why not just get a red marker and write "feral" on my forehead?

As I was trying to figure out how to finish my sentence without sounding moronic, I realized exactly what Bellacia was staring at—my cuff, where my sleeve had ridden back with my arm's motion and gravity.

My unbreakable cuff. As opposed to the removable control cuffs Bellacia and everyone else wore, I couldn't remove mine except by dumping paint loaded with Origin Magic on it.

I smiled falsely and dropped my arm, letting my sleeve fall back into place. "I forgot. I have a thing. And some stuff. With some people. Got to go. See you in class."

Behind me, I could hear Olivia saying something toxic to them—gaining me time, bless her. But I didn't stick around to watch. I channeled Olivia's posture and pushed through the crowd. I didn't look for Neph, for Will, for Delia, for Mike, or for Dare. I kept my gaze focused on the open front door, and upon reaching it I nearly leaped over the threshold and into the free air. Not safe, though; not yet.

I strode quickly to the left, but in the thirty-six-section superstructure that spanned the entire circumference of the Fifth Circle of the mountain, Dorm Twelve was nowhere close to Dorm Twenty-five in the Magiaduct. I picked up my speed.

"Leaving already?"

I looked over sharply to see a tall, familiar shape leaning against a tree, smoking a magic-filtered device. I waved, but didn't pause my quick pace.

Constantine extinguished the tip of the device between his fingers, and his long stride easily allowed him to catch up. "You aren't staying?"

"No," I said decisively.

"Did you spill something on Alexander Dare again? Turn him pink? Maybe with purple polka dots this time? Did I miss the actual fun of the night?"

"I've been very graceful lately, I'll have you know." Constantine didn't need to know that if it had been up to me, pink liquid would have coated Dare once more.

He smiled. "So, why the early exit? Half past ten in the evening is only mid workday for you."

"I'm trying to avoid someone." I cast another look behind me. No one seemed to be following in the shadows, but one never knew with the stooges. "I think I'm in trouble."

One brow rose. "And who is the lucky mage who has the power to make you run?"

"It seems everyone has the power these days," I grumbled.

"Who is making you run tonight then?"

"A girl named Bellacia Bailey."

Constantine's eyes—always sharp—zeroed in on me. "Is she now?"

I took in his facial expression as I continued slicing through the shadows of the Magiaduct. "You know her?"

But that was a silly question, and I knew it as soon as it passed my lips. Everyone of aristocratic consequence seemed to know—or at least know of—each other, even in a campus population of fifteen thousand.

"Yes. She's a cow and terrible in bed."

Gaping and not watching where I was going, I tripped over a tree root.

He easily caught my arm and put me back on stride. "Nothing else constructive to add, I'm afraid," he said.

"That was constructive?"

He shrugged. "That is the sum of the best that can be said of her. I hold my position of 'most-hated' on Bellacia Bailey's list in high regard. Quite the coup."

I sighed. "You dated her and she still wants you." It was a statement, not a question.

"Everyone wants me, darling."

"Constantine..."

"I dearly hope she still falls into that category." He smiled—one of his far-from-nice smiles.

"Would serve that miserable, psychotic friest right."

That word translated very unkindly. I stayed silent for too long, wondering what to say next. He decided to answer my unspoken questions.

"She is an industrious and talented player at the game of revenge, and was singlehandedly responsible for the denial of my petition to work in the Arking Chem Labs in the Fourth Layer last summer. She was also responsible for all of the events surrounding the very public denial of said internship. Even charming and beloved Stuart Leandred took a popularity hit in the resulting wreckage."

I stared at him. Stuart Leandred had to be his father. At some point, I needed to do a news search.

"Never underestimate the media," he said, "and that is the whip that she wields. Never underestimate what they will use as 'facts' when they present their 'worries' to government officials."

He waved a hand at my horrified expression. "I collected a most fitting revenge; worry not. And

I take extra...precautions now. That pathetic experience was worth something in the end, at least."

I remembered the way Bellacia had doubled over in pain in the Dorm One hall from something Constantine had done.

"Does she go after all of the girls who come by your room?" Standing outside his door could not have been beneficial in helping me escape her notice.

"Of course not. She'd never be able to keep up."

If the statement weren't so true, I'd roll my eyes. I shook my head instead. "I hope you have some magical equivalent of STD protection."

"The best that a truly gross amount of money can buy. No mess, no fuss, no application, no—"

I held up my hand. "Okay, okay."

He tried to hide a smile. A real one.

I couldn't help but smile in return. "You are terrible."

"Incorrigible. I should be beaten."

"I'll keep that in mind," I said dryly.

His eyes turned shrewd again. "Tell me what she has done."

I scratched my cuff and tried to shrug convincingly. "It's nothing. She just asks a lot of questions and whispers in my ear." I pulled at an earlobe without thinking. "I'm vulnerable to auditory magic, it seems."

He stopped and put two fingers to each of his temples, eyes closing, as if in great pain. "Never tell anyone that. Ever again."

"Let's face it, you could already do worse to me," I said frankly. "And I'm going to fix the auditory thing so it won't be an issue. It's nothing."

He stuffed a hand in his pocket, and pulled something out. His fingers unwrapped to show a small metal object in his palm. "It's never nothing—not with Bellacia." He stroked the metal briefly with his thumb, then tucked the object into my hand. "If she gets too close for comfort, push this. It will give you a reprieve and make her forget her task for a period of time."

It looked like a child's toy—the kind that made clicking noises when you pressed it. I clicked it, as I would any toy with a moving part that came into my hand. "Wait, what exactly does it do?"

He whipped away the lock of hair that had slid over his eyes, and smiled. "Keeps her from prying into other people's affairs. I hate to part with such an amusement, but keep it in that bottomless bag of yours for the next week. Feel free to click it on my behalf, at least once. When bored or sad or angry too. At will, really."

That sounded...concerning. "It doesn't hurt her, just makes her forget?"

One eyebrow rose. "It will make her forget, and it will protect you."

The metal slipped into my pocket. I kept a finger on it for a moment, before telling myself it was foolish to think that something would protect me from everything. "Thanks."

"Anything for you," he said smoothly.

"You going back to the party?"

"To celebrate Alexander Dare's victory? I'd rather die."

I choked. "Oooookay. You want to work instead?"

"Lead the way."

Chapter Twenty-Four
LUNCHEON COMPANIONS

A T LUNCH THE NEXT DAY, I watched Will and Mike grumble through their hangovers.

"Why aren't you in pain?" Mike whined at me. "You always look halfway to death in the mornings with your usual two point five hours of sleep."

"Olivia was really weird last night." I shrugged. "Dragged me back to our room and forcibly tucked me in. I got ten hours of sleep. Ten hours. I feel awesome. I totally solved your weather vane problem this morning. I'm going to cure death today."

Right after arriving at Constantine's, I'd sent Olivia a note. She'd shown up fifteen minutes later, and read me the riot act so hard about not waiting for her outside the party, that I'd guiltily stood and walked to the door.

Constantine, on the other hand, had been so visibly livid, that I'd had to do damage control just to stop them from killing each other.

Olivia had muttered really strange things all the way back to our room about Constantine "working" while there was a campus-wide party going on. That had been weird. What else would we have been doing?

I chewed my fingernail and focused one portion of my revitalized brain to answering Mike's demanding questions about the vane and used another portion to mull the issue of Constantine's time.

I was using a lot of his time lately. And even though I was making sure to do lots of side projects for him—some without his knowledge—I didn't want to be a burden. Maybe I needed to talk to him about scaling back vault sessions. We had made a huge batch of violet paint loaded with feelings of fealty and allegiance on Wednesday. It would last a few weeks. It was as close as I'd gotten so far to the ultramarine paint I'd made at my Awakening—paint made while thinking empowering, purposeful thoughts, with a protective edge.

A person walked up next to my chair and my gaze rose to meet eyes exactly that remembered shade of ultramarine.

I jerked, tearing off the nail.

"May I sit here?" He indicated the seat next to me.

"Uh…" I automatically looked at the prime combat table on the first tier. Half of the hungover mages there were staring directly at me. And at my table, Mike's fork had stopped halfway to his mouth and Will looked blank. "Sure?" I said.

Dare sat easily and leaned back in the chair with his hands tucked loosely in his pockets, the picture of casual ease. He looked at Mike and Will, cataloged both, then looked back to me.

"Er, so, how are things?" I asked, abandoning my plate of food, having no clue how to deal with this new situation. It was one thing to speak at the party, or while patrolling campus. But to talk or spend time together in the cafeteria was completely new and weird. "Not too exhausted from yesterday?"

The day after the competition in which he had obliterated the school's best fighters in mass combat...and he looked as if he was in the prime of health, flush with healthy color.

"Combat mages live for battle. It becomes invigorating instead of exhausting, didn't you know?" There was that same hint of shared amusement in his eyes that there had been at the party.

"Feeling vigorous are you?" The words emerged in a far more embarrassing fashion than intended. "Ugh. Too much sleep."

His smile was easy, his eyes amused. Wow, it was warm in here. I heard a clatter at a table in his line of sight behind me, and at least one more clatter a few tables over.

"Your schedule today is oddly full for a Saturday," he said.

The Troop would arrive Monday and I could read between the lines. I took a sip from my water glass, my gaze not leaving his. "You are going to make my life hell today and tomorrow, aren't you?"

"Yes, I am," he said with relish. He tipped his head back, along with his chair. He was still smiling. "But there are a few conspicuous black holes in your weekend schedule labeled with interesting nonsense. What are you plotting?"

"Oh, you know, nonsense." I nervously grabbed my pencil at the side of my plate and twirled it on the tray while trying not to think of Constantine, Will, and the leash we would be working on during a lot of those black holes in my calendar. I was wishing, not for the first time, that I hadn't given Dare access to my personal calendar. He had had my class schedule from the beginning, but had run roughshod over my private appointments until I'd given him access to my planner.

Thank God, that like most of my personal documents, my appointments were completely "written" in doodles. Every person had a symbol and each project did as well. It provided an unintentional code that served me quite well in the magic world where information was shared so easily between mages.

Will and Mike had ribbed me mercilessly that the doodles only made sense to me—but it would be a mistake to forget how quickly Dare absorbed and analyzed information then converted it to his advantage.

While I tended to gravitate to people with brilliant minds, Dare's was brilliantly dangerous. There were a hundred different things combat mages had to take into account when fighting, and while I found watching their fluid and dynamic strategies fascinating, I tended to forget that I, too, was prey.

He let my "nonsense" response go, but continued the small talk, as if this sort of happening occurred every day—his sitting casually with me, answering insubstantial questions about his day, and asking me about the events of my day in return.

Finally, I couldn't take the deliberate informality any longer. "Why are you actually here?" I asked.

Dare didn't even pretend to misunderstand. "Without looking, tell me what is happening on Tier Three."

My gaze slid to Tier Three automatically and only a firm thump of his booted foot against mine made me refocus on him instead.

I pushed my tray to the middle of the table, opened my sketch pad and drew a quick, jerky sketch of the room. Flexing my fingers, I took a deep breath to steady my nerves and focused on the threads of magic in the room. The muse-controlled tables were emitting their naturally high beams of calming and focusing energies, but a high concentration from each was extending downward. Toward whatever was happening on Tier Three?

I closed my eyes and followed the magic, letting my pencil line the page.

Shouts interrupted my trance and my eyes opened.

I stared at the picture I had drawn. It was crude, but clearly showed a food fight in progress. I looked, automatically, down at the actual disturbance and saw the first pie as it was thrown. A lemon meringue pie that was already drawn on my page.

"Magic gives warnings and yields intentions." He tapped the side of his head. "You just have to listen."

Insight bloomed like a greedy flower finally exposed to sunlight. "That is why you sit with your back to the room," I whispered.

And why he hadn't even looked up during Freespar.

He smiled and unfolded himself from the chair. "Draw what we are doing at the combat table in five minutes. If you look, I'll make you run combat drills for two hours."

Wide-eyed, I stared. "What?" He would too. Contract magic put me under his authority when we entered any session deemed "training."

His smile edged toward a smirk. "I'll know if you cheat. Don't disappoint." He walked up the steps nearest us, his stride casual.

I cast a glance around me and saw a number of people who normally never looked at our table twice, staring at me keenly. Widening my gaze... Everyone I looked at was staring back.

Even Mike and Will were staring at me. Awe mixed with alarm in their expressions.

"You were born during an unlucky storm." Mike shook his head, finally returning to eating. "I have yet to figure out how to stop the thunder and save you from it."

Olivia's tray clinked next to me. "Okay. We need to make quick work of this. What spell did you accidentally cast last night at the party?" She had her notepad out and was flipping pages before her butt hit the chair. "It is going to take me all day to work out a defense."

"I didn't cast a spell."

Olivia's gaze dissected me. "You were working with him or talking to him. You happened to find something interesting and thought about hanging out, and—"

"No! I..." I sort of had thought something along those lines last night, but there had been no magic involved, of that I was certain. "No, that isn't—"

But Olivia was already nodding and making a note, as if I'd confirmed her accusation.

"Olivia! He is quizzing me. Assignment-related. I didn't do anything," I said, looking around me. People were still staring. "Why is everyone staring?"

"Because Axer Dare never sits anywhere else in the cafeteria," she said calmly. "Even for thirty seconds of time."

"Never?" I asked incredulously.

"Never."

"That's..." The word "stupid" hung on my lips. But then I thought about Freespar and sitting with his back to the room. I looked at the combat table, and the relation of it to everything else in the room. If he sat in the same position each day...and the general population sat in similar areas, and whatever magics the officials pumped through the system came from the same sources, Dare would have a general blueprint to know what was happening everywhere fairly easily. He'd only have to work out small differences, breaking the knowledge into smaller chunks each time, honing the entire process each time he did it.

Like a musician or conductor in the midst of an orchestra, instantly able to identify each of the individual instruments playing around him because he already knew their relative locations. "That's brilliant."

I looked down at my sketch pad, checked the time, and turned to a blank page. I had one minute. Less than a minute now. I took a deep breath, bringing the streams into focus.

"Are you paying attention to me?" Olivia demanded.

"Shhh," I whispered.

Olivia responded in an outraged tone to that and I could hear Will and Mike responding in my defense, but I didn't pay attention to the words. I allowed the streams to permeate.

The muse tables were steady beams of bright eucalyptus. The gamers with Saf and Trick were a competing mix of jasper and jonquil. The scientists were a strong cerulean. An unidentified table between us produced a dark, steady claret. The rest of the tables produced muted, muddied colors, less distinguishable and not as strong—the members weren't working together toward any one goal.

The combat table was swirling opal, crystal, and jet.

I picked each shade apart in my mind, referencing my memorized warding books, the wards I had connected to in the vault, and the ward gallery in the Library of Alexandria. I unfurled the senses of each, and as I did, I let my pencil interpret and deliver. Olivia, Will, and Mike were furiously speaking around me, but I remained steady, thinking of the hues and the shading and how they flickered or beat.

Olivia elbowed me. "Your partner is trying to get your attention," she said.

Dare was motioning that my time was up.

I looked down at my drawing. Sketched figures all had their fingers on the table, bridging magic into an object in the center. The feel of the magic had made me draw the object as round. A protection piece of some kind? No, the magic hadn't felt protective. Draining. There in the swirls at the edges of their hands—the magic was flowing out of the object and toward them, not in.

I looked at the rest of the sketch. The shadows were strangely long. I looked around me, but the shadows were the normal size for the time of day. I had drawn them longer in the sketch. Symbolism?

"What is it?" Olivia asked, looking at the drawing. She still had her pen poised above her pad, but the label at the top of the sheet no longer read as "Ren's Defense." Instead it said "Security Measures."

"I...don't know."

Dare was waiting for me outside the cafeteria when I left. I tried to ignore all of the gazes watching me while I handed him the drawing, then asked the same question Olivia had asked me. "What is it?" I pointed to the object that was the main subject of the drawing.

"That would be telling." He carefully put the sketch in his bag, looking darkly satisfied.

"Why don't you tell me then?" I asked more patiently than I felt.

"Because telling you is not the same as having you work it out on your own." He looked at me calmly. "You solve problems and incorporate information better when you work it out on your own, thereby making it a keen subconscious process."

"I..." I stared at him. That was absolutely true. "How...?"

"We are connected, isn't that what you said weeks ago?" His smile was suddenly edged. I could take any manner of guesses on what he was hinting at and risk being horribly wrong. So I said nothing and followed him past the flagpoles that ringed Top Circle.

Gazes, some old, many new, followed us from every direction for most of the afternoon as we traversed campus. The sun dropped from the sky as Dare flattened me repeatedly in the simulation rooms.

And I still didn't know what the drawing meant.

That evening in his workroom, Constantine stared at me with a particularly dissecting expression as he, Will, and I worked for an hour on the leech.

When only the chemical base remained on the night's list of tasks, Will left. Ten minutes passed with Constantine practically burning to say something as I stirred the ingredients that would eventually form the base of our design.

Finally, I mentally projected a "what?" question in Constantine's direction, too tired to ask it aloud.

"I heard you had lunch with Alexander Dare."

I put my free hand to my forehead. "Not you too." I had heard it nonstop at dinner. "We are working together to secure campus. He's a completely crazy person about it. That's it."

Constantine's expression was unreadable as he wrapped his black ribbon around a finger. "You sound stressed rather than joyful."

"That's because I don't want to disappoint him."

His ribbon started wrapping faster. "You care so much what he thinks?"

"It's...complicated."

"Uncomplicate it."

"He saved me once."

A sneer pulled the corners of his mouth. "He saves everyone. Nothing special in that."

"I know. But the circumstances were...abnormal." I didn't know why I was telling Constantine this, but the words kept coming. "And I can never thank him enough," I whispered.

"You saved him. You died in his place." His eyes pinched. "Your slate should be so clean it squeaks."

I wasn't surprised Constantine would know about what had happened the second time I'd died. He was as likely to have been standing there drinking a martini and watching everyone burn as to have heard it from someone afterward.

But my slate would never be clean, and I couldn't explain that to Constantine. The explanation wouldn't change his opinion. Constantine dealt with a series of debts in a ledger in his mind. One wiped out another evenly, and personal feelings rarely entered in.

"It wasn't the same. The debts don't even out," I said.

Constantine said nothing, he just kept wrapping the ribbon. He finally uncurled from his position and took the rod from me, stirring the concoction with a firm hand until it started to boil. "You make it entirely too easy to take advantage of you, Crown."

"Yeah, yeah. What is the next step?"

"Binding you as a slave?"

"Very funny."

"Add the currant." He pointed at a jar of crushed red flakes. "Ten milliliters should do it. Focus on caged power that pops." He popped his fingers in an upward direction.

"You sure you don't want to add the magic instead?"

"No. My magic is far more sly. It wouldn't be quite as show-stopping for this. You are a starburst."

"You say the sweetest things." I focused on magic contained inside a ten-milliliter pyramid, caged and pushing. I abruptly forced it out and into the mixture.

The light that was always in Constantine's eyes when I used a burst of magic was there now. He smiled in a very self-satisfied way. "Perfect."

"I'm surprised you are happy about me correctly executing the step that will allow the tethered mage—me—to break free," I said wryly.

"Pfft. I am gaining your concrete trust so I can use it against you later. Keep up, darling."

We worked for an hour more before I heard the front door open. Constantine's shoulders tensed, his hand flicked, and the door to his workroom slammed closed.

Holy crap, he did have a roommate. A living one at that.

He shrugged at my surprise. "Gnats are better ignored."

A roommate he didn't like much, obviously. "I'd think you would be magically swatting gnats into paste."

Constantine's mouth curled. "That's a lovely image, Crown. I will definitely consider such an action."

I could hear the footsteps of Constantine's roommate out in the living room. This was the first time I had ever heard sounds of another person living here. I stretched out my magic, curious. The footsteps stopped abruptly. I hastily reined my magic back in before it could touch the person.

The footsteps continued and I could feel the shimmer indicating that wards were shifting, but strangely could feel none of the echo—as if the person had wiped their magical signature clean. But Constantine's roommate had to be taking down the wards on his private door. I yearned to know which wards he was dismantling first.

My magic strained to do my bidding, so I kept a tight hold upon it, forcing the desire down into the brew.

Constantine's eyebrows lifted at the sudden injection. "Trouble, Crown?"

"No. Just thinking. Who is your roommate?"

Multiple emotions flashed across his face, making his expression unreadable except for the dark amusement. "You amuse me."

"Well?"

"Someone you should avoid," he said.

"I think I do that pretty well already." In all of the many times I'd been here, I hadn't once seen another male in these rooms, well, except Will, but he always came with me. And other than Constantine's stuff, there were no personal effects anywhere.

"Mmmm," he said. "Stir."

Who was Constantine's roommate?

Chapter Twenty-Five
DEATHLY CHARMS

ALEXANDER DARE had talked to me at a party, then sat with me at lunch. The two events together seemed to indicate that I wasn't just a shady "person of interest" anymore. To many people, I was now a possible enemy of the state.

Bellacia and Inessa led the charge, and cornered me in the cafeteria for an impromptu interrogation the next morning. I ignored them, until their sudden, extremely smug taunting about 'things to come' for Olivia nearly made me engage. But at the mention of Olivia, Saf and Trick had popped up like, well, magic, and herded me away.

In exchange for the save, they had made me promise to send Olivia their way later that night.

The gleam in their eyes was twenty percent worrying and eighty percent awesome.

The two of them drove her mad, but I noticed that she always went to see what they wanted, no matter how much she complained about it.

Which was stupidly similar to how I always showed up whenever Dare sent me a note to meet somewhere. Stupidly, stupid, since the man was solely responsible for my new "popularity" on campus.

Keeping a low profile? I was obviously going about it the wrong way.

I didn't need to meet with him so often—surely the Justice Magic wouldn't hold me to so many hours?—but I showed up every time he called.

Like now—shaking off tree sap and resignedly thinking about how I needed to look up shower charms. I could seriously use a magical loofah.

Dare put his hand in the dirt of the Midlands. The magic that was still dissipating from the man-eating tree that had stood there a moment ago rapidly reformed under his palm, and a sapling slowly sprouted from the soil. Dare backed away and the tile shifted, taking the new tree with it.

The tree had tried to eat both of us ten minutes past and I was still numb from the bark explosions. But I had to admit that once again, I was a little speechless. Dare hadn't just destroyed it. He had given its energy back, turning the remnants of the bloodthirsty oak into a sapling brimming with vicious possibilities.

Protection could be wrought in many ways, and Dare made use of them all. No wonder the branches and stalks always stretched toward him.

Shadowing Dare was eye opening. It wasn't just battling demons or soul-sucking, flying piranhas or some mage's accidentally realized robot monster—though there were a lot of those. There was also the aftermath and a crazy amount of cleanup.

He had, oddly, about half an hour prior, called forth his form-fitting battle cloak—looking good as new with its many buckles and slightly flared hem. It made for a pretty arresting view. And watching someone who was so deadly revive a plant was a little like looking at a calendar of hot Marines holding kittens.

He pushed dark strands away from his forehead and arched a brow at my, undoubtedly, dumbstruck expression. "What?"

I cleared my throat and tried to think of man-eating trees and not all the hotness so clearly on display. "I've gotta say, since they are now options, trapping and transformation are probably going to be my go-to choices here," I said, brushing the remnants of bark from my jeans in an attempt not to stare at him. "You might have noticed that beating up things is not really my forte."

His lips quirked. "No? But the squirrels in the simulation rooms run in terror when they see you."

That...that had been Draeger's fault. Draeger, and his weird animal curses infecting my brain.

The only thing I was remotely decent at, when fighting Dare in the simulation rooms, was running and setting traps. But his kinesthetic and strategic intelligence was coupled so highly that even when I was winning for a moment,

I usually ended up flat on my back a second later, with Dare's foot heavy on my chest and him smirking down at me.

"Whatever. Tree hugger," I countered.

And there was the much beloved, full-on smirk. "That is why it is essential to carve out the position at the top of the pack right away, Crown. You can express any thoughts you like and do anything you wish, and people will nod along like they are preferences, ideas, and actions of extraordinary value."

"Mmmhmm. Badass apex predator and all, I notice you spend a lot of time doing the dishes." I pointed at his hand, where the healthy, nutmeg-colored residue of the oak's transformation still clung to his palm. "You rarely let the magic go to the recycling plant."

He looked at me for a long moment, as if debating whether to answer. "Excelsine has one of the best magic processors in the entire Second Layer. But relying on backlashes to be taken care of by something or someone else makes mages lazy. And it is useless to fight for something unless you intend to preserve the essence of what you fight for."

"You are only making your new nickname stick harder, tree hugger."

"It's better than some of the others I get." He cocked his head, listening to something in the distance.

"Alexander the Great?"

"Worse." His head stayed cocked, but he refocused on me. "Speaking of worse, the Troop is coming tomorrow. We'll have at least one tagalong for the next two weeks. They wouldn't let me refuse."

He pulled a thin, flexible folder from his cloak. "But before they get here, I want to try something." He handed the folder to me.

It was made of brown, pulp fibers that were bound together with a light dusting of magic. I had made similar folders with Stevens. They were made to hold magical documents.

Unwrapping the string that kept the folder secured, I looked inside to see heavy, blank sheets of parchment. My fingers automatically tugged out the sheet on top, thumb and forefinger rubbing over the bumpy surface. The parchment was laced with magic—heady, old magic.

I looked at him questioningly.

"Draw something," he said, his tone deep and smooth, but there was tension buried deep beneath the words, and something resembling triumph in his gaze.

"What, like anything?"

"Yes, Ren."

The use of my first name, even said in an exasperated way, took me by surprise. I looked down at the blank page—the very expensive, magic-filled blank page. "Er, why don't you give me a more defined instruction?"

"No."

Tiles shifted around us as the Midlands sorted through disparate landscapes, piecing a new puzzle together. One tile clicked in on our right. Ruined cityscape. Ugh. That meant zombies. Another tile clicked on the other side. Stones. That meant trolls. Of course, anything could pop up anywhere in the Midlands, but some creatures were naturally drawn to certain tile types.

I tensely waited for a zombie to spring out from behind one of the crumbling stone pillars. Guard Rock was my zombie fighting wingman. He was great at using his pencil to stab and unhinge jaws on anything that got too close. Zombies got preoccupied when you unhinged their biting mechanism.

Dare cleared his throat in an obvious effort to get me to begin.

Well, it wasn't like Dare couldn't take down a fleet of zombies, especially with his cloak on. This was my umpteenth session with him. I was well aware of what he could do.

He raised his brows and pointed to the paper. I realized, somewhat abruptly, that I was stalling.

We had fought and adventured in the simulation rooms and I had changed the surroundings with a simulated pencil more times than I could count, but it wasn't quite the same thing. He'd seen my dragons, wasps, and maps and hadn't freaked out...and that whole weird thing in the cafeteria had happened. But there was something strangely intimate about this atmosphere and his lack of instruction. Magic was heavy in my hand.

I took a deep breath. I could do this. I could even make something impressive.

He had been going on and on about thinking of defense as offense—containing threats as soon as they presented themselves as such. I suddenly had a pencil in hand and was drawing on the page. The sketch animated as I drew the lines, swirls forming and taking shape as they left my pencil's tip.

The swirls formed into tight, magical rope, knotting together every few inches to form a spider web wrapping around the page and funneling down into a very real holding cell in the middle.

I paused for a moment, surprised, and the line flowing from my pencil tip rippled in suspense, waiting. I was getting more fantastic results with my pencils each week, but this...? It was like the paper and graphite were alive—parts of a sentient picture that had started to form. When I had thought I might draw something impressive, I hadn't quite pictured this outcome.

There was something very special about this paper. I continued drawing, watching in delight as finished lines jumped into motion and began to swirl toward the center, drawing down into the cell I had created.

This was significantly better than my trap for Marsgrove. Better than any I had previously made by pencil—special charcoal or not.

"What kind of paper is this?" I didn't look up from the page, too enamored watching the trap world take effect. I could feel that the trap would work—without paint. It was an unheard of result for me and had to be because of one of the other magical elements in play, namely the paper. The paper I made was good, but this was imbued with something more.

"Something I was wondering if you could use," he said in a distant voice.

His tone made me look up sharply. "Oh?"

Ultramarine eyes watched me in a detached fashion. He didn't respond.

"And?" I nervously pushed a section of hair behind my ear. What kind of paper?

His head cocked an inch farther to the side. "A few months ago, a Department mage told tales of being trapped in a world smelling of charcoal."

I wanted to respond with something vaguely witty and hopefully distracting about the magical world of barbecues, but nothing emerged from my clenched throat.

"He was found wandering around the First Layer, unharmed," Dare said, not waiting for a response. "But with the strangest tale. The non-magical authorities in the First Layer committed him, of course, but when the Department finally retrieved him, mages began investigating the truth to his story."

It wasn't surprising that the brutish man who had been sucked into my gopher sketch on the day I'd truly learned about magic had turned out to be a problem. He hadn't been kind and I hadn't felt too guilty about his disappearance. The episode had provided the initial springboard for my papered traps and storage—a boon from a nightmare. Marsgrove's enchanted paper had done the rest.

Dare snapped his wrist and his staff shot out in both directions from his grip. "Of course, that led to people whispering about magic not seen in decades."

Magic burned suddenly under my skin. The spiraled web on the page swirled faster as I looked at Dare in horror. Whenever Dare drew his staff, he was usually going to take no prisoners. Unbeatable. And he was wearing his battle cloak...had been wearing it for the last half hour, as if in anticipation...

"What do you want?" I asked, my voice reedy. While a normal person might have felt betrayal, I just felt energized resignation.

"I want you to use that paper," he said. A gusty breeze swept the space and the appearance of five serpentine heads formed long shadows on the ground.

Dare swung his staff directly under the chin of the head in the middle. I stared, dumbstruck.

This wasn't some nefarious attempt on his part to end me for the good of all mankind, then. Nor was it zombies or trolls coming out to play.

A straight-up ten-foot monster of legend was striking killing blows.

Dare ducked beneath the next head, twisting in and out of the hydra's five lunging strikes. He twirled the pole as he went, hitting and moving in a fast, coordinated dance.

"She's been tracking us for half an hour," he said in between strikes. "So you can either stay here all day while I play counting games with her heads. Or you can use that paper." He wasn't even out of breath.

"Seriously? You didn't think to mention that a giant monster was tracking us?"

The hydra roared as he broke one of its—her?—necks.

"You're supposed to be paying attention." He smiled, then sliced a head clear off with a blade that suddenly curved out from the end of the staff. Two heads sprouted to take the cleaved one's place.

My resignation retreated like it had never existed at all. "You're a freak." I carefully put the paper on the dirt, keeping my eyes on the six—no, now five again—no, now seven—heads.

"Likewise," he said, spinning, his cloak flaring around him. He made it all look manly somehow.

Then between one moment and the next, he pushed the hydra back toward the paper and the serpentine monster...fell right in.

Schwoop.

A black-and-white, seven-headed monster fell through parchment space then splatted against the cords of the web, heads and necks stilling at odd angles as they affixed to the sticky threads. Dare walked over and we stared down at the stilled picture. Other than the subject matter, the animated blinking of the hydra's seven sets of eyes was the only thing that made the drawing look dangerous.

"How long will she stay in there?" Dare asked, crouching down to get a better view.

"Permanently, I think; if I say so?" I rubbed the back of my neck when he looked up at me. "Don't credit me. There is something extremely special about that paper."

Dare's stare was intense. He rose slowly. "Can you release her?"

I nodded apprehensively.

"Good. We'll let her out near one of the swamps that contain wet caves. She'll hunker down, if given habitable territory."

Release and run? I could do that.

"Okay." I carefully lifted the sheet and held it toward Dare. "Here."

One brow rose. "There is not a chance that I'm touching that."

"You'll fight a hydra, but not touch a piece of parchment?"

"Not that parchment."

I removed the highly magical blank pages from the folder and carefully put the trap paper inside instead. "I can erase the web, later, after we de-hydra it." I had no idea how to erase it, but I'd figure something out. I thrust the unused papers into the air between us. "These are still blank."

He made no move to take them, he just watched me with a dissecting and analytical gaze. "They are yours."

I examined him for a moment, then shook my head. "I know the parchment is special. I can't get this type of result usually without using p... I can't get this type of result usually." Stupid, stupid.

"Mmmm."

He still didn't move, even as I stepped forward into his space and held the papers toward him. He looked at my fingers as I shook the parchment at him.

"Like I said, they are yours," he said.

"I can't take them." They were far too valuable and there was something about the magic in them that sung to me. That was usually a dangerous thing. I grabbed his hand in order to uncurl his fingers and put the pages in his palm.

The second I touched him, something twanged, his cloak rolled up and disappeared from existence, a shield popped, and magic exploded outward, blinding the clearing with white light.

When a troll clubbed Dare in the head the very next moment, I was completely unprepared. Stranger still, so was Dare.

He dropped like a stone, and for a moment, all I could do was stare in shock at his body lying completely motionless on the ground.

Nothing ever got the best of Alexander Dare. He always knew what was coming, assimilating tile shifts and their threats quickly and with seemingly little effort.

I ducked the troll's backswing instinctively, but there were twenty trolls surrounding us now. All motion slowed, and almost unconsciously, I crumpled the papers around the pencil in my fist, crushing them together with magic and forcing images, worlds, onto the pages, before I threw them outward. Paper flew end over end, spreading around me like large leaves blown in high wind. Six trolls absorbed into the papers as they were touched, pulled into the parchments with a horrible squelching sound. A few of the pages continued to turn end over end. Two trolls stepped into papers as they fell to the ground in front of them.

One troll, though, ducked the traps, raised its club, and ran toward me, my death in its gaze. The papers were all too far away for me to dive inside. I called up my magic, but I wasn't going to be quick enough.

Dare, face dripping with blood, slid low across the dirt in front of me, then under the troll, the end of his staff connecting upward and flipping the beast into the air and down into one of the papers. Squelch. But there were still a dozen remaining. I had never seen twenty trolls—a pack? A trollage?—together before. Together, the remaining trolls heaped onto Dare before his maneuver was complete.

I dove for the parchment nearest to me, ready to slap it on the pile in order to suck up whatever I could reach.

Before I could do so, a blast in the middle of the pile blew troll bits everywhere and Dare was pushing himself up off the ground. Relief fired along my veins. Then one flailing, mostly-intact troll who had been blown straight upward, brought a meaty paw down on Dare's back as it plummeted back to earth. Sickly purple burst from the contact.

Dare's shields. Something had happened to one of his shields when I'd touched him while holding the parchment.

Magic leaped to my fingers and I inelegantly blasted the offending troll toward one of the papers on the ground, not watching as the troll was sucked from view. I stumbled toward Dare, who lay unmoving. I dropped to my knees and flipped him over with adrenaline-fueled strength.

His chest didn't rise. Painful silence stretched under the whistle of the wind. Troll parts surrounded us—splayed everywhere in a horrifying tableaux.

Nothing moved. Nothing produced sound. No breaths released from Dare. Dead.

Dead.

My vision tunneled, and my heart rate rapidly approached hysterical as I put my hands on his chest. The litany of resurrection books I had read last term scrolled through my head like a list of movie credits too fast to comprehend. But there was enough knowledge and confidence in my subconscious to form a shaky pyramid anyway, and charcoal made with my own magic covered my fingers. I shoved the magic into his chest.

His body jerked and white light shot out from him like a starburst. The magic washed over me cleanly, but two ground impacts indicated unknown beasts lingering in the bushes had been felled in an automatic defense mechanism from Dare's last shields.

Dare's blue eyes opened above a furious expression. "Where the hell is my twelfth rib?" he wheezed.

Hysterical sounds emerged from my mouth. Alive. Not dead. "I took it. Used it. To revive you." Alive. Not dead.

"What the hell sort of third-century texts have you been reading?" He rolled over and grabbed a twig, then held it to his chest. The twig disappeared and Dare inhaled a deeper breath. His color was rapidly returning and I could see his shields quickly layering back up, one on top of the next. "That was the worst revival I've had since I was six."

Any other time, I would have been avidly observing the rebuilding of his shields and cataloging the magic he was pulling from the environment around us to heal his massive injuries. Instead, I put my hands over my eyes, pressing them against the lids, trying to keep my hysteria in check.

"Hey." His voice was gruffer. He tugged my hands away, but everything was hazy. "It's not a big deal. Got the job done."

"Okay. Sure. No problem. I'm going to go now." I rose unsteadily. "Home." My vision had tunneled completely and I blindly walked toward the pinpoint of light. I could hear swearing behind me.

People died here all the time. Twenty Justice Squad members had died in the first hour of this unholy squad union. I had seen ten people die and get revived in the first event of the qualifier. And judging by his words, Dare had died before—probably many, many times.

But I had never resurrected anyone. Not successfully. I had tried so, so hard with Christian. Desperately. But my brother had been long dead already, and instead of feeling panic, I had been full of steady resolve.

But now... My hands were shaking. A cacophony of sound blended together in my mind—the sounds of Dare fighting and heavy bodies falling around me processed through some strange auto-tuned filter.

How could I think myself capable of protecting anyone?

Dare was swearing, his voice part of the odd filter, and I could hear his feet hitting the dirt as he caught up. "Stop walking, dammit. You aren't even looking around you. They weren't alone. Three dozen of them together, what the hell? Scouts just returned planning to eat you, and there are three more watching in the shadows. Stop moving, so I can safely—"

Safety.

Suddenly my vision jerked painfully clear. Okai's tile screeched into view and Guard Rock waved his stick in agitation for me to come inside.

Dare was instantly half a step in front of me and I automatically glanced at his profile. He was staring at Okai with an unreadable expression on his features.

Danger, danger. Protect Guard Rock and Guard Friend.

My hands stilled and the feel of spilling paint ran along my veins. I motioned with my fingers, the echo of paint on their tips. Guard Rock stamped his stick down in protest, but the tile whisked away.

My magic was giving me what it thought I wanted without the usual filter. I had just called Okai to me then sent it away again in the span of five seconds. I could see other images flashing around me. Things I wasn't even consciously aware of desiring.

But our safety was still uncertain. Dare had said three trolls were still in the shadows. The image of the layer spread out around me like paint poured over a canvas, rolling over three hulking life forms. I focused a beam of magic on each, picked at the layer covering us—at a small, vulnerable section—and shoved. Lightning split the Midlands' gray sky and the earth shifted. The hulking beasts were pushed through the earth like buttons forced through holes too small.

The holes started to open further. Too far. The cuff on my wrist vibrated.

Fingers circled my cuff, pressing it against my skin. Just like Marsgrove had done... Did that mean I should attack? No, these fingers didn't hurt. They were firm. Warm. Protective?

"Look at me."

There were fingers on my chin.

"Look at me."

I focused on ultramarine. Protection.

"Focus."

Long moments of sludge and confusion and alarm mixed together, but in my vision, blue eyes never wavered.

I focused on the color and got my breathing under control. The shaking beneath my feet ceased.

It was another long moment before he let go of my chin. It was a longer moment until he released my wrist.

"Thanks," I said quietly, pulling back my scattered control—testing pyramids like a computer rebooting, checking safeguards—and I pretended that I couldn't read the calculation I saw on his face.

He was going to ask me all kinds of questions I couldn't answer. Like, 'So, trapping things in sketches is pretty alarming, but let's talk about how you just ejected those trolls from Second Layer existence?' Or even more likely, 'So, speaking of threats presenting themselves...'

"You've never resurrected anyone before," he said, breaking through my spiraling thoughts. It wasn't a question, and it was completely unexpected. He continued speaking. "Why didn't you go for help? Or wait for help to arrive?"

"Wait? Leave? I would have lost you. The tile would have moved."

The tiles had moved. I looked around me, we were nowhere near the troll devastation. Dare would probably be dead dead by now.

"There are only ten minutes allowed for resurrection," I said. "What if it took me fifteen just to get out of here?"

"It wouldn't."

I stared at him, numb.

"It wouldn't," he repeated. "Come." He turned and headed back into the heart of the Midlands.

Magic stretched around me, whispering information to me in streams too quick to decipher. He was right. At this moment, I could get out in less than ten minutes. Connecting to the Layer had made me hyper aware, and there was an exit back to the Thirteenth Circle just around the bend. The path wouldn't last, I could feel it already slipping away in a slide, but the ability to feel the changes in the Earth and in the magic of it was there, if I could learn to harness it.

If I could learn to be an Origin Mage.

"I'd like to go back to the dorms," I said numbly.

"We go back and get the papers first." His tone brooked no argument.

"Okay." Gnawing hunger and exhaustion were overtaking me quickly, but I had become adept last term at putting a temporary hold on physical pain and suffering.

Dare led us back to the spot easily enough and stood guard while I collected the papers. An aftershock rolled through the ground.

"We need to release the creatures and leave," he said, sounding tense.

We walked out of the Midlands ten minutes later—one hydra and twenty trolls lighter. I checked the nearest mountain sign. We had emerged on the east side of the Thirteenth Circle. When I stopped abruptly, Dare put a steadying hand against my back. People were shouting and arguing on the green in front of a multi-colored building.

"Campus shaken—"

"Earth mages swear they didn't—"

"Peacekeepers' Troop coming, thank Magic!"

"Department presence—"

"Everything will be better—"

My use of magic in the Midlands had not gone unnoticed on campus then. And I had no idea what Dare had already put together based on his actual observation of the event and the wild speculation that was occurring around us.

"You need to eat. Come on." Dare nudged me into a stride and we passed the terrified gossipers and headed toward an arch that would take us to the west side of the Eighth Circle where there was a henge with an arch to the north side of the Fifth.

"You can't lose control like that again," he said as we walked through the first arch. He unwrapped some strange, perfectly white food from a square package and put it into my hand.

"I know," I said weakly, then took a bite. The white square tasted like...nothing. Rice cakes had more flavor.

"Ever. Especially near the Troop."

"What would they do?"

He looked at me without responding.

"Okay," I said, just as feebly.

"We'll do some resurrections after the competition. Get you used to death."

I shuddered. "I don't want to get used to death."

"Too bad. Death and resurrection are part of this world. People die all the time. Most of the time they only miss twenty breaths."

"Lucky," I said with no small amount of bitterness.

"Yes," he said in a voice that was suddenly almost soothing. "But death is real. The mage who relaxes is the mage who stays dead."

"The papers... They knocked out one of your shields." The magic had passed through my hand to him, but it was no less true.

"Hard to defend against Origin Magic," he said casually.

My heart stopped beating.

He didn't look down at me as he continued striding forward, propelling me along with his hand at the small of my back. "But not impossible. I've got the feel for how the energy starts to activate and will be able to compensate for it next time. Completely worth the shit I'm going to get for dying during a training session."

My legs felt like short, wooden stilts. I swallowed. "Origin Magic?"

"Sergei Kinsky made those papers. Didn't I say?"
He didn't look at me, and his voice was far
too casual. "Cost a small fortune and they are
illegal to own. Hope you have a good place to
hide them." He nudged my suddenly unmoving
form toward my dorm. "See you at Pisces Rising,
Crown. Make sure you eat."

Chapter Twenty-Six
REVELATORY DECISIONS

AT LUNCH, I ate more than I had ever eaten in one sitting.

Still shaking uncontrollably from the whole death and resurrection and Origin Magic revelation thing, I ate and drank and ate some more, and everyone carefully let me do so without interruption.

Finally, I could eat no more. At the feeling of fullness, a white square burst into my mind's eye then exploded, rushing through me and converting all the food I had just consumed into magical energy. Everywhere the white energy streamed, my magic was replenished, and I bodily shook like a dog that had been dunked into a bath.

I stared at my hands, which were now shaking with a different force altogether. It was like a concentrated, alternate form of the energy renewal magic Dare sometimes used on me. He seriously had the best stuff.

"You okay, Crown?" Mike was looking at me dubiously. So were a number of people near us. I hid my shaking hands under the table and tried to stop the rest of me from vibrating.

"Way better." Dare wouldn't have given this renewal to me if he was planning to turn me in, right?

I took a single, eased breath, and that's when the world slowed around me.

No.

The world sped back up almost immediately, and I put my hand to my chest. Raphael had just done something. But it hadn't totally worked.

"The terrorists just partially destroyed a second installation!"

I could hear the whispers traveling the cafeteria.

"But with far less magic. Are they running out?"

Outrage and fear clogged the large, airy hall, but was threaded with the slightest bit of hope. It echoed my own feelings—though normal, crippling guilt rolled through me as well. Partial destruction still likely meant a loss of life.

But, the small cord of hope remained—what had just happened was a far less incapacitating response than I had experienced in the past. We had begun piecing together the leech in the last twenty-four hours and I had been touching materials left and right. If putting leech materials together was enough to limit some of Raphael's power, it gave me hope that we were on the right track.

I looked through the enormous floor-to-ceiling window that comprised one entire wall of the cafeteria—looking out over the mountain. Lightning storms broke in the distance.

Mike inhaled sharply and suddenly, then looked at Olivia. Everyone else at our table looked her way a moment later, and I could feel gazes around us similarly pinning Olivia like a stuck fly.

I grabbed my reader. Raphael had done something and everyone was staring at Olivia.

The newest Information For The People flyer and the Threats to Public Health and Welfare bulletin had hit the metaphorical stands. They were updated with horrible information concerning Helen Price and her failings as a politician on the world stage—and her inability to keep the Department installations secret or secure. Chatter broke throughout the cafeteria, mages eager to pin the blame for the latest security breach.

Since both publications were owned by the Baileys, and Bellacia had used some specific language with Olivia at the party, then taunted me about Olivia this morning, the source of the articles wasn't a surprise. The articles had likely been sitting on the edge of someone's magic fingers, awaiting the right time to hit "send."

I really wanted to push the clicker thing Constantine had given me, just to make Bellacia forget her own name for a little while. Maybe it would cure her of her vindictive streak.

Helen's embarrassment and public ridicule meant little to me—I actually was pretty pleased by that aspect—but Olivia was going to be punished for it, and Olivia knew it, judging by her lack of conversation, clenched body language, and quick excuse to leave the cafeteria.

I hurried after her, but waited until we were back in our room before speaking.

"Olivia—"

"It's fine, Ren. I knew what would happen eventually when—"

Olivia tensed momentarily. I didn't have to ask why. The backlash from the vengeance magic whipped through me in the next moment.

I grimaced and my stomach clenched. But, on the satisfying side, Helen Price had just gotten her backside paddled, pretty literally.

Olivia was staring down at her intact cocoon, bewildered.

I shifted on my feet, pretty certain that I'd be unable to sit in a chair for a good while. I wasn't in nearly the pain that putting the magic into place had caused, but even with the abundance of energy now running through me, the backlash still stung. Magic, like nature, required balance, and it was basically giving me its version of a disappointed parental head shake for misusing it. Vengeance spells, like the one I had put on Helen, weren't full of sunshine and rainbows.

Though, hey... Maybe that would be worse to someone like Olivia's mom. My excess energy and the backlash pain were probably making my brain think thoughts that I should immediately disregard, but the absurdity of Helen Price being repeatedly forced to look at fuzzy rabbits made me smile stupidly. I'd have to consider sending her an overload of cute images in response to whatever she tried next. See if I couldn't do some psychological damage instead.

I bet I could skirt the "vengeance" side of things entirely if I made my brain think of it as "joyful rehabilitation" instead. Food for thought.

My grin widened and I shifted position to lessen the heat on one side of my lower body. That's when I realized that Olivia was staring at me, her eyes narrowed.

"Er, yes?" I wiped my grin.

"Why are you standing there, smiling strangely and shuffling back and forth from foot to foot?"

"Uh, just trying to stretch my legs. Too much sitting lately." I scrambled for a proper excuse. "And I'm trying to recreate some of Neph's moves. Awkwardly."

I tried a little hop, then stumbled into a small, shambling circle to get rid of the blazing pain and cramp.

Olivia watched me through narrowed eyes. "My mother easily connected the Baileys' scathing articles to me. And her response to it should have resulted in far more than the light tickle I just felt."

Filtered through the previous magic in the cocoon, Helen's vindictive attack would have caused the cocoon to burst into a butterfly—absorbing the more anguishing aspects—but Olivia would have still felt remnants of pain.

I pointed at Olivia and couldn't keep the hostility toward her mother out of the movement. "Her response should have contained no violence at all."

Olivia watched me for a long moment, then turned the cocoon over in her hands, examining it. She hadn't examined it since I had given it to her. I had done a pretty good job embedding the second spell, way better than a cursory examination would show, but Olivia was very detail oriented. I knew as soon as she found it. She went rigid.

Her neck bent and her head dropped forward to shield her expression.

Crap. "Er, Liv?"

A shudder ran through her and her hand twitched toward her eyes. "When?"

"A month ago?"

"I'd wondered," she whispered.

That just made me angry again—that she'd wondered why she'd gone so long without punishment. "I'm not taking it off," I said mulishly, crossing my arms.

She pulled the cocoon to her chest, fingers wrapped around it. "Ren—"

"No, you'll let me do this," I hissed. I wasn't angry at her, not in the least, but I was so angry at the situation. I took a deep breath and walked over, kneeling painfully in front of her chair. "Please. At least until it's a butterfly."

Light hands curled around my neck, and for long moments I had an armful of Olivia Price.

When she pulled back her chin was steady and gaze level. "I have a few letters to the editor to write. What say you?"

I grinned.

Once Olivia had started furiously writing and focusing her sight forward, I headed to the Midlands and Okai to work off the overabundance of excess energy Dare had "squared" me with.

Olivia was taken care of for the moment, and I had a longer term plan chugging away for her. But Dare...Dare had died this morning. And no matter what he might know or not, he was firmly in my circle of protection. He had started in it as the stranger who'd saved my life and given me one last moment with my twin, and his importance had increased exponentially since we'd begun working together.

I stroked one of Kinsky's sheets, and set to work.

Two hours later, I walked out of Okai buzzing with spent energy. Locking the door behind me, I stopped cold to see Dare leaning against Okai's wall, casually waiting. It was both a comforting notion and a threat. As suspected, he could find me at any time. I wondered how long it had taken him to get onto Okai's tile. It was one of the trickiest to access—it had taken me a week, a lot of magic, and a drop of paint to do so.

"You were going to be late," he said, a half-smile on his face as he answered one unasked question and left a million others unanswered.

"I would have totally made it with a minute to spare," I said, walking down the front steps while trying to still my racing heart. "I'm awesome at being just on time."

He pushed away from the wall and looked me over. "You ate. I had wondered if I'd find you half-dead here."

"I think I actively offended the table next to ours in the cafeteria with the amount of food I consumed. And thank you for that kick in the jugular experienced soon afterward that made them think that not only was I gluttonous, but demented as well."

I still had a little extra energy running through me and it was doing funny things to my stomach. Had he tracked me down to make sure I was okay?

That made me think preposterous thoughts.

I shoved the little papered creation toward him, transferring ownership as I did. "Here. I made the magic in this one safe for you."

I could feel Guard Rock and Guard Friend watching through the little floor-level window the building had created for them—assessing whether Dare was a threat. How had Dare concealed himself from the three of us before I'd exited? Guard Rock would have seen Dare if he'd truly just been standing out in the open.

Dare examined the small phoenix resting in his hand. He stroked a tail feather and touched the crest feathers and beak. Unlike its slightly crinkly counterparts, the phoenix's parchment had smoothed into a nearly seamless design.

It was one of my best creations. Kinsky's paper was exceptional. I wondered how old he had been—and how long he'd been a mage—when he'd created it. Should I be working harder?

Dare continued to examine it and said nothing. It was excruciating.

"You, uh, you shouldn't use him outside of the Midlands," I said, then chewed on an already chewed fingernail. "You said to keep the paper hidden, and well, ta-da! One piece hidden."

Dare's wasp and dragon swooped down to see their new sibling. My God, I was making him a menagerie. It was beyond mortifying, if I let myself think about it.

"I assigned each a task during their creation," I said, trying to outrun the thought that I was giving him pets in some weird courting ritual. "Sort of like embedding instincts. They can do other things, but their primary instinct will be to complete their task. And I made sure none of them will leave the Midlands without your express permission."

The wasp and dragon were chaotic little beings—and occasionally they absorbed and overdosed on the Chaos Magic around them. I had seen them being mischievous and spiteful to other people traversing the levels, but they always listened to Dare when he spoke, and they followed their embedded directives to a T.

"And the phoenix? What is his task?"

I felt my cheeks heat. Seriously, what had I been thinking? "He, uh, he will follow you." I busied myself with my bag so that I didn't have to look at him. "If you die here, he will immediately alert me."

It should also pull Okai's tile toward him, attaching to whatever tile he was on for a short period of time, making it possible for me to find him if I dropped everything and sprinted to the Midlands. Perhaps the effort of imbuing that magic had made it possible for him to be here right now—that it had somehow tugged him the way that I had accidentally tugged Raphael twice now. I'd have to think about that.

Dare's eyes were unreadable, but he put the phoenix carefully on his shoulder. "We will work on your anxiety after the competition, as I said earlier. But thank you. He's exquisite."

He had said that earlier—that we'd work after the competition. I'd been more concerned with the death aspect of our conversation at the time.

"We, uh... You won't need me to help after the competition."

The tiles slid and a family of goblins and a couple of large ostrich-lion-scorpion hybrids appeared on either side of us.

"Maybe I'll want you to help," he said as he stepped toward the hybrids and left me to talk the goblins down from attacking.

The goblins finally lurched away, and I turned to see Dare give me a calculated sideways glance while the standing hybrid roared over its downed compatriot. Magic was heavy in the air, and the phoenix was spiraling up toward the Midlands' sky. The phoenix had obviously just done something unusual while my attention had been engaged elsewhere.

Which brought us back to things unspoken. I had used Sergei Kinsky's paper to make the phoenix and some of the tasks required in its creation had clearly required rare magic.

"So, you...you know," I said inanely.

"Know what?" He casually knocked the other eight-foot hybrid off its clawed feet with a sweep of his staff. Maroon magic seeped from the end of the staff and made both creatures completely inert.

I fluttered a hand absently. "About..."

"Things? Stuff?"

"You are being deliberately obtuse. I kind of appreciate it." Some of the tight tension in my shoulders drained away. "Why did you give me those papers?"

"Because I thought you would be able to use them." He headed left, and I followed him, catching up quickly. Tiles slid around us, but as usual, he had somehow tethered us together.

"Why did you think that?"

"The puzzle isn't hard to figure out when one studies you. And I had clues that others do not."

I dearly wanted to know what other clues he had, but more importantly I wanted to know... "Why aren't you scared?"

He looked at me, entirely unimpressed with my question. "Why should I be?"

"I don't know. The very notion scares everyone else."

Though that wasn't entirely true. None of the people who knew I could manipulate Origin Magic and who mattered to me were scared. And their attitudes kept me from drowning in the fear of what could be, if I was exposed. External affection suffused me, making me dance a little in place with the extra energy that wanted to do or make something for each one of those people right now.

"My mother is Sera McEllian." Dare said it as if it explained everything.

"Okay," I said, without understanding. Mike and Olivia had talked about Dare's mother and the political ramifications of her marriage to his warlord father, but I had no idea what those ramifications were or why any existed.

Dare laughed. It was a full, deep laugh and it made me shiver. He shook his head. "Feral mages..." He said it almost fondly. "You should probably fast feed a few historical and socio-mage classes or get an app for it when you get a frequency. So you know who to woo and who to avoid." His tone grew darker at the last. "Like the sole known Bridge."

"What's a Bridge?" Some sort of spirit guide? He obviously didn't mean his mother was a span across a river.

A rock-filled river appeared in front of us, strangely befitting the conversation, and Dare took a moment to choose a path to take us across.

"A Bridge is a mage who can create a connection that takes magic from one source and transfers it easily into another, without asking for permission. A natural leech."

The word "leech" was full of negative connotations, even without the baggage it personally held for me, and I could see that he had used the term deliberately in order to gauge my reaction.

"Can it be deliberate? Like particular strands of magic bridged and taken?" My mind was already going in five directions using this new information.

He eyed me. "Yes."

"Like she could remove the extra energy someone has, energy that perhaps makes the person otherwise unable to sleep?"

"Yes." He sounded exasperated, but a smile tugged the edge of his lips. I added a "+1" to my "Making friends feel better" mental tally.

Besides, that skill really could be useful. I usually needed to work quite hard, especially at night, to rid myself of the excess magical energy that was always bubbling up inside of me. I wondered what it would be like to live with someone who could drain and bottle bits of my magic at will. Dead useful and completely terrifying, depending on what she was like. Strange and powerful, and scary in the unknown.

Like me.

"It makes her an excellent healer for people who can't make the conscious decision to have their magic used," he said. "But most people cross to the other side of the street if they see her."

Likely not the life of the party at Old Magic events, then.

Darkness lit his eyes. "Which is laughable. Such a small distance wouldn't stop her, if she wanted to hurt anyone or take their magic."

On the other side of the river, Dare "rehabilitated" a crocodile that breathed poisonous gas when it opened its jaws. Then ran a hand over the oddly wobbling croc-goose it had been attacking. It abruptly coughed then began waddling normally again.

The darkness receded from his expression on his next exhale. "Just because a mage has a power, doesn't mean she is that power. Or that she lets it rule her." He was speaking generically, but his gaze was on me. "Not everyone is frightened by choices not yet made."

Just because I could use Origin Magic, that didn't mean I was going to end the world.

I swallowed around the heady and heavy sensation of those unspoken words and said, "Okay," because thank you was too inadequate and anything else was not enough.

"The Department knows there is a rare mage running around. They will never just let that person be. But if that person can avoid them for a long enough time to make plans and gather allies, there are ways to live inside the fish bowl. Not quite freely, but not quite enslaved either."

"Your mother?"

"Usually stays on our island, quietly away from government eyes and idiotic whispers. Helping as we build our vast armies and make our plans to dominate the world, of course." There was a twist of dark amusement to the statement. "Everyone knows that the Dares are power mad. And we use everything to our advantage. Smart of them to realize that, really, because it's absolutely true."

He conjured a blue ball of energy and a hologram burst from it. An attractive, dark-haired woman stripped one long, black glove off her arm and laid bare fingers on the skin of an ailing man. On the edges of the scene, people resembling the sick man—his family, most likely—stared at her in loathing and distrust.

"But she doesn't withhold help from even the crasseetars who need it," he said.

My throat clenched. I remembered his words so long ago, when he'd been a stranger without a face, and I'd been a girl too bloody to later recognize—that his mother wouldn't have cared that I was ordinary and without magic, and that she would have healed me. Those whispered words and the sentiment behind them were the reasons I was alive today.

He extinguished the hologram in a clenched fist, but his voice was calm. "And one day the fearful will succeed. Someone will finally kill her when she's on some peaceful mission away from home, and the entire Layer will pretend not to be relieved. On the day the world should fear us the most, they will break the dawn with overwhelming relief in their minds, unknowing of what the dark will bring."

I swallowed. "Everyone is in charge of their own actions?"

He tossed the remnants of magic to the ground. "Yes. We are."

The tiles reformed around us once more.

"The irony," he said in a deceptively conversational tone, "is in what people choose to worry about versus what they choose to ignore. While people don't consider how destruction and war can forge creation and health, they also don't stop to think about how healing magic can be used to decimate instead. Knowing the ways to incapacitate or stop parts of the body from functioning? Taking over brain centers—control, perception, memory? Healers take strict oaths. But figuring out how to do such things is the advantage of any mage who can get an entry point into another's magic."

I wiggled my previously broken toe inside of my boot. Dr. Greyskull had fixed it by magically diving down into my system last term.

"Growing up under the tutelage of a mother who heals and a father who wars was a highly useful experience," he said.

"Sounds confusing."

He just laughed. "Come on. We'll go blow the recording devices at the edges of the Midlands one last time before the Troop arrives."

Chapter Twenty-Seven

THE TROOP

THE PEACEKEEPERS' TROOP arrived Monday afternoon.

I had been told by Dare that Excelsine normally used a set alumni roster of exceptional mages who volunteered to return to their alma mater for the same three weeks every year—two weeks to overlap with the student combat mages and one week to take over their duties when the students were at the competition.

As such, usually the first two weeks when the current combat mages and past ones were all on campus was a sort of combat alumni event, complete with playful harassment on both sides and dedicated, mentored practice between the graduates and competitors to prepare the competitors for the competition that would begin two Mondays hence.

The Monday after the qualifier was usually a raucous and cheerful day. And for the Junior Department and most of the Justice Squad, the arrival of the Troop was met with cheery relief.

But for the combat mages... The best that could be said of Dare that morning when we'd met at the goat crack of dawn, was that today was not going to be a good day.

I ducked into the meeting room with a scant two minutes to spare before three p.m.—the time the Troop was scheduled to meet the squads. Isaiah nodded. Peters glared. Camille smiled, coolly civil. Dare looked pointedly at the enchanted clock. I held up two fingers and gave them a little shake, then slipped into a free seat along the right aisle.

I was a little more tolerant of Dare's crazed timekeeping now that I understood it. As each person entered, Dare incorporated them into his schema of the room. The more powerful the person, the more concentration it required for him to adjust the variables into an intuitive pattern that he could quickly convert on.

If he could demand certain people show up ten minutes early to every event, he totally would.

Taken in retrospect, some of the irritation he had shown for me after the Tricorn incident might have been an annoyed realization that there was someone new on campus that he needed to be aware of. Freaky feral power bursts.

Selmarie Senthuss stood tall with Isaiah at the front of the room as they answered questions while everyone settled into seats.

The Troop entered the room on the dot, entering in magical military fashion. Blinks of color flipped shields around them and empty darts of light flashed in ways that demonstrated that such blips could be weapons during battle. Showy.

I stole a glance at Dare and saw his lip curl in derision. I knew his thoughts on the matter. All style and no substance.

There was something weird about the way my eyes traveled over the line-up, though, and it caused me to stop and solve the puzzle presented instead of listening to

Isaiah's opening speech. Without individual study, the thirty Troop members seemed indistinguishable from each other in the line-up—even the tall from the short, the men from the women, and the late twenty-year-olds from those at least in their early fifties. Magically encased in flickering lights, a first glance gave the impression of every mage standing straight-shouldered, with slicked-back hair and an androgynous overlay.

But that was not the truth.

I looked closer. Individual features popped out, then retreated into sameness. Some sort of invariance enchantment was in effect to make them appear similar.

All except the last two. The last man, wearing a multitude of stripes and magic dots on his shoulders, was the obvious leader. The second to last man was dressed in the same uniform as the others and stood beside them in the line, but his thick hair was distinctly blond. He was of indeterminate age but there was something oddly lazy about his eyes that blinked from bright green to gray—as if the invariance magic couldn't totally cover him, and his indolence was on display for everyone to see. It was almost a statement saying that he wasn't drinking the same spells as the rest of the line-up.

Once my gaze hit him, it didn't want to let go. There was something—

A polite clap from the audience snapped me out of my study, as the leader stepped forward. I had missed Isaiah's entire speech.

The leader gave a short bow. "We look forward to working with the exceptional students of Excelsine, and hopefully converting this precedence into a storied tradition."

Dream on, magic man. It had become pretty apparent that no one from the Combat Squad was hoping for the same.

As the leader droned on, my gaze drifted back to the man standing next to him. His lazy gaze was taking in the room, seemingly uninterested and bored, but the minute focus of his leaf-green eyes as his gaze shifted from face to face reminded me of Constantine—projecting an image of disregard, but missing nothing. The man's shifting gaze continued around the room as his leader spoke about glorious opportunities and partnerships.

His build was similar to Christian's and Dare's—athletic and a few inches over six feet. I had never seen this man before, yet there was something so familiar about him.

His gaze met mine and stopped. The color of his eyes flipped from green to gray, and his head cocked to the side. It was hard to breathe and my magic was doing funny things. Flight responses were clashing with a desire to fling my arms around him.

The lazy disregard left his gaze completely as it sharpened on me.

Familiar ultramarine magic instantly tightened around me and shattered the increasingly creepy connection. I swallowed and turned a grateful glance to Dare, who was looking between us with a narrowed gaze.

The leader began to introduce each of the men and women in the line. I heard the names, but the only one that mattered was the last. Emrys Norr, who was still staring at me and had begun to smile.

Isaiah, Selmarie, and the Troop leader shook hands, then Selmarie addressed the room. "We have broken the teams into threesomes and fivesomes based on the original Combat and Justice Squad pairings. Either one pair will have a Troop member join them to make a threesome, or two pairs will add a Troop member to make a fivesome. The Troop member will then work with the Justice Squad partner or partners when the combat mages leave for the competition. This is an excellent opportunity to spread good will and help campus security grow stronger. Assignments are on your tablets."

I looked down, already knowing what I'd see. Magic was a funny thing, and as Dare so often pointed out, it made things connect subconsciously before consciousness was made aware.

Alexander Dare, Ren Crown, Emrys Norr. The last was highlighted purple, and when I looked up, Emrys was outlined in the same dark lilac. He was still staring at me, a small smile riding his lips.

People were moving around me—rising from their chairs and introducing themselves, according to corresponding outlines—but neither Emrys nor I moved.

"Crown."

It took another nudge and a repeat of my name for me to stop the staring contest and look up at Dare. His brows were sharply drawn and there was a hint of concern in his expression.

"Yes?" I answered automatically.

"Up."

I rose mechanically and hooked my bag over my shoulder. Dare's fingers briefly brushed my arm and I felt a small burst of invigoration as well as the echo of a ringing bell, which cleared the haze that had started to gather.

"Thanks."

"Keep it together," he said, his voice tight. "And sleep eight hours tonight, or I'll make you run laps—around the Fourth Circle."

One "lap" on the Fourth was about four miles in length.

"Keep your pants on." At one time, I would have blushed like mad after saying something like that to him, but Dare and I weren't passing acquaintances anymore. "And you are the one who made me get up today at dawn. I'm not running laps," I muttered. "I already have a drill sergeant."

"I do hope I'm not interrupting?" A smooth voice said. We both turned to see our new partner approaching. His green eyes flipped to gray then flipped back to green. The purple corona that surrounded the iris remained unchanged. Whether the purple was from the identification spell or naturally occurring, I didn't know. "Mr. Dare, it is a pleasure."

They exchanged a business-like greeting and handshake.

"And Miss Crown? We haven't met, but it is also a great pleasure." There was something sharp and familiar in his gaze for a moment, and my heart rate spiked. But then a feeling of ease filled the space, making me relax.

"Likewise," I murmured.

When his irises were gray, they were similar in color to Will's.

"I look forward to working with the both of you," Emrys said as we exited the building. His voice was easy to listen to. Masculine, philharmonic tones. Like an oceanic symphony, both crashing and soothing.

Nothing changed on Dare's inscrutable face, but his elbow clipped me and his clear magic spiked through me, ringing me lucid again.

Great. Emrys Norr had been using some form of auditory magic. I was going to seriously have to look into magical cotton balls.

"Where would you like to start, sir?" Dare said, his voice militarily precise and polite, though the lingering magic from his spike made me ultra-aware of him, and there was a deep well of underlying irritation and disgust underneath his polite question.

"Please, call me Emrys."

"Where would you like to start, sir?" Dare reiterated without a pause.

The mercenary looked at me and gave a theatrical sigh. "Is he always so straight-laced? We'll have to change that."

I kept my expression neutral, though my heart rate surged waiting for Dare to destroy him. Dare was anything but straight-laced. He was just very careful in how he rode roughshod over rules.

"Feel free to give it a try, sir." Dare's smile was pleasant and oh, so utterly false. No one listening could say that he was impolite, but in the spirit of the exchange, the word "sir" might as well have been swapped for something far less civil.

"How about we start in the Midlands?" Emrys said lightly. "Terribly interesting strips of land."

Still highly attuned to Dare, I could feel the tightening in his magic. I bumped him back as unobtrusively as I could, and some of the tightness dissipated.

There was a speculative look in Emrys's eyes as he looked between the two of us, and his lips took an unpleasant downward turn, before a full smile bloomed in a manic switch of emotion. "Shall we?"

"Actually, sir, there is nothing you need to know about the Midlands other than how to make sure the barrier magic stays intact. We'll start with the perimeter wards," Dare said, moving in the direction of the nearest henge—a henge full of arches that would send us nowhere near the Midlands.

"Alas," Emrys said, giving me a smile.

I smiled uneasily back and followed Dare.

Dare led and narrated the path through the perimeter wards in the same order that he had when we had first gone through them, but whereas his comments were still direct and correct, they were even more of a textbook recitation than what he had given to the other members of the Justice Squad.

It was extremely boring, but Emrys Norr was just disconcerting enough to keep me on edge. There was something very familiar, and yet strange about him.

"You meet together each day, correct?" Emrys said to me.

"Yes, we—"

"The three of us will meet once a day," Dare cut in, finishing the conversation. "In addition, I'll meet with you separately." He addressed that to Emrys, but I knew, since we'd already discussed it, that he meant me as well.

Emrys was very polite, but I was happy to put his strange eyes in my rearview mirror as he excused himself with a cheerful farewell and a barely visible smirk.

"There's something off about him." Dare's words were flat as we watched Emrys walk over to speak to a number of the Junior Department students who were always following us.

"You would say that no matter who we got stuck with," I pointed out. "And you just met him."

Seeing the charming grin Emrys displayed as the students eagerly chatted with him—while pointing at me—did nothing to make me want to defend him past reasonable argument, however.

"I've seen him before," Dare said. He motioned for me to walk with him to the henge north of our position. "Along with the rest of the Troop's members. The Troop is well-known, and we did our research."

"And?"

Dare frowned. "It's just...off. The whole situation. We should have been assigned to someone else. He's mid-level only."

"Hold on, I'm not sure your head will fit through this arch. Let me go first."

He rolled his eyes. "There's an order to things. And you felt it too—something strange about him."

"A little. Yeah," I admitted as we emerged on the other side of the Eighth Circle. I felt relief course through me almost instantly once Emrys and the Junior Department could no longer see me. "He seemed different from the rest of them. But that could just be your paranoia infecting me."

"It's not. And Telgent isn't right either." At my blank expression, Dare stopped his forward movement and crossed his arms. "General Telgent, the Troop's leader who spoke for the last half hour? Observation involves listening, Ren."

I had halfheartedly logged the Troop leader's whole boring speech somewhere in my memory banks. I'd see about dredging up some enthusiasm to remember it later. "You aren't paying me to do that kind of observing. Let's be frank now. That whole spiel when we began working together was rousing, but you just wanted to get your hands on my sweet, feral abilities."

"I will make you run all over this mountain," he said, overly enunciating the words.

"Yeah, yeah." I waved a hand and began walking again. "So, what, you want to put Emrys and Telgent under watch? Set up some paper animals to follow them?"

He tapped his arm, then shook his head. "I'll deal with it. Just say as little as possible and don't do anything fancy when Norr is around, and do nothing at the group exchange they are scheduling."

"I'll be perfectly dull, promise."

The next few days with Emrys Norr and Dare, though, illustrated the futility of those words.

Emrys tried to bait Dare (unsuccessfully), and to startle me (successfully), into showing unusual magic, as if he was testing us both for rare abilities. He had lots of success with me—I had shot all sorts of, thankfully, unidentifiable and weird magic all over the place in the past few days—and Emrys's success with me was driving Dare spare. But for some reason, I just couldn't feel Emrys approaching like Dare had taught me to feel with other people.

Emrys stalked us in the Midlands, right alongside the Junior Department, every time we entered. Dare couldn't keep Emrys out of the Midlands—the grounds were free for any authorized student or visitor to wander. However, after the third time Emrys startled me, Dare made Emrys's visits there extremely unpleasant in a variety of untraceable ways.

That didn't stop Emrys from trying to follow us, though, or from gathering data on me.

He was being paid by the Department, just like the rest of the Troop. And the Department was looking for rare mages. All he really needed was a stage to showcase the magical way I responded to things, then he could wrap me up with a big red bow.

After a few days of rounds, the Troop, Combat Squad, and Justice Squad convened for the group exchange meant to pull together everything we had been learning, and to facilitate sharing across the three squads. Selmarie and the Combat Squad would be showcasing the defensive lines, wards, prevention steps, and offensive strategies. Isaiah and the Justice Squad would be going through all of the campus rules and regulations, as well as performing the various maneuvers we had learned over the past weeks. And the Troop...would be doing whatever they did.

Dare took me aside to repeat his "nothing fancy" warnings.

"But I'm supposed to be doing things we've been practicing, right?"

"Yes, but don't. Don't do anything I've taught you. In fact, just follow Peters."

I grimaced. Anyone except Peters. "Isaiah?" I asked hopefully, trying to negotiate.

"He's coordinating the exercises with Selmarie and Telgent." Dare gave me a sharp look. "Follow Peters."

"Fine," I said grudgingly. Peters would love that I was watching him for cues.

Dare was looking over my head. "Follow Peters, follow orders, and do nothing more."

Dare's gaze was tracking the movements on the field as the last members of the squads gathered, and I could feel his magic reaching out, wrapping around one person after another, cataloging them in the space. Telgent and Emrys showed last, and I waited to speak until Dare returned his gaze to me, since I knew he was vigorously keeping watch on those two.

"What about Emrys?" I asked. "We are supposed to be working together in the demo."

"No. Don't even glance at him while you are demonstrating."

"That's going to be a little difficult," I said.

"He wants to be seen, and he wants you to be seen. He'll try and get you to do something showy with him in front of the crowd." He pinned me with a heated expression. "Don't do anything showy."

"Okay, okay." I held out my hands in submission.

His lips pressed together and he stared at me.

"I won't, I'll be good," I said. It was what I had said a number of times over the past few days, right before something Emrys did made me blast magic everywhere.

Dare stared hard at me for a long moment more before flicking his wrist. A strip of t-shirt like material appeared in his hand. With his back to the rest of the group, he paused, holding the strip for a long moment. A shimmer of magic caught the sunlight as it flowed from his hand over the cloth. He held the strip toward me. "Put this in your pocket," he said, almost reluctantly.

"Are you giving me a token? Are we in a Medieval Tournament?"

"Ren..." But there was a smile hovering reluctantly on his lips.

"I accept your token and will do honor in your name, good sir." I stuffed the cloth strip deep into my back pocket, trying to extinguish the little thrill that shot through me.

He rolled his eyes and pushed me back toward the gathering group.

Half an hour later, I was appalled at how awful the Troop really was. Emrys's file might have him listed at mid-level according to Dare, but when Emrys was with us, he was clearly better than these jokers.

Maybe I was just extremely spoiled from spending endless hours watching the best combat mage on a campus filled with great ones, but watching the Troop "demonstrate" was like watching the form competition in the Combat Qualifier. All of the moves were perfect and precise and lifeless as they blasted targets that only moved in precise ways, and fought enemies whose moves were already obvious.

Wow.

"Seriously?" I hissed at Dare, who elbowed me in response.

These people put on a dazzling show—better than a Broadway or Cirque spectacle—but they wouldn't last a minute in the simulation rooms with Dare. Dear lord, this group was going to protect campus?

"We are all going to die," I whispered.

"Yup," Dare said, tone dark and resigned. "Set Tyrne will probably be sucked onto campus the day after we leave and destroy the whole mountain in a rage. That is your kind of luck."

"What? Who?" I asked, alarmed.

Camille glared at me and I shut up.
I quickly looked Set-whoever up on my bracelet. Some epic Fourth Layer berserking creature hybrid with three forms—one of them terrifying enough to make me blanch thinking about it—him—bulldozing the Magiaduct in a relentless fury with the torn limbs of his enemies surrounding him.

We were all going to die.

Thankfully, the Combat Squad demonstrations were next, and they were captivating enough to take my mind off our imminent demise. Even watching the combat mages teach the Troop the individual operations for security measures proved interesting.

But two hours later, I was gritting my teeth as I went through really pedantic verbal exercises with Peters in front of the squads. Reciting all of the Justice Codes? Not my idea of fun or the way to use memory slots. Time to get out of here and do something useful.

"And that is the procedure for taking care of an unknown item," Peters finished, thank God. "Yes, Mr. Norr, you have a question?"

Emrys stepped forward, his leaf-green eyes bright. "I found this amazing thing on my last trip through the Midlands. Odd and alarming."

My breath caught as he held up a papered dragon's wing. I managed to stop myself from looking at Dare by keeping my gaze pinned to the wing. It was from one of my map dragons, a wing burned off during our first exercise.

"As opposed to containment," Emrys said, "why couldn't we, say, just do this?"

His hand flicked and the paper caught fire.

Everything around me went abruptly static—the people around me slowing to a time-warped stillness. It was the opposite of Raphael's leeching—I was now the one moving at a faster rate than could be perceived by the others around me. Agony rolled my magic inward, then thrust out toward my dying creation. Unhindered by the control cuff that had been failing me more and more, my magic shot out in a coil to strike the one who dared to hurt it. In the distance, slowed screams shuddered in the air and the ground shook.

Magic edged in ultramarine suddenly, and aggressively, clamped the bared teeth of my subconscious strike and jerked it back. Immediately, the jerk was followed by a sense of calm washing through me, cooling the fire. Dare's magic reached from the back pocket of my jeans—from the cloth he had given me—and took over all my systems. An outside force reining my magic in bit by bit, he took control from me and used my own magic to forcefully soothe the edge of my agony and anger.

I took a deep breath, then another, letting my body relax as he exerted the good decision making that I presently lacked. A strange feeling released from me as he did it—like one of a series of hooks in me had been detached and set free.

Dare's magic let go of me in a puff of air, and the world righted to a normal pace as the group looked at Emrys expectantly while the dragon's wing burned.

Fully under control once more, I realized that no one else had noticed what had just happened in their slowed landscape, and that the screaming and ground shaking had been a forewarning heard only in my own mind—and that such results would have occurred a moment later in that exact way, had Dare not taken control.

But instead, the rest of the group was staring at Emrys, waiting. He had created a loaded silence with his words, and they were waiting for the punchline that hadn't yet been delivered.

Peters looked around, mystified, when nothing happened. "I suppose you can just do that, Mr. Norr?"

Emrys's expression was strange, and his smile was far too tight—almost on the edge of pained. Pained, but at the same time...satisfied?

Emrys smiled and blew the dust from his palm. "Ah, well, then, no issue."

It was a big issue. Huge. I could have done something horrible. And Emrys had wanted...something to happen, though he couldn't have known what. If Dare hadn't taken control of my magic...

I tensely spent the next few hours ignoring Emrys and woodenly emulating Peters. I caught more than one gaze of a combat mage looking at me, then at Dare, in bafflement. As if they'd expected Dare's shadow to do something noteworthy.

When the squads were finally excused, I tripped away to our normal meeting spot to wait for Dare. I perched on a rock and watched the skiers making tracks down the Seventh Circle, going through the bottom arches and emerging from different top arches in an unending run. I pulled the cloth out of my back pocket and ran it through my fingers, shaking.

"You okay?" Dare said when he appeared at my side a few minutes later, expression carefully blank.

"Yes. Other than realizing we are all going to die when you leave, I'm great."

He didn't say anything for a long moment. "I put a lot of pressure on you," he said finally. "But there are a lot of mages on this campus who will help, should something go really wrong. You are strong and have good instincts. You will do fine."

"Like with Emrys and whatever stunt that was? Hardly." He sat next to me and I shakily handed him the ripped strip of cloth he had given to me. "Thank you. I don't know… How did you…" I shook my head. "Thank you for giving me that."

The cloth burst into flame in his hand. The fire burned atop his open palm, but his expression was inscrutable as he watched the skiers. "I don't know what you mean. Give you what?"

"Yes, thanks for that part too," I said. I didn't know what else to say about that expression of trust, about the obviously excessively guarded secret he had just revealed to me.

I wanted to ask how he had stayed unfrozen during my magical tantrum, unlike the others around us. Because of the strip maybe?

But I stayed quiet, and he remained silent as well. There was a last wisp of smoke, then his fist closed over the ashes in his palm. When his fingers opened, his palm was bare.

"Why didn't the Justice Magic on campus charge you?" I asked softly. Dare had exerted control over me and made my magic do what he wanted it to do. Delia never got away with anything half as big as that, and Constantine, Will, and I had talked about how someone would have to take the judicial hit when it came time to test our leech.

"The intention of a caster and acceptance by the person being spelled matters. The Justice Magic takes both into account."

"But you couldn't have known I'd... Okay."

My own level of trust had obviously already been made quite clear.

On the leech front...my mind was spinning. That hook that had detached inside of me? The one that had been in a long line of them? All those hooks were Raphael's leash. And one small piece had been detached by Dare's maneuver.

Dare's eyes narrowed as he looked at the edges of my body, gaze following the outline all the way around. "Where did you get your shield set? I've been meaning to ask you."

"Marsgrove."

"Dean Marsgrove gave you a shield set?"

I grimaced. "He was kind of forced to."

"It's one of the strongest I've encountered in a non-combat mage," he said, his tone giving away nothing of what he was thinking.

"Yeah. It kind of sucks at the same time that it rocks." I shakily met his gaze. "Do you recognize the magic within the shields, at the base?"

Please, no, please, no...

He shook his head slowly. "No. And that is...abnormal...for a set so strong. I can see Marsgrove's fingers in there, now that you say it, but they are like oil in water. Who made the underlying part of the set?"

"Marsgrove knows." That was both true and sounded like I didn't know. Marsgrove was contractually obligated not to say anything about me for another month.

I trusted Dare. With my life. But people got all weird about Raphael. And it would force things I'd rather not discuss out into the open.

"I saw you with Marsgrove, the first day back," Dare said.

"He was escorting his cousin," I said. "She's my roommate."

All true. Just slightly misleading. Marsgrove had been mostly using Olivia as the reason for his escort while he dragged me across campus, but that was better left unsaid as well.

"Hmmm. Come on, the Troop is going to do their 'rounds.' The monster of the hour should come stomping through at any moment. We can hide with popcorn and watch them 'handle' it."

The Troop coordinated their own movements a few hours a day while "on call." Usually, we observed them joking with each other or working casual magic at the edges of their checkpoints—doing little that would be called work. I understood why a little more now.

Aside from Emrys...who always had his head together with students like the Junior Department stooges or the female half of Excelsine's administrative staff. He was always madly flirting around Top Circle—extracting nefarious information about criminals like me, no doubt.

"No." I shook my head. "Pass today."

Dare nudged me toward the nearest Ninth Circle arch. "To Kratos to get rid of your jitters then."

I nodded and rubbed my back pocket absently as we walked to the Battle Building. The emptiness in my back pocket almost felt heavy, now that the cloth was gone. I gave a full body shiver, trying to shake off the feeling that I had lost something I needed.

It had to be the edginess I always experienced after being leeched. That was all.

I rubbed my empty pocket again.

Chapter Twenty-Eight
SPEAKING OF DISASTER

MIKE AND DELIA were doing something with the ski club, so Olivia, Will, Neph, and I met in our dorm room late that night for a power dinner and planning session. Magi Mart wrappers and containers were soon spread out around us.

It was far better than braving the cafeteria with Mike and Delia's empty seats at our table. We'd always been an open and welcoming table, but ever since the cafeteria "incident," strangers had been sitting with us to ask questions about Dare.

Why does he ignore everyone who tries to meet him?

What is he like?

What does he like?

Who does he like?

Does he like me, maybe?

Those were easy. The harder, more insidious ones were about what he was plotting, controlling, destroying, subjugating, conquering, etc.

"Bliss," Olivia said into the companionable silence in our room.

I smiled. Whether she was aware of it or not, she was automatically including Neph and Will more and more in her increasing serenity.

"I know, sorry about the whole cafeteria craziness. That will end soon, though, right?" I asked.

The three of them exchanged looks, then Will and Neph busied themselves with their food.

"What, no? It has to," I stressed. "It was just a novelty, so people are asking questions."

"It was a very concerning novelty to some people, Ren," Olivia said delicately. She had been really putting some effort into thinking about the tone of her words, and I appreciated that at the moment. "Anything to do with the Dares is."

"Ugh. People can be stupid. Dare told me about his mom. Stupid prejudices. Why can't—?" I took in the suddenly blank faces staring back at me. "What? Why are you looking at me like that?"

Olivia put her container down and folded her fingers together. "Axer Dare told you about his mother?"

"Sure. And I looked some things up on her too. She's a great role model. Strong, but warm; powerful, but kind—"

"Ren."

"Yes?"

"When you say that he told you about his mother, what do you mean?"

"He told me what type of mage she is and some of the things she goes through."

Olivia took a deep breath, then decided to take another. "How did you get on the subject of such a topic?"

"Oh, it was during a session last weekend. When he found out. About me. That I'm a…" I curled my fingers in the air and gave a growl.

"That you're a werewolf?" Will looked amused, even as his amusement overlaid deep alarm.

"Hey, yeah, how come we never see werewolves in the Midlands?" I was going to have to ask Dare that.

"Intelligent magical creatures and beasts can overcome the chaotic pull to the Midlands, if they want," Will said, his desire to discuss knowledge overwhelming his concern, as usual. "And unless you are a student or registered as a guest, foreign entities can't leave the Midlands once they are there. And nothing intelligent would want to suffer that consequence. Horrible for—"

"If we could get back on topic, William." Olivia sounded irate.

"Yup," Will said, chastised.

"Now, Ren," Olivia said, overly calm. "Axer Dare. His mother. What he found out about you. Why you were discussing these things at all?" Her words ended in a rushed hiss.

"Oh, he gave me these awesome papers." I shuffled through my things and held them up. "And then he died, then I brought him back, then I tried to blow up campus, then he told me these belonged to Kinsky and were mine now, and talked a little about rare magehood, and yeah..." I shrugged. "Without him spelling out the word 'origin,' I'd bet all on black."

A strangled expletive issued from Will at the same time that Neph threw both hands down and channeled an incredible stream of calming energy into everyone.

"Ren, you can have nothing to do with him anymore," Olivia shrieked. All of the room's magic and my connection to her were filled with her sudden, extreme anxiety, completely overcoming any attempt by Neph to calm her.

I stared at her, shocked. "Wait, you were just fine two minutes ago. And you said I should learn as much as possible from him when we started working together. Become 'not a stranger.'" I held up my fingers in air quotes.

"That was before he started sharing things and knowing things and pretending to befriend you."

"Hey, why does it have to be pretend? I'm not so bad once I stop being awkward!"

"She doesn't want you to be used," Neph said soothingly. "She is saying these things out of concern."

"Concern?" Olivia said. "This is far worse than concern, Nephthys."

"Because of his mom? But there is nothing different today versus yesterday on that subject. And just because someone's a rock, doesn't mean she's a weapon." I looked at Olivia pointedly, using her words.

"She's not you."

"That doesn't mean she's bad!"

"You are not sidetracking me on this. She doesn't matter. No, that is entirely untrue." Her hand cut through the air. "Sera McEllian Dare matters, but she is not the main problem here. That Axer Dare knows what you are is."

"Why?" I asked bluntly. "He's been nothing but kind. Well, kind is perhaps the wrong word when he's all grim and serious, and perfectly muscled, but still lean, and hotter than the sun..." I flailed my hands a bit. "But he's funny and a little wicked and I like him, and he's like Superman, always saving me and everyone else. Or Bautermann, or whatever Mike said."

"Why? Because the Dares have an agenda. And you just admitted he's a little wicked. Weren't you listening at lunch during that Bautermann discussion?"

I cringed. "Only sort of listening. Sometimes I tune out of the political discussions."

"Ren. The Dares are setting up their scion as the protector of the world on purpose. Who can argue against the guy who wins everything and saves everyone?"

I nodded. "Yup. That's why I'm not arguing."

Olivia turned to Neph. "Handle this. I can't do this."

"Liv—" I started to argue.

"Listen," she said, steamrolling right over me and ignoring her own directive for Neph to handle the conversation. "Do you know how many tests the Department has put Alexander

Dare through to see if he possesses the remotest ability to bridge?"

"Judging by your tone, I'd say a lot."

"He has failed—or passed, depending on your viewpoint—all of them, but they make him retake the tests every year."

"Seems extreme."

"Because they think he has the ability, Ren."

The kind of ability that would allow him to give me something that he could then use to control and manipulate my magic when I was about to explode?

It wasn't exactly controlling someone from across a street, like he'd implied that his mother could do, but it had taken him all of two seconds to put magic that could control me into a piece of cloth. Seemed like someone had valid concerns out there. And no way was I going to say any of that out loud.

I would share all of my own secrets, but exposing even the possibility of someone else's—no. And especially not someone who had done nothing but good things for me.

"It doesn't matter what you say about this, Liv," I said gently. "I don't care if he has mad goblins in his family tree."

"Do you know what the Department would do if they thought a Bridge had access to an Origin Mage?" she hissed. "They'd figure out a way to wipe the Dares' stupid island fortress off the map, no matter how impossible the Dares have made it to do just that. A war was fought over Maximilian Dare marrying Sera McEllian. A war their family won. Add in an Origin Mage, and it would certainly send the message that the Dares plan to rule the world."

Olivia said it like that was the message she had already received with this new information.

"I don't think they are trying to add me to their arsenal," I said. "I've only met one of them, his cousin Nicholas. He's sixteen. He was with us right before the Bone Beast showed last term, and sometimes they are training together when I arri—"

"Oh my God, that is not what—" Olivia took deep, heaving breaths. "You're going to be taken. Or killed. And there is nothing we will be able to do to stop it."

"Hey, it's okay." I sent pulses of soothing magic to her through all the streams in our room.

"It's not okay, Ren," she said through gritted teeth.

Will was anxiously looking back and forth between us. "So, let's talk good news instead." He clapped his hands. "Ren, Leandred, and I got a leech working an hour ago!"

"Will!" I hissed. "Timing!"

And that was how Olivia's magic blew my indestructible desk into thirty pieces.

Olivia grimaced as we walked the short distance to Okai at twilight, but gave a brisk nod of greeting to the rocks as they opened the door.

"So?" she asked, after I shut the door behind us. She was still pretty upset with me, but it had manifested into a more resigned world-weariness. And she'd spent an hour using our room's magic to make me a new desk that was even more awesome than my old one. That my desk had teeth that now aggressively stole my schoolwork if I worked for too long had to mean I was almost forgiven.

"You are vibrating with energy," she said. "I have all sorts of scenarios running through my mind about how you brought me here to cover up the tunnel you dug to First Layer China."

"That's a great idea!"

"Ren…"

I laughed and bounced on the balls of my feet, excited. "Not a tunnel." I whipped out the wood chip I had been carrying for the past few hours, waiting to use. Waiting had been agonizing. But Will had spilled the beans about us finishing a leech, and there was no time like the present to put plans to action.

"You've been collecting First Layer playground bits?" Olivia said dubiously. "Well done."

"Anyone who says you lack humor, obviously just doesn't know you yet. No. Look again." I thrust the chip toward her, so excited now that I was literally vibrating with it.

Olivia gingerly took the chip. She knew by now to wait for an explanation rather than to run automatic diagnostic spells on anything Will and I handed to her. Not that we'd meant to electrocute her on Monday. The less said about that, the better. Who checked for poison on a loofah anyway? Olivia was pretty paranoid. We'd just wanted to make and give her a relaxing, magical shower aid, since I had done all that research on shower charms after that day in the Midlands.

But it meant that since she did accept things from me without checking first, that she trusted me a great deal.

"Like Will said…we succeeded. Ta da!"

I held out my hands in a showman's pose. Guard Friend copied the motion, one hand straight up, while the other offered toward the item.

Olivia stilled, her eyes now focused on the chip. A careful tendril of magic flowed down her fingers and wrapped around the chip, gently prodding. The chip pulsed beneath the questioning magic.

"How much?"

"It will allow the user to channel my magic for a five-second period of time. It will only work on me. I refused Constantine's suggestion to start manufacturing nonspecific leeches wholesale." I rolled my eyes. "Hopefully, this will be just enough to start cracking through Raphael's spell."

"I..." She swallowed. "Ren, if you had asked me to do this the week after you moved in, I would have done it and sucked every possible drip of your magic dry in that five seconds. But now..." She shook her head.

I smiled. "Which is why I'm offering! And hey, Constantine wanted me to tell you that he is totally willing to test it instead."

I had expected Constantine to wheedle a first try with the leech anyway, but other than a small, covetous look at it, he had waved his hand to indicate his acceptance of my plan to have Olivia do it. Oddly, even though he ceded the first try to Olivia, his expression had been one of complete satisfaction and anticipation.

Olivia grimaced.

"It's completely safe," I said reassuringly. "It's a small drain with a built-in safeguard. Not enough to control me completely, and easy enough to shake off, if I want."

Like Dare's cloth. He'd taken control of my magic, yes, but it had been an exertion that had consisted of only positive intentions toward the user. If I had panicked, he would have let go. Or at least, that was how it had felt.

I knew this wasn't the leech Constantine sought.

Constantine had been so animated and determined lately. And not only was the leech project going well, but so too was the dodecaplex design and the paint making. We were getting better, a lot better. It made it hard not to smile smugly at Stevens the three days a week that I saw her.

Maybe Will was right—and Constantine simply had been terminally bored. The projects kept him focused and directed. He'd barely crested twelve judicial infractions this week, and I hadn't seen a honey bunny in weeks.

Olivia took a deep breath. "Okay. Let's do it."

We clasped the chip between our hands, then I willed my desire for the magic to work.

White light flared and an internal link of gold was pried away. Another hook detached.

The smile bloomed across my face in reflection of the feeling within. "I can feel part of Raphael's magic breaking free."

Olivia lifted her five seconds of magic use from me, and I only had a second to wonder at what she'd use it for before her outward burst of magic surrounded me in an exact reflection of the lightning blast I had set off at the Festival. Pure joy filled me.

"Olivia, that was wonderful."

She looked relieved that I had liked what she'd chosen to do with the magic. She handed the chip back to me.

I kept my hand out, smile still wide, and motioned to her bag.

"What?" she asked suspiciously.

"I'm going to join the chip to your cocoon. That way you can use a little bit of my magic whenever you nee—"

"No."

I blinked. "But I think it will help. Bit by bit the magic will chew away at Raphael's leash." Dare's cloth maneuver and the first hook detaching had made me think it possible.

"We can do that here, bit by bit, in a controlled setting." She gave me a look. "With Nephthys and William watching next time."

"But—"

"No." She looked weary all of a sudden. "I'm trying to be a better person, Ren. One step at a time, okay?"

I blinked. "You are already a good person."

She stared at me for a long moment. "If everything is fine through the night, we can try it again tomorrow, okay?"

I readily agreed and we returned to our room.

Thoughts of the day wouldn't stop zooming around my head, so I stared at our (still) blank ceiling and babbled instead of trying—and failing—to go to sleep. Emrys was out to get me. The squad simulation had been a horror-fest. The Justice Squad loyalties were split between the Combat Squad and the Peacekeepers' Troop. Tensions were high.

Olivia was generally willing to listen to my grumbles and mad stories, but she was still a little irritated about my inability to see Dare as a threat. Therefore, she issued displeased little noises every few sentences.

I said nothing about the cloth or the dragon wing.

"Working with the Troop is torture. What we need is an awesome fighting force of delinquents," I said, already thinking of the wild and insane abilities and misdeeds that each club member could contribute.

Olivia gave me a deadpan stare, then returned her gaze to her book.

"No, seriously! Think of it! Who better knows the secret ways of campus? Who knows how to skirt regulations and rules?"

Olivia paused in the act of turning a page, then slowly grabbed her pen and held it over her pad. It hovered there for a long moment, then hit the paper with a jolt as she jotted down her note. She crossed something out on one of her many other lists, cocked her head, then penciled over the top.

"What are you writing?" I asked.

"Number Fifty-two."

"What?" I was clueless as to what she was referring. "Fifty-two what?"

"Nothing." She had once more dismissed me entirely, turning her attention back to her book.

I spent the rest of the time until I fell asleep riding high on my success with the leech and amusing myself with thoughts of an awesome imaginary fighting force. Together, the thoughts stopped me from freaking out completely about Emrys, Dare, and all of the watchful gazes waiting for me to screw up.

Chapter Twenty-Nine
CLICK ONCE FOR LUCK

HAD TAKEN to naming my most frequent followers—lizard, stripes, business girl, neon shoes, ribbons, rainbow eyes, tie-dye hair, and twig-man (who was both skinny and easily startled)—and in order to stay sane in the cafeteria, I drew animated cartoons of them being both inept and cunning. Keiren and Inessa, the two mages I knew by name, were often depicted as well. Delia found it all hilarious.

Bellacia got her own comic strip. I called it Bellacia on Report. Just like in real life, she popped up on the page at the most unusual spots and at the most inopportune times to "chat" with the red-headed villain. Trying to catch me when I was most vulnerable and unprepared.

In real life, I evaded the watchdog groups as much as possible, and excused myself from Bellacia when she popped into my path, but unfortunately I couldn't avoid her in class.

Usually, that was true for Keiren too.

However, Will's tireless efforts at working out how to get our group to assemble together paid off big dividends Thursday in Politics when Neph finally slid into the circle of our group. We also pulled in Asafa as our sixth. He had immediately opted into the plan when he had overheard us planning to corrupt the system to be in the same group.

I had tried to help Will with the spells that he had attached to the class chairs, but Dare—running on some crazy pre-adrenaline high mere days before the competition—demanded most of my time. Olivia had finally put her foot down three nights before and told me to delegate.

It had taken an agonizing few hours of being pulled in all directions before I'd asked Delia and Mike if they could help Will on the last few enchantments.

They'd been delighted. I still didn't know how to feel about the whole delegating thing. Guilt, relief, wonder. It was a strange and somewhat heady mix.

Will racked up a demerit in the class log for the spell, but it didn't matter, as whatever group was formed today would be the one assembled for the rest of term. As the group clicked audibly into place, Will gave Bellacia a smug smile.

Every class period, the other assistants moved from group to group, never staying too long in any one—and never approaching ours. Bellacia, on the other hand, spent the majority of each class sitting smack in the midst of our group.

"Ten minutes, assistants. Get names or log magic," Harrow called.

"Please list your names," Bellacia said with a brittle smile, her finger hovering above her classroom tablet. "The room spell will automatically pull you together for projects and discussions for the rest of term. But do be aware that at times the professor likes to mix groups for specific tasks in order to encourage more spirited debate."

She looked to me, her gaze demanding, so I listed our names clockwise around the group, ending with, "Asafa Frey, and Nephthys Bau."

Sharp green eyes speared me. Then Bellacia gave a tinkling laugh, and a warm fairy spirit flowered in its auditory path. Her eyes, though... Her eyes were cold and calculating. Far more faerie than fairy. When I listened to her, all was well in the world. When I looked at her, I knew such was far, far, from the truth.

"Power speaks to power, as always. But so too does danger. Such a group. What was that last name you mentioned? Point her out?"

The table seemed to go still. Alarms blared in my head. Alarms I didn't understand.

"Miss Crown?" Bellacia continued to smile companionably at me, her gaze coldly sliding over Neph, trying to fix in on her position.

Last term, in the cafeteria I had gotten used to people not seeing Neph unless I called their attention to her, but we had formed such a tight table unit that I had somewhat forgotten. I had definitely been unaware that class authorities might be affected. This was the first time we had successfully gotten Neph into our group discussion.

And Bellacia had just asked specifically about her—had recognized her name or the magic of whatever hid muses from normal view. Maybe muses were normally treated as a filled, but empty chair in a classroom. Maybe Bellacia was wondering how I knew Neph's name.

Asafa, Delia, Will, and I were continuous troublemakers—and easily discovered as such if one asked the right person the right questions. There was an anti-gossip enchantment on the Justice Tablets, making punishments and offenses confidential, but names of repeat offenders were easily deduced by those possessing any measure of cunning.

Mike was pretty normal. Neph, who never stuck a foot out of scholarly line, should be considered normal too.

"Miss Crown." Bellacia's voice was lilting again, demanding in its soft, compulsive way. "Point Nephthys Bau out."

Neph should be normal, but there had been all that weirdness back in the First Layer with Olivia calling her by her last name. And the thing with her uncle. And how the muse community shunned her.

Delia bent her head suddenly toward Neph, and Will, Mike, and Asafa, pulled into a tight formation, chairs and magic leaning in to envelop Neph.

"We should get started," I said, pushing at the feel of Bellacia's voice in my ears. I worked at making her voice visible—seeing it as green sound waves undulating in the air—so that I could combat it. I was still highly susceptible to auditory suggestion, but I had been practicing daily anti-audio enchantments with Draeger since the party. I might be new to this world and without the normal defenses people learned from birth, but I was determined and motivated.

"Miss Crown." Her eyes narrowed. "I insist, as a teaching assistant in this class, that you do as I ask."

The frequency of the green waves increased, spiking. The room's Justice Magic rang a peal and Professor Harrow's voice sounded from far away. "Miss Bailey? You just received a Level Two Offense, what—?"

"Miss Crown," Bellacia repeated forcefully, cutting through my ability to hear our professor. "Tell me now. Quickly."

All sound besides her voice ceased. Tell me, tell me, tell me... "No," I gritted out, and my magic repeated the response, trying to push the power she was exerting on me back outward.

She leaned forward, green eyes mere slits, her voice a poisonous spiral of sound. Peals were ringing somewhere far away. "Ren Crown, you will do as I say."

My mouth opened to do as she asked, but my mind screamed and suddenly my hand shoved into my bag.

Click, click, click, click, click! My fingers spasmed around the clicker Constantine had given me. Click, click, click. Forget, forget, forget!!

The insidious sounds that had wrapped around my mind shattered and I looked down to see Bellacia doubled over in pain. Click click, click, click, click, click! My reflexes were completely disconnected from my horror, my panic, and my judgment processing. Everything split apart in my mind due to her attempted mind control and my deep panic—and my fingers kept clicking without my conscious decision to do so as she howled and slid to the floor.

She seized violently on the tiles.

"Professor!" Mike yelled.

A shot of magic hit my chest—magic full of Neph's reassuring touch—and my panic receded just enough that my fingers dropped the clicker. It gave a tinny thump as it hit something in the bottom of my bag. With nothing to grip, I realized I was shaking uncontrollably.

Professor Harrow crouched next to Bellacia and his hands worked medical magic over her, connecting quickly to the first aid enchantments available in every classroom.

I looked around, numbly shocked to find myself on my feet with the rest of the group, in a half circle surrounding Harrow and Bellacia.

Bellacia's interest in Neph had gone past alarming and into the terrifying category for a second—she had been almost frenzied in her need to see Neph—and I felt no remorse for subverting that interest. But watching Bellacia receive what looked like magical chest compressions on the floor horrified me.

Professor Harrow got Bellacia stabilized just as medical personnel swarmed in.

I absolutely would have figured out another way to deal with her, if I had known what that clicker did. And that was on me. I did know Constantine.

He hadn't answered the question about whether it would hurt her—a deliberate omission. He had restated that pressing the clicker would protect me.

I knew better. I knew far better. I shouldn't have taken the clicker during my haze of desperation after the party. I had wanted an easy solution to one of my problems more than I had wanted to look too deeply into what that solution might entail. And Bellacia's interest in Neph and her mind control attempt had unsettled me so completely that my brain had reached for the first thing that said, "Protection."

Ten minutes after class was excused, my tally read:

Protection of friends: +8

Destruction of Constantine's devices: +1

I used an entire batch of the paint Constantine and I had made and destroyed the device with it. Using his magic mixed with mine seemed appropriate.

Also, remembering the conversation I had eavesdropped on between Bellacia and Camille, I ordered a jar of Bellacia's favorite skin cream twenty minutes later, still shaking. It cost me nearly half of my entire earnings—from the Art Expressionists booth, from trades, and from commissions—that I had collected over the past few months. I sent the jar of Tinctly's cream to Bellacia anonymously, then I headed to Dorm One.

Constantine opened the door as I approached, then tsked as soon as he closed the door behind me. "You destroyed it. Darling, you really must stop getting rid of such useful devices."

"Constantine, it did horrible things to her."

He smiled. "I know."

He flexed his arms and below the short sleeves of his black shirt I could see black lines spiraling around his veins. Justice Magic was a tricky thing, and made its own decisions about culpability on a case-by-case basis. Constantine had reaped the repercussions from the black magic backlash caused by the device.

"Didn't know you had it in you, Crown."

I reached out a hand to his arm automatically, then retracted it just as quickly, curling my fingers into a fist. "I didn't know."

"Didn't you?" He sat in his preferred armchair.

I took a deep breath before responding. Constantine taunted and tried to provoke anger when he was attempting to avoid a subject. "I would not do that to her or to you," I said quietly, sitting across from him.

"Let me tell you, Ren..." He gripped the seat of the chair, and the black lines swam around his arms. "She deserved every second of what she got. Do you know what she is planning to do to you? She has four mages watching you at all times and she has given her dear daddy your name. They are combing databases for your home address right now." His gaze became heavy-lidded, and he leaned back. "Lucky for you, your address is protected from memory unless you have given it to a mage specifically."

I looked at him steadily. Constantine had my home address. I had given it to him.

"The same protections that keep you hidden, Crown, will destroy you, if discovered."

Raphael had put the protections in place, and it would mean automatic imprisonment for me, if the Department discovered that I had a connection to him.

I couldn't let myself think about the ramifications of such things, though. Marsgrove had my address and hadn't updated the school records with it. Maybe he couldn't.

"It's a good thing I trust you," I said.

"Foolish of you."

I reached forward and touched his wrist, using the opportunity to send healing magic to him. "I know she hurt you, and you've gotten your revenge a thousandfold. Please don't make another one of those devices."

"If she threatens you, I'll do worse."

"No."

"No? But women love hearing such things." He put his free hand over his heart and his gaze was piercing and seductive. "I will do anything for you."

"No you won't, and no."

He smiled and turned his wrist so that his fingers were reaching up toward mine. "Then what? You want me to turn over a new leaf? To be a good citizen? But being good provides so few possibilities for entertainment."

Sometimes Constantine reminded me of Raphael so much that it was painful. But whereas Raphael was tainted by madness, Constantine claimed bitterness as his closest companion.

"I'm certain that you would be able to find quality entertainment no matter what your end goal."

"You flatter me." He waved his free hand in the air. "Continue."

I sighed. "Don't make another. Please. We'll figure out some other way to deal with her. I don't seem to have any moral compunction about attaching Justice Magic to someone to make their own ill intentions backfire." I grimaced. "But not something used for sport, okay?"

"I'll dwell upon the decision." His fingers curled around my forearm, then slid along the underside of my wrist to my palm. "It may take many nights."

"You can't help yourself, can you?" I gave him a reluctant smile.

"I will keep trying until you succumb," he said lightly.

My fingers slipped from his. "You would hate that. You like the challenge."

The women who fell for Constantine's song never enjoyed it for long. It was as if he was always looking for someone to love him, then was disgusted when they did.

"The chase is my favorite part of the dance. Unrivaled."

"I'm happy to help keep you entertained then." Constantine needed friends, not lovers, and it was never more obvious to me than when I saw him visibly relax every time we were alone and working.

"And about the other thing?" I prodded.

He held his palm out. "I will waste no time this week on a replacement device for that woman."

I nodded. Anything further would be his choice. "You up for working on something suitably destructive, but aimed at me instead?"

"The test went well with Price?" he asked nonchalantly.

"Yes. It was awesome. And bit by bit, it should continue to chip away at the leash."

He smiled, a slow, absolutely satisfied smile. "Good."

I eyed him for a moment. Whatever game he was playing, I was curious to see how it would unfold. Constantine was a planner to the nth degree, and very detail oriented, despite every effort he made to project otherwise outside of this space. And he was starting to make me feel like everything about his outward facade was a carefully created construction to hide what truly motivated him.

"Come." He rose and moved toward his work room. "I wish to speak to you about the stamp I gave you for your birthday."

"About how fantastic it is? I used it to hold three ward designs yesterday that I could enlarge at will." I sat in the chair on the other side of the work table from him and pushed onto the back legs, balancing—I was spending too much time with Dare, obviously. He was always balancing on chairs and trees and precipices.

The black ribbon in Constantine's hand lengthened and I could see magic glinting in the shimmer of the material.

"Think larger, Crown—about how you can use it to defend yourself, if for...oh let's say the group you hilariously call the 'Junior Department' tried to...capture you."

He snapped the ribbon under the table and it lengthened to hit the back right leg of my chair. The leg disappeared and the chair tipped. I flailed unsuccessfully, then fell. My elbow hit the ground hard, but my head hit something soft.

Torso on the ground and one leg sticking awkwardly in the air, I looked at his smirking face peering over the table's edge and sighed. At least he'd conjured me a pillow.

"I can embed small spells and call them to the surface of the stamp, then throw it at something?" I said, absently examining the equations and runes he had written all over his ceiling. "That's awesome. I would actually have remembered that just fine if you'd simply told me."

"But you figured out what I wanted without me having to say anything. And I get to watch you extricate yourself from that position, which is quite the sight."

"I'm very nimble when it counts, I'll have you know," I said as I gracelessly pulled my leg over so I could roll myself upward. The chair was fixed by the time I was upright, so I sat again—all feet on the floor. "Still"—I rubbed my neck—"that is pretty great."

I withdrew the stamp from where I kept it secured under my leather bracelet, and thought about how I could work with this new knowledge. I wondered if I could embed one of the Kinsky papers? Of course, with my luck, I'd probably create a black hole and suck everything in existence inside.

"I have something else for you as well, darling. Specifically tailored. Watch what this lovely substance can do, if you are caught."

A metallic liquid rolled along his knuckles.

I pinned him with a look, even as I leaned forward to see what he had created. "You are feeling guilty for something, and it's not the clicker."

"I have no idea what you mean." He blinked innocently, gaze upon the metal caressing the back of his hand. He twisted his hand upward and the metal surged around the edges of his hand to collect in his palm, defying gravity. "I am merely bestowing an offering to my favorite. One that would gain me an article in the Journal of Scientific Magic and get us both imprisoned."

Constantine was like a deep river interspersed with choppy currents and large rocks.

He showed me what the substance could do—which involved me splayed out on the floor again, but ecstatic at the possibilities. Olivia was certain Constantine would reveal himself as Scylla or Charybdis to go with the currents and rocks analogy, but I was banking on him being something else, in the end.

We pulled out our modified version of Asafa and Patrick's controller and got to work on our next illegal project and leech.

Emrys was unreasonably irritable at our Thursday session, as if something had happened during the night that had infuriated him.

He kept knocking into me and I rubbed my shoulder for the fifth time that session, feeling far more exhausted than I should be.

"Stop." Dare took a deep breath and I could tell he was this close to blasting Emrys off the face of the mountain. "That is not how you call for reinforcements."

"I'm sure they won't be needed," Emrys sneered.

Dare clenched than released a fist. "Do it again anyway."

"Listen, you sniveling brat. I don't care who your mommy is or what competition you've won in the past or what magic you used to get this idiot"—he pointed to me—"to follow you like you own the sun. All that matters to me is—"

One moment Emrys was sneering, then I blinked and he was flat on his back wheezing.

"All that matters is the protection of campus?" Dare said, evenly. "Yes, exactly. Oh, and Crown, did that just register as a punishable offense?"

Mouth agape, I quickly rallied and checked JT's log. "N-no," I stuttered.

"So, tell me when you are ready, Norr. And we will try it again. It's not punishable, so I can do it all day."

Suffice to say, Emrys, for once, did not stick around after our hour was over. Narrow-eyed, he stomped off. His stomp, too, was weirdly familiar. I was going to have to look up his lineage at some point. Or ask Olivia. She knew all of those things.

Maybe I had seen him at Ganymede? The magical Special Forces had been sent out after Raphael en masse, that day.

"I want him gone." Dare stared at Emrys's retreating figure, lips tight. Emrys stopped abruptly before he reached the stairs, then made an immediate left toward the firesnake grove.

"I—" I tried to say something positive, but the words wouldn't come.

Dare's gaze swung to me. "There's something weird between you two."

"Yeah," I said, giving up the argument before it even started. Sometimes it seemed like Emrys wanted to lure me to his side, and other times, he tried to expose me to campus. "I think I've seen him somewhere. He reminds me of someone."

Lots of someones actually, depending on the time of day, the light, my mental state... I was a little concerned for my sanity. I was hoping it might be some innate magic that he possessed to make him seem familiar, rather than my mental state.

A pretty woman who worked the desk in the Administration Building was having lunch on a bench near the firesnake grove. Emrys strode up to her, a large smile on his face. She blushed and waved a hand at the seat next to her.

"Don't trust him," Dare said.

I frowned. "Yeah."

I knew I shouldn't trust Emrys, why did magic keep making me want to?

At dinner, a weird buzzing permeated the air, stretching and curling around the cafeteria's tiers.

"What's going on?" I asked Mike and Will as I sat down.

They looked at each other, then at me. "Two students were taken in for questioning by the Troop and expelled for bringing and creating an illegal port on campus. And four more were expelled for possessing illegal devices."

"What?" I said, jaw dropping. I thought of idealistic Provost Johnson who thought I could be rehabilitated with a billion hours of community service. "Expelled?"

"Yeah, two of them were guys from my transport class last spring." Will looked sad. "Good experimenters. A student group turned all six in."

I thought of the things the stooges had been putting around campus all term. "The student Department flunkies have been planting recording devices," I said numbly. "To locate disturbances."

Mike nodded as if this confirmed his thoughts. "I locked up all of Will's portal projects."

My head jerked toward Will, who looked chagrined. "It's true. I got a lecture from Neph too. No more portal projects until the furor dies down."

"But—"

"No." Mike interrupted me and looked at Will, unapologetic. "I'm not letting you get expelled. You can work on something else for the next few weeks, then resume operations in the spring."

I chewed a fingernail. Mike didn't know about the extremely illegal projects we were working on with Constantine. "The other four students—what devices did they possess?"

Mike frowned. "Some sort of control devices. Unspecified."

My neck swung Will's way. He shook his head minutely and relief made me sink in my seat. Not Asafa and Patrick then. And not Constantine. No one in our sphere.

But we were working on control devices.

"They said that anyone possessing control technology will incur instant expulsion," Mike said.

I thought of all of Delia's little toys with their suggestions. And even Bellacia with her voice.

Will looked around surreptitiously and leaned in. "People are talking. The club is not pleased. There's talk of implementing some...reverse action."

A club of delinquents was assuredly thinking up some truly horrific things.

"What happens when a student gets expelled?"

"It depends on the infraction. You can apply for admission to another university—though no other school is nearly as good as Excelsine," Mike said in a purposely boastful tone designed to lighten the mood. "But the Troop, and therefore the Department, was behind their ejection, and the Department carries a lot of weight in granting admissions throughout the Second Layer. They function behind the scenes in everything."

Will made a skydiving motion with one hand. "They can sink you before you start."

"And if you can't enroll at another university, they plunk you in work camps designed to make sure you can control yourself until you turn twenty-three. Either that, or you can elect to wear a null cuff," Mike said.

"Nullifies all internal magic," Will added.

Last term, expulsion had meant not being able to resurrect my brother—an unthinkable thought. Now, it meant the loss of my magic and friends, as well as probably getting leashed by some crazy government operative. Magic had crept into my being completely, and now it was like a second heart I needed in order to live.

"That's—"

"That's bad timing," Mike said decisively. "People are crazed all across the Second Layer right now. Which is why Will is going to be on the straight and narrow for the next two weeks. Once the competition is over and the Troop is gone, things will go back to normal here, and you weirdos can experiment to your heart's desire."

Will and I exchanged quick looks—we'd have to discuss whether or not we'd continue the leech experiments, or whether to hold off until the Troop was gone. The good news was that Olivia and I had pried two links from Raphael's leash with the chip—one last night and one earlier today. Along with the one unhooked with Dare, the damage had to be making a nice little dent in Raphael's plans.

I was about to give my vote to put everything on hold, when a bright and shiny girl sat down to the left of Mike and smiled broadly at me.

"Hi! I'm Torvessa. And I wanted to know if you could introduce me to Alexander Dare?"

I sighed.

Chapter Thirty

MIDNIGHT IN THE GARDEN

T HE TROOP CONTINUED to run raids on student rooms, and four other students were suspended over the course of the second week. It was becoming more obvious that the Troop was more interested in regulating and discerning student life than in worrying about campus safety and Excelsine's monster-of-the-day phenomenon.

The major rule breakers on campus knew how to hide things, but the Troop was starting to circle them like predators around a bait ball. Constantine's rooms had been searched three times already, Asafa, Patrick, Delia and a slew of others had been raided twice, and charged words between Dare and Emrys made it obvious Dare had received at least one visit due to his "living circumstances"—whatever that meant.

Will, Olivia, and I had made it out clean so far by keeping everything at Okai. Olivia and I continued to use the chip leech there in the Midlands each night—where we couldn't be tracked and where Administrative rules didn't apply—and each night she did something really awesome with my channeled magic. We'd even started making it a game. She'd even managed to somehow port herself to the other side of the main room in Okai, startling Guard Rock completely.

The second week with Emrys and the Troop, on the other hand, fell into an uneasy routine. Patrolling with Dare alone was great. With Dare and Emrys? Not so much. Emrys was increasingly grumpy, manic, and short-tempered. And Dare made sure to make Emrys's day worse each time we met.

When all three squads gathered, things grew even more tense. It was obvious the Combat Squad was not pleased with their replacements, and that members of the Justice Squad were feeling overworked and unappreciated as the intermediaries.

Outside of squad work and Troop irritations, I deflected people who asked perky or pesky questions about Dare, and stringently avoided Bellacia, who had been livid when she'd gotten released from medical.

She had been charged with a Level Three Offense—upped from a Level Two due to her refusal to stop—for the magic she had used on me. Everyone in class assumed her convulsions on the floor had been a Justice Magic punishment. The upside to the whole event was that Professor Harrow had banned Bellacia from assisting our group for the rest of term. The downside was that Bellacia and her minions had been following me outside of class like hounds on a hunt ever since.

Not that I cared about that when there was something much worse to worry about as the second week of the Troop's presence on campus drew to a close. Worrying, distressing, freaking out, tormenting, harassing, not sleeping! Not sleeping! Not sleeping!

Because the combat mages were leaving.

Tomorrow, the combat mages would depart, the tumbleweeds would roll, and I'd be the new sheriff in town.

One week. I just had to get through one week, get Dare and his crew back on campus, then I could dive into a coma for a little while.

One week. I could do that. It became a steady mantra in my head.

I was exhausted, and it was pretty late, but I had a brainstorm for Constantine's dodecaplex project, and Dorm One was on my way back from one of Neph's bi-weekly recitals. The recitals were open to the student population and all kinds of awesome. It had been a varied line-up with different styles of dance, and many performers, but in my completely unbiased opinion, the other muses didn't have half Neph's mojo or spirit.

I knocked on Constantine's door, which was not a good sign. Usually he opened the door before I made it to the threshold. Not answering meant he was either not home or busy.

I grimaced. It wouldn't be the first time he answered half-dressed with a girl giggling somewhere in the background, but such a thing hadn't happened in weeks and I'd gotten used to not seeing a different girl with every wardrobe change.

I started to turn, rooting in my bag for my tablet in order to send him a note, when the door opened. A rueful smile lifted my lips and I turned back. "I was just…"

My words trailed and my smiled dropped. Constantine wasn't the one standing on the other side.

Dare, barefoot, hair slightly mussed, in a white shirt and loose sweats, had his hands outstretched between the doorjamb and the edge of the door, physically taking up the space.

My mind went blank. "Uh…" My gaze went to the number on the open door, sure that I had it wrong. But Sixty-Nine with an "I" in front of it—Constantine's stupid joke—stared back.

"What's wrong? Nothing pinged me." Dare started to lean back, probably to check his tablet. "I knew I should have stayed out. Seriously, the whole 'get a full night's sleep before the competition' directive," he mimicked, "always seems to invite the opposite effect. But you didn't have to come here. I would have answered your note."

"Er, right." He was Constantine's roommate?

For all of the hundreds of notes he had sent me detailing various places to meet him around campus, Dare had never asked to meet in the dorms. I had long wondered if I should feel offended that he didn't want me stopping by his room.

His eyes narrowed on my assuredly gobsmacked expression and all movement in his body stopped. "You're not... You're here for Leandred?" He made it sound like I was actively trying to contract a sexually transmitted disease.

I felt disparate urges to defend myself and to defend Constantine. Okay, well, Constantine earned every bit of his reputation and reveled in it. It was always a little hard to defend him.

The first thing that tried to roll off my tongue, 'We are friends,' was quickly swallowed. No one ever believed that. "I... We do business."

"Business?" His tone implied exactly what he thought any business with Constantine might be. Extreme disappointment laced it.

"Not that kind," I said, flustered. "The kind with favors. Business favors." Hi, I'm a hooker! "Legal ones! Well, not legal, but not prostitution! I mean, the kind of favors that you exchange with business partners."

His expression was still tight, but there was a little amusement there too, now. "Business favors."

"Exactly." I tapped the edge of my bag nervously. "Why are you here?"

His expression turned deadpan. "I sleep here."

"That's...weird." The look he gave me caused me to rally. "I've never seen you here before."

"You've been here so many times then?" His tone was back to being unreadable.

The answer was close to triple digits at this point, but I didn't think that would be smart to say. "Enough to be surprised at the presence of a roommate, let alone you. All those wards," I murmured, "suddenly make sense."

As did Constantine's delight whenever something bad happened to Dare. Oh my God, Constantine had been amused when I'd asked him about his roommate directly after he had quizzed me about sitting with Dare in the cafeteria. I was going to kill him.

Dare's eyes narrowed further. "You've been inside?"

"Oh, please. Constantine invites everyone inside."

I felt a layer of magic lift from me—pulled from me. The magic flew out, scattered, and settled around the room in hues of red. The heaviest path, bloody in its consistency, led to Constantine's workshop. A more moderate level of crimson stretched to the chair I always used in the living room. No path led to the bedroom. A light pink path led to a spot inches in front of the room that was always heavily warded. I had tried to study the wards a few times. Dare's wards... Great.

Which was somewhat embarrassing, to have that laid out in front of him.

"I didn't know that was your private room," I said quickly, feeling the need to defend myself. "I just thought the wards were fascinating."

He was studying the paths, though, his expression unreadable again. "He lets you in his workroom."

"There's no bed in there!" I clamped my lips together and shut my eyes. "You know what...? No. I don't have to defend myself."

I turned to leave. He reached out a hand to my arm. "No, you don't. I'm sorry. You took me by surprise. And I...was a little disappointed that you might be interested in Leandred that way."

He was probably disappointed whenever anyone was interested in Constantine, because he obviously held him in extreme dislike. "Why do you—?"

I stopped the question. I knew the answer to the question of why they roomed together. Their magic had to be highly—extremely—sympathetic. That was the only reason two people who despised each other would room together at Excelsine.

I wondered if Constantine also was protected from expulsion by rooming with Dare. Constantine's father was obviously highly placed and influential, but roommates were a big deal. The magic involved made the mages stronger, more rested. Dare was both feared and worshiped on campus—by the students and faculty.

If that made them more lenient with his roommate, that leniency probably pissed Con off just as much as his father's influence.

"So...you've never answered the door before," I said, somewhat lamely.

"Everyone knows not to look for me here. I wouldn't have answered it now, but I felt you on the other side."

I blinked, flustered. "Is there something set up in the room that allows that?" I really needed to read that how-to document for our room.

"No." His face was unreadable again. "Leandred knows when you are here?"

"He always answers the door before I arrive."

His expression tightened, and he tapped his fingers against the door. "Are you going to wait for him or do you want to leave a message?"

"Uh…"

He watched me for a long moment, before coming to some decision. "Come in." He held the door open. "I'm not sleeping anyway, and he usually drags himself in early, between midnight and two, when he has a Sunday session with Stevens."

I didn't want to sit around and wait for Constantine by making small talk with Dare—especially if it might take two hours—but my body didn't listen and my feet took me across the threshold. They then moved me toward the antique chair that was my favorite—the one that looked like the least comfortable option in the room. Initially, it had seemed like the best non-seduction chair in the area—straight-backed and armless. The chair was extremely uncomfortable looking, and I'd bet anything that I was the only one who ever sat in it.

But looks were deceiving when it came to Constantine and his furniture choices, and he found petty delight in small things like making chairs that looked comfortable impossible to sit in for a long period of time, and vice versa. After a minute, the hard chair always conformed perfectly to my shape.

"I'll just wait fifteen minutes," I said, cursing whatever urge had made me enter. "You should sleep."

"You should get a frequency."

I sighed. "I know." I started to sit.

"Wait."

Dare waved his hand, and furniture I had never seen before appeared in the living room, replacing all of Constantine's pieces as if they didn't exist in Dare's world. Four leather club chairs appeared in a center circle instead of Constantine's large, imposing armchair that usually lorded over his visitors' far less comfortable ones. But their furniture choices had the same classic style. I found it oddly hilarious that instead of old and traditional versus sleek and modern or some such thing, both men showed similar taste.

I completed my movement and sat in the deep, cozy chair. The magical leather instantly warmed.

Dare paused and I could see something dark flit over his expression, then he waved a hand toward the door. I didn't try to track the clear magic. Dare's magic was hard to follow when I was at the best of my abilities. And after thirty hours of work, I wasn't even going to put in a token effort.

I dropped my bag on the floor and tucked up into the club chair, leaning my head against the arm. Whatever mad urge had possessed me to enter the room had deserted me fully. This was going to be awkwardly epic, I could already tell.

"So...you don't get involved in...?" I was trying to ask how he dealt with Constantine's many offenses. Constantine so often misbehaved that an entire Justice Tablet could be devoted to him. And Dare's rooms being raided because of his "living situation" made complete sense now.

"I have nothing to do with student prosecution. Combat mages are responsible for defense and protection only. And I made it clear a long time ago that I would not be responsible for him in any way. It was just my luck first year to walk in here and see him." He grimaced, leaning back in his chair.

That seemed to indicate that they had known each other before coming to Excelsine. Maybe in one of the prep schools that most mages attended.

"I deliberately bi-ward against anyone who is visiting him. I don't want to know who is here or why, and I make it so that they gain nothing about me. Not even a scent." He tapped a finger on the arm of his chair and splayed back a little more, his gaze upon me. "The hallway, however, doesn't factor into that."

Warding against visitors or not, my magic must have known he was the roommate walking through the common areas. It had tried to reach out toward the person too many times.

Great.

I pressed my fingers against the bridge of my nose and harshly smoothed them outward over my eyebrows, pushing against the gathering headache there.

"Don't let him take advantage of your grief rebound," he said, a little too rapidly.

I blinked at him through my fingers. The expression on his face revealed that he hadn't meant to say that. It was a weird sort of role reversal—him blurting something out.

"What?" I asked, confused, letting my hands drop. We had spent a lot of time together by this point, but I had no idea what he was talking about.

He grimaced. "It's none of my business. That is exceptionally true. And you aren't Leandred's normal type of visitor. He never, and I do mean never, lets anyone into his workroom, but he's…" He waved a hand, grimacing again. "Let's just say that he's a really shitty roommate."

"What do you mean by grief rebound?"

"Your boyfriend died."

"My what?" But my thoughts outpaced my mouth, like usual. He remembered.

"Your…" His eyes narrowed, constricting with the same knowledge that forced my heart to feel as if it was being squeezed into a chest suddenly far too small. "Not your boyfriend then. Who was it?"

"You remember," I said, my voice far away. "When?" When had he realized? My mind tried to sort through memories looking for differences.

"The search spell. As soon as you thrust your magic through mine, I knew. There's a difference between feeling and experiencing someone's magic. You felt familiar before, but the actual touch was the same as the essence of the broken, ordinary girl who fought on a street in the First Layer to get to her fallen companion."

"I hadn't Awakened then," I murmured.

He said nothing.

"You heard me talking to the book in the library about not letting anyone else die," I said just as absently, stitching past events together in my mind. "I received the firework the next morning. You sent the firework to me."

Even irritated with me for hitting him with the search spell, and for using an avoidance spell against him, he'd sent something anonymously to offer help. I stared into ultramarine eyes and swallowed heavily. This boy was always giving me a last, priceless moment, patching me up, unaware that the wounds he was healing went deeper than skin.

He didn't acknowledge the gifting of the firework verbally, but I could see my guess was right.

"Who was he?" he asked.

"My brother. My twin."

"I'm sorry."

I nodded, and had to clear my throat. "I tried to bring him back to life all last term. That was all me. Everything on campus. It was unintentional, but still my fault."

I numbly met his gaze. There was nothing worse that I could admit to, except being leashed by Raphael. But...the firework. One more emotional piece that had mended something inside of me. He had anonymously given me that healing. I clasped my hands together to stop them from shaking.

"I know," he said quietly. Leaning back, he watched me through half-open eyes. "Not that you were trying to resurrect anyone, but that you were somehow responsible for the magic imbalance. It wasn't hard to put two and two together after our first few outings."

Which is why making friends was the most dangerous thing I could do in this world. Everyone always guessed. I practically served myself up on a platter. Raphael had told me months ago to seek out allies, not friends. But I couldn't regret my choices when they had brought me what I had now.

"Why haven't you done anything?" I asked.

"About what?"

"About me. I'm a threat to the school."

He laughed. It was not a happy sound. "So is everyone enrolled here, whether they choose to acknowledge it or not."

I looked into his eyes. The same cautiousness they always contained was present.

He looked away, then pulled himself up. "Since you are here, I have something for you."

He walked toward his warded room, passing close to my chair. I leaned over and caught his forearm before I could lose the courage. His muscles rippled under my fingers. He turned and I looked him in the eye. The color of his eyes swallowed me in Last Judgment blue, and redemption mixed together with the touch of skin.

"Thank you." My fingers pressed slightly, echoing the sentiment non-verbally. "You don't know what it meant to me to..." Have that last moment with Christian, to feel that last meeting of warm skin. And at the festival, to launch that firework.

"You wouldn't have been trying to get to him so forcefully and brokenly, if it didn't mean so much. Your actions prompted mine. Determination and loyalty." He leaned toward me, and the action forced my fingers to move around the band of his arm. "Why do you think I wanted you working on my team so much?"

I swallowed. "To keep an eye on me?"

He stepped back and I released my grip. "Trouble follows you, Ren Crown. But so do other things."

The front door opened and I looked over my shoulder. Constantine strolled in wearing a fitted, charcoal, full-length wool coat. The tall collar wrapped around his throat and buttoned up to his chin. His lip curled unpleasantly as he saw the changes wrought to the living room. He tossed the hair from his eyes and moved toward the bedroom, his long stride unhurried. He ignored Dare and his gaze sped over me with little interest.

Then he stopped cold, his gaze backtracking and freezing on me. He tried to cover his surprise by looking down and flicking his fingers over his frame. His long coat unbuttoned, slipped from under his bag, and peeled off his arms, disappearing completely as it rolled into itself.

In the quarter of a moment that the removal took, his gaze rose and his expression was completely under control again. He posed, unmoving, his bag still slung over the shoulder of his gray shirt, looking at Dare, who now had his back to me. Constantine's eyes were iced caramel. "Well, well. Whatever do we have here?"

"Hey," I said, a little lamely in the tense atmosphere. And seriously...why had no one told me they were roommates?

Constantine tipped his head to me, but his gaze was completely fastened on Dare. And as Dare backed up and casually dropped back into his chair—delaying whatever he had been planning to retrieve for me—Dare's expression was dark and anticipatory.

Constantine swung his bag toward his workroom. The door opened to accept it, then slammed shut after it was through. The casual use of magic and the crackling in the air indicated damage was about to occur. Constantine flicked his hand toward the chairs and I could feel the fight in the very fabric of the air as he tried to change Dare's enchantment. The magic tugged back and forth, nearly screeching, then with a crack, the two extra chairs disappeared and Constantine's chair appeared, forming a closed triangle.

Constantine folded into his seat, but there was an energy vibrating under his skin. He kept his hands on the arms of the chair, but the fingers of his left hand twitched ever so slightly as if he wanted his black ribbon in them. It was nowhere to be seen, though, and for some reason that seemed purposeful.

He lazed back in his seat, crossing his long legs. "Well, I didn't anticipate such fun this evening. And just when I thought I was almost rid of you." He looked at Dare, his gaze far too casual, his fingers drumming against the chair's arm. "Casting a suppression spell on the door? Devious. Do your handlers know their uptight wonder boy has such a slick side?"

There was a tight tension underlying the lines of Dare's body too, but he kept his words just as casual. "Does Daddy know you have taken an interest?"

Rage flashed across Constantine's face, then was chased into studied insouciance. "And here I thought you had all of those lovely little spells in place to ignore whatever I did. If I had known you were so interested, I would have spun you a lovely tale of poison."

"You two sleep in the same room?" I blurted out, unable to hold it in. "And are still alive?"

"Amazing isn't it, my level of saintly patience?" Constantine said, still not looking away from his roommate.

This then completely and definitively explained Olivia's acceptance of me as a roommate in the first place, and old magic users' "means to an end" philosophy in strengthening their magic.

I pressed a hand to my forehead. "Okay. I came to talk about—" No, I couldn't say anything about that in front of Dare. "Then I had a thought on—" No, I couldn't say anything about that in front of Constantine.

Train wreck. That was the only description that sufficed.

I waved my hand around. "Both of your projects are progressing. I should go." I put a hand on the strap of my bag.

"Darling, no. Stay. This is about to become most interesting."

"Interesting, like, hey, we have common interests, let's discuss them? Or interesting in the multiple ways that blood can splatter?" I asked weakly.

Constantine tilted his head as if contemplating the matter. "More of the latter, I think."

Dare didn't respond, but he was far too still. The kind of stillness that preceded explosive destruction.

"Oh, my God," I said feebly. "Could you two be any more of a Superhero/Supervillain cliché?"

"Alexander prefers 'villain' for his own designation. I, however, will retain my super status, thank you, Ren."

"Con...why...what...how...? I'm going to kill you," I said.

"You will not. You indulge far too many of my games. More than is good for you."

"Kill."

"Well, if you really must, it will be my preferred method of death, coming from your hand."

"Feel free to begin at any time," Dare said in a far too casual manner, leaning back nonchalantly.

Dorm One was not going to survive the night. I was about to watch an explosion of gorgeous body parts. I mean...it was a wonder their room hadn't already imploded due to the sheer level of hotness it contained. It seemed like a room should have an attractiveness quotient.

I realized that I might have said that out loud at the same time that I registered that they were both staring at me.

"Oh, would you look at the time?" I said, and bolted from my chair. "Good luck on the bloodshed. Gotta go!"

Strategic retreat? No. Wise course of action? Most definitely, yes.

Chapter Thirty-one
PLAN FIFTY-TWO

I TRIED TO maintain an air of nonchalance the next morning as I followed Dare on our last round together. He wisely said nothing about the awkwardness that was our three-way meeting the previous evening, but he seemed cheerful in a way that made me think maybe I'd check on Constantine later and bring bandages.

Having an actual conversation about the previous night would have induced a small panic attack on its own, but worse than that, Dare was leaving campus in three hours. Leaving campus and expecting me to have everything completely in hand. He was leaving me here alone in three hours and I was freaking out.

"So, what if I just wear a camera and do rounds and then you can watch those?" I was proud of the well-modulated sarcasm I had included to hide my terror.

"You are going to journal me each night with your observations? Good thinking." He turned and started walking toward the exit point.

"What?" I hurried to catch up. "I was being sarcastic and I didn't say anything about writing to you."

"It's a good idea."

"I don't want to journal you every night!"

"Why not? Am I so distasteful?"

"What? No, that's not what I—" I saw his smirk and let out a sigh. "Just...fine. I'll do it. Don't expect Shakespeare."

He cast me an askance glance. "It will be fine. You won't let anything happen to campus."

I flung my hands into the air in a complicated gesture meant to show my complete incompetence and terror. "I am the antichrist of this campus. What were you thinking?"

He laughed and watched his dragon and phoenix swoop together overhead.

"Everything will work out just fine. And when I get back, we'll have a very interesting discussion," he murmured. There was something very unsettling in the way the edges of his eyes crinkled.

~*~

"Ren, you look terrible," Olivia said at dinner, 6.2 hours after Dare and the rest of the combat mages abandoned campus. "You should go to bed early. Gaming is unnecessary, I already told you." She looked a little too eager to avoid going to Asafa and Patrick's.

"What? No. We have been practicing. We are totally going to do battle with my creations and take Trick to the cleaners. Saf's going to help. And I'm fine." I bit the end of a fraying fingernail nearly in half. "Fine. Hurry up and finish."

Olivia had promised that she would do a focus spell on me after lunch. I needed that spell. Dare's energizing spell had worn off two hours ago and I had to get back out on the grounds.

A quick circuit around campus, then I'd do some quick, quick gaming for Olivia's sake, then I'd get back out there again for another circuit.

"That salad looks really delicious," I said, pushing it closer to her.

Will slowly put down his hoagie. "You do look a little green around the skirk gills, Ren."

"I'm fine." I stared at Olivia's bowl, willing the leaves to launch into her mouth so we could leave. I pushed her bread roll closer. "Eat." Maybe the water would do it. I pushed her glass closer. "Drink."

"Is this where we call the men with the white coats?" Mike asked. "Isn't that what the non-magical world does?"

"Yes. I mean, no," I said. Olivia hated olives, but always ate a few in her salads because of their nutritional value. They always took the longest for her to eat. While she was looking at Mike, I lifted the three black spheres from her bowl with magic and wrapped the olives in my napkin. "I mean, yes, that is what they do. No, I don't need the men with the white coats."

Unless they would help me take down rogue monsters and villains. Would straitjackets work as a defense?

"You're making less sense than usual, Ren." Mike pointed his fork at me. "Will does this when he is stressed."

"Stressed? If we are pointing stressed fingers," I pointed sharply at Will, then Olivia, "how come no one told me that Alexander Dare and Constantine Leandred are roommates?"

Will blinked. Olivia frowned. Neph waved a gentle hand trying to even the group atmosphere.

"What do you mean, no one told you?" Olivia asked. "You are over there all the time, or with one or the other of them."

"You didn't know they were roommates?" Will's voice came out in an incredulous squeak as he stared at me.

"Everyone knows," Olivia said, now frowning in disbelief.

"No, everyone did not know."

Delia's laughter rang out as she sat down. "Oh that just begs the question of how you found out then. Full details."

Mike shook his head. "Seriously, Crown? Only you." He looked at Will. "And maybe Will."

"Hey!" Will said.

Olivia narrowed her eyes at me. "Is that why you look terrible?"

"I'm just making sure campus is safe." I waved a wild hand. "I have to do that, you know? I have to watch and make sure nothing weird is happening and that no creature gets in and rampages the grounds. And that the people temporarily guarding us don't keel over while the combat mages are away." It all came out perhaps a little more maniacally then I meant it to. "And I will do it! I have it under control! I'm fine."

Everyone at the table except for Olivia stared at me, mouths opened and food forgotten.

Olivia nodded briskly, lips tight, as if this entire conversation reinforced something she had been thinking. "I thought this might happen."

She magically took a note on her pad. "We are implementing Plan Fifty-two."

Her brisk certainty broke through my spiraling thoughts. "What?"

"It is the optimal solution for your health and well-being." She nodded sharply again. "I don't have to like how much you are taking upon yourself, but since there is nothing I can do to make you stop caring, I can do this."

"I'm fine. I'm great! Just hurry up and eat, then spell me. Quick. Hup to it."

I nudged her roll closer. Though...if she ate it, I calculated that it would cost us at least forty-five more seconds. I grabbed the roll and stuffed it in my mouth.

Olivia nodded aggressively again. That nod meant that she thought I was behaving irrationally and she wouldn't be convinced otherwise.

Self-preservation kicked in. I swallowed the roll with difficulty, my throat dry. If Olivia thought I was being irrational, then she might knock me out and take me back to our room.

A smile pulled painfully on my cheeks. "You are right. There's no hurry." Hurry! "Take your time. Eat. Then we will go after," I said, attempting a soothing tone but producing something like "strangled raccoon chatter" instead.

Mike had a weird little smile hovering around his lips and he was scrutinizing Olivia like he was seeing her for the first time. "Plan Fifty-two?"

Olivia looked at her list. "Plan Fifty-one isn't enough, and Fifty-three has too much fire power." She nodded decisively, looking up. "Fifty-two."

We all stared at her. Mike was still smiling. Delia's expression was completely unreadable.

"What plan, Olivia?" Will asked, almost gently, in the way one might address a mental patient.

Wait. I looked at him suspiciously. That was the tone they had been using on me for the past few minutes.

"Not here." Olivia was briskly magicking line items on her pad. "Your assignments will be sent and we will meet in our room tonight at...eight. Yes, eight." She nodded at her pad. "You are all free at eight."

"You have all our schedules in there?" Mike asked.

Olivia looked at him blankly. "Of course."

Mike looked astonished.

"Oh, please," I scoffed. "Of course she has them. She has all your transcripts too, don't think she doesn't." I looked at Olivia. "Now that we have that all settled. Eat?"

Olivia took a slow bite.

"You are deliberately messing with me," I said a little desperately.

She pressed down on my hand and I could feel her concentrate on the connection between us. She gave a tentative push—it was the first time she had pushed a feeling to me like this since the stomach sickness weeks ago. "Calm down, Ren." The push became more assured as I accepted it without reserve. "It will be fine."

"Yes, that's what I keep repeating." But for the first time in 6.3 hours, I actually believed it.

~*~

Our room was packed at eight that evening. The game tourney had made spreading the word easy. And the expulsion procedures the Troop had begun implementing made students eager to gather and discuss options. It was rather amazing how many delinquents responded to the call. They hovered in chairs near the ceiling and around the edges of the room, creating an intimate amphitheater effect.

According to Olivia, we were only waiting for two more.

"Barbarians," she muttered.

I held back my smile with difficulty as Olivia answered the knock on our door.

Patrick's head popped in a moment later. He immediately brightened as he entered. "Our fellow delinquents," he greeted, inclining his head to me then to the others in the room. "And the Queen." He gave Olivia a little bow. Her fingers were gripping the door knob so tightly that I thought she might crush it.

Patrick turned his head and stage-whispered over his shoulder. "Her Highness answered the door for us, Saf."

Asafa pushed him inside, easily following behind. "It is good to see you, Your Highness."

Olivia's lips tightened. "It's either Your Majesty to go with Queen or Your Highness to go with the title of Princess. Pick one. Better yet, pick neither."

"Never a princess." Patrick looked horrified. "You are too commanding and worthy of exaltation already."

Patrick sounded so serious. My smile broke through along with a giggle. Olivia gave me a look as if my reaction was a betrayal of the deepest kind.

I poked her with magic.

She sighed. It tickled me that these two could get to her so well. They liked to buzz around her when we visited them. Setting her feet up on a tuffet, getting her tea in china cups. Visiting was always hilarious.

On a serious note, they had paused their weekly game tournament for an entire hour so that we could do this. They had glibly cited eating needs, but I'd bet anything that neither took as much as a five-minute break usually. Pizza could be shoved down eighteen-year-old throats in less.

Olivia reiterated what she had said to everyone who had stepped through the door. "You received your notes and are here, so you accept this assignment and the offered payment for your service?"

Two mismatched grins greeted her. "Absolutely. We have the most fantastic idea for a campus snare."

She nodded and marked something on her list. "Excellent."

As it turned out, in a room full of rule breakers and delinquents, a lot of people had fantastic ideas for ways to cause mayhem, especially after Olivia assured them that if the campus were under attack and we implemented the plan, that full responsibility would fall on our shoulders, not theirs. After it became known that Olivia and I would be taking all judicial punishment, we had to rein in the bloodthirsty nature of their campus protection suggestions. But bloodthirsty, or not, we jotted down every single one.

"We will create five teams—Alpha, Beta, Gamma, Delta, Epsilon—and split personal and technical skills between the five." Olivia kept charge of the meeting, moving it right along. "Olivia, Ren, William, Delia, Michael, and Nephthys on Alpha. Saf, Trick, Lifen, Bryant, Kita, and Dagfinn on Beta. On Gamma—"

I tuned Olivia partially out as she went down the long list of mages. My team, the Alpha team, was comprised of the people who knew most of my secrets, and who would protect that knowledge.

Everyone started talking and throwing out ideas.

"We can combine a number of our specialties and strengths and create some seriously wicked magic," Patrick said.

I thought of the combat qualifier and how each of the individuals in Dare's group had competed against each other using their own specialties, but how their real power increased when they worked together as a unit, as they had when fighting the Bone Beast last term. That's what we needed to do. Create fighting teams for campus protection. Units that combined individual specialties to render maximum destruction.

"We should set up a separate communication network. Unattached to the Frequency Grid. Never know who is listening," Dagfinn, a twenty-one year old paranoid communications mage and frequency hacker, said. "We don't want to be hammered by some sketchy ops group or one of those idiots who thinks they are fast tracking to the Department."

"We can embed a communication link in something wearable. Keep all communications in the loop. Infinity scarves?" Lifen, a seamstress, nodded to herself, as if the decision was made, and turned to Delia. No one argued, and they started discussing construction, fashion, trickery, and destruction.

Destruction was definitely a strength of the people in this room.

I was never going to be the fiercest fighter. However, I could be a tricky one. I could use my strengths to get myself out of a situation and help friends who were in one.

Using my magic, Raphael could make the earth swallow people whole, and could force space to close around others. Such actions caused immediate backlashes, and Layer tremors that I didn't yet know how to avoid, but they were possibilities in my asset bag.

And all those around me right now could be just as tricky.

As the group argued, discussed, and manically suggested ideas and counter recommendations, for the first time since Dare left, I felt if it were attacked, that campus might be okay.

Constantine had rolled his eyes when I'd told him about Plan Fifty-two and how the team planned to disrupt, disable and neutralize any creature security breach if it occurred, until the combat mages could get back. He called us morons. Olivia hadn't even, at any point, tried to include him in the plan, and she had been against me telling him. But I nudged Constantine into participating anyway—a team of one, reporting directly to me on the Alpha communication loop.

Dare, on the other hand, was delighted about Plan Fifty-two. I briefed him on every aspect of it via hologram journal that night.

The magic in the journals echoed the feeling of his absolute satisfaction, and his words to the other combat mages in the library that first day back on campus resounded in the back of my mind.

Overlooked assets.

He had deliberately chosen me. He had wanted this group to form.

Olivia's previous warning came to mind—members of the Dare family always have a plan. The words echoed, along with the feeling that I was doing everything according to Alexander Dare's.

I waited until Olivia got into the shower, then lunged toward her desk. Everyone had a plan, and I had a contingency.

Fumbling quickly with the newest chip leech and the cocoon on her desk, I pressed the two magics in my creations together. Closing my eyes and concentrating, focusing and pushing, the magic from the chip seeped out and into the cocoon, making the cocoon glow forest green for a moment.

The chip was a leech, but the cocoon connected directly back to my magic. I had just leashed myself.

Tucking the empty chip back into my pocket, I hurried back to my side of the room and grabbed my tablet as Olivia emerged, already magically dressed for bed.

Trying not to blurt out what I'd done, I fiddled with my tablet and babbled to her about all the traps we had placed and the diabolical nature of some of the minds at our school.

So many plans—perceived and invisible—were in motion now, and it just remained to be seen who would be left standing in the end.

"Ren, stop fretting," Olivia said as she tucked herself in.

I let my head hit my pillow and stared at the ceiling. "Are you sure about this? Fifty-two? It's a lot of work for one week," I said.

"It is helping you."

I chewed on my fingernail. "I don't want you to sacrifice your free time just to relieve my anxiety."

Olivia didn't say anything for a moment, then I could feel her move magic along the wards that connected to me. "Ren, being your friend is never a sacrifice."

I touched the wall, sending magic back. "Good night, Liv."

Chapter Thirty-two
APPETIZER TO DESTRUCTION

EVEN THOUGH DARE was gone and the Troop was in charge, I wasn't free of squad work, and Emrys cornered me for rounds every day.

Dare despised and distrusted him more than he did the other Troop members, and I knew I should feel the same way. There was no doubt in my mind that Emrys was out to get me in some way—even if it was only to expose me as a feral or rare mage to campus at large. But the odd familiarity and occasional comfort that he exuded, messed with my mind and made me want to trust him.

As such, I tried to limit my time with him as much as possible. Fifteen more minutes with Emrys and his disorienting presence, then I could check in with the people with whom I really wanted to case campus.

Asafa, Patrick, Will, and I had been working together to create a hex that when activated would hit any "tagged" creature and suck them inside the nearest arch. Will had created a way to make the tag alert in a particular manner, and a few of the other plan members had contributed jinxes to zap anything registering as "tagged." Campus was going to be littered with those spells by the end of the day. Hopefully, any beast terrorizing campus that got away from the Troop would just need to be tagged by us, and then be taken care of in a series of blasts—after being sucked from arch to arch.

Since I couldn't just suck creatures into papers around campus—not if I wanted to continue to breathe free air—this made a wonderful backup plan, in case we had another bone beast type of incident.

Bless Olivia, for saving my sanity with Plan Fifty-Two.

Emrys held out a companionable hand to my shoulder. "So, Ren—may I call you Ren?"

I gave him a quick nod and extricated myself from his touch, trying not to yawn. Doing rounds with Emrys exhausted me.

"How long have you been at Excelsine?"

It was a question he had asked before, in a different way. I repeated my cover story about transferring from Four Corners.

"I have quite a few friends on the faculty of Four Corners."

"A lot of people do." I showed a little bit of tooth with my smile.

As we checked the strength of the perimeter security, I concentrated on one ward in particular. The ward that sealed off the Eighteenth Circle from the Nineteenth—and all the levels below—was so depleted in strength, that its color was nearly transparent. I marked its location and sent a note through Justice Toad to Mbozi's most advanced warding class. Students in the class rotated as the on-call mage for campus wards, and whoever was on-call would have the Department-initiated ward back to full strength within the hour and would issue an administrative report on what had caused the problem so it could be patched going forward.

"I must say, that is a truly beautiful scarf you're wearing again today, Ren."

I smiled and touched the scarf automatically. It was beautifully made, and loaded with the communication spells Delia and Lifen had woven in with their quick and dexterous seamstress' hands the night before last. Looping us all together, when needed. A few of the more quirky members of the group had already been using them for small group tricks that wouldn't actually register as campus offenses.

"Thanks," I said. "I'm helping out with a friend's fashion project this week."

It was our standard line.

My smile fell as I looked at the ward again, and I frowned. It bothered me that it looked so fragile. I had checked it yesterday and it had been fine—and it should have been checked by at least three other patrols already today. I scrolled JT, looking through the checklist program that had been put into place just for this week. All previous Justice Squad patrols had checked it off as "normal."

It was possible some magic spike from campus had interfered—or something from the resident and business levels below. My fingers were already itching to grab the administrative report the on-call mage would produce.

This wasn't a Red Alert problem. Not yet. The Administration Alarms hadn't sounded, and the other campus security measures hadn't kicked in like they would if someone breached the perimeter. The ward was still working. I shouldn't really be as bothered as I was feeling. In order for a threat to get in, someone would have to disable a number of other security measures before tearing through this one. Such events were highly unlikely.

Still, I sent another more urgent note to the on-call mage to take care of it posthaste.

"Look at you, taking security so seriously. So devoted," Emrys said.

He sauntered next to me as I forced myself to move on to the next checkpoint. Emrys checked nothing, obviously not caring one whit about the safety of campus. Emrys had attended a different school—Dare had read his transcripts and given me the basics—so in addition to having zero professional concern, he also had no personal loyalty to campus. But unlike some of the other Troop members who still got turned around on campus and regularly took the wrong arches, Emrys always seemed to know where he was and where to go. Likely juiced with an Administration spell from one of the staffers he courted.

He even looked physically brighter than he had a minute ago—like he had ingested a sun spell that made him glow from the inside. I blinked and shook my head. He must have cloaked himself when the last crowd of students had walked by, then poorly removed the cloak. The Troop was so weird sometimes while trying to integrate into the student population. Everyone knew who they were. If they thought they were some secret fighting force, they were seriously bad at their job.

Which was exactly why the combat mages didn't want them here.

"So devoted to this mountain after such a short time," he mused.

"It's a wonderful place," I said sincerely. I loved school. It wasn't a secret. Maybe I could infuse some of my love for it into him.

"And working with Alexander Dare doesn't enter into your love of it, of course."

"He's very dedicated to the defense of campus," I said diplomatically.

"He is indeed. So dedicated." There was an emphasis to the words. "One wonders from where such dedication springs."

"I assume it springs from a desire to protect."

"He does seem so earnest in that aim," he said, odd leaf-green eyes focused on me. "It's almost enough to believe."

"You want me to turn against my teammate," I said, as I turned to examine the wards surrounding the one that formed the perimeter barrier. "You are baiting me, trying to get an emotional response." I had one, but I wasn't going to let it show.

"I'd never think to do such a thing, Ren, never. You seem very...fond of him. I would never think to come between young love, however ill-advised it is."

"You wield words like poison," I said absently. I knew quite a few people with that skill, which made the tactic obvious. "You do it quite well, though."

He laughed, a full-throated, delighted bark and squeezed my shoulder a second time, then put a hand on my wrist, over my cuff like he was trying to weirdly shake my hand. "Oh, I do like you."

"I don't know why," I said frankly, feeling tired again. Merely sharing air with Emrys was exhausting. I'd been energized before we'd begun our route. I disentangled myself from him.

He smiled at me as his fingers drew the last inch over my cuff and he stepped back. "Words are like weapons, like magic. They can cause untold pain. That you appreciate my attempt to drive a wedge between you and Mr. Dare just makes the game more exciting. You are quite a loyal soul, aren't you? What would it take to make you feel betrayed by him? What would Alexander Dare have to do?"

I took a step away from him and touched my leather bracelet that held Constantine's stamp underneath. There was a rune in the stamp that would give me a thirty second window to get away if I hit Emrys with it. "Listen, I realize you are just trying to do your job all nefariously and the like, but I'm not that interested in social politics and picking sides."

"Everyone picks a side eventually, even if it's their own side. Neutrality ends in fiefdom and subjugation."

"Sometimes neutrality ends in peace and happiness."

"Tosh. The only time neutrality works is when the person or country with the biggest stick allows the other entity to have it."

"That's pretty depressing. I'd like to think that people can work to better what they have instead of seeking to take what they do not from someone else."

"You must sympathize with the Third Layer cretins, then." His eyes sparked and his smile grew. "The whole struggle is fascinating, don't you think?"

Participating in this conversation was the worst thing I could do, but I felt impelled to say, "I think it is sad."

"Mmmm. Perhaps we are just different kinds of personal engineers in the end. You work with what is—always trying to capture and protect the spirit of a person without changing them—while I'm always looking at ways of creating anew, based on what has worked, or destroying what has not."

His words caused my pulse to jump unpleasantly. It indicated a deeper knowledge of me and my past than I was comfortable with.

The reaction must have shown, because he smiled. "Discussing such things always makes people nervous. So poor of me to make you uneasy. You seemed so less...stressed...this afternoon. And it is a guilty pleasure to see you somewhat content."

A small part of me relaxed at the sudden change in the tone of his voice, which was infused with comfort and kinship. "Some friends are helping me with a project." I touched my scarf reflexively.

"That sounds like an interesting tale." His voice was enthusiastic and his eyes mischievous but kind—like Christian's had always been. It was easy to see how he had enamored some of the students and admins. "Do tell."

"It involves me and I'm quite dull, unfortunately."

"Nothing could be farther from the truth, I'd say."

We checked three more access points. It was odd that Emrys had quizzed Dare on anything and everything campus related for two entire weeks, yet here we were alone and he wasn't trying to wheedle campus and Midlands secrets out of me. Dare had been nervous about that.

But, no, instead, Emrys was trying to wheedle personal admissions and making me feel suddenly companionable to him. He was the most insidious type of Department plant. And I was easy prey.

"Why did you join the Peacekeepers' Troop?" I asked. Might as well attempt my own digging for personal information.

"A delightful question. A previous engagement was ruined, but an alternate opportunity presented itself, and I took it."

"What was your previous job?"

"Training. I was in the midst of training the most perfect specimen. But then—"

"Norr!" The leader of the Troop motioned sharply to Emrys from twenty-five yards to the east of us. "Turn your frequency back on and let's go!"

Emrys's gaze narrowed unpleasantly on the man, and he tipped his head as if debating some sort of violent retribution.

Adrenaline poured through me at the very familiar gesture on an unfamiliar face. I listened to my body and backed away slowly. "Well, you should see what he wants, and we are all done for the day...so see you tomorrow!"

He regarded me for a moment before tipping his head to the other side, increasing the weird sense of jumbled familiarity. "Perhaps sooner than you think, Ren, my dear."

He turned and strode toward General Telgent. His comment along with the way he moved was extremely upsetting. He walked like Christian.

I turned and ran. I ran right through the group of Junior Department members who had been following us again. They gasped and scattered and I didn't bother to apologize as I ran through the Fourteenth Circle West arch. I immediately took another arch to Sixth Circle North.

I'd pay later for running them down, but at least Keiren and his friend that I had nicknamed 'Stripes' were gone—they and a few other high profile students had been given permission to leave campus and had been collected by their parents and a Department escort yesterday. They had bragged about going to watch the competition in real time, instead of via projection and feed as the rest of us were doing.

I was surprised Bellacia hadn't gone as well, but she was hosting special news reports for her father's papers about Excelsine, in anticipation of the school placing first in the competition.

Justice Toad croaked an alert, startling me and making me almost drop the tablet.

All-hands meeting for the Peacekeepers' Troop, Justice Squad, and Neutralizer Squad—report to Dorm Eleven <u>immediately</u>, the screen read.

Great. No wonder Emrys had made that comment. I looked at the Magiaduct one level up and started reluctantly tromping toward Dorm Eleven.

Emrys had gone from fearsome Department lackey to serious creeper. He was seriously creeping me out. Why was I seeing my brother in his movements?

My control cuff squeezed my left wrist hard, and I stopped and stared at it blankly. It gave a more vicious squeeze, waiting for acknowledgment. Seriously? Now?

I put my fingers around the cuff and let my acknowledgment seep inside. Dean Marsgrove was calling me in for our review. Relief at getting out of the squad meeting vied with irritation at Marsgrove.

I'd figured that we wouldn't meet until next week or the week after, since the Excelsine staff held their quarterly and yearly meetings during the week of the Combat Games. While

the students were busy watching the games,
the teachers gathered and held a symposium,
probably discussing things like, how to make
classes more brutal, and what to do with
the troubled mages on campus—feed them to
the Blarjack or assign them more community
service?

But Marsgrove hadn't forgotten me, and the
contract magic I had signed upon enrollment
would force me to answer the call in a painful
fashion, if I didn't do it on my own.

I shook my left wrist. My cuff felt weird and
it hurt—like the metal had split somewhere
and raw edges were now curling down to
pierce the flesh underneath. There was a slight
ultramarine hue to it now too. What had
Marsgrove done? How did he know to associate
that hue? The morning after my Awakening, he
had only seen the brown sludge aftermath of my
blue painted massacre.

Regardless, it was not a good sign.

I sent Isaiah a note saying I couldn't be at
the squad meeting and that I'd catch up later,
then jumped through three different arches
to reach Top Circle and the Administration

Building. All the way up the mountain, my magic was doing things without my conscious say-so—small things as I passed people who were heading to the battle field, like changing their eye color to match Dare's, simply because I was thinking about the hue—so I wrapped fingers around my cuff, trying to keep control and not freak out.

My increasingly panicked thoughts couldn't wrap around the blurred data points that were jumping around my conscious thought—or those thoughts simmering on the edges, waiting to come together to form a picture. Unable to do anything else about my panic, I alerted Beta Team to go on immediate rounds. On the off-chance that something was wrong with campus, rather than me, I needed an unbiased second opinion.

I increased my pace, swearing under my breath. I didn't want to go to an all-hands meeting with the squads on campus, I didn't want to see Emrys, and I didn't want to see Marsgrove. What I actually wanted to do was to join the majority of students on campus on the battle field in front of one of the giant hologram, or "Jumbogram," projections showing the remote competition live, and to soak in the excitement of the matches, and the brilliance of the competitors—namely one competitor.

But if this was an appetizer for how my day was going to go, I'd be lucky to catch any of the action later on repeat feeds.

I sent a quick note to Olivia, letting her know I'd called in Beta and was on my way to meet with her cousin. She was, unfortunately, in the midst of a scheduled social debate despite the rest of campus having already flocked to the large areas that were projecting the combat competition live. A quick reply from her said to stay calm, say as little as possible, and remind Marsgrove of the contract he was under.

Sinking slowly onto the straight-backed metal chair in Marsgrove's mixed modern and traditional white and brown office, I mentally scrolled through questions he might ask.

Origin Mages. Raphael Verisetti. Kinsky's painting. Cuffs. Stolen golems. Leeches. Leashes. The Troop. The community service network and underground black market. The Midlands and Okai—had he discovered Guard Rock and Guard Friend?

Gray eyes regarded me coldly. "You are working with Alexander Dare."

His opening statement was not at all expected. But maybe that's what the ultramarine overlaying my cuff was meant to be—some sort of weird forewarning about what Marsgrove wanted to discuss.

Honestly, no wonder Dare never spoke to anyone outside of his crew. Everyone was always digging for information about him.

"Yes, I'm aware of that," I said. "I just spoke to him two hours ago."

He'd been all tiny and hilarious sitting on my desk, like a dangerous little Muppet. Hologram communication could be enormously entertaining like that. I wished my parents' journals could work with holograms.

Marsgrove tapped his fingers impatiently on the desk. The sound pulled me back to the present.

"You can see him too—he should be on the field soon," I said. "He's doing really well. First in all staffs, first in offensive wards, first in dismantling, third in swords and a list of other placements. The three-person team competition is up soon and they are expected to kill it. It'll be a great time to fanboy out. No need to pump me for info."

Marsgrove's chilly visage grew...chillier. "Take care with your tone, Miss Crown."

I really wanted to get out of here. I needed to gather my scattered thoughts. The pattern, just out of my reach, was trying to form, waiting for me to relax and think it through. I touched my cuff. The sooner I left Marsgrove's company, the better.

I disliked him, but I was well aware of the power he had over me on campus as a dean, even if his title was the inexplicable Dean of Special Projects.

"What do you want to know?" I could give Marsgrove all sorts of empty information with zero real content. I was pretty used to answering these sorts of questions. "Yes, Dare got stuck with me and I'm helping with campus security. Yes, I'm putting effort into it. Yes, he's good at his job. No, I don't think he's interested in your love spell. No, he has not told me of his world domination plans. No, I didn't bespell him, and you are delusional if you think I could. Didn't he beat you in competition, Dean Marsgrove?"

Will had said something to that effect back in the info dump he had given me when we'd first met.

"Are you quite done?" Each word was deliberately enunciated.

Okay, maybe in my litany of memorized answers I shouldn't have tacked on one about Marsgrove getting beaten by a teenager, military wunderkind or not. "Debatable. Are we?"

"I haven't asked you an actual question, and yet you spew words without a shred of control."

I pointed at his face. "The questions are all there in your unfriendly expression. It's a family trait. Though I'm happy to say that Olivia is blooming like a sunflower away from you people. How is Helen, by the way? I hope she isn't in pain these days."

Olivia was going to murder me.

Marsgrove's eyes narrowed. "You play an increasingly dangerous game, Miss Crown."

I absolutely should be saying nothing more. Implying to Marsgrove that I was in any way responsible for reverse-spelling Helen Price's care packages was stupid. Saying anything at all was unwise. But now that it had arisen, my rage couldn't be swallowed back down.

"It's not a game. You know what she does to Olivia. You know and yet you sent her to our room, knowing what she would do to her daughter. You are a terrible dean and a worse family member. You tell that—" What word had Constantine used? "—that friest that worse will happen if she touches my roommate again."

From the look on Marsgrove's face, Constantine's word was stronger than even my dictionary had translated.

He leaned back and examined me like a bacteria-infested microscope slide. "I owe you no explanation, but to set the record straight, I didn't send her to your room. In fact, I sent Olivia a warning as soon as I saw Helen. And I won't even get a chance to flatten you in a month when I'm out from underneath our 'contract.' You will already be dead from gross stupidity. Congratulations."

I smiled, showing a lot of teeth. This was
the man who had tricked me into enrolling
at school, then kept me prisoner under
suppression and calming spells, trying to make
me into a complacent vegetable until he could
do...whatever he was planning to do with me.
The fact that he hadn't sent Helen to our room
didn't change my opinion of him. He obviously
knew what his cousin was capable of and he had
sent a warning. Yippee.

"You underestimate my unfortunate ability to
stay alive," I said through clenched teeth. "But
celebrate my stupidity, please do. It will serve
your agenda just fine."

"You don't know what my agenda is," he said
coldly.

"You hate me. As soon as magic releases you
from your bargain with Olivia, you will turn me
over to the government."

"Hate implies far more emotion than I feel for
you."

That sapped my anger better than anything
else he might have said. There was nothing
to be gained from arguing with Marsgrove. I

needed to save my strength for other things. I wasn't going to change his mind about the risk of me continuing to draw free breath, and he wasn't going to change mine about what a rotten human I thought he was.

My shoulders dropped. "Why did you summon me? I thought we were doing a great job at ignoring each other." I got to pretend that I was a normal person attending magic school, and he got to pretend I didn't exist.

He frowned and his shoulders tensed. "I summoned you because we needed a review, and it seemed like a good time."

I sat forward in my chair, unnerved by the thin thread of underlying confusion in his voice. He wasn't completely sure why he had summoned me? He should be at one of the staff meetings currently in session, not meeting with me.

Marsgrove grimaced. "Enough. I want to know what Alexander Dare is teaching you. And why he picked you."

Without argument, strangers always accepted my false answer that Dare had gotten stuck with me. None of the Junior Department stooges or anyone else who had moderate contact with Dare or with me ever accepted that response.

"He's teaching me how to guard campus. And..." I sighed. "You know why he picked me. I'm powerful, and it's obvious."

Enough people had told me so, and I wasn't delusional. Power attracted people, just like any other charismatic trait. It didn't make people have to like me, though. I was lucky to have found good friends, and I was going to keep them.

"And what have you told him?" Marsgrove asked, eyes narrowed and pen tapping a funereal beat on his desk.

I was lucky to have found good friends, and I sure as hell wasn't going to sell any of them out.

"The only thing Alexander Dare cares about on campus is keeping it safe. And it would be against my best interests to tell anyone the things that you are insinuating."

Of course, that last statement would only be true if I had any actual self-preservation instincts when someone I considered "mine" wanted something. Dare knew plenty of my secrets, including the one Marsgrove didn't want him to know. One, because Dare was extremely sharp, and two, because when he asked, I answered.

I'd sell myself down the river, if asked by one of eight people in the world. I sure wasn't going to let Marsgrove know that, though.

"You know, I don't understand you people," I said, not waiting for Marsgrove to respond. "Do you think he's going to take over the world on his lunch break? Shouldn't you be more concerned about the motives of other mages. Like your former buddy?" I tapped my finger in echo of his joyless rhythm.

A knock on the door interrupted the beginning of what was likely to be a scathing rebuttal on Marsgrove's part.

"What?" He called in a surly, but commanding voice.

The door opened and his attractive secretary stuck her head in. "Delivery for you, sir."

He waved her forward and she put a small, package wrapped in brown paper and twine on the edge of his desk.

"Checked and cleared, sir."

"Thank you, Sylline."

"Of course, sir." She exited.

My gaze went to the package, wondering idly what could be in it—the trapped soul of some hapless student?—then shifted back to Marsgrove as he exhaled.

The interruption had caused something in Marsgrove to lose steam. He ran a hand along his face, and for the first time I saw weariness there. Fatigue that was bone deep.

"Miss Crown, you don't understand the game that is being played."

Fatigue painted across Marsgrove's normally militant features was alarming. I eyed the package again. Maybe it contained magic pills to handle stress. Maybe Marsgrove was hyped on them all the time and needed a recharge right now.

He shook his head, drawing my attention back to his face. For once, his steely eyes looked to me in appeal. Weird. Really weird. Even the air around me was starting to feel freaked out about it.

My eyes immediately returned to the package. I felt compelled to look at it. Another spark of unease shot through me.

Marsgrove reached almost absently for the wrapped paper and twine. "You have no idea what—"

As he reached out, a line of magic materialized around the package—a gold line stretching toward him as his fingers drew closer.

My magic reacted before I even realized consciously what was happening. Marsgrove's chair rocketed backward and the package shot off his desk and hit the wall. The box dropped, clunking awkwardly to the floor. A spent pyramid was rotating in my mind, drawing in more magic in case the package—now pulsing gold—erupted.

But an outside force smothered my magic, shattering my mental construct and yanking away my ability to connect to it. Just before the magic sealed, my scarf tightened, communicating distress to the Alpha team before it too was sealed away from me by Marsgrove's spell.

Marsgrove stood before me, his shields fully raised. "You attacked a dean of this school." He looked furious, but the emotion was edged with a dark satisfaction. "And it will be my pleasure to—"

"Not...right," I croaked. Whatever Administrative Magic he was using made it hard to speak. I cast pinched eyes at the package, unable to find the right words or to lift a finger. "Not right."

The grip on my magic paused.

Marsgrove would be a far less dangerous enemy if he were stupid. He cast an immediate suppression bubble that encased the package, and a flurry of cataloging spells flew toward it even as he watched me. He would be a far less dangerous enemy if he weren't powerful and controlled—I couldn't even hope to split magic and mental focus into multiple streams like that yet, and he did it easily.

He pointed to the package without looking away from me. "What do you see on it?" The Administrative Magic loosened enough for me to speak and focus, but I was stuck to the chair, unable to move.

"Gold." With an additional thirty seconds to process, it was obvious whose magic was all over the package. "Raphael."

Marsgrove's expression didn't drastically change, but there was a tightening around his lips and eyes. It reminded me again that the two of them had history. Normally, I wouldn't care, other than to know they hated each other and I hated both of them. But now...

"Why can't you sense it?" I demanded. The package was fairly glowing now. "And how did it get through your security procedures?"

His secretary had said the package had been "checked," and Marsgrove should have been able to identify the feel of Raphael immediately. He had recognized Raphael's magic on me right off.

Marsgrove was already moving to the door and flinging it open. From my stuck position, I could see Sylline crumpled on the floor as if the strings that had been holding her up had been cut. Her styled auburn hair and neatly tailored gray suit looked incongruous on the cold tiles.

Marsgrove was silent as he checked her, then he finally murmured to her, "Grey will be here in just a minute, hang on."

He had obviously contacted someone—I was betting on Dr. Greyskull—via frequency.

All of the spells holding me to the chair collapsed and Marsgrove suddenly loomed over me. "Open it."

I stared at him for a moment, flexing my fingers and toes now that I had the ability back. "No."

"Open the package."

"No. No way."

I waited for Administrative Magic to make me do it, but nothing happened. Bitter relief swept me. He couldn't force me to do something, then, unless I finagled myself into a magical contract like I had with the Provost last term. The magic Marsgrove had just used could only suppress and restrain.

Marsgrove relaxed slightly at my negative response.

Realization bloomed. "You thought I might be in on it." It wasn't a question.

He didn't respond, making my anger erupt again.

"I saved you. From a package that should never have been able to be delivered. What kind of mail system do you have here? Allowing students and family to be maimed under your watch?"

Even if everything else resolved itself, I would never forgive him for allowing Helen Price's poisonous packages to get into Olivia's hands.

Any previous loosening in Marsgrove's posture was gone. His expression indicated he was past furious and approaching savage rage, but I didn't care.

"I thought your mission in life other than to subjugate me, was to hunt him down?" I said. "Shouldn't you have some sort of basic signature detector for mortal enemies, Dean Marsgrove? He was a student here once—with you, probably—and I know the school records student's signatures."

"I should be asking you about his magic signature." His tone was bitter. "You are the one who fed him additional magic."

That was completely unfair, but I gripped the verbal response tightly between my teeth. The mental voice I had incorporated from debating with Olivia said arguing about my guilt and lack of consent during my Awakening would be useless. Marsgrove didn't care about fairness. Not in this, and not with me.

"And I'm the one who just saved you from that magic," I said. "And now you owe me."

"Get out."

"Gladly." I was on my feet before the end of the word exited my mouth.

I gave the still-glowing package in the corner a wide berth and slipped around his fallen secretary.

I got as far as the grassy center of Top Circle when my journal to Dare shrieked in my bag.

"Ren, perimeter ward failure where Norr is—" The transmission cut off abruptly.

Light exploded behind me. I whirled, along with everyone else on the circle as the Administration Building glowed, pulsed, then went dark, sealing shut. I sprinted between two buildings and to the edge of Top Circle, gasping as I looked down the mountain.

Light exploded, rippling down the mountain, in every direction. A dome sealed over the battle field stands, and a ring of light encircled the Magiaduct. All the ports lit as one, then darkened. I saw a student on the Third Circle run through an arch and emerge on the other side of it, as if he'd passed under a simple decorative stone construction.

My God. I stared at my bag and the dead journal transmission as my brain processed and shoved together the data that had been hovering.

The combat mages were all at the competition.

The administrators, staff, and professors were all gathered in the Administration Building for planning sessions.

I could see some students walking the grounds, but the vast majority of the population was either in the stands at the battle field or in the dorms watching the competition remotely.

The Justice Squad and the Troop—and even the Neutralizer Squad—had been called to an emergency meeting in the dorms ten minutes ago.

A package had been sent to neutralize Marsgrove.

The perimeter ward had been breached.

The tracking spell Dare had placed on Emrys Norr had registered him at the breach.

Emrys Norr, who Dare had researched, and who had never felt right to him.

I ran, pulling everything I needed from my bag as I sprinted straight for the Blarjack Swamp.

Campus was under attack from the inside, and the only thing that now stood in the way was me.

Chapter Thirty-three

RED ALERT

DARE HAD NEVER trusted Emrys to actually complete the safety checks he was required to do, and although there had been nothing Dare could do about the Troop's presence, he had put a spell on Emrys's tablet to directly track his movements around campus.

I fished out my tablet and simultaneously checked Dare's spell and the state of campus. Minutes ago, Emrys had been logged by the spell at the exact spot where we'd checked the weak perimeter ward less than half an hour before. Then...nothing. The tablet had been either destroyed or taken off campus.

State of campus? Locked down, with all off-campus transmissions and ports blocked.

And all I could think of was Emrys.

Creepy Emrys who was aware of all our security measures—who had been trained to be. Perfectly positioned and operational, he, like each member of the Troop, knew every emergency procedure. He'd also been having lunch with blushing admins and members of the staff who kept operations information.

My imagination was starting to get ahead of me and it was telling me that at any moment on-campus transmissions might be disrupted as well. I pushed the panic button on Justice Toad.

"All hands! Perimeter ward breached, Administration Building sealed, battle field stands and Magiaduct sealed, ports sealed. Isaiah, are Norr and Telgent with you?"

"General Telgent is here," Isaiah responded immediately, voice dark but commanding. "Every Troop member except Norr is here. And every Justice Squad member but you. We have no outside communication. What is going on?"

"I think...we are under attack. I think Emrys Norr took down the perimeter ward on Eighteen."

Justice Squad voices shouted back that I was insane, and I could hear outraged Troop voices demanding that I explain myself. They had been suddenly, inexplicably trapped in the Magiaduct because they had been called to a surprise squad meeting, and they wanted me to explain why I thought something bad was happening?

If this wasn't just a notable collection of random events, then this setup had been planned and timed perfectly. Whoever had done so had waited until most of the staff and students were contained and vulnerable.

Everything in me said this was not a random series of events. The question of why—why would someone affiliated with the Department attack campus?—would need to be answered later.

I gripped the scarf at my neck, opening the line of magic that allowed anyone wearing one to hear me. The magic connected to me and pulled on my energy. "Olivia, everyone, Red Status, repeat, Red Status! Anyone free, meet at Rendezvous Point Zeta. I repeat, Red Status!"

I ignored the yelling, expletives, and invectives issuing from my tablet and scarf, as I grabbed Dare's journal from my bag and commenced the spell that would record everything that happened around me in a mass cloud and dump it to Dare when he eventually made it through a blocked port or perimeter ward.

Until then, it was all on me.

No, I thought, as I saw Olivia, Will, Neph, Delia, Mike, Saf, Trick, Kita, Lifen, Bryant, Dagfinn, and five others running toward Rendezvous Zeta—the entrance to the Blarjack Swamp—it was all on us. Anger and relief crashed through me with so much force that I stumbled.

"What the hell is going on, Price?" Bryant shouted as he ran.

"I don't know. Model up with a live feed now!" Olivia barked, as we all converged.

Saf, Kita, and Will slid to their knees and Trick looped their magic together. A model of the mountain grew—constructed as quickly as I had ever seen them model anything, then they forced their collected mass of magic to make it a real projection to track and record where the disturbance—or disturbances—were emanating from. Dagfinn saturated the hologram in Communication Magic aimed specifically at the massed disturbance darkening the Seventeenth Circle, and Delia and Lifen pulled the threads of the communication-enhanced magic through the air and attached them to Olivia's scarf, which activated the magic in all of ours.

"A lovely backdrop for a massacre." A booming voice burst through the audio enchantment, and the sharp features of Vincent Godfrey appeared in our hologram as he strode dramatically across one of the battle fields with his arms outstretched in the open air. "Look at this view. Almost as magnificent as it used to be in the Third. Let's return some of this beautiful magic back where it belongs."

"Dear Magic," Will whispered, horror in his voice. It was a sentiment repeated verbally by at least three others. The voices coming through Justice Toad suddenly changed from condemnation to terror—people trapped in the stands were likely relaying via frequency that Vincent Godfrey was on campus and walking toward them.

Vincent Godfrey—the man responsible for the carnage in Sassraf, and the man who had appeared in the hijacked feed and demanded that the Second Layer concede. Here was definitive proof that this was an attack. But not by the Department—by Third Layer terrorists.

I frantically checked my wrist and the other places where gold glowed—but the color was not pulsing any more brightly than it had earlier in the day, which meant Raphael hadn't suddenly appeared. Terrorists in the top ten must work alone. I let out a strangled noise of relief and Delia looked at me as if I'd lost my mind.

In the hologram, Godfrey gazed into the dome encasing the stands. He smiled and gave a little wave. The campus news feed had reported that ten thousand students were expected to watch the first day of competition live at the battle fields. Ten thousand students.

"Communications up now," Godfrey said to one of the five minions behind him. His gaze narrowed on the students trapped inside the dome. "And why are they speaking in there like that? Shut down all internal campus transmissions immediately, you idiot."

"Isaiah!" I shouted over the yelling from my tablet. "Make Telgent t—"

Abruptly, Justice Toad went silent and nearly everyone around me grabbed their ears and throats.

"—talk," I finished loudly into the silence.

The hologram of Godfrey wavered. The scarf tightened around my neck, and my right knee buckled in surprise as magic was yanked out of me in order to keep the communication of the scarves active and alive.

Most of our assembled group looked at Olivia in surprise as the hologram continued to show the six terrorists in live motion. They slowly removed their hands from the physical points hit by their broken frequencies—looking for an explanation as to why the hologram and scarves were still active when all other communications were not.

"Price, you actually did it?" Dagfinn asked, impressed. "You carved out a block of magic separate from the school's communications?"

"Magic has been made available, yes. Track his channel, Dagfinn," Olivia said tightly, gesturing abruptly to the hologram.

Dagfinn nodded, smiling, and initiated the magic. I startled again under the pull.

My movement did not go unnoticed this time.

"Price? Dear Magic, Price." Dagfinn was staring at me in horror, along with the others around him. "The block of magic... Did you hook our communications into her?" Dagfinn whispered oddly.

"Track the channel, Dagfinn," Olivia said furiously. Her fierce, angry gaze bored into me before switching back to Dagfinn's group. "We don't have time to discuss."

It was the argument I had used when I'd initiated the leech, and Olivia meant the angry barb for me. She hadn't liked this modified part of the plan at all.

A more aggressive pull began as Dagfinn did exactly what was asked of him. I wasn't surprised this time, and I forced myself to relax and not reflexively grab the streams of magic slipping away from me. If I stopped the magic, we might not get it restarted.

When Dagfinn, a twenty-one-year old communications mage, frequency hacker, and steady delinquent, had suggested hooking the scarves into a separate power source so that we'd be out from under control of "the man," it had been obvious even at the time that he had been thinking of some sort of hijacked space in the mountain.

We hadn't had time to configure that, so I'd hooked the metaphorical jack up to me with help from Will. With my complete consent offered to the magic and our practical leech experience, it had been ridiculously easy.

The Frequency Grid was powered by magic the government allocated for communication. Anyone trying to shut down communications would, without question, take it down first. I didn't have a frequency like nearly every other student did. I was an island. I was the perfect battery.

"They are opening eight channels. Trying to piggyback now to see if we can get a signal through with theirs, then I'll hold a channel open for us, in three," Dagfinn said, holding up three shaky fingers. He, and everyone around him, kept shooting anxious glances at me. "Two, one, got it."

Much of the pull on me lessened as Dagfinn opened a small channel beneath one used by the terrorists. I took a deeper breath.

In the hologram, Godfrey smirked at the men and women lining up in front of him. "This is going to be a day for the books, folks. Let's make the Baileys' print run red."

Even from here, I could feel the dome encasing the students. I could feel it inside of me—hollowness, like a watermelon scraped of its fruit. The dome was made from Origin Magic, but tainted and fouled by ill purpose. I looked at the Administration Building—which we could see partially through the trees that surrounded the swamp. Different dome, with a different purpose, yet there were streaks of illness in there as well. Jagged edges that could detonate if not handled correctly.

Delia cursed and pressed her lips together as the holographic view zoomed outward. "Where did they all come from?"

There weren't just six terrorists. At least a hundred battle hardened men and women had stepped into the frame of the projection.

"A perimeter ward was breached," I said. I looked at the men and women in front of Godfrey. "There are probably even more of them beyond the image's range."

"We need a body count, Asafa," Olivia said. "We need to know…"

We needed to know what? I could hear the question echoed in the silence of the others. These were men and women who had been successfully terrorizing the entire Layer and its military forces for months. We needed to know how many we were going to…fight?

"In order to do what? We are not combat mages. We are not soldiers. We need to hide, now," Bryant said. A few other faces looked like they agreed.

"Tracking the foreign signatures on campus, Olivia," Saf said, his voice strong and certain. He, Trick, Will, and two guys from Epsilon were running the spells with Dagfinn. "And initiating character location and scenario mapping."

There was a small tap in my scarf, then a dot popped up on the hologram of the mountain that Saf was stretching between his hands. Sixteen other dots appeared around mine—registering each connected scarf—and an equal amount were grouped together in Dorm Five. It was just like one of Saf and Trick's games—except the mountain was the setting and we were the game's protagonists armed only with full life bars.

"Frey, you can't tell me you are going along with this change of plan, this war game, this utter tripe?" Bryant addressed Asafa incredulously. When Saf didn't answer, Bryant turned to Olivia and pointed sharply at her. "We are not soldiers, Price. I am not a soldier."

"Do you see who that is, Bryant?" Olivia jabbed a finger at the first hologram where Godfrey was smirking and strutting outside the domed battle field stands. "They will kill all of us. They will kill everyone in the stands at the battle field, probably as soon as they gather their audience. As soon as those eight channels are answered, that dome will house the burial ground for ten thousand trapped ducks. You are either an asset or a liability to us," Olivia said, locking gazes with him. "Which one is it going to be?"

"That so?" Bryant looked both incredulous and angry. "You going to take me out if I'm not in on your absurd little war game?"

Olivia's gaze was uncompromising. "I wouldn't waste my energy or time."

"What the hell. You? Going to save campus?" Bryant laughed. "I was all for this stupid plan when we were talking about creating havoc and screwing with people, but fighting? Putting our necks on the line? What's in this for Olivia Price?"

Olivia's gaze unwittingly slid my way for a moment.

But Bryant was looking through the trees, over the grassy central circle, to the Administration Building. He gave an unpleasant laugh. "You got war bonds or political plots riding on this? Mommy set you up to make us martyrs?"

"You are released from your commitment, Bryant. Leave your scarf. Go hide." Olivia turned to Dagfinn's group, turning her back on Bryant and hiding her expression. But the magical and emotional feedback from her was overwhelming—violence, drowning sorrow, rage, love, determination.

"Oh, you can bet I'm going. Those already trapped are as good as dead anyway. You are the idiots who are going to die with them." Bryant dropped his scarf and made a rude gesture at Olivia, then swept it across the air to encompass the rest of us before disappearing into the foliage surrounding the swamp.

"Anyone else?" Olivia asked. Silence greeted her.

Delia's gaze was fixed on Olivia. A few moments later Bryant's scarf flew through the air and landed in her hand.

Neph put a hand on Olivia's arm. Silent communication passed between them—I didn't know whether they were not including everyone else, or not including me specifically. The communication magic in the scarves was based on Frequency design, and the intent of the speaker directed the message to an individual, three people, a select team, the whole group—or everyone except for one person.

A moment later, Neph ran toward the nearest flagpole.

"A perimeter ward was breached on the Eighteenth Circle for five minutes," Saf said, manipulating the section of air filled with code, maps, and the magic that they were all working with—normal magic, not magic drawn from me. "It was closed again—the magic changed and reinforced—but we might be able to break through."

Olivia nodded briskly. "The combat mages and the Department will be looking for any entry point onto campus."

At the base of the mountain, far below the student levels, we could see flashes of fire and color. People fighting.

"The campus ports and mage-made travel options are closed. It will take fifteen minutes to get to the Eighteenth Circle through the natural travel systems," Lifen said, pointing at the Blarjack Swamp, a natural port that didn't rely on Administrative Magic. "And that doesn't take into account how long traversing the Midlands will take or the fact that the enemy is on the Seventeenth Circle, and likely guarding the hole they created, even if it's patched."

Hundreds of yards away, Neph was doing complicated magic around the flagpoles. The magic flowed in a current from one flagpole to the next.

"I'll check the perimeter ward," I said, already moving.

Olivia grabbed my arm. "No. Lifen's right. There are undoubtedly guards positioned there. And we need you elsewhere." Her mouth pinched unhappily.

Everyone looked uneasily between us. I couldn't even imagine what they were thinking—no blips of emotion were coming through the scarves. Everyone except for me was a frequency user already, and they had adapted to using the scarf communication properties quickly and easily.

"I'll be fast. Someone has to check the ward who knows it," I said.

"I'll do it," a new, but familiar voice said.

Everyone spun to see Constantine casually leaning with his back against a tree at the edge of the swamp.

"What are you doing here?" Olivia demanded. Then her gaze swung to me. "No, I know what he is doing here."

I held up a hand in apology. "He is helpful?"

"Are you insane?" she hissed.

Constantine smiled. "I'll do it, Price. Unless you want to send Crown while you continue to drain her?"

Olivia smiled thinly, which meant she was livid. She hadn't liked it when I'd insisted on hooking the communication spells of the scarves into my magic, but Olivia didn't waste resources, and she well knew I could function at far lower energy levels than this. Dagfinn's open channel was taking most of the load now, too, which was far better than expected.

At least something was exceeding expectations. Because for all of the stress relief and fun Plan Fifty-two had become, we had not prepared for an incursion—especially not one that would rely solely upon us to solve.

I had been worried about monsters, yes. Anxious about keeping campus safe, most definitely. Actual emotional preparation for a military assault of campus with no combat mages, no teachers, no Troop, and no backup? No. Not even close.

We had been far more certain that a creature rampaging the grounds or some diabolical magic getting out of control would be our problem. And we hadn't planned for what exactly a Red Alert would mean.

Olivia had implemented Plan Fifty-two in order to manage my stress level—this had never been a war strategy.

Constantine didn't wait for Olivia to respond. "Give me the extra scarf. I'll check the perimeter ward on the Eighteenth Circle immediately and try to reopen the breach. On my magic, I so do vow."

For a moment the only sound was of the Blarjack swimming around the swamp—waiting for one of us to jump in so it could catch a meaty two-legged meal. Everyone stared, dumbfounded, at Constantine as the Contract Magic, still perfectly in effect as natural magic, settled around his shoulders and bound him to the promise.

"Fine. Give him the scarf, Delia," Olivia said. "Perhaps the enemy will save us the trouble and take care of Leandred permanently."

Constantine's expression didn't change, but something satisfied settled in the connection I could feel to him. He took the scarf from Delia, then strode to the edge of the swamp.

Constantine was... Well, Constantine was a lot of things, but putting himself on the line as a scout was out of character.

He winked at me over his shoulder, then threw powder into the water. The Blarjack recoiled and dove away. Constantine stepped on the speckled black water, and his coat flared out as he was sucked inside the natural port. The black water sealed over the top of him.

"Ren," Olivia snapped. "Pay attention."

Rocked and conflicted, I tore my gaze away from the empty space where Constantine had stood. "Sorry."

"Dagfinn?"

"They have six of the eight communications already open, live, and frozen—two Department heads, the three Council members of the Alliance, one ambassador. Waiting on one more Department head, and the eighth comm is a frequency to Roald Bailey's office."

Bellacia's dad—the head of the major news networks.

"Based on the connection time of the others, we have three minutes max until the last two are up," Dagfinn said.

"Five hundred and eleven foreign signatures detected on all non-Midlands levels," Saf said, magic curling like swarming fireflies in the afternoon air as he populated the mountain hologram with each relevant dot.

"Fine, we have three minutes, five hundred plus professional combatants, and eighteen of us," Olivia said.

Someone in the back whispered that we were all going to die.

"Which means we must be smart," Olivia said briskly. "Best case scenario is that Vincent Godfrey performs another long-winded, tedious speech and we free everyone while he is windbagging."

"We should get the teachers out first," someone said. "And the staff, so they can reactivate the Administrative Magic."

"No," Olivia said harshly. "Think. What will Godfrey do if the Administration Building is freed, defenses go back up, and the teachers come streaking down the mountain? Or, if whatever forces are fighting at the bottom of the mountain make it through? What does an animal do when you corner him next to the self-destruct button?"

"They'll kill everyone at the battle fields," I said numbly. I thought of Raphael. "Probably blow the dome completely hoping to take down the mountain. The perfect statement."

More than one person winced. It was hard to concentrate on the flurry of the others' responses over the beat of my throbbing pulse.

Olivia nodded sharply. "The dome around the stands at the battle fields must be dealt with first, then the Administration Building, then the Magiaduct. We have only one thing on our side—the element of surprise."

"They are Origin Domes, Price," someone said. "What do you want us to do to them?"

"They are made of magic," Olivia said briskly, undaunted. "And we are all criminally exceptional magic users. Figure it out."

Saf looked up from what he was doing and the skin at the corners of his eyes crinkled in pleasure.

"Beta Team, you are on the Administration Building," Olivia said. "Figure out the dome's magic without triggering it. Use whatever is needed to free the professors and staff after we get the students at the battle fields released. Once the field dome goes down...it's going to be a bloodbath. I have no idea how they got the Administration Building and the Administration Magic locked down so completely, but freeing the adults as soon as possible after that is our absolute best bet for campus to survive."

For most of our classmates to survive.

No one said that, but Beta Team nodded grimly.

Minus Bryant, Beta was in full force as a result of the call I had made preceding my visit to Marsgrove. And Alpha was in full force due to

the personal alarm sent through my scarf when
I had been with Marsgrove.

Both teams had been mobilizing on the
grounds when the domes had been raised.
Unfortunately, most of the Delta, Gamma,
and Epsilon members were trapped under the
domes with the rest of the student body. The six
with us were the only ones free.

"Remaining members of Delta, Gamma, and
Epsilon, go to the dorms. Same procedure there.
Figure out the magic to free our classmates after
the battle field dome is taken care of. Round up
stragglers to help." She pointed at the twenty
or so mages who had gathered around us while
we'd been speaking—students who had been
walking the grounds or in other buildings when
the domes had gone up, and who were now
desperately looking for information. "Take them
with you and get them to gather others. Form
chant circles. If you see soldiers, hide and spring
the traps we spread."

Olivia pointed at her scarf. "We have people
on the inside who can hear this and they are
already working on their ends. The Justice Squad
got the warning before their communications

were suppressed, and most of them are not stupid, so they should be working on a plan from the inside. Look for areas in the domes that can be weakened by striking from both sides. Our people will figure out their part."

Everyone nodded.

"Alpha Team deals with him." She pointed at the hologram of Godfrey. "Ren?"

I nodded, flexing my fingers. They were only trembling a little now. "Ready."

"The third Department head is online," Dagfinn announced. "Just waiting for Bailey now. His secretary is in tears trying to explain how even though Bailey always answers his frequency immediately, that right now he is in a non-magic zone, but will be out in two minutes."

"Roald Bailey is never without a frequency connection." Olivia smiled unpleasantly. "He should have been the first to answer.
He's stalling, which means Bellacia got a communication through before the domes went up. She was monitoring us, or more likely, Ren. Something good came of her incessant snooping for once."

"Price, eight units are splitting off from the main force and are heading up campus in a compass sweep," Dagfinn said. "They noticed our magic use. They are planning to put down all pockets of resistance that they find. They are using a copy of an Administrative spell to locate students in groups."

Everyone exchanged grim looks.

"Use the scarves," Olivia said. "Keep slightly scattered. We have two minutes to get in place. Everyone knows what to do." Everyone nodded, packed up their things, and those kneeling on the ground stood. "Update any students or faculty you find. Hide and be smart. Three students won't attract attention. Seven might. Go!"

Everyone except for Alpha Team, Saf, and Trick, sprinted away.

Olivia turned to me. "Ready?"

"Yes." I held out my hand and Olivia grasped it. She pulled out a cord and started to wrap it awkwardly around our hands.

It seemed almost ludicrous that we were doing this, but Contract Magic didn't care about emergencies and contingencies. The magic would make sure that we held up our end of the bargain now that Plan Fifty-two had been implemented. And it was better that we took a moment to control this now rather than let magic enact punishment at an inopportune time—like ten minutes from now when we were fighting for our lives.

Trick stepped forward and held out a hand for the cord.

Olivia looked at him sharply. "The magic will count you in our culpability."

"You'll never hear an O'Leary spin a finer tale then the one I will spin after this. You need a witness and we need to hurry."

"You don't have to—"

"I'm pleased to do it, Your Majesty," Trick said. He made a grabby hand motion for it, but waited for permission to touch the rope.

"I—"

Saf touched Olivia's shoulder. "He'll get it done."

Olivia's lips pinched, but she nodded and handed Patrick the cord that we had "borrowed" from the Law Department during a routine community service "cleaning" of the office building two days before. Patrick wrapped it quickly around our hands, then began reciting the words that would activate the binding in the scarves. All of the punishments and havoc that would be wreaked today by anyone wearing a scarf would be assigned to Olivia and me. It was part of the promise we had made in the contract signed by everyone participating in Plan Fifty-two.

"Olivia," Asafa said, "What was the code for the implementation spell again?"

When Olivia looked at Asafa, Patrick's gaze slid to me. I nodded. His thumb slid along the cord, gripping it far more in my direction instead of at the midway point between Olivia and me that she had planned. It was an 80/20 accountability imbalance now to me.

I would be getting expelled today.

Patrick quickly finished the binding while Olivia's attention was on Asafa, then slid the cord smoothly free of our hands. "All done."

If Justice Toad could, he would have given a loud series of four croaks, registering the illegal use of the cord. Level Four Offense. I had looked it up when we'd decided on this plan. Using the cord had automatically earned me a trip to Provost Johnson's office and the review board.

I looked at the Administration Building. I wished the trip was possible right now.

Olivia looked at her hand strangely. If she had even a fraction of a minute to think about it, she would know what I had done. She didn't have that minute. "Okay, good. Thank you, Patrick. Now, go destroy."

Be safe.

"We will be very, very bad, Your Majesty," Patrick said with a wink. "Promise."

He gave a little bow, Asafa nodded to both of us, and the two of them strode quickly to join their Beta teammates who had already started casting diagnostics on the Administration Building from the shadows of a nearby structure.

Neph rejoined us. "The flags are all set. The community was split between Dorm Thirty-six and the battle field stands for crowd control purposes when the bubbles were erected. When they are freed, they will be called here en masse."

I wondered what the muses would then do.

Olivia gave her a swift nod, then looked at me. "Ready?"

"Ready." My heart clenched as I looked around the group.

Olivia turned to Delia. "I know you can get us to Eighteen in less than a minute without using any arches."

Delia and Olivia exchanged a long, charged look.

"You are going to trust me to be on your side, Price?"

"You are on this team. I put you on this team," Olivia said curtly. "What do you think?"

Delia stared at her for a moment longer, then gave a curt nod. She turned, waved her hands in opposing figure eights, and flicked her fingers toward the Blarjack. It made a bleating noise and fell sideways. I patted Justice Toad through my bag. When the Administrative Magic caught back up, that would be another croak.

Traveling through the Blarjack swamp for the second time was only a tenth as traumatizing as the first time had been. The tree roots shot us out onto the Sixth Circle and we jogged into the flipping petals of the perisim trees. They enveloped us and spun us onto the Fifteenth Circle.

A pinch on my skin made me pull up my sleeve. Constantine's familiar black script appeared along my forearm. Perimeter ward will be eaten through in twenty-five minutes.

"Constantine will have the perimeter ward down in twenty-five," I said. I decided against mentioning how. People sometimes got a little weirded out by what his chemical concoctions could do.

I touched the skin beneath his writing and thought back at him—We need you at the Administration Building. With the leash.

Everything was happening far too quickly. If only I could have thought things through before he'd taken the scarf and left. Constantine could take down the Administration dome using me while I was on the Seventeenth Circle.

The words—Deliciously tempting, maybe later. Busy now—came back.

Constantine!

There was a caress against my skin, then his words disappeared. His threads still pulsed with healthy life, though, so he hadn't died.

"If we can stall things until the perimeter ward goes down, maybe...?" Mike said, echoing many thoughts—maybe we could all be saved.

My scarf shivered against my skin.

"Price, everyone," the voice of Kita, one of the members of Beta Team, sounded in my head via the scarf's enchantment. "Dagfinn says Roald Bailey just answered the call, so all initial parties have been contacted. But they've initiated a general call as well—and it looks like it's a hijack feed for the entire Second Layer."

Godfrey was planning a show. That wasn't good news.

"Concerning our assignment," Kita continued. "Students started skulking around the

Administration Building. And not in the 'we are attempting to free anyone' type of way. More in the 'secure the building' sort."

A visual of the referenced students seeped through the scarves and showed wispy images of each person in my mind's eye.

"Three of those are students I've seen Emrys speak to," I said. I took a deep breath and pulled the visual memory of all the students I had seen him with and sent the images back through the scarves. "These are all the students I've seen him with. Watch for any of them. You can't let them alert anyone down here."

"We'll take care of it," said Asafa grimly.

I wiped a shaky hand along my forehead. There were so many things that could go wrong. So many intangibles over which we had no control.

Delia couldn't quite hide her apprehension and fear as she led us to a large stump. She paused, then vaulted up and disappeared inside. The rest of us followed.

When we emerged in a small silver, gold, and rose-colored grove east of the battle field on the Seventeenth Circle, I turned to her and whispered, "You made that trickster map you gave me my first day on campus, didn't you?"

"I come from a long line of nature, fiber, and timber mages." She gave me a shaky wink, and squeezed my wrist, but then looked at the men—the terrorists—in the distance, pacing in front of the dome. Her expression was torn. She looked at me, then Olivia, who was watching us. "I do have sympathies and connection to the restoration movement," Delia said to her. "But not for this. This is not the way. And this is my home too. I will defend it."

She turned and touched the ground with Neph, coaxing the trees into hiding us.

"Alpha is in position," Olivia whispered through her scarf. "Video feed activated."

Beta Team and the others would be able to access video shot through the brooch attached to Olivia's scarf.

"There is a defensive field around Godfrey and the others," Will said through his scarf, after speaking softly with Mike and someone on Gamma. "Storm Magic. Secured by wind. Any magic done in or to that field will be noticed."

A number of voices offered suggestions and ways to disable it. Our people trapped in the Magiaduct and at the battle fields could still hear us and contribute—and unidentified voices could be heard in the background as people trapped around them sought to help as well. A scuffle heard through multiple Beta scarves said whatever was happening with the campus betrayers was happening now.

I could almost feel the ghostly echo of Justice Toad vibrating the stream of alerts and offenses as Beta sprung the numerous traps on Top Circle. Other than around the Magiaduct—which was purely due to the convenience of the casters—Top Circle was our most heavily fortified level. An attack had been expected to happen at the top of the mountain, not through the wards the Department had secured below.

Then again, everyone had been expecting an outside attack, if any, not an expertly executed inside job.

We crouched together and prayed Beta would triumph.

The mass of fighters, battle fields, and spectators spread before us. It was both a strangely similar and completely different view than what the six of us had seen a mere two and a half weeks ago at the Combat Qualifier.

Without announcing our presence, this was as close as we could get to the dome that had ten thousand of our classmates trapped inside. But Godfrey made it easy for us to see what was happening, even at our distance. He was, indeed, preparing a spectacle, and he had made sure that all of the trapped students had bird's eye views.

The holograms and projections of the combat competition that had been in place for the students to watch had been replaced with eight three-dimensional images. And Godfrey was addressing eight angry, austere faces. Helen Price's image appeared alongside a man who looked like an older and kinder Constantine. The image of a very menacing-looking man stood on her other side. The other five projections were arrayed around them.

As she stared at the profile of her mother, Olivia was as tightly strung as a violin string the moment before it snapped.

"Emrys Norr isn't here," I whispered, touching the back of her shoulder.

Olivia nodded and her muscles relaxed enough for her to fiddle with her scarf. "Send a picture of him through the channel anyway."

I did, along with a visual name tag under his face. Emrys's absence lent credence to my opinion that he had abandoned campus once he'd let the enemy inside.

"We have your children and the children of your most valued underlings," Godfrey said, continuing the speech that had been occurring prior to our arrival. "If you want them to perish, please do continue trying to send your special forces across the river below."

The flashes of fire from the base of the mountain ceased abruptly.

"Ah, excellent." Godfrey smiled at the eight faces. "I think we might have found a bargaining chip finally."

"We will not—"

"Negotiate? No? Let's widen our network."

Pictures of Second Layer citizens appeared in image squares on a grid that grew tighter and tighter, each picture shrinking smaller as fifty more appeared in another square, then fifty more again. Soon the grid montage contained thousands of squares filled with anxious faces.

The hijacked general feed had been opened.

"People of the Second Layer, your leaders plan to sacrifice your children. We are offering a simple exchange. An exchange that will be contractually binding between governments. The lives of the students at one of your finest institutions for the immediate replenishment of half the magic you've stolen from the Third Layer."

"Only half?" Helen sneered.

Godfrey put a hand to his chest. "We aren't ogres, Madam Price. We know you've used your ill- gotten gains over the past decades to build things that your society now rests upon. We will grant you three months to remove that infrastructure before seizing the other half of our stolen magic as well."

"You say you aren't ogres, and yet you hold children hostage, threatening their mass murder?"

"Ah, but they are soldier age and grade, are they not? You send just as many soldiers of this same 'child' status to strong arm us. Your pitiful attempt at sympathy is without merit."

"They didn't sign up to be soldiers."

"We, all of us, must battle for our freedom," Godfrey said, with a mirthless smile. "Isn't that right?"

"What have you done with the Peacekeepers' Troop?"

The man spread his arms wide, his smile disturbing. "An interesting question. They were checked and approved to protect your hallowed halls. By you and the rest of the Council and Alliance, Madam Price. You allowed us to be in charge here, and for that I thank you."

"The answer is no," the menacing-looking man at Helen's side said coldly. "We will not negotiate with you."

"I'm sure your audience is despondent to hear your decision, Stavros."

The parents inside the image squares were yelling and screaming.

Godfrey shook his head in mock sadness. "You need to listen to the citizens more, Stavros. And spend less time on the questionable projects you oversee in the Department's basement."

I had to mute my scarf as everyone on our line was cursing and sending violent mental images. Underneath all of the hostility and aggression coursing through the scarf network, though, was a deep resignation that I understood from taking Layer Politics. The Second Layer could not give up the appropriated magic in the way the terrorists were demanding, and everyone swearing violently knew it. If the governments had planned and implemented a return of the magic before now, then yes, maybe. But in the next ten minutes or even ten hours? Not a chance.

And the governments didn't want to give up the magic. After a few more attacks and massacres...maybe. It might be demanded of them, if the "might makes right" side of the equation switched to the terrorists' side.

But there wasn't a thing that could be done to resolve Godfrey's demand.

People were going to die. Godfrey had raised the dome himself—I could see the same onion peel shade flashing through it that flashed around him—which meant he would be able to manipulate or destroy it using whatever device he had used to raise it. There was no device visible, though, and he was absurdly well protected. Getting the device before he could use it was going to be ridiculously hard.

Unless...

Thoughts whirled through my mind as I stared at the dome and thought about containment and traps and all of the other various crazy things I had been doing with Dare. If a magical creature or being was unable to access its magic, it became easy to trap. And on the flipside, if magic was trapped under strong magic, the magic underneath couldn't be accessed until the trap was freed.

I didn't need to touch the dome or the device. I could trap the dome.

North, south, east, west, top... In my mind, a grid drew over the dome, along with anchor points.

I touched my bag and removed my remaining five Kinsky papers. Of the original seven, the one I had turned into Dare's phoenix was out of my reach, as was the "hydra" net I had kept intact and stored in Okai. But I had five to work with. I could create anchors with five. Just like the visual pyramid I used to manipulate the cornerstones of magic.

I scooted to the far side of the grove, away from the others as Godfrey and the adults continued their verbal warfare. I drew quickly, trying not to let my shaking hands influence the nature of the lines as I let my mind bend the cornerstones. Anchor points. Anchor points for a containment dome of an entirely different variety.

I looked at Olivia, then pointed sharply to my ear then my scarf.

As she strode over toward me, Olivia nodded and touched her scarf. "Muted."

I held up the finished papers in the folio, gripping them hard to try to stop my shaking. "I can secure the dome. Trap it—put it in stasis—so that Godfrey can't use his dome underneath. We can keep the students completely out of harm's way until this is over. Then we can dismantle Godfrey's dome appropriately and in all the time we need."

She didn't say anything for a moment, and indecision chased anger across her face. "Everyone will know, Ren." She stared at me, demanding that I understand what she meant.

I understood that Professor Mbozi would pass me so hard in engineering class, if this worked, that maybe I'd even get a rare smile from him before they carted me off to some top secret facility.

"Are we going to let them die?"

She said nothing for a long moment then closed her eyes. "No."

"What are you two discussing?" Mike asked, crouching closer. Like the rest of us, his face was blanched of healthy color and his expression was drawn.

I stared at him and a moment of inappropriate elation overcame me. I put the papers down and grabbed his wrist. "Wind. Can you influence the winds without drawing attention to us?"

"Through personal enchantment?" He glanced between us, then nodded slowly. "Yes. But it is weaker magic than what you've seen me use before because I can't use the campus systems. The terrorists shut down the campus weather magic like everything else administrative. All my snow is melting," he said trying to wanly inject humor before growing horribly sober again. "And I can't do anything to that defensive field. They have three weather mages inside—powerful ones—holding it."

"Personal enchantment only. Your smallest and least detectable wind charm. Feather light." I let go of his wrist and scooted back a foot, then spread out the five papers. "Just enough to fly these into a sloped pyramid formation around the Origin Dome and keep them suspended there until I tell you to release them."

Something strange registered in Mike's eyes as he looked at the papers, then at me. Delia, Neph, and Will came closer, huddling together with us too. Delia and Neph were still holding the strands of magic to the ground that were keeping us shielded within the trees. Mike looked at Will, whose eyes were beseeching, then back at me.

Mike nodded even more slowly, and I could see that he was fighting an innate desire to put more distance between himself and the papers. "I understand." He understood far more than my need to attach a few papers via a wind charm. "I understand a lot, now. A conversation perhaps best saved for later."

I smiled tightly. "I can do that personal wind enchantment you showed me a few weeks ago and encase each paper as a buffer so that your magic won't touch them." I could only float things an inch or two and not for very long, but it should be enough. It had to be.

A tug on my scarf indicated someone was about to speak through it.

"Administration Building perimeter secured," Patrick was panting and his words were halting.

"All those traps we set on Top Circle… Loudon, man, when we get out of this, remind me never to get on your bad side. We're baiting the traps again for the soldier units trekking up the Fourth. About ten minutes." His voice strained at the last. "We'll get it done."

Sixty war-hardened soldiers against the five remaining Betas? I shut my eyes. They might trap half. They'd probably trap half. And then…

I opened my eyes, brutally pushed the thoughts aside, and started wrapping each paper in air.

Another voice chimed in. "This is lone Delta. We are hooking up remote detonations for the Magiaduct. The magic is thinner here than on the Administration Building—they probably had to stretch it too far. So the intention in the magic is focused on restraint only—keeping the mages inside cut off from magic and secured—unlike the explosive nature of the other two domes. I think we can blow it as soon as we get the go-ahead. The Midlands should be able to handle the backlash. And we've gathered dozens of strays. Trick, we are sending them up behind the soldiers, to help you take them out. They are wearing conjured blue scarves.

Unconnected to ours, but still something to identify. Ten more minutes here, then hopefully we'll all head up top."

I looked down at my wrist. Constantine's scrawl ticked each minute. Twenty minutes until the perimeter ward came down. We could all be dead by then.

I showed Olivia the time remaining.

"Crown," a new voice said. "I split off from the others to check the Midlands boxes, and Holy Magic, I see your—"

Flashes of color swept my mind as a member of Epsilon tried to send an image, then the color cut off abruptly alongside the gurgle of Tilsia's unfinished statement.

A flurry of shouts to Tilsia issued via the scarves, especially from her Epsilon teammates.

"Asafa, identify her position," Olivia whispered harshly. "Then two members at the Magiaduct, go get her. Approach with extreme caution. We need to know what she saw, but we can not spare anyone else to find and resurrect more of you."

Tilsia was dead. Our first. Dead from something she was trying to identify for me. I shut my eyes. We had ten resurrection minutes to find her.

"Everyone else, hold position and wait for the signal," Olivia said.

The voices in the scarves abruptly silenced, people taking to individual threads to yell or grieve.

Godfrey stepped in front of the dome, smiling at the thousands of students populating the stands inside. "Perhaps if your Alliance had actually made a good faith effort during the fall negotiations, you would be having an unexceptional winter term. Alas."

As Godfrey turned back to face the active holograms, Mike and I focused harder on our enchantments. We weren't going to be in time for whatever Godfrey was about to do, but we were close, and we had to keep going.

"An appetizer for you," Godfrey said, his voice ringing out. "As your children, in this nice, fattened crowd we have collected here, experience what the Third Layer deals with daily—a loss of air and magic."

The dome rippled, and thousands of gasps and shouts resounded, then abruptly silenced. The silence was horrible. The scarves horrifyingly went silent with them. I felt the ripple of magic over my skin as the magic of the dome pressed down. I shuddered and concentrated.

"Oh, already some casualties," Godfrey mused aloud. "Dropping like flies in there. You aren't a very hardy lot in the Second Layer, are you? Hmmm...and the dwindling magic inside is making resurrections taxing for your best and brightest."

"Stop this, Vincent," Constantine's father said, his voice steady even as the expression in his eyes was not. "This will not end well for you. This is a battle that can only be won politically, not through violence."

"Unlike the rest of the Alliance, you do practice what you preach, Stuart Leandred. Sacrificing your own revenge on the altar of politics has bought these students eighty seconds more. Ten seconds for each of your eight years of lost vengeance. What will you do with those eighty seconds? Will you save them?"

He released the spell and air and magic filtered back into the dome.

"Mike," I said. There was no more time.

Mike nodded jerkily and a thin breeze drifted between his fingers as the papers lifted.

"Will, I need you to—" I pointed between the three of us, trying to convey my need. Will snapped forward and activated a lesser form of our magic share ritual. It would guide Mike to where the papers needed to go by using the intentions in my magic. And once the papers were locked in place, the dome would sustain itself.

Olivia crouched at my side, legs in position, ready to run. "You do this, then we jump back to the Fifteenth Circle immediately," she said grimly. She closed her eyes, and without waiting for our response, touched her scarf, activating it again. "Alpha is implementing on the Seventeenth. Ten seconds. We can wait no longer. Everyone get ready...and may Magic be our ally."

"What say you, Madam Price?" Godfrey taunted. "What is eighty seconds—seventy now—in the scale of our negotiations?"

"You, and every Third Layer citizen will be held accountable for each death that happens today," Helen Price said. "And we will find out who helped you."

Godfrey smiled at the eight faces. "That might prove an unpleasant surprise for some of you."

With Will's direction forming a conduit between the two of us, Mike lightly placed the first three papers.

The gaze of the dangerous looking man—Stavros—who stood next to Helen Price abruptly shifted to look at the paper that had just settled into the north position. His posture stilled, making his projection static, then he immediately started scanning the grounds in a very dissecting and disquieting way. He didn't even pretend interest in the proceedings any more. He was trying to track the magic back to a source. A shiver of unease ran over me.

The fourth paper hovered in place.

"Shall we try our negotiations again, Council members of the Alliance?"

Mike settled the fifth paper on top. I shut my eyes and activated the mental pyramid that would connect them.

I wanted this. This would happen.

And just like that, the magic of Kinsky's papers clicked into place, blazing gold. A smooth rumble of thunder sounded overhead, shuddering through me in response. Unlike the one beneath it, my protection dome felt right.

"Go, go, let's go!" Olivia hissed and grabbed my arm. Delia, Neph, Will, and Mike were already up and running.

Godfrey's gaze snapped to the dome and one of his minions sent a line of copper magic toward it. As soon as the line touched, the man dropped like a stone—like Marsgrove's secretary, cut from her strings.

Fierce, primitive satisfaction made my knees shake as I sprinted toward the stump with my friends. The ten thousand students at the battle field were secured. I could hear voices shouting and cheering in my head via my scarf. It was only three small jumps back up and a sprint to the Administration Building. We could make it. We could save everyone.

The stump—our exit out—exploded. And Delia, who had been vaulting toward it, flew backward into Mike.

Chapter Thirty-four

DEMONS FROM A CHECKERED PAST

THE GROVE BURST around us. Rose, silver, and gold leaves rained upon our skin. The sunlight reflected the shimmers and the leaves fell almost in slow motion. It would have been beautiful in any other event.

I pulled all magic back into my shield set. Voices in the scarves stuttered.

A force hooked around my waist and violently tugged. I went flying back through the air, my friends along with me. Mike cut his hand downward through the unnatural wind current and we abruptly dropped fifteen yards from Godfrey's feet. It was only the barest bit better than at Godfrey's feet.

"What do we have here."

The six of us drew together and rose, all shields active.

"The Dare scion's pet," Godfrey said, voice still magnified, eyes narrowed at me. "I was shown your face, but you were supposed to be taken care of." He turned to four soldiers at his side. "One by one to four," he said cryptically.

Then he motioned abruptly to the minion who had gotten the communications up.

Helen Price's virtual eyes narrowed briefly on her daughter, then the feeds to the outside world went abruptly dark—the eight holograms and all of the hijacked feeds vanished.

"Don't worry," Godfrey said, smiling unpleasantly at us. "We'll get them back online after you've been dealt with and after whatever miserably small magic you just put in place is removed. Then we'll make a proper example out of you. Until then, five units, go to Plan B. Verisetti may want to coddle whatever pets he has here, but I've wanted to obliterate this mountain for the longest time."

A hundred soldiers headed for the stairs to Sixteen.

"Track them, Saf. Everyone, head to wherever they are going." Olivia's mouth didn't move, but her voice echoed thinly through my scarf, dominating the panic that had taken hold through our communications.

We really were all going to die.

The trapped—now secured—students started emptying the stands, freed from whatever magic had kept them in their seats beneath the dome. Would they survive the destruction of the mountain? Droves of them ran to stand at the edges of the now-doubled dome. Some wore mystified expressions, many looked fiercely determined, and five in the front had distinctive scarves wrapped around their throats. They stared at us.

There was no port—natural or mage activated—for us to run to.

Bellacia and Inessa pushed forward to stand with our scarf-wearing members under the dome. Bellacia's narrowed gaze connected with mine.

"Now why don't you start by telling me where you got that magic?" Godfrey said, striding our way, and forcing all attention back to him. Soldiers numbering in the hundreds spread out behind him, and two dozen were already moving to surround the six of us.

"No," Olivia said, and activated every "security" measure we had put into place on the Seventeenth—hoping to hinder the five units going to Plan B, hoping to give us time to get the hell out of our current predicament.

Snares, compulsions, and nightmares burst upward. Music to ensnare the senses, dreams to trap the unwary, personal storms that hit and battered, impulses to sleep for a thousand years, false games that played against whoever tripped the magic, desires and unrequited needs forced up and demanding completion.

We turned and ran, dodging through the illusions and traps. The nearest soldiers to us were immediately snared. Dozens more followed the first wave into nightmares. A hologram replaying the Freespar competition was doing the best job, as a number of the soldiers thought the combat mages had suddenly appeared.

But it was a fleeting win, and we had nowhere to go. We ran alongside the front face of the dome, hoping to move around it enough to put a curve between us and the enemy. Solemn faces watched us as we sprinted past. With the grove gone, the nearest natural port was now miles away. A shouted command from Olivia caused us to veer left as fire and lightning rained down on the troops. Our teams at the Magiaduct and Top Circle were working together to form the magic.

But the soldiers were battle hardened fighters. They raised a stronger shield. And each fallen soldier was quickly revived and released by comrades. Five hundred soldiers accustomed to working and fighting together.

And for all our planning, we had barely touched the Seventeenth Circle. Everyone lived and played on the top of the mountain, above the Midlands, most of the time. We had booby-trapped the hell out of the first six levels, expecting any huge monster fight to be held there. Hindsight was cruel.

Mike went down first—was cut down in a long red arc—his shield like warmed butter to whatever knife had been cast. His thread snapped directly from my chest, leaving ice in its place. I touched my chest, trying to weave it back.

Delia dropped to his side and immediately started resuscitation procedures.

We surrounded them and put all energy into our shields.

A spell bounced off mine, but Neph winced as something hit her arm. I stepped out front and pushed more magic into my shields, spreading them larger. A flurry of spells flew all at once, battering, testing, and threatening the mixed shield set gifted to me by enemies. Raphael and Marsgrove did excellent work. But even their magic would eventually fail.

Godfrey threw none of the magic aimed our way. He simply stood in the midst of the barrage directing his forces.

Voices shouted through the spells in the scarves, silent to Godfrey's ears, but a cacophony in mine. Our allies fighting up top, those watching remotely through the brooch on Olivia's scarf, and the ones under the dome with a firsthand view were all yelling—directions, expletives, enchantments—punctuating the jarring barrage of magic hitting us.

Godfrey cut a hand through the air and the onslaught stopped along with the steps of the soldiers.

"Aren't you the little Excelsine spitfires, ready to join your comrades bathing in Third Layer blood. But that was merely a taste. A promise. Let's try my question again," Godfrey said, gaze never leaving me, even though Olivia had been the one to answer in the negative the first time.

Answer or die—his unvoiced message was clear.

"No," I said.

In a slash of almond brown, a pinpointed slice of magic curved around my shield and Delia fell across Mike's chest. Her thread to me snapped too. Neph and Will immediately began resurrections on both as I tried to curve my shields around all of us.

"Olivia, Ren, those units are heading to the Midlands. Do you copy?" Asafa yelled. "The processor in the—"

"You won't be able to save them," Godfrey said, smiling. "No matter what you do."

I blinked at the sudden white spots in my vision—born from fury at his confident words. The spots tunneled into a vortex and a too-crisp picture replaced my view. Emotion ceased.

A cold smile rose in me, and from under my leather bracelet, I casually withdrew the stamp Constantine had given me for my birthday. I held it between my fingertips and rolled onto the balls of my feet. Equations and diagrams coldly snapped together with doodled schematics and intention.

Throw magic my way, Vincent Godfrey, so that I may end you.

"Ren," Olivia said under her breath. "Your shields will hold for the time needed to reach Sixteen. You can run and make it. Go." Abandon us and release the Administration Building, Olivia's voice urged silently through my scarf.

I held still, poised and emotionless, my magic on the pinpoint of my mental pyramid. The twelve pictures I had drawn on the stamp material two nights ago, while Constantine had watched, were awaiting activation, depending on what I chose to do. And the single drop of paint I had placed inside swirled, waiting as well.

Godfrey's gaze narrowed on Olivia, as if drawn there by her whisper. "Do my eyes deceive me? Is this the Price spawn standing before us? What a truly glorious day. We'll deal with you publicly."

Magic flashed from one of Godfrey's minions. Will fell, and the thread between us started to unravel. Seconds were ticking a cold, dead beat in my head, approaching one minute for Mike, thirty seconds for Delia, and ten for Will. Nine minutes remained on the ten minute resurrection clock.

They would never make it if I ran to Top Circle. And there were plenty of public ways for Godfrey to make sure they could never be resurrected, no matter how much time remained for them.

"Bring them back, Neph," I said mechanically. "No matter what."

"Run!" Olivia's mental voice shouted.

"I'm tired of waiting," Godfrey warned. "I will give you a choice for how you die."

I had a choice. All I needed was a piece of the enemy's magic. Godfrey's magic. A key. And a personal taunt to get it. I activated the two wards I needed while pulling my fingers against my chest.

"We don't deal with losers who can't even keep their Layer safe," I said harshly.

Godfrey threw the bolt instantly. A sweet citrus hue. I didn't care what horrible thing it was going to do. It was mine now.

Fifteen other bolts flew with Godfrey's. The shifting chessboard settled into a single move.

"Ren—!"

I mentally released Kinsky's papers and the protective covering over the dome fell, leaving only Godfrey's dome behind.

I whipped my hand to the left, then right and the stamp extended in both directions in front of us like liquid mercury soaring through the air before snapping into an eight-foot banner. The sixteen combined beams of magic were sucked inside, activating the first ward. I twirled like Neph had taught me to do in order to keep magic active and constant, and the banner snapped and recoiled into a ball that I immediately threw at the dome containing ten thousand of our classmates. Just like tossing footballs with Christian in the backyard.

The second ward activated in the balled stamp and the mutable material grabbed Godfrey's magic—the magic that had been used to erect the dome, no matter if it was through a device—and thrust it to the surface of the ball alongside my drop of paint. The ball of magic hit the Origin Dome with a splat.

Cracks immediately formed a spiderweb on its surface.

Olivia shouted into her scarf and Neph pressed hands against Will's chest.

The dome shattered. The mountain shook. Something split within me, sucking magic free as the magic in the dome mushroomed out. The enemy troops shouted. Shouted about Plan B. The Midlands.

I made the magic mushrooming outward swirl upward, up, up, the mountain, then down into all of the Junior Department's boxes that Dare and I had tagged over the weeks—I twisted the magic, and flipped the box spells into projecting a barrier instead.

"Holy shivittrails!" Trick's scarf voice yelled. "The Midlands have been shut! I repeat, nothing is getting in, and that includes magic. Backlashes already gathering around the edges, watch yourselves!"

Someone yelled my name.

Students were spilling out around us. Some started fighting. Some ran.

The ones left behind simply stood, frozen in place.

Olivia was screaming at them to move.

And Godfrey...Godfrey looked as if he was being physically shattered as well with the dome's backlash. But through the pain—and as his soldiers started cutting through my classmates—he stared at me with an incomprehensible look on his face that slowly morphed into painful glee.

"Grab her! Grab whatever device she is using!"

He was swallowed from view and Olivia yanked me backward. I held out my hand and called Kinsky's papers to me.

I felt Will's thread trying to snap back into place under Neph's sure hand. I saw Delia and Mike crawl—alive—into the surging crowd, leaving a trail of red behind.

Emotion rushed back into me, abrupt, soaring...horrific.

Students streamed around us, and everywhere, classmates fell.

Parchment crinkled in my fist. Parchment which had been put in place to save every one of these people, but that now resided in my palm.

Two girls fell to a flash of sapphire.

A swirl of meringue blew a group of five off their feet. A slice of gunmetal cut across another. Slaughter. The colors shot around me in a dizzying and sick array of light and intent. Lime green cut off a boy's arm. Coconut burst into a dozen milky shards that pierced flesh.

We were in the middle of Freespar, but this wasn't a war game people had signed up to play.

It was a nightmare that shouldn't be happening. Not on campus.

Sheer student numbers were winning in a few places—a group of soldiers went down in one particularly violent charge. But like Dare and the other top-flight combat mages had been able to do, the soldiers took out massive amounts of lesser opponents all at one time. Freespar had taken less than ten minutes, and this...

I rejected the images, thoughts spiraling out and away from the carnage—and especially away from seeing the clear magic pulses that sliced through the air without warning. Magic hit my shields repeatedly, battering against them.

The papers in my hand dropped to the ground as a bolt made it through and three of my fingers sliced free. A man ran toward me, hand raised to finish the deed. I drew back my foot and kicked a paper at him, sending magic through my toes to direct its path. It curled around his face and sucked him inside.

The world tilted. Everything grew cold.

A man beside me gutted a tiny blonde girl. She dropped like an unwanted doll cast aside.

I scooped up a paper with my intact hand and screamed incoherently as I thrust my hand through the air and against his neck. I heard the crack as he was bent in two and ingested by the parchment. It fell from my hand.

I stared down at the splayed girl, a crimson angel on the grass. I should have protected her.

A burning slice split my right side.

Everything was going hazy, and my cheeks were wet.

"Ren's going into shock," Will's voice yelled from the fabric at my throat. Alive.

The feel of Neph's magic immediately washed through me. "Olivia, I can't get to you. Ren's magic—her command—made it so I have to stay close to Will, Mike, and Delia and revive everyone that falls, and everyone keeps dying. But I can give you forty seconds." Her voice was thin and strained and I wanted to help her.

A blast of Neph's magic burst from my chest and made everyone around us stop in slack-jawed awe—staring at something only they could see.

Olivia's hand was suddenly clenched around my chin. She jerked it downward to make sure I saw her pointing at the blonde girl. "Resurrect her."

"I don't know her." I was only responsible for her death, not her life. I was responsible for Olivia's life. Will's. Neph's. D—

"Ren." Olivia growled.

I dropped to my knees and laid my intact hand on the girl's torn stomach. Magic spilled into her. There was a cloud of magic still extending outward from where the dome had exploded and I grabbed it. Sunlight shot everywhere, haloing out my sight. Christian?

I pushed the enormous amount of magic into fixing everything in the body beneath my hand.

Magic—in a dazzling and sickening array of colors—was flying everywhere around the river I was channeling downward. Traps were springing in a perimeter around us one after another in technicolor brilliance. Olivia was holding concave shields made of magic and shooting colored balls at the soldiers. Nameless and faceless students ran, leaped, shot, fell, then rose again.

My gaze met Bellacia Bailey's in the mass. Her green eyes were slitted and her perfectly styled hair had violently loosened around her face. Her expression was apocalyptic. I wasn't going to be able to do anything against an attack from her. She drew her hands back, took a deep breath, threw her hands forward and screamed.

Sound waves burst from her. In the thick magic of the field, they visibly rippled the air.

The sound waves shuddered the air above me and I could hear bodies falling behind me in the first wave of it—dropping enemies that had been drawing closer to me in my unaware state.

The waves turned into ripples and Bellacia stumbled, drained. Then Inessa was there, shielding her and pushing Bellacia toward a magical barricade some of the students had formed.

"You will finish this, then you will answer. You will!" Bellacia yelled at me as her friend manhandled her back.

Arms wrapped around my neck and words spilled into my ear in a foreign voice, as the blonde girl I had just resurrected clung to me.

"I think I'm responsible for you now," I said absently. I let go of the conduit of magic and flared the rest outward toward anyone my magic considered a friend. The girl continued to utter words in my ear like a vow. "You need to hide," I said.

She said something else incomprehensible, then sprinted off into the fallen grove like a pixie wearing shoes taken directly from the feet of Hermes—dodging between fighting mages, magic making her feet move faster.

I rose, and the gash in my side magically knit itself together, as did the repaired fingers on my damaged hand. The magical tingles were laced with Neph's remote magic.

"I didn't mean use that much magic," Olivia hissed, flicking her fingers to finish stitching the job on my side. "You need to save some for yoursel—"

Will gasped, "Olivia, watch out!"

My mouth worked silently as the pull on my magic engaged and a violent blast of magenta impacted an inch from Olivia's chest. The barest hint of wings shimmered, and a butterfly rose in front of her, then burst into a hundred shards of smaller butterflies, each absorbing the magic, pulling a piece of my shield from me, then shattering. Saving Olivia. Saving her exactly as the caterpillar life cycle creation had been designed to do.

I clutched my head and tried to rebuild my shield set. Triumph mixed with other intense emotions. My magic had saved Olivia. The remote leech had worked. Exactly as designed.

I saw her look down at her hands in disbelief.

But I had no time to process her reaction as Godfrey's face came into view and his expression indicated that he had been granted every wish he'd ever made. His gaze followed the thread of magic in the air right to me. "It's her, it's her, not a device."

And that's when the dome around the Magiaduct blew. The explosion rocked the entire mountain and everyone automatically ducked. Magic burst from me in response to the Origin Dome's collapse and I stumbled and fell. At my loss of control, I could feel the Junior Department's boxes explode, opening the Midlands once more, magic sucking through the boundaries and coiling inside.

Justice Toad gave a weird, ear-splitting shriek, ending his silence. It was very, very possible that even without the Administrative Magic, the tablet realized I was now truly expelled.

Contrarily, relief surged through the combined magic of the scarves as Delta, Gamma, and Epsilon yelled that the muses were taking up their flagpole posts and were calling all students. Everyone in the Magiaduct was streaming from the building, heading up to help the muses and to free the Administration Building.

Trick cackled in delight.

The teachers would be freed. And Marsgrove would hie down the mountain at top speed to arrest me. We were almost saved. The scarves were crowing with it.

The students around us started swarming, en masse, up the mountain, toward Top Circle as well—heeding the call of the muses to free the Administration Building, to end this.

But I couldn't move, hands curled into the dirt, shaking. The Layer was shaking. And no one seemed to be aware of it or else they would be freaking out too.

"Grab her, now," Godfrey repeated, clutching his chest. As the originator of the magic, connected to whatever device or enchantment he had stolen, he was obviously also affected by a second dome shattering—and the magic was pulling on anything connected to it (Godfrey) or kindred in spirit (me).

His footsteps lurched toward me. "All personnel, to me. Now."

"You will not touch her."

The words preceded a flash and then Olivia was in front of me, battling like a demon freed from hell, throwing devices and magic toward the foe.

But Godfrey was also a demon possessed. "Forget the students. Forget the processor. Forget the mountain," he yelled. "Here. All personnel to me, now!"

I crawled and tried to cover Olivia's back as she moved forward, offensively blasting enemy after enemy. All of the students were streaming away from us and up the mountain, and the soldiers were streaming after them, trying to cut them down from behind—either not hearing Godfrey or not able to hear him in his stumbling state. The Layer was shaking and it was all I could do to keep it steady and protect Olivia at the same time.

"Wait, wait! Don't abandon the battle fields! Neph! Get everyone back down here! Everyone! Everyone!" Will shouted mentally through my scarf. I could hear him throwing devices left and right in the background and I could hear Mike and Delia fighting as well. "Ren and Olivia need help! Neph!"

My elbows gave out and I face planted in the dirt. So much for Epsilon's theory that they could just blow the dome around the Magiaduct... Magic was sucking out of me as the detonated magic in the Origin Dome continued to spread outward. Black lightning crackled in the distance and a rip sounded. A tsunami in the First Layer, or a flood in the Fourth, or a plague in the Third...some natural disaster had just occurred somewhere in response.

I seemed to realize it subconsciously before consciousness grabbed hold. All of those things that had been occurring... Origin Magic backlash. Build a house of bricks, then remove a few bricks at the base willy-nilly, and disaster occurred.

Just like in the Third Layer.

Scarf chatter was suddenly shouting about backing off from touching the Administration Building's dome. They too now understood the danger.

"—Layer cracking!"

"—can't possibly—"

"How did you get the battle field dome down, Crown?"

"By Magic, everyone, stay away from the Midlands, I repeat, _stay away_."

"Crown? Answer!"

I couldn't answer. I was doing everything I could to stabilize the magic spreading outward and to guard Olivia's back.

"Constantine," I croaked out. "Help. Leech."

But Constantine didn't answer.

Fifteen balls of fuchsia burst around us, blowing back the students who were turning around to help.

Olivia was holding her own, but there were just too many enemies and we were too far away to layer our shields together. My shield was doing triple duty and incurring heavy damage just trying to keep me alive.

And the magical cloud was expanding, shuddering across the surface of the Layer.

"Just grab both of them, for shivit's sake!" Godfrey yelled.

I rose and used every tactic Dare had taught me, every tactic that I had observed and that our ragtag group had been practicing to dodge, trap, and evade. Wind enchantments threw the papers at charging enemies, swallowing them inside, but others just kept coming. And the shakiness in my limbs and the horror in my head kept increasing.

"This is a decided case of finders keepers," a new voice said. "You always were behind the ball, Vincent."

Emrys. He hadn't left.

"And such a keeper. With some sparkling new additions," he finished. His voice was somewhere off to my left.

I released a stream of magic forward and tried to sweep a paper toward a man trying to kill Olivia, while at the same time my peripheral vision saw a dart headed my way. A dart would bounce off my shield like a paper airplane, so I ignored it and concentrated on holding and dispersing the cloud of Origin Magic.

Only the swirl of gold magic in the dart made me look at it twice. My shield pulsed companionably in response.

To the gold. No. No.

There was nothing I could do to stop its impact anymore. In a millisecond, mathematical equations of angles and speed rushed through my mind. Whatever was heading my way had been created by Raphael. And with my magic releasing elsewhere, I couldn't form enough preventive magic soon enough to intercept it in time. It was going to pierce my shield and do...something terrible. The satisfaction in every line of Emrys's body made that apparent.

I thought of Christian.

My gaze met Olivia's. Horror, fury, and despair. Her expression compressed, then become determined. The empty cocoon was already in her fist and magic was flaring outward, pinching space. No. No.

Magic yanked inside of me, pulled, leeched, and hands pushed me, shoving me from the path of the blast. I landed hard on the grass. Cracks formed in the sky as the cloud of Origin Magic abruptly released from my grasp.

Splayed out, hair falling in my face, I saw Olivia standing in the position of space that I had just occupied. In a horrible, horrifying repeat of what I had done for Dare last term, Olivia had used my magic to impossibly port herself across campus and into my position of space. She had been practicing porting with a leech inside the Midlands—where Administrative rules didn't apply. She had been practicing for fun, a smile on her face.

And when her cocoon had hatched into a butterfly a few short minutes ago, she had figured out that I had put a leash to me inside. She had used it to port to me. She had taken my place.

Gazes connected, I could see satisfaction mixing with her underlying terror. She had known, and she'd chosen to port to me anyway.

Olivia's skin burst into gold.

"No, nonononononono!" I scrambled upright, but she was already disappearing, her body breaking up one tiny burst of gold at a time, starbursts of golden light vanishing pieces of her body bit by bit, like Lightning Festival magic. "Nononono!"

"Stop! Don't touch me!" Olivia threw a hand forward as I stumbled to try and reach her.

And that was the problem with leeches—even the ones we created. They rendered the leeched mage magicless during the leech's use and for precious seconds thereafter.

"Olivia." I stumbled, lurching forward uselessly like some horrid nightmare. I wasn't going to make it in time.

She gripped her brooch and tore off her scarf, throwing it away from her disappearing body. The working of her bare throat showed her anxiety as the shimmering burst faster. Gold dust puffed out as the scarf fell on the grass. Her hazel eyes were a maelstrom of emotion.

Then they too burst with gold and vanished. The scarf was the only thing left to show that she had stood before me. The world swam as I fell on it. I saw the blurred image of a man readying another dart as the group of soldiers closed in around me.

The aftermath of the leech ended. Magic rushed back into my control.

Coldness. Numbness. Rage.

Rage.

The waiting cloud of Origin Magic dove into me like a meteoric swarm, then pulsed outward as I threw my arms to the sides, blowing away everything in my vision. Black shapes toppled like dominoes in a broad circle around me.

The earth cracked and creaked.

My hands hit the ground roughly and a trench opened in front of me. I could wrench the earth in two. Force this world to eat itself. Here, on the edge of existence.

A pull, a crack—tiny in the melee of destruction that I could wield—yanked at me and footsteps sprinted toward me. A strong forearm diagonally banded my chest, then I was being pulled upright and hauled away from the trench. The arm felt familiar. Someone was pulling me away from the edge, and it didn't matter if it was friend or foe. The enemy had killed Olivia. Olivia had sacrificed herself for me.

Coldness. Numb rage. Right in my chest. Right where Olivia's thread pulsed green. Still...pulsed... green?

Numb rage turned to fire, and my magic exploded.

The arm holding me dropped. The earth thrust back together. Mountains in the far distance shook and crumbled. I thought of Dare in the Midlands.

Dare.

A wave of the dome's magic ripped from me and the spells blocking the ports blew open with the explosive sound of a million shards of detonated glass.

Mouths opened in screams, and terrified student faces—with gazes focused on me—were rejected from my view. I didn't have time for fear. Only for rectification and retaliation.

I tore the magic away from the ports in a fast flowing mist of piercing screams. Connected to campus, I could feel Dare and the rest of the combat mages streaming through the port on Top Circle. Coming through so quickly, as if they had been balanced on the balls of their feet on the other side, notified and waiting for this exact moment.

I could feel Dare. I could feel his magic enveloping the dome around the Administration Building. Then the connection to him snapped. Dead. Dead. I lurched and fell forward. Then the connection snapped back into place—almost too quickly for me to truly process his death. A moment later the mountain rocked as the Administration Building burst free.

Cheek pressed against the Earth, I could feel Marsgrove too—his magic striping the air. There were dozens of unfamiliar touches as well—other combat mages or Department types—but the figures were moving too fast for me to keep track. Justice Toad was back online and croaking gutturally and burning my lower back through my bag. And I...I just didn't care. I threw my bag to the side and rolled to my back.

I was shaking. I realized it the moment that sound returned. I was shaking uncontrollably, and I felt empty. Exhausted. Drained. No one was still standing in a fifty-yard radius surrounding me, and that included a portion of the level below. From above, it had to look like the blast radius of a detonated bomb.

The connection to campus was draining quickly—a tenuous thread, barely supported by the empty well of my magic.

I was fried. I gripped my chest. Olivia was alive. But I had no idea where. She had been taken via that golden burst, and a mathematical proof or artistic rendition wasn't going to help me. I needed magic, and someone up top had already funneled all of the magic from the Administration Building's dome. It had to have been done immediately—so quickly that the dome's magic must have been the only thing that concerned whoever had done it. In the midst of a thousand deaths, some official had done that first? That wasn't reassuring.

Through clouded eyes, I stared at the scarf puddled on the ground next to where Olivia had stood. She had shed it. She had shed the scarf so that the enemy didn't get it. The scarf that controlled the others.

Adrenaline sputtered from some hidden well, and I rolled and grabbed the scarf, and yanked it on over mine. Frantic questions and shouted directions immediately assailed me, and I realized that I had ended the communication magic threaded through my scarf at some point—and probably through everyone's scarves—but now that Administration Magic was back in play, our communications were online naturally again, at least for everyone else.

I yelled directions through Olivia's scarf to assist and update the combat mages. The enemy forces were still actively fighting all over the mountain. Dare would have told his own forces at this point about aiding anyone wearing a scarf. And as far as I was concerned, he was back in charge.

I unwrapped the scarf again, and crouched on the spot where Olivia had stood. I put my palm to the earth and pulled a portion of the combined magic from the scarf network into my other hand—we had set up the scarves to allow the lead scarf to use a small portion of embedded magic from all of them, if needed. I needed.

I pressed her scarf against the ground and focused the magical circuit. I pressed down on my more unhelpful emotions—loss, despair, failure—and concentrated on the question I needed the remnants of Olivia's presence and magic to answer. Where did you go? An indecipherable six-sensory response shot through the loop and I shakily captured it in the scarf's threads.

I let go of the combined magic in the scarf, and wrapped it back around my neck.

Voices were shouting even more loudly. Over-buzzed on emptied adrenaline and mortal peril I could hear Neph and Will, thank God, and a stream of other voices I was happy to hear yelling at me. Friends and associates who were alive and accounted for.

The battle was still raging, but their voices were crowing that the tide was turning. Exactly as the attackers had foreseen and tried to prevent, once the combat mages were back on campus, the teachers released, and the students no longer contained, the extremists were unable to maintain control. The terrorists excelled at being a hit squad, not warriors on an equal battlefield. Sections of the enemy force who had realized their fate were starting to flee.

Still, with my hands gripping the dirt and only the smallest bits of magic recharging in me, I was seriously vulnerable. Even with the thick ring of downed bodies from the blast surrounding me, there had been plenty of time for magic to arc over the top of the ring and end me. I looked around, slightly confused by why I was still alive.

Constantine stood behind me, wielding his ribbon like a whip in an eight foot circle around us, snapping each piece of magic that ventured close. Blood was dripping down his forehead. His right fingers, hand, and forearm were bubbling with burns. Comprehension was swift. Constantine had been the one who had grabbed me.

There was a very interesting smile on his lips as he studied the chaos around us, and as he looked at the reactivated arch nearest to us. His burned arm hung at his side as if of no consequence. He batted away streams of magic coming at us with easy motions of his left hand. As with the fight in the First Layer, he didn't lift a finger to aid anyone else. Bryant's scarf dangled from Constantine's back pocket.

I shakily pushed myself upright and put a hand on his arm, activating the shields in both scarves that I was now wearing and spreading them to his as well.

"Get what you needed?" He asked, somewhat distantly, as he wielded a blast back at the woman who had thrown it. Most of the attackers were now fleeing in earnest.

"Hopefully." I touched Olivia's scarf, then the crisped flesh of his wrist as gently as I could. "I'm sorry."

"Never be sorry for such magnificence of magic."

"If you weren't so hot, you'd be a dork," I said, voice shaking like everything else in me. I could feel the magic of our latest leech prototype in his belt, under the edge of the scarf. I unclasped the metal stud, flipped it, and pressed it against the burn on his limp arm. "Heal."

I was burnt out and my magic channels were raw—magic itself was like a severely overworked muscle that I didn't feel I could flex again. But there was a little leftover juice from the scarves running along my skin and Constantine knew how to heal himself.

His eyes, heavy-lidded with amusement and pain, were fever bright. "You simply do not understand danger, darling."

Before he even finished the sentence, he began pulling the last dregs of the scarves' magic out of my body. His crisping skin sizzled and smoothed to pink, then tan. Gold seeped down his arm and a full bodied shiver rippled through him.

He scraped through my magic—burned out as I was, the feeling was akin to fingernails raked down the inside shell of a melon, as if he was trying to dig out the last bit of fruit.

"What have you done to yourself, Ren? Any magic you try to channel will be a horrible mess. We can't have that."

His magic thrust through me and gripped the gold edge of the Layer hovering around us.

The ground shook. Shouts echoed. The mages fighting near us stumbled and fell. Constantine was looking around us with a strange, dark anticipation, as if waiting for something.

"Constantine."

At my strangled call, he looked down. "You should know better than to give me such toys to play with, Ren." A grinding sound echoed and he pulled the magic through me, rehydrating the husk of my body. Magic flowed over me and healed as it went. I flexed my fingers as the leftover ache in them eased. The magic connecting me to the leech released.

The earth trembled again.

I squeezed his newly repaired arm, digging a nail in. "If that caused anything other than some poor woman's toilet to explode in the First Layer, I will beat you."

"Bound to have made some woman's day more exciting, and don't make such lovely promises." He flexed the newly repaired flesh of his wrist.

I gave a shaky laugh. I had to find something funny right now, otherwise I was going to sob.

"You always were a smart boy, identifying the real prize," a rough voice said. The leech was blasted from Constantine's fingers.

Constantine pushed me behind him as Godfrey rose from the dead. Godfrey looked terrible—scorched and drained—but his eyes were manic.

I couldn't call up a thread of magic, but I expected Constantine to blast Godfrey. Instead, he was carefully examining each face as the soldiers rose to completely surround us. Godfrey's personal force had obviously been laying in painful wait.

"Blow the Midlands," Godfrey said to a soldier at his right. "The combat mages are in there right now and the muses will never be able to hold campus together without them."

"I can't reach the men, sir," a soldier said apprehensively. "The combat mages engaged our forces and are sweeping through the processing factory, dismantling our bombs and traps."

Dare was in the Midlands. Relief rushed through me. He would take care of everything. And Constantine would whip out some insane device at any moment.

"No finale today, then," Godfrey said tightly. "But we are gaining something far greater than terror. Leandred." He beckoned forward with his hand. "Bring her here."

Constantine was still carefully examining each face surrounding us. "That is not part of our agreement."

My stomach dropped.

Godfrey's eyes narrowed, as if he was contemplating strange new information.

"Interesting. Come here, girl." Godfrey's voice pulsed.

My foot took a horrifying step forward. Constantine grabbed my arm, the only thing that stopped me from completing the command.

Godfrey's sharp intake of breath turned to an exhalation of glee. "Sit, girl."

I sat horrifyingly fast—my arm ripping from Constantine's fingers.

Godfrey's words were not insidious like Bellacia's, they were a flat out command that didn't try to hide the auditory magic control laced within them. Far more obvious than Bellacia's, but also far more undeniable.

Godfrey laughed gleefully. "Oh, Leandred. You have made me a happy, happy man."

Constantine's eyes were dark and he cast a brief, almost involuntary glance toward the Midlands as if looking for someone there. He shrugged. "You haven't fulfilled your end of our bargain. You said he'd be here."

"And he is. Rise and come to me, girl," Godfrey said.

I began walking. Panic didn't come close to describing the horrid, sick, weeping feeling inside of me. I thought I had gotten a lock on auditory magic, but this was none of the cajoling that Bellacia legally employed. This was a steel handcuff.

I had been practicing. But nothing in that practice had prepared me for someone using auditory magic illegally against me. Not like Bellacia's Level Two Offense that I had subverted just enough to use Constantine's vengeful device. This was far worse. Jail sentence worse. But Godfrey already had a death sentence waiting for him. Illegal magic was just magic to terrorists.

"You cannot take her," Constantine said, voice rising.

"I beg to differ. I am doing so right this instant." Godfrey pushed and maneuvered me between the bodies littering the ground. "You should focus on your own goal. He came here, just like you thought he would. And I now understand why he did so. But if you cannot figure out where he is, that is your problem. Forgive me if I don't stay to chat."

"I invoke Penalty Two for a broken contract." Constantine's palms were out at his sides.

Godfrey froze and turned slowly. "You are playing your trump card now? All of those little debts you've been saving, making all of those little contraptions and vortexes for us, and this is what you are turning it in for?" He looked at me, even as he still spoke to Constantine. "You will never be able to keep her. I'm not the only one with eyes on this mountain."

"It doesn't matter. Let her go."

"Hasn't your father slammed his dreary speech about your poor life choices into your brain enough times already? No?" Godfrey snapped his fingers and motioned to the men surrounding us. "Don't touch him, not while arbitration is active. But don't let him move while we quickly iron out this little problem. Shields up at a maximum."

I could feel contract magic swirling overhead as shields rose around us.

Godfrey leaned down and said to me in a low voiced whisper still meant to carry to Constantine, "Do you know how I knew you were susceptible to auditory magic? Leandred told me exactly how to incapacitate the most powerful mage on campus. I had asked him the question as part of our agreement, assuming the answer would yield Alexander Dare's weakness, of course. But the puzzle pieces have assembled together in a rather different fashion. What do you have to say, little mage?"

His words twisted in my ears, hooking into me by magic.

"I'm not the most powerful mage on campus," I said, gritting my teeth and trying to fight the compulsion to answer whatever he asked.

"Ah, you believe that. But power is sometimes nothing more than perception. Like you perceiving that you have less than others. It is a truth to you. While Leandred's truth is believing something quite opposite. That could be for any number of reasons, of course. Mages can word things in astoundingly devious ways. Like, what Leandred might have meant was the mage with the most power over him. He is a rather clever boy."

Those last few lines weren't meant for me. Godfrey was looking at Constantine and his words were taunting. A question to see if he was right.

"He hates his roommate so much and has no attachments to anyone other than Alexander Dare, that I never even questioned the answer would be about anyone other than the Dare scion. I never questioned his betrayal. An artful double blind. Of course, he would think I needed more than a few auditory spells to hold someone such as you. Might have even thought his betrayal wasn't a betrayal at all. But no one can anticipate everything."

He snapped something roughly around my throat. All ability to touch magic froze inside of me.

Constantine dropped his show of indifference. "No."

Godfrey smiled at him. "I stole that from Verisetti after he left the base. I wondered why he had it—always playing his little side games—and now I know. Now I know from where he was getting all of that Origin Magic. Filtered and created through an actual Origin Mage. But he shouldn't have let you run free, little girl. The old legends about letting Origin Mages reach their full potential are ridiculous. You can use them up at half-strength just as well."

There was a metallic flash across Constantine's knuckles. A silver ring changing properties to liquid and moving across the hills and valleys of his hand, waiting. I knew what that liquid metal coating his knuckles was—he had pored over the details of it with me.

He had pored over the details with me at the same time that he had given elaborate instructions on how to use the stamp to greater effect—and how to protect myself, if caught. That he had done all of that...was interesting in the current course of events.

"Con, you told them about my weakness?" I asked distantly, trying to focus my thoughts and ready my magic, even though I couldn't touch my magic with whatever Godfrey had put around my neck still in place.

Constantine looked straight at me. "Yes."

"And the perimeter ward?" I focused on readying for a single blast.

"I left the mixture to destroy and regrow it in a specified location near the Midlands."

"He is a betrayer," Godfrey said. "Like every mage in the Second Layer. Only good for death."

I stared at Constantine. Olivia would agree with two parts of Godfrey's statement. I was the only one who believed he was not firmly on the path of destruction—even when faced with his betrayal, surface-level or otherwise. Constantine wasn't like Raphael or Godfrey, at least not yet. His soul was conflicted and screaming, not dark with black magic madness.

If someone had healed Raphael, who was equally brilliant, of that rift—what might he be inventing now? What good might he be doing?

Godfrey kept speaking. "He used you—set you up for a cold, sterile cell."

An expression finally sparked in Constantine's eyes. "You underestimate the place in which I would ever set her." He turned to me and his expression was deliberately lazy and offhand, but there was an intense sort of wrath underlying his gaze that was not focused on me. "It would be canopied and blanketed with velvet, and there would be at least two over-sized tuffets. Very plush."

I reached out a hand, as if to touch his wrist, and his expression calmed somewhat.

It wasn't okay—not at all—his actions had enabled Olivia's kidnapping—but Constantine never did anything without five reasons. I would hear them out.

I nodded slowly at him and something akin to painful relief flashed across his face. The liquid metal was nearly coating his hand now, but it needed another fifteen seconds.

Godfrey motioned to his minions. "Time to go."

Constantine's jaw worked and his ribbon flashed out with cutting magic from his other hand. The minions stopped in their tracks. There was a cruel, savage aspect to his expression. "You don't touch her. You don't leave with her. This is not the deal we agreed to."

Godfrey sliced a hand through the ribbon and Constantine's magic, and Constantine fell in a long arc of blood and magic. Blood splattered to the ground in a long line. The minions inched closer around us.

"Your arbitration time is up and now the point is moot. You didn't word the magic quite carefully enough, boy. Teenagers—always thinking you know more than you do."

Godfrey knelt next to Constantine, pulling his head up by the hair on top. "Sad, really. Such a disappointment you are. Even to your enemies. So much power, yet so little direction."

There was blood on Constantine's lips, dripping from his mouth. His eyes drifted up toward the Midlands, then back to Godfrey. "You will die."

Godfrey sighed. "You say that as if you have any use or life expectancy left. For your help, you will have your ten minutes, but nothing more. And in this battle zone, that will count for little. Had you simply stayed quiet, you might have lived to see another sunrise. What did you hope to accomplish by keeping her from us? To have your own secret pet? She is far too valuable. Verisetti tried to keep it quiet too. His stupid games will get him killed, but not now, I don't think, by you."

Godfrey tutted. "Sad about your revenge. I was hoping you'd end him for me."

"You will die," Constantine repeated.

"You should have just given her up—made a nice deal of it," Godfrey said, like a mentor forever disappointed in his students. "Maybe asked for Verisetti's head on a pike. Our superiors might even have considered it. She is obviously the one the informants have been reporting about. It was merely a matter of time before she was exposed completely, yet you didn't exchange her. I think I see why now. But, it matters not. I have her now. I will be celebrated, and the Third Layer will rule again. We will be the ones with the leash to the entire Layer system in hand."

Constantine looked...unhinged. Vicious and deadly and without care for his own safety as he pushed upward. "So you think you are the only one who knows what they hold?"

"I am the one with my fingers on the prize," Godfrey spit. He held out a hand and

Constantine's fallen leech zoomed into his palm. "And I will wield that ownership to glory."

The metal coating Constantine's broken hand glowed the moment before he flung it toward me. It splashed against my chest, then flowed upward, traveling against gravity in glops of goo, seeping into my skin as it did. Magic vibrated up through me and cracked the band at my neck and the spell in my ears. Already ready, I immediately blasted the broken spells outward, just like Dare had taught me, and the men went flying.

I lurched to Constantine and quickly sketched a healing rune on the underside of his forearm with my finger, sending the dregs of my magic through it as best as I could. Our skin contact seemed to be working better than the rune.

"Sympathy and connection," he responded to my unasked question, blood coughing from his lips.

I could see the men starting to rise. Constantine didn't wait to heal more fully, he rolled and let out a concussive wave of energy through the living magic that still coated his knuckles—the remnants of the liquid magic he had thrown at me. The blast rippled, bending the air as it went, and the men went flying. They landed at odd angles.

Godfrey panted on the ground, back arched strangely. Constantine's blast must have cracked half of the bones in the man's body.

Constantine pushed himself up unsteadily and stepped over to the man. He put his foot against Godfrey's throat and pressed down. "Well, look at that," he said bitingly, then coughed briefly into his elbow. His hair fell into his face but did not hide his vengeful expression. "I must not have worded my magic carefully enough."

"Con?" I touched his arm. I tried not to look at Godfrey as Constantine pushed harder.

"Do you know what he would have done with you?" There was something savage in his eyes as he looked down at the leader of the group, even as he addressed the question to me.

"No. Knock him out and let's get Marsgrove."

He leaned over Godfrey. "I'll give you your ten minutes, and not a thing more." His foot pressed down and I blocked my ears to the resulting sound.

Constantine yanked the leech from Godfrey's fingers and stepped over his body. The lines of his face were calm again, but his eyes were vindictively pleased.

I lifted a leaf and transformed it into a bandage. It would only stay a bandage for a half hour or so, but it would have to be enough. There was no way I was letting Constantine do another leech maneuver. Not when Godfrey's body lay so near.

I wrapped the bandage tightly around his arm. "Does this hurt?"

"A bit."

I gave the end tie an extra tug. "Good."

He smiled.

"You led those men to us in the First Layer."

"Yes."

I nodded sharply. "Why?"

He had been looking for someone on the battlefield. He was still looking.

People were fighting a hundred yards in the distance. How had we gotten so far removed from everyone? As I stepped around and in between the bodies of the fallen, I tried not to look down at them in answer to that question. "Why did you make a deal with Godfrey? Who are you after? What do you need?"

I was pissed, but I would help. Constantine seemed to understand that.

"All I've needed for months was you. My very own angel."

"Con."

"In more ways than you could know, darling." He smiled, but his expression tightened. "I'm hunting someone. Someone I can never find. But someone who should be here. He should have come through the perimeter ward, but I searched and found nothing. I was promised that he wouldn't miss whatever was going to happen here. And you are here. And you broke his—"

Emrys appeared in front of us so suddenly that I jerked. Constantine's expression reflected my astonishment, then as his gaze moved from Emrys to me, then back again, it morphed into some sort of horrible, bitter realization.

He threw one hand toward Emrys and the other—the one that held the leech—toward me. His hand wrapped around my forearm, but Emrys was already in motion.

A cord of magic whipped across Constantine's cheek, snapping his head to the side. He fell like a stone dropped from a cliff. His fall took me with him and he landed on top of me, knocking the wind from my lungs.

Emrys kicked him off, ripped the leech from his hand, and stared down at Constantine, expression loathing. Air wouldn't re-inflate my lungs fast enough for me to do anything but stare.

"I would have left you alone, an endearingly bitter little boy," Emrys said. "You amused me with your attempts to track and undermine me. But no more, not after you dared." The leech burst into flames in his hand. Green eyes reflected the promise of imminent, irrevocable death.

Air returned and I rolled partially onto my knees, hunching over Constantine, hands thrust upward toward Emrys. "Stop!"

Emrys looked physically hammered, as if pieces of him were a moment from breaking and falling off. He had been nearest to me when I'd blasted the magic from the Origin Dome outward. All of the time we had been arguing with Godfrey, Emrys must have been piecing himself back together and biding his time—but despite his physical wounds, his expression was of a man who didn't understand limits.

Constantine reached around me and the end of his broken ribbon licked Emrys's chest, leaving a small paper behind. I could see the dodecaplex cells on the paper rotating for a split second before the edges of the sheet grabbed Emrys's chest with a crumpling paper sound, then a pulse of electric blue rippled over his body, thrusting him back a few steps.

Something...something strange was ripped from Emrys...but he remained standing. A little pulse of gold magic rolled over his body and dissipated out into the air.

Constantine grabbed my wrist, palm pressed over my control cuff. His palm was laced with the same liquid paint that had been on the dodecaplex paper. My paint. His fingers scrabbled over the metal, trying to get it to release. To set my subconscious magic free.

Emrys's green eyes were looking down in mild surprise at the paper attached to his chest. "That might have actually worked, had this been another situation. Clever, idiot boy."

He threw out a hand and Constantine's head slammed against the ground. Constantine didn't rise, and the magic I was frantically sending to him—his fingers still connected to my skin—wasn't working. I gripped his cheeks between both of my palms.

"Get out of the way, butterfly," Emrys said.

Magic leaped to my fingertips and I flung them toward Emrys, panic and terror giving my magic added strength, but he grabbed my wrist and the magic shoved right back up my arm, internally igniting me with pain.

He dropped my wrist abruptly, but pain lingered along with the feel of my magic being unnaturally stoppered. I stared numbly at the man above me, the puzzle piecing together from my nightmares.

Marsgrove had once told me that my shield set would give me tremendous advantage and protection, but that it would also make me especially susceptible to Raphael, whose spells were inextricably woven all over me.

I touched Constantine's cheeks again, then grabbed his hand, but only the tiniest drip of magic was making it out from whatever had been done to stop my magic.

But there was a drip. I looked at the paint on Constantine's fingertips, it was slowly seeping into my skin.

"Clean-up is beyond dull." The man above me sighed and rubbed his eyes as he paced. Green eyes bled quickly to gray than turned to a sapphire ringed with teal—the colors that made up my own irises. His blonde hair darkened and lengthened. He looked down at his chest, poking it strangely. "And that maggot actually broke something. How utterly delightful, though, that he failed so miserably in his revenge at the same time. Eight years. Delicious," he said through the lips of the vessel I had come to know as Emrys Norr.

But the real Emrys Norr, wherever he was, had never been on rounds with me. The real Emrys had likely never stepped foot on campus this term.

Almost nothing physically remained of the blond, green-eyed man I'd been doing rounds with. The vessel in front of me now looked...like Christian.

I knew exactly what stood before me. I had shaped the features on its face.

"All this time," I bit out. "I'm surprised the body count isn't higher."

"I thought you'd figure it out sooner, I have to say, even with the tedious task on my part to act like that buffoon Emrys most of the time. His body style fit your creation best, unfortunately. Alas, on the body count. I had a very nice plan in place in case you uncovered my identity before today."

The dolls at Alexandria. The familiarity of Emrys. I should have figured it out—the person on the other side of Emrys's flashing eyes.

"And Constantine?"

My golem poked his chest again. His body was slowly growing taller and even more athletic. "The Leandred spawn's lovely, celebrated mother was shopping in Salietrex the day I wiped the town from existence. One of my first pieces of art. A little messy, that one. I've gotten better, of course."

"No," I whispered.

I could see Dare running for us, casting magic left, right, and straight at us as he did.

"I've gotten far better, and with you, butterfly, I've become divine."

His fingers twirled, and the air cracked and earth shook as magic pulled from the ground through me. A dome shot around us, twenty feet in diameter, trapping us inside with Constantine, Godfrey, and an obscene number of bodies—both minions and students. Dare's spells impacted the dome and ricocheted away.

Dare skidded to a stop a foot before he splattered against the side. His gaze met mine, then immediately started probing the dome's magic, looking for a way in.

Movement beyond the dome registered in only the vaguest way.

"I hate you more than I've ever hated anything," I said numbly.

And I was tired, beyond done, with having my magic cut off, turned back on, and cut off again, like some sort of magical faucet controlled by everyone but me. I pulled my wrist slowly and deliberately along Constantine's painted fingertips.

Raphael watched Dare methodically examining the dome's magic and flashed him a smile halfway between a smirk and a grimace. Dare spared a moment of his examination to exchange a look with him that promised death.

Raphael pulled a fingernail along his own throat in a long draw, then turned. "Come, butterfly. We have appointments to keep. And these last few weeks have truly exercised my patience."

I gave a short laugh. "I'll bet they have." I exchanged my own look with Dare. A far different one. Stall, his said, and five fingers were open on one hand indicating the minutes required. I turned back to Raphael. "You stole that body from me."

"And such a glorious one it is." My golem—controlled remotely by Raphael somewhere probably miles from here—pulled a tube of paint from his pocket and gave it a wiggle.

My lips tightened in fury. "A drop of my Awakening paint to keep you going when you needed it? And to keep me under control whenever I start to slip your grasp?"

I gripped my wrist and willed the paint to seep in faster. My sudden bouts of fatigue every time Emrys touched me were stupidly, easily explained now. And why Emrys had been furious the other day—the day following the loosening of Raphael's leash. And the sudden need to have control devices become an expelling offense.

I looked down at my control cuff with the new violet stains from Constantine's fingers, and the older, blue stains upon it. "My ultramarine paint." Emrys had touched it—right before it had started malfunctioning strangely.

"You make such useful tools, butterfly."

Behind Raphael, a resurrected Godfrey was regaining his feet with help from a minion. Raphael's gaze followed mine and turned malevolent. His hand raised, then he obliterated Godfrey and the minion against the inside of the dome.

Overwhelming nausea bent me over. "Oh, God."

I couldn't hear anything outside of the dome, but I could see Dare's increased motions.

"Vincent was so eager to play at being an Origin User. Do not rue his destruction, butterfly. He would not have rued yours. He would have tried to use you, chain you too early, and I can't let that happen now, can I? Not when you are on the edge of true potential."

He smiled. It was Christian's smile, so achingly familiar—but it was also the gold-tinted smile of the person I hated most.

Months ago, I had shaped the roughened features before me into the contours of my brother's face. And Raphael had stolen the form and shaped it further. Changing the features, making them less recognizable, but keeping just enough elements to capture my attention when the facade of Emrys blinked.

It might look like him, but it wasn't Christian standing in front of me.

Emotion rocked me. I grabbed the anger and launched myself over Constantine's body and at Raphael. Unprepared for that response, my golem tripped backward under my weight.

I whacked his head against the ground and tore the tube from his grip. "You bastard. You utter—" I got in one more whack before Raphael bucked me off.

We grappled with the tube and paint squirted out of the top. I rolled into it, dragging my arm and cuff along the painted blue path. The ground started to shake.

"Look at you," Raphael said, eyes gleaming strangely. "Breaking free of each control cuff that is stronger than the last. And when they stop you no more? What then?"

The golem smoothly crouched into a fighting position, familiar gold eyes shining brightly, finally shaking all other color free now that the person on the other side had taken complete control of the vessel in order to fight me.

He called the spilled paint on the ground back into the tube, and the earth abruptly ceased its quaking motions. He capped the tube with the thumb of the same hand that held it, never taking his gaze from me. "Don't be wasteful, butterfly. We have work to do. Especially with you trying to detach one of my finest creations from draining your magic and abilities when I need them. You have chosen to repay the freedom I gave you in such a duplicitous way. I don't know whether to praise you or beat you," he said.

My lips pinched together. Raphael had been rifling through my soul spells when I'd entered our room to find him there after the bone beast incident at the end of last term. And his magical experience far exceeded mine. He had taken my creation and looked at the exact spells I had planned to use—the ones that matched up with the golem's physical creation—then improved it. Improved it to a point where I hadn't even recognized my own work. He had used the inherent familiarity of it—the bits of Christian I had imbued—and kept me off balance with the threat of the Department.

None of which meant I was useless in my lesser knowledge. I smacked my painted hand to the dirt and shot a soul-separating enchantment through the roots traveling the ground between us. With the thrum of splattered paint gaining momentum inside of me—supernaturally revitalizing my entire well of magic—the full force of the spell snapped toward him.

His eyes widened and he jumped to the side, narrowly avoiding the blast. The magic hit the dome and sizzled upward, strengthening it. I could see Dare swearing, but I was already shooting off another.

"Butterfly, you might scar me." Delight tinged Raphael's voice, uttered through my brother's mouth. "I had planned to use this body for something far more divine. Perhaps with a copy of your brother's soul and wearing his skin. He could have been the general of my army. Oh, the pain that would have brought you. You, who wanted the real thing and would not settle for a magnificent copy."

I didn't bother speaking through my sudden tears and fury, and launched another attack, twisting soul spells and blasting them forward. If Raphael was going to use my creations as bases, I would warp things back my way.

We traded shots, ducking, diving, and rolling. But even thought I was flush with Awakening paint, Raphael had far more tactical, physical, and magical experience. He anticipated what I would do before I did it. I was shaking and running on angry fumes.

And he was wearing the face of my brother.

The only reason I wasn't flat on the ground was that I was delighting him. I could read it on his face, and it just made me angrier. Made me give into the anger and devise new strategies, pulling magic from the earth that would backlash and break something elsewhere, which further gave Raphael what he wanted.

And I couldn't stop. I was so angry.

"Those scarves are exquisite, butterfly. You rendered them able to bypass a communication shutdown by lightly leashing you to them. And all of those pieces of you, the tokens you gave to your friends...what is the difference between our beautiful box—worthy of Pandora herself—and all the tokens you've given to your allies? Is it simply a scaling concern in your mind?" he mused as he shot a bolt of cyan that would temporarily shut down my internal organs if it connected.

"Friends," I emphasized as I dodged, trying another soul separation spell. The dome pulsed and sang. "And I willingly gave them parts of my magic. Of me."

"And you willingly gave this—" A picture of the box rose in the air "—to me."

"I did not."

"You did. Don't you remember?" His voice dripped with deliberate hurt, and his golden eyes taunted me.

"Don't play word games. And you know that I do not." I somersaulted from the path of an almost lazily thrown bolt of electricity.

But... "You can't recharge the box like you were able to before," I said in stunned realization.

His eyes narrowed.

"It worked," I said numbly. "Better than we planned."

"I will cede that you and that boy combined motivation with genius. But it matters not, now." He smiled and blasted me off my feet.

Unable to draw breath, I stared at the dome above me. The dome pulsing with Origin Magic.

A thin line drew from the top of the dome into a vortexed dot of black. Detaching from the dome, the dot spiraled outward to form a black-and-white circle rotating in the air. Patterns and graphics moved and morphed as it spun. I knew what that was. It would open at any second, and the real Raphael, with his box, would be on the other side.

The golem stepped toward me and smiled, its gaze on the destroyed gold cuff on the ground. "Your options are few. I saw Stavros looking, and I can feel his minions here. Head of the most insidious branch of the Department—he will spirit you into a dark cell and chain you there before anyone realizes you are missing." There was something dark in his eyes, like memory. His smile twisted. "I do have plans for you to be captured there someday—the day Stavros's life will end—but I have too many moves yet to savor.

"I have accomplished what I needed to on this mountain—though your little boyfriend tried so hard to keep me from doing so. And you've learned enough on your own to be of use to me."

"No."

He smiled at me and tilted his head. "Your friend—so valiant in her sacrifice will not survive for much longer. I know you want to check on her, butterfly. Tick tock. If someone else chances upon her first, you will never see her alive again."

I swallowed. My fingers closed around Olivia's scarf and the magic I had gathered within it to trace her location. Helen Price's daughter would be a grand sacrifice, used by some terrorist like Godfrey...and Helen would not save her.

I raised my free hand.

Raphael's stolen smile turned elated.

Someone shouted, "No!"

Raphael's head whipped around in surprise at the sound. We had been in our own bubble this entire time—what...?

The thought didn't complete in my mind before the dome was fracturing around us, Dare's magic splintering the surface in twenty directions. The dome shattered. The transportation circle burst.

And Dare fell.

Chapter Thirty-five

REAPING WHAT YOU'VE DRAWN

T HE ELATION DISAPPEARED completely from the golem's face and a deep, underlying wrath whipped across its stolen features. Marsgrove was the one who had yelled, and he stood six feet away from me, just past where the dome's edge had been, steadily hacking toward us as he fought a group of four assailants who must have taken it upon themselves to defend their leaders. He was holding his own, and had been holding Godfrey's forces back while Dare had torn through the dome, but fighting multiple assailants required movement and Marsgrove was forced into a less desirable position for a single, crucial moment.

Raphael whipped a sickly yellow blast at Marsgrove's side and I launched forward, over Dare, to push Marsgrove from its path.

Marsgrove took a green blast to the chest and my arm went numb under a thin violet wave, but the yellow missed both of us and erupted in the crowd of assailants, piercing straight through two of them and killing them instantly.

Marsgrove would never have survived that hit, shields or no shields. That kind of blast was the sort not often used, as it took so much magic that the user couldn't channel another blast, not even defensively, for a few seconds—a critical amount of fighting time.

Marsgrove seemed to understand at least something of what had just happened, because he rolled with my airborne tackle, his arm moving past his chest, fixing whatever had been done to him and healing my arm at the same time. The same arm flew out as we continued to rotate and sent out a concussive blast at the remaining men—most of whom, due to Raphael's magic, had been blown off their feet—then let me fall in a tumbling roll to the ground, as he somehow landed on his feet, whipping around to face the golem.

Marsgrove didn't bother to go through the mental arithmetic or verbal questions that I had.

He seemed to instantly understand who he was facing.

"A cockroach really does always know how to hide." He fired off a spell at the same time as he uttered the last word.

Raphael smiled darkly as they began fighting. "So disappointing. Your attention has been so far away, yet all along..."

All along he had been right under his nose.

I pulled myself along the ground toward Dare—unwilling to consider that his dismantling of the dome and my magic had irreparably harmed him—as spells meant to maim and kill flew and shuddered in the air between the two men, like a deadly dance they had learned and practiced a long time ago.

When we had first met, Will had said that Dare had beaten Marsgrove the previous year and that that had been a feat. I could see why.

Raphael controlling a golem body wasn't quite as fast as Raphael in person. Controlling the vessel from a distance would require a lot more mental processing than him fighting on his own.

And the vessel didn't have my box of doom to make up for the lagged deficit.

Marsgrove's blade slid through the golem's left hand. An answering pain snagged me, and I rubbed my own.

Dare's eyes opened a moment before I reached him and he shot a spell over my head that impacted one aimed our way. "Didn't die this time. Progress," he said, as he threw an extra shield around both of us.

"Progress," I echoed vacantly.

Hands tipped my head back and examined my eyes and rubbed the space behind my ears, checking for some injury. "Just a little longer, Ren. Hold on."

He tossed another shield over me and one to Constantine, then took out the remaining enemy combatants surrounding us, leaving Marsgrove and Raphael to battle alone. I numbly crawled back to Constantine—who was barely breathing, but alive—and put his head in my lap, trying to heal him as I joined our Dare-gifted shields together. I watched Marsgrove and Raphael fight while Dare brutally kept any of the remaining terrorists—or bloodthirsty students—from interfering.

Magic flew from fingers, foreheads, and every pore. And it became quite, quite, obvious from the tossed out taunts that Raphael and Marsgrove were more than simple enemies.

Then Raphael was in the wrong position, both arms hanging uselessly at his sides, and with the magic of the vessel depleted. "But I have what I came for and also what I need, don't I?" Raphael said, smiling at me. Olivia. "Delivered to my door."

Marsgrove pulled his arm back. The vessel was going to die.

"Alas, that your glorious construction comes to an end all the same." The light left the golem's eyes a split-second before Marsgrove's blast hit. The empty vessel fell to the ground.

Pain and emptiness ran through me, then the connection to the vessel terminated completely, leaving me with another kind of emptiness.

I held onto Constantine.

Marsgrove's piercing gaze stayed on the vessel for a long moment before turning to me. "Where is Olivia?"

Agony.

"I don't know," I whispered. "But I will."

Anger burned in his eyes during the first three words, but Marsgrove's expression turned unreadable at the last three. "You do not realize what you've started."

I didn't care what I'd started. I only cared that I would end it. "Raphael is not dead."

"No. Cockroaches don't so easily die." He pushed the golem over with his foot. "Yours?"

"Yes," I whispered.

Fire rushed forward and burned the body with instant, scorching flames. I watched my creation burn in five scant seconds, as if it was a piece of lined paper caught by gas flame.

"Never leave anything behind," Marsgrove said, his eyes narrowed at me, rightfully accusing. "We will discuss this after I get these crasseetars off our campus. Speak to no one." He strode away.

1000

I looked up to see a paper phoenix diving from the sky, eating magic as it went, following behind its master as he swept the grounds. The magic that I had given Dare was probably going to come back to haunt me as well.

I could feel the campus magic pulsing, Administration Magic sweeping through, the Muses doing crazy magic on Top Circle, the Midlands rhythmically breathing, one breath, at a time.

Marsgrove, Dare, and the others wiped the scattering troops away.

I looked back at the ashes flying free from the disintegrated body of my golem and saw the gleam of white. Lifting my hand, I called it to me. The magic of the object knew me and the tube flew easily into my hand. I curled my fingers around the half-empty tube of paint.

I squeezed out a single ultramarine drop and wiped it across Constantine's forehead, then concentrated. The blue glowed for a moment, then seeped into his skin. I numbly put the tube in my pocket.

Dare blitzed back into view a second later. His expression was hard to read as he looked down at his roommate, but he touched my shoulder before he lifted Constantine.

Chapter Thirty-six

NEVER A SACRIFICE

P ROTECTION OF FRIENDS TALLY:
Devastating

The earth was scorched. But it would be fixed. Just like last term. Many things were fixable with magic.

But not everything...not always.

Asafa and Patrick drew closer with Will, Neph, Delia, Mike, Kita, Lifen, Dagfinn and the others. They closed ranks around me on Top Circle, where everyone on the mountain had been called by Administrative Magic to gather. We looked down at the scarf I held.

"Self-sacrifice in a Price?" Delia's expression was unreadable, but there was a tightness to her voice, and a resolution to action.

Asafa and Patrick exchanged looks, communicating in their quick, nonverbal way. Patrick nodded, and there was a strange glint in his eye.

Farther off, I felt Dare watching us even while his head was bent to speak with his uncle. He would have seen everything that happened up until the ports blew open—I had programmed the journal magic to stop and throw everything to him as soon as communications reopened. I pressed my fingers against the pulsing, ultramarine thread connected to my chest. He was going to ask a thousand penetrating questions, and I was going to have to figure out how I was going to answer.

Roald Bailey and Bellacia were talking rapidly, and magic steadily lifted into the air behind them as if on airwaves.

In the background, Helen Price and Constantine's dad and all of the heads of the Department—including the man they'd called Stavros—joined a dozen other authorities demanding answers in loud, commanding voices.

I wondered what Marsgrove would tell them. For this small moment of truce, I didn't think he would try to get around the contract restriction in order to out me. But he might not even have to make the effort.

Voices clamored.

"Where is my daughter?"

"My son is barely alive!"

"Where are the students who are responsible for the massacre at the battle fields?"

"Who blew the ports? I want to know that right now."

"—was completely obliterated. The Fourth Layer is demanding answers."

"Where is that girl? The one Godfrey was talking to when the transmission cut out?"

"—General Telgent and the Troop? Where is Emrys Norr?"

I didn't care to answer the questions being asked or to hear the answers being given. I didn't even know if I was still a student at this school.

"Where is my daughter?"

I gripped Olivia's scarf. Raphael would be waiting for me, wherever she was.

There was one thing I was sure about, though, and it was the only thing that mattered.

I would get her back.

About the Author

Anne Zoelle is the pseudonym of a USA Today Bestselling author who loves writing about college-aged protagonists who get embroiled in complicated adventures. Split between the midwest and west coast, she writes books for all ages that feature sentient libraries, rock guardians, and people finding family.

You can find her at www.annezoelle.com.

Or contact her directly at:
anne.zoelle@gmail.com

9 781954 593329